Praise for *Following Polly*

"Funny, intelligent, accessible. *Fo~~ll~~~~owin~~*
makes Karen one of my favorit~~e~~
—Jim G

"*Following Polly* is a delicious de~~light~~ ~~. . . the tour is~~
most fun, and Alice Teakle is so clever and quirky a protagonist—or is she a perp?—that you won't be able to stop reading. Bergreen is a wonderful new voice in the mystery world."
—Linda Fairstein, author of *Hell Gate*

"A murderous romp . . . highly entertaining."
—*Mystery Scene Magazine*

"A laugh-out-loud page-turner." —*The Huffington Post*

"Part cozy mystery, part romance, and all parts outrageously funny." —*Las Vegas Review Journal*

"A fine first novel: polished, acutely observed, and delightfully mean. What fun!" —Susan Isaacs, author of *Close Relations*

"Karen Bergreen has created a lovable heroine who is a bundle of totally unique neuroses. I couldn't put it down and I can't wait for the sequel!"
—Susie Essman, author of *What Would Susie Say?*

FOLLOWING POLLY

• • • • • • • • • a novel • • • • • • • •

KAREN BERGREEN

ST. MARTIN'S GRIFFIN
NEW YORK

FOLLOWING POLLY. Copyright © 2010 by Karen Bergreen. All rights reserved. Printed in the United States of America. For information, address St. Martin's Press, 175 Fifth Avenue, New York, N.Y. 10010.

www.stmartins.com

The Library of Congress has cataloged the hardcover edition as follows:

Bergreen, Karen.
    Following Polly / Karen Bergreen.—1st ed.
      p. cm.
    ISBN 978-0-312-57109-2
    1. Murder—Investigation—Fiction. 2. New York (N.Y.)—Fiction.
I. Title.
PS3602.E756F65 2010
813'.6—dc22

                                                    2009045742

ISBN 978-0-312-57358-4 (trade paperback)

First St. Martin's Griffin Edition: August 2011

10 9 8 7 6 5 4 3 2 1

For Victoria Skurnick.
Thank you!

ACKNOWLEDGMENTS

I am extremely grateful to anyone who has said a kind word to me throughout this entire process. More precisely, I thank Elizabeth Beier for her editing skills and snacks and Michelle Richter for being more organized than I could ever hope to be. I could not have written a word of this novel (or sold it, for that matter) without the encouragement of my agent and good friend, Victoria Skurnick. I am also indebted to Elizabeth Fisher and Monika Verma, and the entire Levine, Greenberg Agency. Thanks to Susan Ginsburg for all of her help. I also appreciate the support of my parents, Barbara and Bernard Bergreen, who, thankfully, are nothing like Mother and Barnes. Thank you to my mother-in-law, Dr. Lita Alonso, for her medical expertise and suggestions. I love all my friends and cannot say thank you enough for the emotional support and suggestions from Daniele Campbell, Kathleen Chopin, Nona Collin, Adrienne Crowther, Cari Shane Parven, Susan Kozacik Rodgers, Stacey Shepherd, Debby Solomon, Julianne Yazbek, and Brad Zimmerman. I'm giving a special shout-out to Maria Verde, who put up with all of my nonsense. Also, to my children, Danny and Teddy, who give me a reason to get up in the morning (and let's face it, they will get a kick out of seeing their names here). And finally, to my real-life Charlie, my dreamy husband, Dan Alonso.

ONE

· ·

FOLLOWING POLLY

I started following Polly Dawson two hours after I was fired from Mona Hawkins Casting, Inc. I know that this isn't a good thing to do. Phrases like "compulsive voyeur" and "invasion of privacy" come to mind. It's not the first time I've done this, but it is the first time in almost twenty years, and I wasn't that proud of it then.

The fact that I don't want to stop seems to be yet another signal that I should.

But I can't. Besides, Polly Dawson is a loathsome human being.

Why did Mona fire me? It wasn't incompetence. Even *she* admitted that I showed incredible promise in casting. Though even my growth called for fear tactics. "Don't even think of going to work for Farron Moore." (Her only real competition in the New York City casting world.) "I'll ruin you."

While I didn't dump Mona for one of her competitors, I was—in Mona's eyes—disloyal. She had been casting *Only at Sunrise,* next year's sure-to-be mega-blockbuster. The director extraordinaire, Humphrey Dawson, had been on her to cast the sultry Jenna McNair as Kate, the leading lady. But Jenna didn't do movies, only *films.* Her agent insisted that she was allergic to blockbusters—even if they were directed by Humphrey Dawson. Humphrey offered her really big money.

"Not gonna work, Humpy." Mona had a nickname for all of the men in her life. "Jenna McNair isn't about money. Let me handle this one."

So, Mona held general "auditions" for the female lead at our hip town-house offices on Twenty-first and Sixth. We had four or five rounds of callbacks, narrowing the list for female lead each time. Mona was very hard on each of the actresses. As usual, she disregarded Screen Actors Guild rules restricting waiting time and made them sit in the cramped, airless anteroom for hours. No one dared report her.

"You do know that the role of Kate is meant to be played by a pretty, *thin* actress?" she asked several insecure auditioners.

They all read extremely well under the circumstances, though most left in tears. After six read-throughs and a staged screen test, Mona finally told the waify, lavender-clad Lissa Purcell that she would be calling her agent at LTA to offer her the part.

But Mona didn't call anybody at LTA. She never intended to. She'd been reporting to the press about the emergence of an "unknown," knowing that the faux casting of Lissa would be the perfect remedy for Jenna McNair's "reluctance." Jenna and her agent had an eighteen-minute conference call with Humphrey and Mona. They sealed the deal. Jenna would be playing Kate.

No one called Lissa. She found out that the part was no longer hers from an item in *Tell Me* magazine. Furious and hurt, she showed up at Mona's town house and asked what had happened.

"I just don't get it," she sobbed. Her butterfly choker was bobbing up and down. It looked as if it were flying.

"You were really close," I reminded Lissa.

"I don't have the stomach for this. I thought they liked me." She cried even harder, her lips pursing in a way that would have done the role of Kate proud.

In retrospect, I should have given her a hug. Instead, it all came pouring out so fast I can't even remember exactly what I said. I might have disclosed that she was used, manipulated, taken advantage of, and that her being offered the role and then Jenna's being offered the role was premeditated and no reflection on her acting ability.

"Keep going," I advised her. "It'll happen for you."

Lissa was heartened by our little discussion.

Mona wasn't. She had hung on my every word as she listened with her ear pressed against the wall. She stormed out of her office. Lissa saw Mona and ran away. I was terminated immediately.

I loved my job and I didn't want to leave. At least not yet. I was content moving up Mona's casting ladder. When I started there, my responsibilities were limited to ordering lunch. Three years later, I was placing all of the day players in NBC's hottest sitcom, *Slip 'n' Fall,* featuring the professional and romantic hijinks of an accessibly handsome personal injury lawyer.

But no more. Tears welled in my eyes, but I willed them to stay there as I held on to a semblance of dignity. I wish I could say the same for my ex-boss. As Mona was criticizing my ethics, fashion sense, and desk design, she kicked a garbage can and stubbed her toe. She blamed me for that, too.

Now I'm left with a lot of time. On the one hand, this holds a certain appeal. I can pursue all of those things I've really wanted to do all of these years.

On the other hand, there isn't anything I've really wanted to do. I've never even had a real hobby, unless you count watching television. I love, love, love television. My best friend, Jean, a partner at Lowry, White & Marcus, says I watch it to escape. Maybe she's right. But what's wrong with that? A well-scripted drama-filled life is much more fun and fascinating than my own real one.

Jean is always amazed at how accurately I can predict the plot of any TV show. The truth is, I have a weird memory. Once I see something, it never leaves. Show me the first two minutes of any episode of *Law & Order,* and I can spout off the identity of the killer. Jean always tells me I'd be a good detective if the casting thing doesn't work out. I think I could have been the Internet, if only someone hadn't invented the computer.

Right after Mona fired me, I ran out of her plush Chelsea office town house for the last time. I felt empty. I had no love life. And now I had no career. Mona, the most powerful name in East Coast casting, would make certain that no one would hire me.

I really would have to find something to do. I took a few deep breaths—something I learned from the entire Women-Changing-the-Course-of-Their-Lives Lifetime movie genre—and decided I would change the course of mine.

I went to Mother's.

I don't know if going to Mother's was the perfect response to my crisis. She has been so relieved that I am in a job that I finally like.

Mother's an actress, not a big star or anything, but someone you might recognize if you see her. She works mostly in the theater but has also been on a lot of the soap operas and every other show that films in New York. She usually plays the vulnerable but stalwart matriarch who is faced with overcoming tragedy.

She had been so pleased with my progress at Mona's. She had gotten me the job. Before that, I had worked as a paralegal and at a nonprofit. I was disgruntled as a paralegal and my nonprofit was nonfun.

I got off the elevator at the sixth floor of their sumptuous Fifth Avenue apartment building and let myself in.

"Hello, Alice." Barnes was there as usual, his moccasined feet resting on the claw foot of his precious rolltop desk. "Your mother is rehearsing in the next room."

"Hi there, Barnes." I gave him a perfunctory kiss on his alarmingly smooth cheek. I could tell he was pleased to inform me that Mother wasn't available. He delights in limiting my access to her.

Barnes is my stepfather.

"I'll wait," I told him.

I took off my coat and plunked myself on Mother's bumpy old crimson and gold silk sofa in their study. Mother is in an off-Broadway play, written, directed, and produced by a playwright friend of hers. They were using Mother's spacious velvet dining room for rehearsal space. Barnes was reviewing the *Wine Enthusiast* at the desk and was happy to continue with his reading while I stared up at myself in their scalloped, mirrored ceiling medallion.

After forty minutes, Mother finally walked in. Her blond hair, in a ponytail, looked as if she had it in rollers all morning. She was wearing drawstring ivory pants and a brown cashmere cardigan. She had no makeup on, and her face was glowing. She looked fourteen.

"Mona fired me." I forgot to plan a speech.

"What did you do?" Barnes asked, demonstrating his confidence in me.

"What will you do?" Mother came in quickly.

"I don't know. I never really thought about this possibility," I said to her truthfully. "On the bright side, I've saved some money, so I can support myself financially for at least six months or so. But I just don't understand. I was doing so well."

"Obviously, not that well," Barnes interjected.

I watched Mother, hoping she, for once, would chastise her husband, but she ignored his comment and looked at me.

"Do you have a plan?" Barnes looked at me, as if he were waiting for the PowerPoint presentation detailing my five-year career forecast.

"I thought I'd lie in bed with my television remote in one hand and a box of chocolates in the other."

Barnes's eyebrows were moving at warp speed, so desperate was he to add his two cents.

Finally, he asked, "How do you see yourself at thirty-three?"

"A year older than I am now," I answered.

Exeunt Barnes.

"Alice, did you have to be so flip?" Mother asked.

"You're right." Truth is, I didn't know what to do, and flip usually helps me out in those kinds of situations. "I felt attacked."

"Barnes is just concerned, sweetheart. He wants to help you." Mother so longed to believe what she was saying.

"I guess his help isn't the kind I can use right now."

"Maybe it's not." Mother finally hugged me. "You know Barnes. He sees a problem, he wants to fix it."

And Barnes likes to keep me working so that he can have Mother all to himself. I let it go.

"I know, but it's more complicated than that," I said.

"Maybe Barnes and I are too close to you. Maybe it is too complicated. Why don't you see someone professional? This may be a good time to assess where you are in your life."

Here's where I am: I'm alone and jobless.

"You mean, like a shrink?" I asked.

"Whatever you want to call it."

"Shrinks are for people who have employers who will pay for their health insurance," I reminded her.

"I'll pay for it," Mother told me.

"Thanks. I'll think about it. I have to go now." I gave Mother a quick kiss, pretended to wave down her long hall in Barnes's general direction, and ran out the door.

Before there was Barnes, there was my father. He was a very nice man. Mother and Dad met at Northwestern University. Mother was a theater major. As a pretty, blond freshman, she was cast in two experimental theater productions. The first was an account of the sinking of the *Lusitania* done in mime, and the second was a science-fiction piece about mind control, where she was cast as Woman Number Two.

When she was a senior, Mother was accepted into Company, a seminar offered by Northwestern's most popular professor. That professor was none other than my father, the athletic, dark-haired, hazel-eyed, albeit disheveled Austin Teakle. All of the students were assigned a position in the fictional Company and each week Austin would present the team with a goal or a problem it had to solve. Mother, having selected this course for its popularity and having no interest in running a business, was chosen to be the team's chief operating officer. Terrified by the prospect of such responsibility, she sought Dad's advice.

She said something like this: "I'm not cut out to be the COO. I'm really an actress. Maybe you should demote me."

To which he responded something like this:

"Ms. Anderson."

He knew her name. She was stunning. She had blond hair, light brown eyes, and fantastic legs. I'm sure he tried not to notice.

"The point of this seminar is to teach so-called nonexecutive types to have the confidence to make major financial decisions."

"I understand, Professor—"

Forgive me if I don't have the dialogue right. It has been thirty-five years since they had this conversation, and I wasn't there.

"I'm really at Northwestern to act, and I feel that it would be unfair of me to take this job from an aspiring mogul."

I know for sure that this is the part when Dad gave Mother a huge smile. I know because he always smiled at her that way.

He smiled at me that way, too.

"Maybe we can make a mogul of you yet. Why don't I take you to lunch and we can work on your business future."

Dad's rugged good looks were not lost on her, either.

They went to lunch at the faculty dining room, and even though Mother and Dad were obviously attracted to each other, they were perfectly appropriate. He was her teacher, after all. In a climate where many of his colleagues were enjoying the perks of their institutional allure, Dad preferred to keep things professional. The two went to lunch every two weeks or so, always with the intention of discussing competing business methodologies, but instead talking about this and that.

Mother graduated in May but stayed in Chicago to star in the original play *Taken.* Two weeks after graduation, Dad "accidentally" ran into her in the Drama bookstore. This time, he asked her to dinner. I don't know all the details of their date but I'm pretty positive that the evening ended up in somebody's bed.

The timing could not have been more perfect. Dad was leaving the university that spring. He had a business idea, a design for a series of cleaning brushes. He was moving to New York City. Mother would go with him, of course. They were completely and totally in love.

They got married, and soon Dad's brush business was making millions of dollars. Then, as if their life wasn't perfect enough, Mother gave birth to a fantastic little boy, my brother, Paul, and two years later, they had a cute, charming baby girl: Alice. Me.

Paul was the serious one. With his thick, unruly coffee-colored hair and inset eyes he was the spitting image of Dad. With the same personality to match. He ran a lemonade stand on Eighty-third and Madison Avenue that actually made a lot of money.

"If I charge a lot, the people will think they're getting a superior product," Paul informed Mother, as he stirred the A&P-brand lemonade mix into the tap water.

While there was a vague family resemblance, I didn't really look like either of my parents. As far as my hair was concerned, I didn't have the shiny blond of my mother or the rich brown of my father. It was decidedly mousy. Mother called it chestnut. And, whereas Paul had the physique of a young swimmer, I looked like an overcooked noodle.

I was a mix of my parents. Personalitywise, like Dad, I loved school. Like Mother, I was something of a performer, but I didn't have Mother's flair for drama. Instead I chose to be a ham. When I was three, my teachers told my parents that I had a gift for humor. I played elaborate pranks on all of the authority figures, often informing teachers beforehand to try to enlist their participation in a joke. One Sunday night in first grade, after viewing Hayley Mills in *The Parent Trap,* I called Mrs. Schoettle to inform her that I would be attending school as my long-lost twin from France. I borrowed one of Mother's wigs, a curly short-haired number, and fooled the whole class. Mrs. Schoettle, irritated as she was, went along with the gag.

Our lives were perfect. That is, until December 31, 1985. Dad and Paul, then ten years old, went for a "men's" snowshoe trip in Canada. Their plane took off from Killarney, Ontario, and crashed into Lake Huron in Michigan. All seven passengers and the pilot were killed.

Mother's reaction to the plane crash was simple: She took to her bed. Gorgeous and near death herself, she was a real-life sleeping beauty. The plane crash was her prick from the spinning wheel. From then on, she cared for me in a somnambulant haze, and did—under the circumstances—a decent job. I wasn't undernourished. I never missed school or doctors' appointments. I just missed Mother.

It wasn't that Mother didn't love me. I know that now and I knew it then. But my presence only reminded her of her dead son and her dead husband.

As Mother retreated from me, I retreated from home, choosing instead to reside, for the most part, with my close friends,

Stephanie, Pauline, and Daphne. Their parents were especially welcoming after learning of my bad fortune. They all had plenty of room and were happy to add an extra plate at the dinner table and carve out some space for me to sleep, study, and store my clothes.

Although Stephanie had the nicest home, a town house near school with an entire floor all to herself, I was partial to staying at Daphne's house, as she had a television in her room and a consistently impressive supply of baked goods in the pantry. Pauline's mom was the closest I had to a parental surrogate. She showed an interest in my academic progress and often picked up a thoughtful gift for me when she was running errands.

I'm not sure that I thrived emotionally under this system, but, on paper, I did very well. I continued to be a stellar student and had a stable of friends.

When I was thirteen, five years after the plane crash, Mother got out of bed. At the urging of her theater friends, she went into therapy with Dr. Richard Reuban. Within a year, she was on stage again. No longer cast as the lovely ingénue, Mother had evolved into the brave-in-the-face-of-adversity character. She was still remarkably beautiful, but she was drained.

When I was fifteen years old, Dr. Reuban urged Mother to try to meet someone.

"I was never a dater," Mother told him.

"Don't put labels on it, Angela. The last thing you need is pressure."

Finally, an opportunity presented itself. Our upstairs neighbors, Michael and Margot Berman, were having a small dinner party. They invited Mother.

That was how she met Barnes.

Barnes Newlan was taken with Mother the first second he saw her. And he didn't mind that she was tired. He was good at taking care of people, and Angela Teakle looked as if she needed taking care of.

Mother liked Barnes. Blind to his distractingly large forehead and oversized hands, she found him attractive.

I'm not being fair.

At first glance, he is appealing. He has a full head of bright white hair and a nice set of choppers. I rarely use this word in reference to teeth, but Barnes's are ample and always in sight. He has very smooth skin for a man of his age. He lacks the natural leanness of my father, but remains in fairly good condition so as to avoid his inherent tendency to become pear shaped.

From time to time, Barnes appears to be a boob. That said, he has an extraordinary knack for investing and spending money well. He took Mother's notable fortune and converted it into a more notable one. And over the years he transformed her elegant nine-room Fifth Avenue apartment into an extremely elaborate homage to the Bourbon Monarchy, replete with enormous tapestries, precious objects, and slightly uncomfortable furniture. When Barnes was not managing Mother's investments, he was managing Mother. Soon, she was working fairly regularly on television, in movies, and in the theater. She gained back fifteen of the twenty pounds she had lost. Her ash hair was back to its New York blond. She was, once again, her creative self.

She had met her prince.

But in this sleeping beauty tale, there is a hitch. Me.

Which takes me to why seeing a therapist might not be such a bad idea.

As I left Mother's to head back to my rent-stabilized Hell's Kitchen grotto, I realized the rest of my day—not to mention my life—was free. I stopped for a snack at the Land O' Bread. They have the best, you guessed it, bread, in New York. The place is always packed with unsuspecting pedestrians who couldn't pass up the aroma of warm cheddar buns. I walked in, grateful that there was only one customer ahead of me. In the mirror, I saw her face.

It was Polly Dawson.

Oh my!

Not exactly the person you want to see when you're feeling bad about yourself.

I met her my first day at Harvard. I had just entered Thayer South's cobwebbed but otherwise unremarkable entryway, when I noticed a very striking girl trying desperately to unlock her room.

"Do you need some help?"

"Is it that obvious?" she said, and gave an exaggerated sigh. "I've never been good with keys."

There was something endearing about this beautiful and to-gether girl admitting that she was not good with something.

I tried the door and was equally unsuccessful.

"I hope Harvard isn't trying to say something," the girl said modestly.

I laughed, my loneliness starting to melt. "Wait. I have an-other idea." I pulled out my fresh ID and wedged it in the door. Nothing happened.

"Just like MacGyver," I said bitterly.

"Thanks, Alice," the girl said warmly.

She knew my name. I was flattered and at the same time con-fused. How did she know? I hadn't told her.

She read my mind.

"I'm not a witch or anything. Your name is on your little break-in gadget," she said, chuckling, "and I noticed that you and I have the same birthday: April second. We could be twins."

Oh sure, twins. I was awkward, with brown hair and an iffy complexion, and she was the Breck Girl.

"This is not a bad picture. I wish I could be half that photogenic."

"Let me see," I asked, curious to see if this pretty girl could actually take a bad picture.

She reached into her pocket and pulled out her card. First, I saw her name: Polly Linley. Then I saw her picture. It was the most perfect photo I had ever seen. In person, this Polly was not flawless. Her face was a little pointy, and her blond hair, though straight and shiny, was a little thin. None of these imperfections found their way into her cheap school ID photo. Polly not only looked flawless, she looked warm. I glanced at my own card. My hair was flat on my face and I had several burgeoning pimples. The photographer also took the picture before I got a chance to smile.

"Maybe we could use your ID. Your picture might open a door that mine can't."

It was worth a shot. I had seen enough episodes of *This Old House* to know that Massachusetts locksmiths were not at the top of their game in the 1880s.

Polly handed me her ID and I put it in the door. Voilà, click, the door opened.

"Great job, Alice," Polly said warmly. "I can tell we're going to be the best of friends." Polly went into her room and, for lack of a better expression, closed the door in my face.

I didn't see Polly until later in the week at our official dorm welcome party. When I came in the door, she headed toward me.

"Hi, Polly," I said enthusiastically.

"Oh." She did not look at me but rather through me. "Hi." And then she effusively greeted the gorgeous hockey player who came in behind me.

Polly had not only lied about my photo being better than hers. She had also lied about not being a witch. We didn't speak for the rest of the year. Nor did we speak for the three years after that.

"She's a user," my roommate and now best friend, Jean Middleton, had told me when I relayed the story months later. "And she'll get hers."

Jean was wrong. Polly Linley was a shining light at Harvard University. Sure, she was charmed to some degree, but added to her natural flair and good fortune was her relentless drive. She studied hard, and was a terrific student. She was up at 4:45 every morning for swim practice. She had men all over her. She had women all over her. And they were always the most successful, the most popular people on campus. I was useful to her as a one-time locksmith, but I lacked the requisite social résumé to have any other role.

She also produced Harvard's first-ever fashion show. Initially, the university's population was skeptical: Such a superficial display would never go over at an intellectual hotbed like Harvard. Boy, were they wrong. Polly unapologetically selected the best-looking undergraduates. She even asked Jimmy Kagen, the funniest guy in the Ivy League and now a successful comedian, to host. The fashion show catapulted Polly's popularity. She became nationally known, appearing in many magazines and even landing a guest visit on *The Tonight Show*.

"Some people peak in college," Jean said when we saw Polly on the cover of *Boston* magazine. "In ten years Polly Linley will be an anonymous frump."

But it has been more than ten years and Polly Linley is about as far from anonymous and frumpy as anyone could get. She is stunning. Even at the Land O' Bread. Her natural blond hair still looks natural enough. She's fit, tall, and effervescent. I saw her face in the mirror, but she didn't see mine. I was now, as I was then, invisible to her.

I saw that other people at the Land O' Bread were staring at her. Polly is pretty recognizable. She's married to the famous director Humphrey Dawson. In fact, he's directing *Only at Sunrise*, the film I was working on at Mona Hawkins Casting until today.

Humphrey is Polly's second husband. She's thirty-two: exactly my age. After college, Polly eloped with Professor Jack Birnbaum. Ninety percent of the female students and at least ten percent of the males fantasized about Birnbaum.

Ironically, Birnbaum taught a class called Morality in America. It was my first exposure to the concept of integrity, and Birnbaum seemed to embody it. He was ordinary looking: balding, medium height, with a doughy body and a wardrobe only the Jehovah's Witnesses would be proud of. But the man had appeal. He was extremely passionate. I recall one classroom discussion of laws that prevent spouses from testifying against each other in criminal cases. We, of a sanctimonious age, so far away from thinking about the emotional complexity of marriage, were outraged by a policy that could protect criminals. Birnbaum tried to convince us otherwise, stating emphatically and dramatically: "I would—without a doubt—perjure myself for my wife."

The women in the class gasped. Jean swooned. I was crying outright.

Two months later Birnbaum left his wife. He married Polly the day after graduation.

A year later, Polly left him. She found that the life of an academic's wife wasn't as glamorous as the life of an academic's mistress. It was even less glamorous when Harvard's president invited Birnbaum to his home for tea and then asked him politely to resign.

Birnbaum, it was rumored, begged his first wife to take him back. She didn't.

Polly then moved to New York, where she conquered the

city's social scene. In no time the daily tabloids dubbed her Princess Polly, and, ultimately, the Principessa. Taking advantage of her newfound fame, Polly launched the Principessa lingerie line. Within two years, she had a corner in Barneys. A year later, she was in all of the major department stores. Five years ago, she opened her very own store on Madison Avenue. Today there are Principessa stores in every upscale mall in the country. And she's famous for always modeling her newest lingerie trend on the cover of her catalog. Polly's romantic life has always been perfect for her image; she has dated politicians, heirs, captains of industry, and entertainers. The relationships were never long, usually because she terminated them before they got serious.

"She may be successful, but she'll never be happy," Jean assured me.

And then, about three years ago, when Polly demanded a top director for the launch of her arty big-budget Principessa ad campaign, she met the always dashing, sometimes aloof Humphrey Dawson. They fell in love in an instant. ("It was truly barfy," Jean always says.) They had a very public, very romantic courtship and have been married for almost two years now. They are a golden couple.

Jean and I are single.

I looked in Land O' Bread's mirror, and I saw Polly and me. She is beautiful and I am on the ordinary side. We are the same height and weight, but I'm gangly with bad posture and she looks like the patron saint of Feldenkrais.

We both have long, straight hair, but hers is bright blond and full while mine is two shades darker with a hint of wind tunnel. Her bone structure reinforces her good features; my bone structure reinforces my bone structure.

She looks like a million bucks and I look as if I'm about to do laundry. We went to the same college. She's a mogul and I'm an unemployed assistant.

FOLLOWING POLLY • 19 •

How did this happen?

In truth, I don't want to be Polly, but I could use a little of whatever it is that makes her tick. I don't need to be involved with a famous director, but it would be fun to have a boyfriend or even a really good make-out session. I don't need to be a mogul, but it would be nice to have a job.

What is life like for Polly? Who does she talk to? Where does she go?

Polly left the store, and without much thought, I was right behind her.

Polly walks very quickly. With some huffing and puffing, I match her pace. We walk over to Lexington Avenue and Eighty-sixth Street. She descends the staircase for the Number 6 train, swipes her MetroCard, and goes through the turnstile.

Polly Linley Dawson has a MetroCard?

I, unfortunately, do not have a MetroCard. Mine has run out. I run up to the machine to put my credit card in and a train comes and goes, taking Polly with it.

Why was she taking the subway? Polly was always portrayed in the media just as I remember her from college: a person who enjoys the amenities money can buy. Even back then she wore expensive perfumes, carried luxury handbags, and trotted about in designer shoes.

An afternoon ride on the Number 6 in unseasonably hot weather is not comfortable. Polly Dawson's hiding something. I have to know what it is.

Okay. I want to know what it is.

I'm up at 7:45. I make my coffee and then turn on the TV. Michael Ledyard, the most annoying guy in the world, is on *The Today Show* touting one-on-one private "straight" camps wherein gay people are cured. He's been everywhere in the past couple of months: *Larry King, Hannity & Colmes, Newsline.* Ledyard, who claims to have cured his own homosexuality and charges a minimum of twenty-five thousand dollars to cure others, clearly finds Matt Lauer attractive.

I have to wait another hour before calling the therapist that Mother recommended for me. I check my e-mail. Ooh, good, one from Daphne Feller, my best friend from high school.

Hey there,

How's showbiz treating you? More specifically how's crazy Mona? Guess what? I'm coming to town for a couple of days to celebrate my parents' fortieth anniversary. My sister is planning a soiree, and she wants me to do a little retrospective of their marriage. Like I have the time. Help please—you're the genius. What in the world did we do for the 20th? I know you were there (weren't you?). Something about Santa Claus or something.

I'll be in for two days, and then I have to fly back Christmas Day. Can I see you? When are you coming to California?

Daffy

I write back to her immediately.

Daph:

So good to hear from you. I have left show business. More to the point, Mona banished me. On to more important things. Of course I was there for their 20th anniversary. Your parents had a small dinner party at Aquavit—you and Samantha and your parents and me. And then Samantha got to bring her best friend, Rachel Goldbaum. And your father had his friend from junior high school and his wife there. They were living in Sweden, I think. Anyway, your mom ordered the reindeer with Lingon-berry, and Rachel flipped out that your mom was eating rein-

deer on Christmas Eve. She said that it was disrespectful to Rudolph and the gang. And then your father started laughing because someone named Goldbaum was showing a little too much sympathy for a Christian folk hero.

Is that helpful? Don't forget to use the thing that happened four years later when your mom forgot about the anniversary altogether and left your dad standing in the rain outside the Martin Beck Theater with two soaking-wet never-to-be-used tickets to see Guys and Dolls. *And then when he screamed at your mom, she, without a missing a beat, started singing "Sue Me." How great was that?*

I hope that's enough to work with. If you want any more help, e-mail. You can call, too. I have some time.

xo
Alice

The therapist has a cancellation this morning and agrees to see me at ten.

"How can I help you?" She asks this as if we are in a department store. I am sitting on her well-worn mustard-colored couch. The room is filled with hanging plants.

I'm shopping for a new life. I explain that Mother wants me to be in therapy.

"And do you want to be here?"

"Sure. Mother has a point."

"Why do you call her Mother?" she asks right off. I admit it does connote a nineteenth-century sort of relationship. My college friends all made fun of it, but then they met her and started calling her Mother, too—to her face.

The therapist's name is Dawn Moses. She asks me to call her Dawn.

"If my patients call me Dr. Moses, their expectations could

be too high." She laughs right as she says this. I can tell she has recited this introduction with this laugh at least a hundred times.

We talk about Mona and why I was fired. She asks if this was the job for me.

"I don't know," I say to her. "I hadn't pictured doing anything else."

"Casting is a unique line of work. How did you get into it?"

"Mother got me the job."

Does she think I'm Mother's puppet? That I only work at jobs and see therapists she sends me to?

"Oh," she says.

We sit awkwardly facing each other for a few seconds. Dawn is tall, fair skinned, with long hair, long earrings, and absolutely no makeup. She wears a crocheted vest over what looks to be a flowing blouse that must have been designed in Flanders, 1452. I bet she has an herb garden and bakes her own granola when she goes camping.

"She was trying to help," I say in Mother's defense. "It's not as if she were pushing me into a life of casting. At the time I needed a job, I was in my twenties, a little aimless, and Mother had a friend who knew Mona. I liked the job. I was good at it. And even though Mona was an unpleasant presence, I didn't mind her. I found her behavior entertaining, except of course when she fired me."

"Your mother is in show business?"

"Yes she is. That's how I got your name."

"And did you ever think about going into show business?"

"Sure, when I was small. I wanted to be just like my mother. Show business looked like fun."

"But you didn't have a lifelong dream about being in show business yourself?"

Wow. I've never had a lifelong dream, except, of course, for the one in which my father and brother would show up and say that it wasn't their plane that had crashed and that Mother was Mother again.

I tell her about the plane crash and Mother's subsequent seclusion. Dawn is adept at getting me to open up. I tell her about how the Upton School community had rallied around me during the years Mother was so remote. My friends and their parents provided me with unending hospitality.

"It sounds like you coped in a very healthy way," Dawn said. I look around the office. Her shelf is filled with academically oriented mental health books, half of which include the word "disorder" in the title. I'm pretty sure she doesn't consult *Mars and Venus Go to the Shrink*.

"Yeah," I told her. "I guess that's why I've never been to see a shrink before. Maybe I was too young to feel the weight of my father's and Paul's absence."

"But you felt your mother's absence."

"I did. But I understood. Even then. That this was more pain than a mother could bear."

"But did you feel pain?"

"I wouldn't say pain, exactly. I don't think I knew what that was. I felt numb. I mean, I remember doing stuff, but it was almost as if someone else was doing it and I was watching. I think that's why it was so easy for me to live my friends' lives."

"Do you still live through others?" Dawn asks.

My mind flashes to an hour before when I was chasing Polly into the subway.

"Not really," I say quickly.

I elaborate a little, telling her that I may just be a vicarious person. When Jean made partner in her law firm, I was probably as happy and as relieved as she was. When Pauline Johnson opened her own creperie, I gobbled five crepes and told everyone I knew to go there. When my friend Stella won five awards at the Sundance Film Festival after writing, producing, directing, and starring in her very first film, I helped throw her a party. The article listing Daphne Feller as one of the top five doctors practicing sports medicine in California is posted on my bulletin board. I love watching my friends make it. I even like watching my nonfriends make it. I'm happy for Gwyneth Paltrow every time she has a baby or stars in a film or looks fantastic in a photo shoot.

Dr. Moses doesn't say anything. So I keep talking.

"When people ask me what's new, I tell them Jean broke up with Hugh Price, Sarah's finally scoring with her take-out crepes, and that I'm hopeful that Lindsay Lohan will pull her life together. So, it's not just Jean."

Dr. Moses still doesn't say anything.

"And it's not as if I'm a gossip or anything. If I can brag about anything, I can tell you that I'm not mean-spirited."

As Jean's gay ex-boyfriend Bram says: I'm schadenfreude-less.

"Well, I would say that's a terrific quality," Dr. Moses says. "But ultimately the question is whether your generous reaction to the lives of others is enough to provide you with a complete and full life?"

"I don't know. Sometimes I think it is. That's why casting was such a perfect gig. I was so happy for the actors when they got their roles and I was happy for the producers when their problem was solved."

"But what about doing something you like to do for yourself?" Dawn asks me.

I'm stuck. "I don't expect you to come up with a perfect career idea for me. So don't worry."

"Why don't we see how it goes?" Dr. Moses says.

"What do you think? Are you going to have me committed?"

Dawn smiles. "I think we have a goal for you in this office."

"What?" Jean will like this. She's very goal oriented.

"Our goal is for us to see if you can come up with a lifelong dream."

"So I can never fulfill it and be disappointed and miserable for the rest of my life."

"That's how I stay in business," Dr. Moses says, and winks at me.

At least she's funny.

That was surprisingly fun. No wonder everyone sees a shrink. It's like writing a memoir without fearing its failure. Jean says that therapy is the best relationship she's ever been in. Seeing as I've been relationshipless for quite a while now, I'm game.

I leave Dr. Moses's office energized in part by her ministrations of therapy but more out of anticipation. I've decided to follow Polly again.

First, I get a MetroCard.

I run over to Polly's building. The Beresford, 211 Central Park West. Right off Eighty-first Street. I know the address because Mona had me drop off some audition tapes for Humphrey Dawson's movie about five months ago.

I wait outside the building. I've brought a copy of *The New York Times* and a coffee with me to pass the time as I lurk on her block.

Around noon, Polly emerges. Her hair is in a ponytail. It looks thicker than it did in college. She's wearing enormous dark glasses and an aubergine pleated silk dress. I notice that she's carrying a large Chloe satchel. I hope she's not going out of town.

Polly once again enters a subway station. It's four yards from her lobby. We're heading downtown. I sit next to her.

She doesn't want to be noticed, and I, for obvious reasons, don't want her to notice me. But it is irritating that the woman doesn't recognize me. We went to school together for four years. We lived in the same dorm, for goodness' sake. Is she that self-absorbed? Am I that unnoticeable?

Evidently, I am.

Once on the subway, Polly opens her Chloe and pulls out an enormous gray sweater, which does not in any way befit her dress or the sweltering subway conditions. I figure she's trying to avoid being recognized so that people won't harass her. I can understand that, although, if we are going to be honest, I am stalking her.

We get out of the train at Canal Street. I follow her. Polly, oblivious to me, heads up the stairs. We walk a couple of blocks. She keeps her head down the entire time before ducking into a small, shabby Victorian apartment building on the north side of Chambers between Broadway and Church Street. It will be impossible for me to follow her upstairs. The question is, do I wait here or do I head home? Of course I should go home. The building has no lobby area, and the block is utterly stoopless and stairless. We are near a lot of city and federal buildings, a huge security zone in post-9/11 New York City. I have no choice but to go home.

And yet I stay.

I imagine Polly is on the top floor, because shortly after she went into the building, a translucent curtain magically appeared, covering an entire bay window.

What is she doing?

When Polly was in college, she always did the unthinkable. When she realized that her freshman roommate, Melinda Jacobs, was on a work-study program, Polly offered a salary twice what Harvard was paying to keep the dorm room clean and do her laundry.

Our dorm master was skeptical of Polly and Melinda's employer/employee relationship, but Polly pleaded her case.

"It makes both of us happy. I don't want to spend all of my

free time sweeping and folding laundry, and Melinda will be able to work fewer hours cleaning toilets in the Radcliffe Quad."

"Are you sure you're comfortable with this?"

"Yes," Melinda assured him.

"Wait till Polly starts making her wear a maid's uniform," Jean had said to me when word got around.

Melinda never wore a uniform, but she did wear Polly's hand-me-down clothing. Polly also bought her a set of cleaning brushes (ironically the ones developed by my father) for her birthday. They took a lot of the same classes, and Jean was convinced that Polly had Melinda taking notes for the both of them.

"They're not even friends," Jean shrieked. "This is sooo wrong."

At the end of the school year, Polly hosted a soiree in her room. She paid Melinda to help decorate and then encouraged her to "stay out of sight" during the party.

"Unless you want to work it," Polly chirped.

I didn't see Melinda after freshman year. Rumor had it that she transferred to Brown.

Six hours later Polly emerges, looking exactly as she did when she went into the building.

What was going on in there?

I stay as close as I can to Polly on the rush-hour, packed train. It's democracy in action underground. Rich people like Polly who prefer the speed or anonymity of New York's subway, and the rest of us. But of course Polly gets a seat. She reaches into her large bag and pulls out a book—the huge bestseller *The Golden Pillow*. And even though she keeps her head down, she bites the left corner of her lower lip, an affectation, I had determined in college, she developed in order to appear pensive. We get off the subway at Eighty-first Street, and she heads upstairs.

I feel as if something really important has happened. I almost skip all the way home.

When I return to my apartment, I see that there is a message on the answering machine. I press Play. It's from Mother.

"Barnes and I are very proud of you, Alice."

I've developed a routine with Polly. I get up every morning at seven, drink my coffee, and put on my Polly outfit: black pants and turtleneck and a black suede jacket. I have some old Jackie O sunglasses that Mother gave me several years ago. Polly and I get on the subway together and go to our assorted destinations. She, for the most part, heads into an apartment building or an office for a few hours, while I wait patiently outside. I tell myself that these excursions are educational.

Okay, I'm nosy. There, I said it. More to the point, why doesn't she recognize me? The combination of my curiosity and my sense of pride leads me to the irrefutable conclusion that I'm justified in spying on her.

Is she cheating on Humphrey Dawson? Is she on drugs? I'm tempted to call Jean and report what has been going on. She often has insights that I don't have. She, for example, told me that I haven't really fallen in love because I'm still not over the death of my father. That makes a lot of sense to me. And is something I will probably bring up with Dr. Moses.

More significantly, Jean would eat this stuff up. A phone call with some Polly gossip would make her day. But she'd probably tell me that what I'm doing is unethical. Jean just made partner at her firm. I don't want her tarnishing her reputation by having an unethical best friend.

In truth, I don't know if following Polly has given me any insight into my own life, but it certainly is fun. Okay, it's a little more than fun. I love it. At least I think it's love. When I wake up in the morning, I'm in a hurry to get out of bed. I rush to Polly's building, flushed with anticipation of the day. When I'm not following Polly, I spend my time thinking about it. I review the places that I've gone with her, and contemplate the places I will go.

I'm addicted to following Polly.

Am I ready to stop?

Not yet.

I like the person I am when I follow Polly. I'm a superhero with the power of invisibility. What am I fighting against? Polly and people like her. When I follow her, it takes away some of her power. I'll teach her not to notice me. Ha, I'm conquering her overconfidence by injecting myself into her secret world.

A world so secret, I have no idea what she is doing.

I could probably learn much more about my attraction to this behavior if I hunkered down and told Dr. Moses. But, let's face it, this activity can't in any way be considered mentally healthy. She would tell me to stop; or worse, she would make it seem so unappealing to me that I would decide on my own to stop. I'm not ready to do that. I'm having way too much fun. I'll tell her soon. Better still, I'll stop.

In a day or so.

I'm late for my appointment with Dr. Moses. I show up with barely twenty minutes remaining in our session.

"Is everything okay?" she asks me.

"Subway stuff," I answer quickly.

In truth, I spent most of the day at Silvercup Studios with Polly as she offered her fashion-conscious admirers select treats from her wardrobe menu: a sleek Armani coat dress, an asymmetrical Mizrahi number, and a Luca Luca tangerine-hued, beaded suit. She's been making the rounds with each of the males from the cast and crew. Today it was Preston Hayes, the handsome male lead. It almost went beyond flirtation; they seemed intimate. Interestingly, she was doing all of the talking—not the usual Polly. She usually speaks only when absolutely necessary. Especially with men.

"Men love to hear themselves," Mother has always told me. Yet every guy I've ever dated has told me I'm too tight-lipped.

Tight-lipped works with Polly; she comes off as sylphlike, whereas I seem like I have nothing to say. But today, she's chatting away. And she has an annoying self-satisfied expression.

Are they an item? Could be, but only yesterday she was talking to the film's other hunk, Ian Leighton.

"If you carried a cell phone"—Dr. Moses brings me back to the present—"you could have called to tell me you were running late." She's wearing a berry-colored peasant blouse. Normally I'm not a fan of square-dance attire but this suits her.

"I assumed that you had figured that out," I rejoined, trying not to sound too snotty. Dr. Moses has on several occasions pressed me about my lack of a phone.

"I rarely feel the urgency to speak with anybody," I continue, "and there are still a fair number of working pay phones in the city if it's really important to call somebody. I'm okay not being in contact every second of every day. Isn't that a testament to my mental health?"

I also saw something on The Today Show about how they cause brain tumors, and it freaked me out.

"Fair enough," says Dr. Moses.

I definitely prefer her response to Jean's; she repeatedly accuses me of being a Luddite. You may have healthier brain cells but you're probably missing opportunities, Jean scolds. You are, in effect, removing yourself from the day-to-day.

In our abbreviated session, Dr. Moses is showing an interest in my romantic history. I don't say anything about Charlie. She would put me on medication.

Charlie is the man I have had a crush on since college. He doesn't know I exist.

Maybe I should spice up my relationship history. Bob, my last meaningful boyfriend, courted me for months because he liked the fact that I didn't turn everything into a huge drama. He hooked up his PlayStation to my TV set and came over every day after work with a bag of Cheetos in one hand and a chocolate Yoo-hoo in the other. He broke up with me a year later, informing me that he was "prepared to be in love" and I was apathetic. I don't know whether I was apathetic or simply apathetic about Bob.

"Have you ever been in love?" Dr. Moses asks me.

Maybe I should make something up, but I want to be as truthful with Dr. Moses as I can. I am, after all, seeking a lifelong dream.

"I said 'I love you' to my college boyfriend, Mark. And then I've had some stuff after that, but I don't believe that I've ever been in love."

Well, that's not true exactly. I've been in unrequited love since college. I only allude to it with Dr. Moses, because I'm afraid that she'll analyze it and ruin it for me.

My college boyfriend, Mark, the pre-med, was a comic book fanatic. One evening, he admitted he was initially drawn to me because I bore an uncanny resemblance to Lois Lane. He was cute in a Richie Cunningham way, but it's difficult for me to conjure up any sexual memory of him. He was a fine diagnostician, though. Jean is a hypochondriac who does in fact get sick from time to time. Mark correctly diagnosed a series of urinary tract infections, strep throat, and tendonitis without conducting any sort of physical examinations. I felt closest to him at these times.

After college, I took my first job as a paralegal, where I had a series of what Jean calls para-relationships: little three-month stints with innocuous men. During that time I attended quite a few social gatherings where I would meet guys who would ask for my phone number. They'd call for a date; we would go out once or twice a week for two or three months and then I'd start not answering the phone.

When I was twenty-five, I quit my job at the law firm so that I could "help people." Julianne London, an old friend of mine, and her older brother Freddy had founded K.I.N.D., an organization to help start nonprofit groups. I told Julianne that I was impressed, and she offered me a job authoring manuals they could provide to start-up nonprofit organizations. Except for acting as a "big sister" to an inner-city kid during my sophomore and junior years in college, I knew nothing about public service. But they seemed so eager to hire me. I took the job and read every manual of every nonprofit group and virtually plagiarized their policies.

Did I mention that I didn't get paid for this position? I realized after six months that Julianne and Freddy wanted me aboard because I wouldn't have the courage to ask them for a salary.

Freddy and I became involved a few weeks after I started working. As the weeks went on, he began spending more and more time in the office, hanging out by my desk and asking a lot of questions. There was never much of a through line to his conversation, and I assumed he was a little lazy and trying to avoid his job responsibilities. One night as I was leaving the office, he asked if I wanted to have dinner. We went to a Chinese restaurant, and he paid for me, telling me that it was the least he could do, given my lack of salary. We talked about the office and Julianne. I realized he was kind of cute. He had the body of a dancer, a large head, and pronounced features, which were further intensified by fiercely rectangular sideburns.

After dinner, he asked if he could come to my house. There was nothing pushy or even romantic about this gesture; I sensed he didn't want to go home. He took off his coat, hung it in my closet, and asked if I smoked pot. I told him that it didn't interest me, and then he asked if it would be okay if he smoked in my house. I said sure. He smoked a joint, and then asked if he could stay over with me. Sure, I said again. We slept in my bed. He didn't try to kiss me or touch me, but when he was asleep, he hugged me tightly. Two days later, he asked if he could come over once more. He took me to an Argentine restaurant three blocks away from my apartment. After the meal, he came over without asking, this time dumping his coat on my couch before extracting a joint from his trousers. We continued with this ritual for months.

"He's gotta be gay," Jean told me when I finally offered her the details of the relationship. "That's the only explanation as to why he's not all over someone as gorgeous as you are. He should want to fuck your brains out."

I didn't tell Jean that I wasn't sure if I wanted him to. I was comfortable with our arrangement. And I was ambivalent about the sideburns.

Freddy and I finally had sex. It always happened in the middle of the night. Freddy would caress my body until I woke up. Then he would make love to me very softly. He always thanked me afterward, unsure of my own enjoyment.

Was it blissful? No. But it was nice. I liked the company. After a year, he put me on salary—for the manuals.

Our relationship continued throughout my tenure at K.I.N.D., almost four years exactly. One day, when Freddy failed to show up at work, Julianne told me that he was deeply unhappy in New York and had moved to Colorado.

Jean was furious. "You gave him the best years of your life," she screamed to me, "and he doesn't even have the decency to be decent."

I was more upset with Jean's describing the last four years as the "best" in my life than I was with Freddy for leaving.

A few weeks after he left, I received a letter from him in the mail.

Dear Alice:

It's very hard for me to write this letter. As you know by now, I am particularly terrible at expressing my feelings. I don't know what Julianne told you about my move. I haven't even told her the real truth behind my leaving. And I couldn't admit it to you until I was 1,600 miles away. You must know how deeply in love with you I am. I have been since I first saw you at your crappy little K.I.N.D. desk. Every morning I'd see you, and I'd try to think of ways to impress you and I always came up blank. I hung out once on the front steps of our offices prepared to strum my guitar and sing a James Taylor song as you strolled into work, but I chickened out when my sister got there first. How many times have I tried to tell you how beautiful you are, how delightful you are, how smart you are and instead ended up talking about al Qaeda or moss. I thought I'd relax when we were sleeping together. But it was clear I was feeling something intense and huge and your mind was elsewhere. I've tried for a couple of years to convince myself that it's okay. I'm shacking up with the hot chick from the office, but it's not okay. I need to start again. I love you, Alice, and I wish you a terrific life.

Freddy

"Wow," Jean exhaled when I showed her the letter. "Thank God. I was beginning to think this man had problems."

"And this doesn't mean he has problems?"

"No. It means he acts like a jerk when he's in love. Now I know why he was so lame."

"You think this is for real?" I asked her.

"Alice. Look at yourself. You are stunning . . . a knockout. You're funny. You have a decent work ethic, which could be great if you applied it to a job you loved. I have three goals in life: I want to make partner, I want to marry a great man, and I want you to realize that you are irresistible."

Yeah, I'm funny. As to the rest of it, I guess that's why you have a best friend.

Dr. Moses asks whether I find women attractive: I talk about Jean in many of my sessions and she asks if that is meaningful.

I think about it. Jean is very attractive, the kind of attractive that men don't appreciate in college but find beautiful at thirty. She's got a runner's body and dresses impeccably; she has blue eyes, curly dark hair—she calls it frizzy because she hates herself— pale skin, and a long nose. She is, without a doubt, my closest friend. But even she tells me that I have intimacy issues.

"You're the only friend that I don't hug," Jean has told me from time to time. She always says this in a lighthearted manner, but I know that it annoys her.

"Maybe it confuses her," Dr. Moses says slowly as if she is leading me to a homosexual epiphany. She's on the wrong track.

It's not her fault. There's all that information I omit. I don't tell her about Charlie. I'd rather she think that I'm not in touch with my inner lesbian than that I have wasted the last thirteen years pining for a man who has no interest in me. He's the standard by which I judge other men. They don't even come close.

"It's not about Charlie," Jean has told me countless times. "You've picked a nice guy who's out there but not available. This is about the death of your father."

I tell Dr. Moses.

"Jean tells me that I can't really fall in love until I address the loss of my father."

Dr. Moses nods her head yes, which I have noticed she does when she is about to disagree with me.

"Funny, I was thinking that falling in love might be hard because of the loss of your mother."

And our time is up. We had only twenty minutes.

"You seem really good," Jean tells me after I have been following Polly for almost two weeks. We are sitting in Ducks, a completely uncool bar on the Upper West Side that makes the most phenomenal cheeseburger in Manhattan. We're waiting for our friend Bram, who, as always, is running about thirty-five minutes late.

Bram is Jean's closest male friend. They dated briefly in college before Bram made the surprise announcement that he was gay. A surprise really only to Jean, who'd found it flattering that, sophomore year, Bram dressed as Jean for Halloween. Jean survived the blow of the breakup and the two of them forged a tight friendship. The two spent and continue to spend most of their time discussing their romantic entanglements, competing for whose situation could earn the label for most toxic. Like Jean, Bram has always been a high achiever. He's now on the verge of making partner with a management consulting firm.

"I am good," I tell Jean, wishing I could spill about Polly.

"Hi, beauties." Bram swoops down and gives Jean a kiss on the mouth. He's wearing a jet-black jacket with a mandarin collar, which looks quite dramatic in concert with what appears to be a very recent Roman gladiator haircut.

He turns to me. "Some affection, please."

I give Bram the warmest hug I can muster. He's actually fairly good at eliciting physical contact from me. We talk for a while about Jean's latest fling, which Bram has labeled "Inappropriate: Exhibit Twenty-four." Jean is sleeping with her paralegal at work.

"He could sue you for sexual harassment," Bram admonishes her.

"I'm pretty certain he's in love with me," Jean says. "He'd never want to hurt me."

"Famous last words," Bram says, but he still manages to ooh and aah over all of the dirty details. "Too bad he's straight."

"How can you be so sure?" I joke.

"I'm done with gay boys," Jean says. "You were my last."

"Jean. I will tell you now, as I tell you every time I see you. You have the worst gaydar since Mrs. Cole Porter."

"Hear, hear," I say as Bram and I clink our glasses.

"What's doing, sister?" he asks me.

"Alice got fired." Before Bram is able to offer his condolences, she assures him, "It's okay, she's in therapy with a top shrink, named Moses."

"I'm loving this already. And by the way, Miss Alice, may I say that unemployment suits you. Your hair looks divine, and you're actually smiling. I never knew you had teeth. Now, tell Brammy everything."

So I go through all of the details of my termination with "Brammy" and Jean. Bram tells me to sue Mona Hawkins Casting and Jean tells me that I should move forward, that the firing was an opportunity for me to figure out bigger life questions. The two of them discuss me. I listen in.

"The only thing bad about the timing here is that Alice could have given us some juice from the new Humphrey Dawson movie. Lots of hot hunkies in one little picture."

Jean always sounds like a fourteen-year-old in 1982 when she and Bram get together.

"Humphrey Dawson." Bram thinks for a minute. "Didn't he end up marrying Polly Linley?"

"Um, hellloooo, welcome to the world. They've only been married for three years now."

"Um, helloo. Thank you, I've been in Africa trying to help several governments develop a comprehensive medical plan," Bram responds. "My *Juice* magazine subscription didn't reach Djibouti."

Bram and Jean spend most of the evening interrupting and complimenting each other while I moderate. This is our typical dynamic. It's both familiar and comfortable. For a couple of hours I'm happy to be distracted from the fine points of Polly Dawson's unpredictable schedule.

"When you worked for Mona, did you ever see little Polly Princess?" Bram asks me as we are walking out.

Only for the last thirteen days.

"Never," I tell him. "It's Humphrey's movie. She's got her own thing."

We're out on the street now. I'm eager to return home. I'm not comfortable lying to my friends.

"Boy, does she ever have her own thing," Bram says, eager to gossip and reminisce some more. "That is one selfish broad. I've spent the last nine years traveling the world, and I've never met a more egocentric bitch than Polly Linley."

"Or competitive," I agree. "I love how she used to invite girls over to her room and say, 'Let's measure our thighs.'"

"Remember when we were having a dorm meeting in the first semester about whether birth control should be free for all students? Polly insisted that it should be and then Frances Stein offered a counterargument that some girls might feel more pressure from boyfriends to have sex if the stuff was so accessible."

Jean doesn't want to go home; she loves telling this story.

"Polly announced to the entire Thayer South that Frances was only saying this because she was a virgin and had confided to Polly that she was terrified that she was frigid. What was the term she used, Alice?"

"Abnormally sexually averse."

"You remember that? That was like fifteen years ago," Bram says.

"Actually, thirteen," I correct him. "How could I forget that kind of language?"

"Bram, how could Alice forget anything? She probably remembers what we ate for dinner that night."

"We had granola."

"Okay, now you're bullshitting me," Bram says.

"No. I'm not. It was broccoli cheese pasta that night, and Jean and I always had granola when it was broccoli cheese pasta because we thought it had fewer calories."

"Dare I ask how you knew it was broccoli cheese pasta night?"

"Because that was the day that O.J. was acquitted. Drew Gordon choked on his broccoli when he heard the verdict, and Alan Shickman gave him the Heimlich maneuver." I remember wondering if I would have been able to do the same.

"How do you know it was all that same day?"

"Bram, never question the memory," I tell him.

"You're right. We are sitting with little Miss Wikipedia. And now, I would like to get back to how evil Polly was toward Frances about her sexual insecurity."

"She had no respect for other people's privacy," Jean says.

"Maybe she's just not that secretive," Bram says.

"Everyone is secretive," Jean tells him as I air-kiss them both and wave good-bye. "Polly just doesn't care about other people's secrets. I bet she has a bunch of her own."

Polly doesn't limit her excursions to the downtown apartment. We've made several other trips in the last few weeks. She meets often with a ginger-haired, heavyset woman in her mid-fifties who wears only beige. Last week, the three of us visited the Metropolitan Museum of Art. Could it be that Polly has a renewed interest in the fine arts? She is spending an enormous amount of time studying Manet's *Déjeuner sur l'Herbe*. There is no way she could be delivering a lecture on the painting. More likely she is trying to work masterpieces into her ad campaign, and replacing all of the masterpiece nudes with pictures of herself in her underwear. Edouard Manet would be proud.

As for the ginger-haired woman, she and Polly seem to hang out quite a bit. The other woman always carries a weathered tote bag with the initials D.M. I've ruled out any sort of sexual relationship between them; D.M. seems way too uptight around her. I've lunched with them at Lever House several times and we've made three trips to the Four Seasons. I'm going broke doing this. It's only a matter of days before the credit-card company calls and asks how I expect to pay for all of this.

I've developed a knack for the restaurant missions. I always bring a popular bestseller and pretend to be engrossed in it, while in reality I'm engrossed in the famous woman sitting two tables away. Of course, it helps that Polly is so self-absorbed.

Polly and I have also made several visits to the New York Public Library. Polly always goes in through the side door, again careful to disguise herself. She heads up the marble staircase, transforming her gait from that of a glamour girl to that of a no-nonsense librarian in a pink Chanel suit.

Polly Dawson has a lot of secrets.

I continue to hear Jean's voice in my head. "Polly Linley will get hers."

Dr. Moses is asking about my friends. Jean and I were roommates freshman year, but we didn't have a real conversation until just before the winter break. She thought I was shy, and I was. Jean always had parades of people in our sparse dorm room, sharing coffee and Pop-Tarts. I envied the ease with which she made friends. She envied my apparent ability to be alone.

Jean and I united that December when her contact lens scraped her cornea and the University Health Services told her she had to go to a real hospital for treatment. I navigated our way from Harvard Square to the Massachusetts Eye and Ear Hospital. We bonded immediately over our dislike for Polly. According to Jean, Polly had been friendly to her the first few days of orientation but distanced herself soon after learning that Jean hailed from the über unchic Fairfield, Vermont.

"Does she even know that Chester Arthur, twenty-first president of these United States, was born in Fairfield, Vermont?" I asked Jean with bogus solemnity.

"Ow—I'm in so much pain, but you actually made me laugh," Jean said. "How did you know that's Chester's birthplace? Have you been to Fairfield?"

"No. I have a good memory," I told Jean.

"You should be a history major."

The hospital visit lasted almost four hours. Jean and I exchanged stories about our families. She was completely fascinated by the tale of how my parents met—I think it had special meaning for her as a college freshman, as she was a bit stuck on Jack Birnbaum (this was before he left his wife for Polly).

The year I met my best friend was also the year I fell in love.

I was a freshman when I first saw Charlie. We were both taking a spring semester History of Paris class. Jean had insisted that I couldn't go through freshman year without a single romance and she instructed me to develop a crush on a male within the week and report back everything. I was eager to find someone so Jean would stop harassing me. On day five, I found him. He was always easy to spot because he wore the same blue oxford shirt to every class, and he wore it the same way every time: sleeves rolled up, about halfway on the left and a sloppy one-quarter on the right.

The class was taught by a Professor Flatineau, an actual French person himself, born and raised in Paris. And while the course had advertised a focus on the social, political, and economic history of Paris, Flatineau spent most of the semester recollecting anecdotes about his obviously privileged upbringing on the Left Bank. To make matters worse, he often lapsed into French. The class ate this up and laughed heartily when he made a little French joke—desperate they were to show him that they understood the French language and the nuances of French humor.

One such time, I caught a glimpse of the guy in the blue shirt: He was rolling his eyes. He caught me staring at him, and smiled. That was good enough for me. I ran back to the dorm and reported everything I could about him to Jean. I was surprised by how much I had picked up. He was on the thin side, though I thought of him more as lanky rather than skinny. His wavy dark hair seemed to grow up and out. He had pronounced cheekbones and thick brown giraffelike eyelashes, which could have made him look feminine but for the fact that he had a large but rather well-appointed nose. Jean was delighted with my progress. I thought she was satisfied until she started to cross-examine me on every detail.

"Does he have a girlfriend?"

"I don't know."

"Is he an upperclassman?"

"I don't know."

"Where's he from?"

"I don't know."

"What's his major?"

"I don't know. I just liked the way he rolled his eyes at the affected people."

"Well, that's a start, but you've got to learn some basic things—like his name." Jean had a point.

My recollection of spring semester was (ahem) spying a bit so that I could fulfill Jean's assignment. And, funny, the more I focused on him, the more my pretend crush became an actual crush. I started thinking about him outside of Flatineau's classroom. Soon I was daydreaming about him on a regular basis, harboring fantasies that he and I would be stranded in a classroom or a library nook, leading to a dramatic and passionate exchange. When I listened to him speak in the class, my stomach would do a somersault.

After weeks of glancing at the contents of his bag, I deduced that he was a junior living in Quincy House, majoring in history. Jean thought that showed compatibility, as I had settled on history as a major. I also figured that he was thinking about law school. He sometimes rearranged his bag revealing LSAT preparation books and law school guides. He was from New York City; I knew that because he used an Amtrak train ticket from the Thanksgiving break as a bookmark. I didn't know if he had a girlfriend.

A few days later, I scored a major coup. I was taking an afternoon seminar at the business school across the river, and I saw Charlie decked out in sweats and a Walkman, running on the bridge. He was there, like clockwork, every Tuesday and Thursday. I found myself trying to come up with excuses to go to the business school even though I didn't have class there on Monday, Wednesday, and Friday to see if I could catch a glimpse of him.

"What's his name?" Jean asked me after two weeks of information about his running habits and his tendency to nap for maybe a minute or two during the slide portion of the class.

He was just the guy with the blue shirt. But I knew Jean would be disappointed with that answer.

I panicked and looked at a copy of *Madame Bovary* that was lying open on my desk. "His name is Charlie," I told her, naming my crush inaccurately after Emma Bovary's doltish husband.

"Charlie's good." Jean changed the subject.

My crush grew and grew. I reported this to Jean, who instructed me to make my move. She told me to ask him if he wanted to study for the final exam together. That way we could work late one night, and the mood would be set for some romance to happen. My stomach turned at Jean's suggestion. I think I experienced shortness of breath.

"I'll think about it," I told her.

And I did. I thought of nothing else. I pictured the two of us holding hands in the library, laughing at the Francophiles and even hosting cocktail parties, similar to the ones Mother and Barnes would have liked except that they would be held in a dorm room and Barnes would not be there. Charlie (as he had become to me, even though I finally learned his name and revealed it to Jean) would come to visit me in New York during the summer, and I would go visit him in Washington. Why Washington? One day his knapsack spilled during Flatineau's class and among his notebooks and history texts was an orientation packet for his upcoming summer internship at the White House.

But I had never spoken to Charlie. In fact, I don't know if we ever officially looked at one another. It would've been strange to invite him to study with me. Aside from that, he was an upperclassman and might not want to be quizzed by a clueless freshman. Jean had no patience for my resistance. She had already dated two seniors and was accustomed to initiating flings.

"Your mother should never have sent you to an all-girls' school," she told me as she was getting ready for the final spring dance. "You're way too scared of boys."

She was right. I was scared of boys.

I still think about Charlie. I learned recently that his family is going through some public trouble. The papers all report that his father, a major bigwig in the pharmaceuticals industry, has been going to prostitutes. This must be difficult for Charlie. He works at the law firm of Pennington & Litt, which represents Kelt Pharmaceuticals, his father's company. I know this because I worked as a paralegal at Pennington & Litt right after college. Everyone at the firm was aware that Kelt was a big client. Everybody at the firm knows who Charlie is. Only, they don't know him as Charlie.

Dr. Moses asks me if I think we are making any progress in the therapy.

"It's only been a couple of weeks," I tell her. "I thought I was on the lifetime plan like Woody Allen. It's probably going to be years before I have my big breakthrough."

"That may be true," Dr. Moses says, "but I'd still like to check in with you and see how you feel."

Hmm. I certainly like it here. Although sometimes it cuts into my Polly time.

"I mean . . . I guess so. I haven't yet figured out my lifelong dream."

"That'll come. Right now, we're just trying to get to a point where you agree it's okay to have a lifelong dream."

For some reason, I start crying.

"Do you need a Kleenex?" Dr. Moses asks, reaching behind her couch.

"No—it's okay. I've got it taken care of." I'm using my shirtsleeve. The tears keep coming.

"You okay?"

"Yeah, I'm fine. I don't know why I'm crying like this. Maybe I'm tired or something."

"Are you getting enough sleep?" Dawn asks warmly. "Do you feel tired?"

Of course I feel tired. I spend at least three mornings a week chasing Polly around the Silvercup Studios lot, watching her flirt incessantly with Preston Hayes and Ian Leighton. The other days she's running around the city with D.M. or engaging in some no-good activity down by City Hall. I really could use a vacation.

"I'm not a big sleeper," I tell her. At least the crying has subsided. "I never have been."

After the plane crash, I could only fall asleep when I was with Mother. The quiet of my room was overwhelmingly lonely. Mother let me fall asleep in her bed every night. That was our best time together.

When I was eleven or so, I stopped sleeping in her bed every night but was happy to know I had the option. It all stopped when she started dating Barnes. He wasn't a frequent overnight guest or anything, but Mother said that was an inappropriate habit.

I heard Mother telling Barnes about the fact that she felt bad for me.

"It's really hard for her," Mother explained to him.

"Angie, she needs to learn. She can't go running to you every time she has a tough night."

Jean calls me this morning to tell me the big news. Charlie is taking a leave of absence from Pennington & Litt. The public story is that it's for health reasons; the real story is that Chip Pennington has told Charlie that while the entire firm appreciates all the work that he has done, clients will associate him with his father. And they told him that it would be best for him, both out of firm and filial loyalty, to leave for a short while.

Jean loves to tell me Charlie news whether or not I want to hear it. In January of my freshman year, not long after I realized that my crush was somewhat obsessive, she told me she saw him holding hands with Polly Linley on a movie line in Harvard Square.

Charlie and Polly were on a date? My life was turned upside down. I felt betrayed. Although Jean had vowed never to speak to Polly, she was concerned about my well-being. She casually asked Polly if she was dating the upperclassman who liked running and history.

"Oh, that guy," Polly sneered. "We went out a couple of times, but he doesn't have any style. I got rid of that one."

Jean encouraged me to find a new crush, reasoning that I shouldn't long for a man who longed for Polly. I was able to push the short-lived couple to an unused part of my brain, and my crush remained intact. Jean can't let it go.

Today she admits to me, however, that while she enjoys the salacious quality of Charlie's work situation, she's also disturbed. She feels that her own job is threatened by this turn of events. Lowry, White & Marcus is a similar firm, and Jean had always assumed that once she earned her partnership, she could expect job security. I remind her that her father is a retired classics professor and will have no impact on Lowry, White & Marcus's financials. Jean tells me that doesn't matter. If they feel that anything you do could hurt their client image, they will throw you out. Charlie, she reminds me, had spent three years in the District Attorney's Office and then four years in the United States Attorney's Office, prosecuting corrupt officials. Jean doesn't need to remind me of this. I'm well aware of Charlie's impressive résumé.

It's cold today and, while we have two weeks until it's officially winter, the trees are bare and the sidewalks are brittle. The streets in my neighborhood look sterile.

I'm betting that Polly hasn't left her house yet. Today is Thursday, and for some reason Polly seems to get a late start every Thursday. So I dawdle at Mother's a bit. She and I chat amiably until Barnes enters the room. He hands me a file folder.

"Alice. I've done a lot of research on your career path and the job market. And I think I have narrowed your options. You should go to law school."

"Thanks, Barnes. I don't want to be a lawyer."

"Law school gives you three years to figure out your future. With that memory of yours, you'll probably be at the top of your class. You'll be buying time, Alice, without wasting time. If you haven't figured it out by the end of law school, you can work as a lawyer indefinitely until you figure out what you want to do."

"I really appreciate that, Barnes," I say, although I don't appreciate it. "But law school is tough and working as a lawyer is hard. It will be almost impossible for me to come up with a—" I want to say "lifelong dream" but Barnes cuts me off.

"Alice, most people work at jobs they don't want to do. What makes you think you're so special?"

I look at Mother, hoping she'll say something about me being special, but she doesn't.

"Thanks, Barnes, but I think I'll put off the LSAT for a few months. I've been making some real progress."

"Some."

"Really?" Mother's face brightens. "Anything you care to share with us?"

Barnes is staring me down. He can tell I've made no progress, and he's angry that I'm rejecting his law school idea.

"I've been taking some meetings," I say in my most CEO-like tone.

"Taking meetings with who?" Barnes asks.

"I think you mean 'whom,'" I tell him.

"Who's at the meetings?" Barnes bellows. His face is red, and I'm suddenly enjoying myself.

"A classmate from Harvard. Perhaps you have heard of her: Polly Dawson?"

"You're taking meetings with Polly Dawson." Barnes's voice is dripping with disdain.

"Sure," I tell him. "We've had a couple of lunches at the Four Seasons and have been sort of exploring New York together."

Sort of.

"That's wonderful," Mother says, relieved that her decision to push me into therapy was the right one.

Barnes looks suspicious.

"We always had this bond in college," I tell him. "Remember? We lived in the same freshman dorm. We have the same birthday."

"That's wonderful," Mother says again, and Barnes looks defeated.

"I have to go and pack for my backgammon convention," he announces.

"We're really proud of you," Mother tells me.

As I leave, I realize I sound like those crazy people who stalk celebrities for months and months, and fabricate a personal relationship with them. If Mother were to approach Polly and ask her about me, Polly would have no idea what she was talking about.

This is a big wake-up call. The following has got to stop. I need to find a real career for myself. Then I can tell Mother that it didn't work out with Polly—I can even tell her that the Principessa is a major *B-I-T-C-H.*

But alas, I find that my calendar is still rather clear for the rest of the day. Maybe I'll just go by Polly's apartment building and see if there's any activity.

Okay, so I've been standing outside Polly's building for more than an hour. I know I just said I was going to stop, but the day has gone to waste anyway. I might as well see what she's up to. Tomorrow, I'll do something productive.

Polly emerges.

She's in her public outfit. Her hair is cascading down her back. She's wearing some sort of light-colored animal skin. Knowing Polly, it's a polar bear. I remember a few years back when animal-rights groups tried to boycott Principessa products to protest Polly's wearing a tiger skin on the cover of her Principessa catalog.

Polly shot back at the groups.

"If a tiger could drive a car it would," she announced at a press conference, "and it would run over every animal-rights wacko out there."

Initially, the business world gasped at Polly's outburst. For days, there was talk that Principessa would go out of business. No such luck. Polly's little eruption transformed into a lucrative and unexpected trend. Her store sold baby tees, pajamas, and boxers decorated with little tigers driving cars. Since then, Polly rarely goes to a public function sans animal pelt.

It turns out we are going to Gracie Mansion.

The mayor's home.

My first thought is: I can't get in there.

My second thought is: I'm not dressed for the occasion.

I'm able to sneak by security. Well, not exactly. I notice that the mayor's office is hosting an event for high-profile women. When the bouncers ask me for my name and identification, I grouse, "Don't you know who I am?"

It works. They are mortified. I sneak into the mansion's drawing room and look for Polly. She is just there to make an appearance. She kisses the mayor on the cheek; I give him a polite but uncalled-for curtsy. She waltzes out the door, and I do the same.

Today Dr. Moses wants to know what I think about Barnes.

"It's complicated," I tell her.

"Try me."

"The man 'saved' Mother. He virtually brought her back to life. Something I couldn't do."

I remember so clearly meeting Barnes for the very first time. I had just turned sixteen and was thrilled to meet him. My friends thought I would be freaked out that a stranger would be replacing my father. But I was relieved. This stranger had given Mother a second chance. It was a miracle. I had never even thought of him in the same category as my father.

"Do you resent him for that?"

"For being able to do something I couldn't, you mean? No. I think I may understand it. I was too young to take care of her."

"I sense a 'but' in there somewhere," Dr. Moses says as she removes her clogs and brings her legs up on the couch.

"It's just that I feel ripped off. I'm happy that Mother met someone. I just wish he were different. Mother started off married to Indiana Jones and she ended up with Marie Antoinette."

"I can see how that would be a comedown."

"I know that Barnes doesn't want bad things to happen to me. He has just made it abundantly clear that he wants to be the most important person in Mother's life, so he tries to limit my access to her. I'm less likely to intrude on his time with her if I'm employed. It's just who he is."

"But is it who your mother is?"

"It's not how she was," I say. "Maybe it's who she is now."

I leave Dr. Moses's feeling sad. To make matters worse, it's too late to catch Polly today.

Today we go to the apartment on Chambers Street. We are only there for an hour before she comes out. She's not alone. She's with a man. Not even a man. He looks like a boy. He's wearing cargo pants and unlaced hiking boots. Oh my! He has a soul patch. A soul patch?! Doesn't he realize she's wearing Pucci?

Polly Princess is a big cheat. This is not the flirtation dance I witnessed at Silvercup. This is sneaky.

I decide to skip my therapy appointment. All the work that I have put in: I have to see it through to the next step. Dr. Moses would understand—if she knew what I was doing.

We go to Mee-Hop, a restaurant in Chinatown. It's completely un-glitzy except for the nine thousand Christmas lights all over the place. I have been so consumed with Polly that I forgot Christmas is in two days. That's okay. Barnes ruined the holiday a long time ago.

The place is packed. Polly is sporting her understated but beautiful look. Her perfect ponytail effortlessly bounces on the back of her head. She's wearing a slate-blue tunic over black leggings and tall black boots. Most of the patrons are Chinese and don't seem to recognize Polly. The two find a little table in the corner. As I glance around the restaurant looking for the perfect seat, I hear a familiar voice behind me. I feel that tingling sensation. It's Charlie's.

I head toward the restroom so that I can assess the situation. I should abort my mission. Charlie might see Polly. I wonder if he would say anything to her. For all I know, he's still pining away for her.

My eyes keep wandering to Charlie's table. I find him so appealing. He is still thin and he is slouching ever so slightly. His dusty brown hair remains untamed. I read somewhere that chemistry is not necessarily determined by looks. Jean says that it's all smell. But all that I smell now is the scallion pancake that sits before me.

Charlie's back is to me. He's sitting across from a cop. I know this because he's wearing a uniform, with a name badge on it. KOVITZ, it says. Maybe he's talking to Kovitz about his father.

Polly's becoming less and less interesting to me. She's staring into her lover's eyes. He's looking proud. The relationship has "going nowhere" written all over it.

You'd think I'd consider this day a great success. Polly slipped up. I saw her and I saw the guy. But I feel less resentful of her than ever.

I'm too distracted by Charlie and Kovitz. I cut my mission short.

The next day Dr. Moses tells me that I seem preoccupied—more so than usual. She may be right. I'm jarred by the Charlie spotting. Not just because it involved Charlie, but because it happened during an operation. I can't tell the therapist because that would entail discussion of Charlie and following Polly, neither of which I'm prepared to do.

My two secrets, I think as I leave her office.

I can't shake the feeling that someone is watching me.

Today I'm ready to change my life. My most recent Polly excursions have been more annoying than interesting. I have been so caught up in following this woman that I missed Daphne's visit to New York. Besides, I have a feeling my secret missions aren't so secret. Yesterday, when we emerged from a shopping spree, she quite suddenly turned around. While looking right at me, she started screaming, "You. You. You. I knew it was you!" I was trying as fast as I could to put together a sane-sounding explanation for my behavior when I heard a voice behind me.

"Chérie."

It was the deep voice of Maurice Fantin, the celebrated Corsican parfumier. The two embraced in the street, their attraction for each other charged not by a sexual force but rather the natural exhilaration experienced by purchaser and purchasee. Once I realized that Polly had not been looking at me but rather through me, I was interested only in removing myself from the scene. I tasted, for only a second, the humiliation of being found out. I didn't like it. This will end.

In five days, we'll be starting the New Year. And I'm making my resolution early. I'm going to stop following. Today will be the last time.

I go to the bagel shop right around the corner from me before I head over to Dr. Moses's office on the East Side. There is nothing to eat or drink in the house. And I remember that I haven't eaten for days. My intense Polly excursions coupled with my recent Charlie sighting have made me feel crazy.

The bagel place is almost empty. An old man is sucking on his bagel at the other end of the shop. I eat my bagel and drink two coffees. I feel invigorated. Off I go to Dr. Dawn Moses.

I think I know my lifelong dream.

It's Charlie. It always has been.

And then, just before I walk out, I see her! Polly's here. In my bagel store. If I didn't know any better, I would think *she* was following *me*. It's a sign. But of what? To keep following her? No. I know it's wrong, and I'm committed to stopping. I have to stop. I have to move on. Maybe she's here so that I can come clean. No—not fully clean. Not, "Hey, Polly, remember me? I helped you break into your dorm room at Harvard, and now here I am trailing you for weeks on end for no particular reason."

I couldn't admit to that.

But maybe there is some other way to stop following Polly. I could act as if our dual presence at the bagel shop is serendipitous. I could ask if she remembers me from Thayer South. I could be casual about it. After all, I'm a Harvard graduate. For all she knows, I'm a private investor looking to sink my funds into a lingerie company. This is perfect.

This is the closure I need. After I'm done with her, I'll figure out a way to meet Charlie, really meet him. And if my dream isn't realized, I'll at least know that I had one. I look in a mirror for a second to fix my hair. I wish I didn't look quite so shabby. I jump into the restroom to finger comb my hair. I step out, and Polly is gone.

She's next door at the tailor. I wait outside, pretending to look at the junk shop window next door. It's only eleven-thirty. She emerges and immediately sticks out her hand and hails a cab. Without much ado, I stand behind her with my hand sticking out. The first cab stops for Polly. I get another within seconds. The driver asks where we are going. I tell him to follow the cab in front of me. He's confused but I explain that the person in the cab has bronchitis and that I'm pregnant and don't wish to catch her ailment by sitting so close to her, but that we are attending an important meeting, and she was coughing so hard when she gave me the address that I couldn't hear her, but I didn't want to ask her again because she kept coughing on me. The driver has no idea what I'm talking about, but is moved by the fact that I'm pregnant, and he tails Polly's driver like a pro.

It turns out our "business meeting" is at Otto & LuLu's, a clothing emporium in NoLita, a once-gritty, now-trendy area south of NoHo and east of SoHo. The place looks like a brothel. There are rugs and scarves and Tiffany lamps everywhere. Necklaces and gloves and masks hang from lighting fixtures. There's a ficus tree in the middle of the store, and two spider monkeys roam around. A sign explains that the larger monkey is Otto and the smaller one is LuLu. There are armoires all over the place filled with clothing, and chests of sweaters. I look for Polly, but I can't find her, as the armoires and chests create a labyrinthine atmosphere. The décor does not inspire me to shop. In fact, despite the small customer turnout, I feel claustrophobic. There are also about twelve different flavors of incense and candles vying for aroma-dominance. Suddenly, I hear music. I will find Polly, say my hello, and leave.

I realize she must be in the back of the store. I see no sales-people, but I keep looking. There's a large space in the back cordoned off; it must be the dressing area. I grab a dress from the armoire behind me. I'm eager to leave this strange store and try to start my life. I climb over the ropes. There are three small rooms, with curtains for doors. The first one is completely empty. The second one is filled with clothes. The curtains to the third one are mostly open, so I go inside and look. It takes a second to sink in. Polly is in here, but she is on the ground.

"Hello," I say softly.

She doesn't answer.

It suddenly registers: Polly is covered in blood. I'm afraid to touch her. I've never seen a dead person, but she certainly does not look alive.

"Hello," I say, and I look at her face. Her complexion is off. Her eyes are open, facing me, but she doesn't blink and the parts of her skin that aren't covered in blood have an eerie quality to them. I touch her. I expect her to feel cold and stiff, but she's warm and pliable. Maybe she's alive.

"Hello," I call out. But no one is there.

I hear something. Someone's coming back here. I am still looking at Polly's bleeding body.

"You should call an ambulance," I say.

No response. I look around and realize that I'm talking to either Otto or LuLu. This freaks me out completely. I vomit. I must get out of here. I find my way out of the store, and I run.

One thing is for sure: Polly Dawson finally got hers.

TWO

ON THE RUN

I don't want to leave my house. I am, to borrow a phrase from Jean, freaked out. I turn on the television to see if Oprah has any suggestions about my spirit, but the show has been interrupted by a breaking news story: Polly Dawson, wife of critically acclaimed director Humphrey Dawson, has been stabbed in cold blood in NoLita, a perky journalist reports.

I can't believe that Polly's death has bumped Oprah.

The perky journalist starts to list Humphrey's film credits. I turn off the television.

I realize I haven't removed my suede jacket even though it is sweltering in my apartment. There is a dried splotch of blood on my sleeve. Polly's blood. The blood of the wife of critically acclaimed director Humphrey Dawson.

The phone rings. It's Mother. I let the machine pick it up. Mother talks very quickly when she's excited. She wants to know if I heard that Polly Dawson was dead. She remembers that I had reunited with her. Did I know her husband? She then switches gears a little to congratulate me on leaving the casting office before this whole thing happened. It can be very "toxic," she explains, to "work in that kind of environment." Not casting in general. Just in an office with such close ties to a homicide.

I don't pick up the phone during this long message. Mother can be a little exhausting. She was always very curious about the daily goings-on at Mona Hawkins Casting, and she'll be impossible to get off the phone now.

Jean also leaves me several messages. She's less concerned with Polly Dawson than she is with me. She says things like "How *are* you?" and "I just want to know *how* you are." A few times in a very long-winded message she also manages to tell me that her twenty-three-year-old paralegal dumped her rather abruptly and that she'd been depressed but that this whole thing with Polly Dawson has put everything into perspective. She finishes the phone call with another "Just wanted to know *how* you are doing." I'll call Jean later.

There are some more messages. Everyone is concerned but excited by the news: Clare Ransom comes right out and asks if the director husband did it. Bram calls from an airport in Africa and leaves me a message. "It's a gay thing, I bet you."

Dr. Moses calls me to tell me that she is worried that I missed my appointment. Would I like to make it up?

But I don't.

Dr. Moses calls again. She says that it might be beneficial to see her and that of course there is the matter of—

The matter of what? The machine has cut her off. Whatever curiosity I may have about her message is outdone by my limitless inertia. No need to erase all the messages. Any new ones that come in are bound to sound like the others.

The phone rings every now and then. Usually the caller gives up after five rings or so, but there's obviously one caller out there who is willing to give me ten rings. This is clearly someone who has never been to my teeny-tiny apartment. I'm only vaguely curious about the identity of this persistent individual. I don't have caller ID on my phone. Jean romanticizes this and tells me that ultimately I'm a fan of mystery and suspense and caller ID kind of ruins that.

The phone continues to ring. I continue to ignore it.

I think it has been a full two days since I have eaten. There's nothing in my fridge other than capers and some moo shu chicken from last week. I don't feel hunger.

I don't feel anything.

I don't turn on the TV. I'm sure that there will be more information about the murder, but the gossipy tone of the news reporters is sickening.

I finally take the phone off the hook. I'm no longer interested in the identity of the caller. I'm tired, but I can't sleep.

There's a knock at my door. I look in the peephole. It doesn't show much, but it shows enough.

Kovitz.

A police badge with the name Kovitz.

Charlie ate lunch with a policeman named Kovitz in Chinatown the day I saw Polly with her young lover.

More knocking.

"Ms. Teakle, are you in there?"

I don't even answer; I open the door.

"Ms. Teakle, my name is Phil Kovitz. This is my partner, Ray Seminara, and Officer Donnell Bristol. We have some questions for you. Would you mind coming to the station house?" Donnell, chocolate-skinned and burly, looks like Mr. T would have had he gone into a more conventional line of crime fighting. Kovitz is shorter than I am, pasty in the face, and balding with a crew cut. Seminara, mustachioed and tall, has an acne problem.

Now, I know what you are thinking. I should say, "Yes, Detective Kovitz, I would mind going to the station house." But the truth is I am sort of looking forward to it. A change of scenery would do me a world of good at this moment. I haven't left my house in close to three days; I'm hot and bored. I smell something unpleasant. It's me. I haven't showered in three days, and I've been sweating through the same outfit.

I ask if I could freshen up a bit, but Officer Bristol tells me that freshening up isn't necessary. He's only lightly touching my arm, but I'm in no position to test his physique.

I go outside. My block is unrecognizable. The air is thick with snow. I can't see anything. I walk with my hands outstretched like I'm in a zombie movie. I hit an object covered with snow. It's a parked car. A parked police car.

Officer Bristol tells me that this is his vehicle and encourages me, with his hand on my arm, to get in as quickly as possible. I do, but I take a second to grab a handful of snow and wash my face.

Kovitz sits next to me in the backseat of the car. I'm eager to ask him about Charlie but I know that would be inappropriate.

We drive with the siren on.

It occurs to me that this isn't a friendly encounter. So I do what I do best: I keep silent.

We stop in front of the fifth precinct station house. Kovitz opens the door and leads me inside.

Should I ask for a lawyer? I was, after all, a paralegal at Pennington & Litt, and they have hundreds of them.

I doubt they remember me.

I could call Jean, but she does mergers and acquisitions. Whenever I watch *Law & Order,* I call her to ask if that episode's legal maneuvers would really happen. She always tells me she doesn't know.

Then there's Charlie; he knows Kovitz.

The problem is, of course, he doesn't know me.

I wonder if I should call Mother. But she would get all dramatic and turn what promises to be a short and simple interview into a Sally Field feature film. And Barnes? Well. No. I'll do this alone. I'm good at alone.

Kovitz and Seminara take me into a room. They ask me if I know Polly Dawson.

"Not well," I tell them.

"You were aware that she was murdered three days ago," Seminara instructs me.

"Yes."

"What was your relationship with her?"

Relationship?

"I didn't have a relationship with her?"

"But you knew her."

"Yes."

Kovitz interrupts us and remarks that I look cold and asks if I would like a coffee. I'm not cold, but I'm famished and tired. I tell him to add a lot of cream and sugar. Usually I like milk and no sugar, but I imagine the station house fare needs a little help.

"What was your relationship with the deceased?"

The deceased.

I tell Seminara that I worked at Mona Hawkins and that we did the casting for her husband's film *Only at Sunrise*.

"How would you characterize your relationship with her?"

This is the third time Seminara has alluded to a relationship between me and Polly Dawson.

"I had no relationship with her. I don't know that we ever spoke since our first day in college."

"Ms. Teakle, we have reason to believe that you were on the premises of a store called Otto and LuLu's at or around the time Polly Dawson was murdered."

Kovitz puts the coffee in front of me. It smells like old milk, but I'm dying to take a sip. I grab the cup and put it near my lips when I see the only thing that, at this point, ties me to Polly's body.

I decline to drink the coffee. As I told you, I watch *Law & Order,* and the police always tempt suspects with beverages and cigarettes so they can get DNA from their saliva.

I don't fall for it.

"Ms. Teakle." Seminara has raised his voice and his left cheek bulges a bit. "We have an eyewitness who claims to have seen you enter the premises of Otto and LuLu's at or around the time of Polly Dawson's murder."

I don't say anything.

"Better yet"—Seminara is louder still—"our eyewitness has

firsthand knowledge of you tailing Polly Dawson from a location at or around Midtown Manhattan to the premises of Otto and LuLu's. In fact, Ms. Teakle, our eyewitness tells us that you ordered him to follow the decedent and that you utilized a ploy involving a story of Polly Dawson being pregnant and of you having bronchitis."

Actually, I said that it was Polly who had bronchitis. I was the pregnant one.

I still don't say anything.

"Ms. Teakle. We also found a fuchsia button looking an awful lot like the buttons visitors to the Metropolitan Museum of Art get once they have paid their admission to the museum. We just happened to check your credit-card records and we learned that you were at the museum several Thursdays ago. And we happened to check with the Metropolitan Museum admissions office, who told us that they were dispensing fuchsia buttons to museum visitors several Thursdays ago when Polly Dawson was there."

But I returned my button to the museum recycle bin.

I still don't say anything.

"Ms. Teakle, we also found at the crime scene matchbooks from the Four Seasons, Lever House, and other restaurants Polly Dawson frequented. You were at those restaurants at the exact time she was. You left credit-card records. Also at the crime scene, we found a sample of Denis G. hair wax. And our records also happen to show that you received beauty treatments at an establishment known as Denis G. at or about the same time Polly received those treatments. And Ms. Teakle, our records happen to show multiple incidents of trespass at Silvercup Studios and in the mayor's mansion during an exclusive party Polly Dawson attended. We have it all on videotape."

Their records happen to show a lot.

I don't say anything.

"We are in the process of confirming with your psychiatrist that you missed your appointment during the precise time that Ms. Dawson was attacked."

"Psychologist," is all I can say.

"Excuse me?" Kovitz turns on his tape recorder.

"Psychologist. You said I missed my appointment with my psychiatrist; she doesn't have an M.D. She can't dispense medication. She's a psychologist."

"Don't be smart with me. Not all of us went to Harvard," Kovitz says.

"That isn't . . ." I try to defend myself.

"You may think you have the upper hand now because of your Harvard education, but you aren't going to get out of this. Ms. Teakle, the police are at your house searching for the weapon that was used to kill Polly Dawson."

The police are at my house!

"They won't find any—"

I lift up my hand and I see the blood on my sleeve.

But Kovitz doesn't notice.

"I'd like to call a lawyer," I tell him.

He pauses.

"Okay."

Someone knocks on the door. Kovitz goes to answer and the two whisper. I'm curious to know the content of the conversation because I know it's about me.

"We have to go to another room," Kovitz informs me.

We leave our room. I grab the coffee cup. I guess they don't need my saliva if they're at my house right now. I left loads of DNA behind.

Kovitz directs me to a chair outside. He tells me that he has to take care of something and that I should "sit tight." Seminara and Bristol are nowhere in sight.

I sit tight per Kovitz's instructions. The station house is busy and loud. My eavesdropping skills have improved over the last months, so I'm able to pick up significant portions of conversations.

There's a baby-faced woman a few feet from me begging an officer to seek an order of protection and press charges against her abusive husband. The officer looks through his notes.

"Do you realize that this is the fourth time you've been here to get the police to take action against the same individual?"

"Yes, sir." She's looking in her lap.

"Do you know that every time you file a report, the District Attorney's Office expends a considerable amount of time and resources following through on your request?"

"Yes, sir." She doesn't look up.

"And you must know that you always drop the charges?"

No response.

"You probably don't know how difficult this is for the District Attorney's Office. Do you?"

No response.

"And demoralizing, too," he adds.

She's crying. No—she's not the one crying. She has a baby in her lap.

I turn my head. There are NO SMOKING signs everywhere and yet the room smells like a bar.

Police officers keep walking by me. They don't look at me; they don't know I'm being questioned for the murder of Polly Dawson. It's amazing how different they look from each other in spite of their uniforms.

They all have guns hanging at their waists.

I hear a familiar voice from across the room. It's loud enough so I can hear it and atonal enough so I can identify it. The voice belongs to Officer Bristol.

"Positive ID on the Dawson murder weapon. It's Teakle's."

Then I hear, "Let's do it."

It's Kovitz.

These people believe I killed Polly Dawson? I thought they were giving me a hard time because they thought I was a witness or a weirdo. But they think I did this? It makes no sense, and yet they're certain. The police always make mistakes on *Law & Order*. Usually, they figure out where they went wrong during the trial, but occasionally an innocent party ends up in jail.

Could that happen to me? Jail for the rest of my life? Because of a museum pin, some video footage, and hatred-slash-stalking of a former dorm mate?

Jail looks pretty crappy on TV.

I'm not an ambitious person, but I have recently—in the past second or so—developed a new lifelong dream: no prison.

And I know how to achieve it.

Bristol and Kovitz are talking, laughing even.

There's an EXIT sign across from me. So I do what I do best: I sneak out unnoticed.

I'm on Canal Street. The precinct house is two blocks from me, but it feels as if I've crossed the Iron Curtain. There are no cops out here. The air smells delicious—a mix of coconut from the Chinese bakery behind me and the lamb kebab from the food truck across the street. It's still snowing, but all I'm wearing is my T-shirt and suede jacket. I think I'm freezing, but I'm grateful for circulating air. I can't go home. The police are in my house. I can't go to Mother's. The police are probably there questioning her. If they checked all that stuff on my credit card, they would most certainly have staked out my family. It's probably too risky to contact Jean right now. Even if the police have not spoken to her, I don't want to get her in trouble with her law firm. Just think, if Charlie's firm ousted him because his father is a suspect in a prostitution ring, who knows what Jean's firm could do when her best friend is a murder suspect?

A murder suspect. And probably not just *a* murder suspect. *The* murder suspect.

Me.

Of course it's ridiculous and yet I almost think I am guilty. I followed Polly to Otto & LuLu's. And I have no credible explanation for it.

Then, of course, there are the museum receipts.

And the restaurant receipts.

And Silvercup.

And the mayor's party.

But I threw out my museum pins; I never took matches from the Four Seasons and Lever House. And I didn't even know Denis G. was doling out hair wax samples. I certainly never touched the murder weapon.

Someone has been following *me*.

I do the only thing I can think of.

I look up Charlie in the phone book. He's easy to find. He's the only Walter Redwin in Manhattan. Walter Redwin. That's Charlie's real name, but he's way more of a Charlie than a Walter.

Charlie lives in a town-house apartment on East Sixty-fifth Street between Park and Lexington. I take the subway to Hunter College on Sixty-eighth Street. I emerge from the station. The light blinds me, but the sun is devastingly deceptive. It's freezing, and I'm still wearing only my suede jacket and a filthy T-shirt. I curl my hands up into my jacket sleeves to walk the three blocks. It's odd; this area is usually packed with college students hanging around outside the buildings and the subway station, but today it's completely deserted. I pass a church. I look across the street; there is a store that sells only white wicker.

Suddenly I see about fifty police cars. Have they been tracking my movements underground? No. They're parked. There's a police precinct on Sixty-seventh Street, but no one seems to be tailing me. I get to Sixty-fifth Street and I walk in front of Charlie's building. The residential block is completely isolated except for a small booth. I look across the street and I notice a small house, the size of a phone booth, with a huge POLICE sign on top. There's a uniformed officer inside reading the *New York Post*. He doesn't realize that he's in the presence of a murder suspect. This could be the big break he has been waiting for; they could finally let him out of that microscopic booth into the big city. But no! He isn't looking for a promotion at this moment. I know that I can't take his complacency for granted. If I remain on this block too long, he may notice me and start poking around. On the other hand, if I want to make contact with Charlie, lying in wait at his apartment is probably my best bet.

I remember that it's New Year's Eve. Charlie may be away for the holiday. I'll stake him out another time. The sun is starting to sink and it's bringing the temperature along with it. If I want to survive the night, I need to be inside. I run five more blocks downtown and push myself through the by-now-familiar revolving door at Bloomingdale's, one of Polly's favorite hangouts. It's packed with people returning Christmas gifts and people desperate to find something perfect to wear tonight. I'm one of the latter.

I go to the ladies' room to freshen up. After I wash my face and run my fingers through my hair, I don't look so bad. I improve myself at the Clinique counter, where three women in lab coats give me a makeover. I make it clear to them that I'm not going to buy anything. They enjoy my honesty and tell me that I have a lot of potential in the beauty department.

Hardly flattering, but I'm completely dependent on their kindness. They wash my face with two kinds of soap and then they massage my head a little before dabbing me with toner. Then we get to a base cream, a base powder, and a base mix. A crowd begins to circle me. The women are using my head as a demonstration. No one is looking at me as a dangerous killer. I am, after all, only a learning tool.

After twenty more minutes of eye artistry and lip work, the Clinique scientists release me. But not before they thrust a mirror in my hands. I must admit, I look pretty marvelous. I bet I'm the best-made-up murder suspect in the greater New York area.

I head up the escalators to the fourth floor. The shoppers have incredible focus.

"I need something midnight blue with one percent spandex," a customer tells a salesgirl as she maintains one eye on the rack. "That's my look."

I too have focus. I go through the stock with tremendous speed. Two salesgirls ask me if they can help.

"I'll know it when I see it," I tell them.

Of course, I can't tell them I'm looking for that one item of clothing that lacks a security tag.

I find something. It's a deep purple wool dress: a turtleneck that falls just below the knees and is four sizes too big. Not exactly right for a New Year's Rocking Eve, but at least it's not too small. I take off my suede jacket and go to the dressing room and I pull the dress over my head. I pull my jeans above my knee. I'm wearing my orthopedically friendly, therefore ugly, shoes and argyle socks; I'll have to lift some tights on the way out. If the regular cops don't get me, the fashion police are sure to put me in lockup.

I walk by the salesgirl who had offered me her help. She doesn't notice that I'm wearing a completely different outfit.

Or that it's four sizes too large.

Even with my makeover I'm invisible.

I go to the coat section. At first I think my only option is a white ski jacket with rabbit trim; I decline to take it. I may be a thief and a murder suspect, but I don't wear fur.

I have an idea. I grab the ski rabbit thing and I go back past my salesgirl into the dressing rooms. I find a Prada purse sitting on top of a sensible navy wool coat. The coat does not have a security tag; it is not for sale. It belongs to a customer. Well, not anymore. I put it over my new outfit. I dig into the Prada purse and learn that Diane Paynter will be going to her Park Avenue apartment sans coat. I memorize the address; I will send her a fruit basket and a check when this whole mess is straightened up.

I realize that my moral center has taken a turn for the worse. The following was strange, but at least it wasn't illegal. But I have crossed over from quirky to outlaw. I didn't report Polly's death, I escaped police custody, and I have committed two thefts (three if you count the tights I plan to steal on my way out). With the exception of stealing Diane Paynter's coat, which I agree is deplorable, I really didn't see a way out of my situation with law enforcement. I have to prove them wrong, and I need to be warmer to do it.

I leave Bloomingdale's with the tights. No need to return to Charlie's street. I have to approach my stakeout parsimoniously if I'm going to avoid the policeman noticing me. I'll wait elsewhere.

I hang out at a Starbucks two blocks from Bloomingdale's. It's fairly warm and comfortable, and no one seems to care that I'm not buying anything in exchange for this temporary shelter.

In fact, there's a man who has taken over the back of the store; he has a laptop computer on one table, five enormous textbooks on another, and some legal pads on a third. He doesn't appear to be eating or drinking anything. He gives me a dirty look, so I stop looking at him.

The barista announces that due to New Year's Eve, Starbucks will close early tonight: only fifteen more minutes.

"Fuck, fuck, fuck, fuck." The laptop guy says it—not me.

I leave Starbucks. Diane Paynter's coat is not warm enough for me to stay outside indefinitely. Any other day, I could probably hop from store to store for twenty-four-hour shelter, but this is New Year's Eve and everybody seems to be itching to go home. I head over to the Fifty-ninth Street subway station. It seems especially grim tonight, but there's a Downtown Local 6 train approaching. I get on.

I like the subway less when I'm not following Polly. When I was with her, there was a certain level of suspense involved. I'd ask myself, Is this the stop? What will we do once we get there? Now there's no suspense, unless of course you take into account that the fifth precinct is after me. But the decision-making is more or less in my hands, and that makes me uncomfortable.

I get off at Spring and Broadway. This may be a stupid decision, as I'm only seven blocks from the precinct, but I'm in the heart of SoHo, which will make for more activity. I pass a Victoria's Secret, where I pity the mannequin displayed in the window wearing nothing but tap pants and a padded bra in this brutally cold weather. I pass a Sephora. They advertise free New Year makeovers. I almost go in until I remember that I had the Clinique makeover a few hours ago. I can't take my eyes off the window display. The packaging of jars, tubes, and compacts looks like a candy display. I'm salivating over lip gloss. I espy a Dean & DeLuca across the street and confirm that I'm starving.

Alas, I'm penniless. Not a single sou in Diane Paynter's coat.

I go in. My mouth is watering. I haven't eaten for days and their presentation is inviting. The vegetables are so abundant and bright, they look unreal. The string beans are tumescent. They have six different kinds of oranges and fourteen species of pear. I walk past the vegetables by the prepared foods hoping for a little sample. There's nothing to taste, but there's a huge selection of goodies for sale: chicken pot pies, flavored hummus; platters of ribs are being advertised as TODAY'S SPECIAL. I see a jowly, aproned man hawking all sorts of hams and meats. He's slicing prosciutto with one hand and giving it to customers with another. One is saltier than the other, he tells a customer who by now must be on her tenth slice. He looks at me.

"Can I help you?" he asks.

"What is so special about Prosciutto di Parma?" I'm hinting for a free taste.

"It is all in the breeze," he tells me, not offering me a slice.

"The breeze?" I ask, staring at the carcass.

"The breeze from the Apennine Mountains. It makes for perfect drying conditions of the ham."

He still doesn't offer me anything.

"May I have a taste?" I ask rather meekly.

"No."

I leave Dean & DeLuca, hungry and outraged.

I open the door for myself and keep it open for a couple behind me. The woman is holding a bundle of dark orange flowers and the man is holding a very large cake box.

"Do you think this is enough?" she asks him.

"Enough? We go to this party every year with food and flowers and every year the food sits in the kitchen unopened. I keep telling you, Kirsten, you don't bring food to a catered party."

"I know, Toby, but I feel so stupid going empty-handed."

"It's a waste of time. Why don't we give the cake to some homeless person?"

Like me, I want to say. Coat by Anne Klein. Makeup by Clinique.

"Let's just go to the party, and we'll give them the cake and tell them they can spend all day eating the cake in bed."

I've been following Kirsten and Toby for several minutes now.

"I wish we could find a better New Year's Eve party." Toby's voice has a distinct whine that makes me feel almost sorry for Kirsten.

"It just goes to show that you can have all the food and all the booze in the world, and still throw the worst party ever."

"On the bright side, the food is good."

"And there's so much of it."

"I think that Justin and Felisha must expect more people than actually show up. And the only people who show up are the losers who didn't get invited anywhere else or have the self-esteem to stay home on New Year's Eve."

"Toby, you just insulted me."

"No. I insulted *us*. And the Siskins."

"That's okay. More lamb meatballs for me."

"And more Peking duck for me."

Lamb meatballs! Peking duck! I don't care how boring the Siskins are. I'm going to their party.

I follow Toby and Kirsten around for two and a half hours. It turns out that they live in Greenwich, Connecticut, but they wanted to get to Manhattan early enough to park their car and to avoid drunk drivers. So I guess we all have to kill time before going to the Siskins' for lamb meatballs and Peking duck.

I enjoy following Toby and Kirsten. They don't skulk around like Polly did; they announce their destinations to make it easy for me. We just went to a Duane Reade so they could buy gum, and then we go to the Angelika theater to see a Czechoslovakian

FOLLOWING POLLY • 77 •

film. Well, I don't see it. I don't have the money. I probably could slip by the ticketers, but I don't feel like committing another crime, especially within walking distance of Kovitz. Besides, the movie poster brags that it is "a tour de force—albeit a depressing one." Maybe this isn't true for Kirsten or Toby, but there is enough depressing tour de force going on for me without having to read subtitles.

So I wait for them right inside the Angelika. No one bothers me. I pretend to peruse the *New York Press* while I fantasize about the menu at the Siskins' New Year's Eve party. Like Toby and Kirsten, I typically dread the pressure of the New Year's party—of any party, really. But my hunger is so powerful that I find that I'm more excited about going to this party than to any other party I have been to in my entire thirty-two years.

Toby and Kirsten disagree about the movie. He tells her that his seat was too uncomfortable for him to sleep in and she tells him that his inability to appreciate anything other than overly produced Hollywood garbage sickens her. They don't speak for several blocks. He asks her if she still has the cake. She holds it up for him. She asks if he has the flowers, and he lifts them up, pulls out an orange lily, and gives it to her. She rips off the stem and pockets the flower.

"So the Siskins don't find out," she tells him, and kisses him on the cheek.

We get to Broome Street and walk about halfway down the block.

"I always forget the building," Kirsten says.

"There it is," Toby tells her without pointing anyplace in particular.

"You know, Toby, if you really hate this party so much, we can go back home or go out to a restaurant."

Please, Toby. Don't say yes. I need to eat. Just get me in the door.

"Kirsten, that is so 'sweet of you, but we're almost there already. I think we should show our faces. Let's at least get a little credit."

Toby heads to the door and looks for the Siskins. A buzzer rings and they head upstairs. I decide to wait for the next guest before I poach entry. I've been with Toby and Kirsten long enough, and I know that the lamb meatballs are minutes away.

I wait fifteen minutes or so, and three women walk to the door.

"Here goes nothing," one says, and we are buzzed in. We walk up one really long flight of stairs. I hear music and I smell hot food.

"I'm giving this one hour," one of them says to the other two.

A head pops out the door.

"*Hiiiiii,*" the head and three guests scream in unison. There's a lot of simultaneous hugging and coat removal.

"You look great."

"Ugh, I feel disgusting. You look great."

"Doesn't she?" I tell her.

"I am so glad you guys could come."

"We wouldn't miss it."

"You should have heard us raving."

I lose track of who is saying what as I try to sneak past the three girls as they chat, presumably with Felisha Siskin.

"May I take your coat?" a voice asks.

"Sure," I tell a man in a top hat. Oh God, I hope this isn't a costume party.

I hand him Diane Paynter's coat as I try to find the Siskins' food court.

"You might want to take off your shoes," Top Hat tells me as he stares at my sneakers. At first I think he is giving me some sort of imaginary makeover, but then I see a wall of shoes staring at me. I take mine off but Top Hat is still staring at me. Does he recognize me from the news? I see he looks down at my feet again. No, he's not staring at my feet but rather my legs. My jeans have fallen back down to their rightful place, and I look ridiculous.

"Can you remind me where the bathroom is?" I ask him.

He tells me that I can use the second door on my left. I walk in a couple of steps, and I'm in the coolest apartment I've ever been in.

Don't get me wrong. Mother and Barnes live in a nice place, but their apartment is conventional. Expensive but conventional.

The Siskins, it turns out, live in a loft. The apartment is brightly lit—I'm not sure of the source because I don't see a light anywhere unless you count the picture-perfect fire taking place in the stone fireplace. The ceilings are tall—at least fourteen feet. If you look up, you see a balcony—not unlike the mezzanine at Macy's. Clusters of people are on the balcony, disappearing occasionally into what must be bedrooms and closets. Every so often I hear a "Wow." A few people ask to move in. The floor is a lightly stained wood. If I were the Siskins, I would not only forbid shoes on the floor, I would forbid feet altogether. The walls are also wood, but they have been stained a darker color. There are no hangings on the walls, rather there are television screens inlaid every few feet or so. All of the televisions are on. What are Kirsten and Toby talking about? How could they disparage a couple with this many televisions? If I weren't a fugitive from justice, the Siskins would be my new best friends.

CNN is blaring in the house.

Please don't switch to local news.

I take a break from the tour and head to the bathroom. The walls, floor, and ceiling are marble. There is even a little television facing the toilet. I clean myself off a bit and remove my suede jacket and my pants. I look under the sink for a bag or something to put them in, but there is only a huge basket of pot-pourri. I wrap my clothes in a little ball and tuck them under my arm. Maybe I will give them to Top Hat.

I exit the bathroom and a very blond man hands me a glass of champagne.

"Roger." He says it in such a way that I'm not sure if he is identifying *himself* or guessing *my* name.

"Alice," I say, wondering if I've already shared too much information.

He lifts his champagne glass, imploring me to clink my glass against his. Roger's furrowed face suggests several years of fierce acne. I'm not certain I want to drink. I haven't eaten in days, I'm not a big drinker, and I'm on the lam. On the other hand, I'm hungry, and this is the closest thing I have to food. I take a sip, vowing to find the lamb meatballs within sixty seconds.

"How do you know Justin and Felisha?"

"Oh," I take a gamble, "those guys." I point with my chin in the general direction of the girls who got me in here.

Roger pauses a little.

"Don't believe anything they say about me. I'm really a good guy."

"I'll keep that in mind." I'm uncurious about his past. "I'm starving."

"Well, you've come to the right place. Shall we?"

Roger thinks we are on a date. I follow him to a table filled with delicious offerings. There's roast suckling pig flanked with grilled vegetables and plantains, a wide assortment of sushi, cheese fondue, and a huge roast beef alongside a cluster of individual herb Yorkshire puddings. Some of the meat has been sliced, but the roast remains mostly intact. There is a huge carving knife resting comfortably in the cooked flesh. I think for a second about the knife that had been thrust into Polly Dawson, and her dead, silent body oozing blood. Someone went to serious lengths to kill her and then plant the weapon at my house. Who would want to kill Polly? Who would want to frame me? I'm distracted by a waitress who stands before me with a tray of lamb meatballs and a cup of toothpicks.

"Would you like one?" She hands me a napkin.

"Maybe I'll just take two," I say as I take three.

I overhear one of the guests telling another that he's been nervous on New Year's Eve since the Egyptian guy bombed the Seattle airport a few years ago.

I want to maintain limited visibility, so I struggle not to remind him that Ahmed Ressam was Algerian and didn't bomb anything. He smuggled bombs into the Seattle airport in mid-December with the intention of blowing up LAX during the millennium celebration.

"So?" Roger says.

"So," I say back, half expecting him to ask why I took three meatballs.

"What are your resolutions?"

"Oh," I say, "I didn't realize there would be a quiz."

"You have to earn the food somehow."

Oh, I earned it.

"Well, I resolve to get myself out of this mess I got into this year."

"Anything else?"

Anything else? Other than getting cleared from a slam-dunk murder charge and trying to stop living off my parents.

"To be happy in my life." I remember the studio audience clapping when someone on *Oprah* said it.

I look around for more meatballs and remember Kirsten and Toby's promise of Peking duck.

"Do you want to hear mine?"

"Hear mine what?"

"My New Year's resolutions."

"Oh, sure." I can't see the duck anywhere.

"I'd like a new car."

"Isn't that more of a wish than a resolution?"

"Okay, then. I resolve to get a new car."

I see now why Kirsten and Toby were so reluctant to come to this party.

". . . and . . ." He is still talking. "I resolve to fall in love with a beautiful woman." He pauses and whispers in my ear, "A very beautiful woman."

Sounds like another wish.

"Well?" he asks back in his normal voice.

"Well what?"

"Well, what do you think of my New Year's resolutions?"

"Aim high," I tell him. "Shall we eat some pig?"

Roger puts his hand on my back. Despite his nettling presence, I feel protected by him. We stand around, not saying much. I glance at my surroundings. The others at the party aren't big talkers, either. Everyone seems fixed on CNN. They're more concerned with the hour than the news: There's a full hour and twenty minutes until midnight. The guests are trying to mastermind a way to round off the rest of this year.

"Couldn't they just say it's the New Year at eleven?" The voice is familiar. It's Kirsten's. Toby gives her a look and grabs her hand.

Roger seems to have lost interest in me. He's clinking glasses with another woman.

I take another shot at the food table. I notice that the Siskins have also provided finger sandwiches. The first one I taste is filled with bacon, arugula, and egg. I taste another: It is steak and caramelized onion. I taste another: crab cake, this time. I'm in love with this food. I take another: It's peanut butter and jelly.

"I can't believe they have peanut butter and jelly," I mention to another woman at the table.

"I believe Felisha is calling it peanut spread and chutney," my comrade says.

"It's tasty," I say as I saw myself a hefty piece of roast beef and add to it an especially large portion of Yorkshire pudding. I gather some sushi but have to plop it on top of the meat once I realize there is no more room on the plate.

"How do you stay so thin?" the woman asks. I do admit that the enormous dress gives me an unexpected emaciated look.

"I starved myself the last few days."

"Me too. I figured if I was going to stuff myself here, I would feel less guilty about ringing in the New Year."

"You look great," I tell her. "Eat away."

"Thanks. By the way, I'm Jill." I like her. She reminds me of Jean. Friendliness comes easily to her, and she's unapologetically neurotic.

"Alice." Was that stupid to tell her my name? I already told Roger. If I tell her some other name, I may forget when she addresses me. The whole fugitive thing is new to me.

"Are you friends with Felisha and Justin?" Jill asks me.

"Not really." I spy Toby and Kirsten, giggling, rushing out the door.

"I'm more friends with Toby and Kirsten." In a way I am telling the truth.

"I haven't seen them all night."

"Oh, I think Kirsten isn't feeling so hot," I confide.

"Alice, none of us here feels well." Jill looks over at our host Justin, who is sporting a velvet smoking jacket and polishing a cigar. Barnes has a disciple.

I laugh.

"I don't know if you're interested, but I'm starting a book club. Fiction. No men. Don't get me wrong: I'm not a man-hater;

they just don't read the books and they still manage to take over the conversation. Any interest?"

I'm interested, but under the circumstances . . .

"Sure." I blank as to how to lie my way out of this one.

"Do you have a card or an e-mail or something?"

"Oooh, my work doesn't do that."

"Really, what kind of work are you in?"

I look up at one of the televisions and there's a report from Baghdad.

"I'm in the army," I say a little too loudly.

"The army?" Jill asks thunderously, and it's clear that Justin has heard.

I pause. This can't be good. There are going to be all sorts of questions about foreign policy and travel. I know nothing about either.

"I'm in the Salvation Army."

"That makes more sense."

I look at my huge dress. Of course it does.

"Did I just hear you say that you're in the Salvation Army?" a voice from the balcony bellows.

"Yes," I say meekly. I've never had this much attention in my entire life.

"Wait, wait, wait, wait, wait." Felisha starts jumping up and down.

She says it again.

"Wait." She runs away for a bit, and I look at another television. I see that the scroll at the bottom of the screen reports:

Polly Dawson Murder Suspect on the Run in NYC: Extremely Dangerous

At least they don't show my face.

"I've been meaning to call you people." Felisha thrusts two enormous shopping bags in my general direction.

I'm about to tell her that I don't deal with the used clothes when it dawns on me that I could use them. I look at the crawl on CNN; it says something about a new breed of rubber tree.

"I don't know how much you guys will be able to use." Felisha smiles; she has enormous teeth. "This is my old riding gear."

I look in one bag. There are new riding pants, a helmet, riding boots, and two plaid horse blankets.

I mull over the homeless equestrians who are going to suffer as a result of my lies.

I grab the bags.

"I'm sure we will be able to put this to good use."

Felisha waves her ponytail at me in thanks.

There's a new story on TV. It says BREAKING NEWS LIVE FROM NEW YORK CITY. There is footage of the Fifty-ninth Street subway station.

"Police are now trying to follow the tracks of Polly Dawson's alleged murderer. She last used her MetroCard to get into this subway station."

The camera zooms in on the reporter going through the turnstile.

"Police have determined the suspect's last known whereabouts because of this little card."

The camera further zooms on a MetroCard.

I see a familiar face on the screens; it's Kovitz.

"We are able to piece together the suspect's whereabouts by reviewing her MetroCard history. A MetroCard which she bought with a credit card just like this one," the reporter says.

The camera zooms over to the MetroCard machine and zooms in on the credit-card slot. Suddenly a hand appears in front of a machine holding a Citi Card.

This story is about me. Of course. My MetroCard. I paid with a credit card, and they can track me when I use it.

They don't have my Citi Card, though. The reporter's using

his. The story is powerful enough; they don't have to stage a dramatization of my credit card.

Roger comes over to our area and puts his arm around my shoulder.

I shudder as I try to concentrate on the story.

"I was just giving . . . ummmm . . ." Felisha looks at me for help.

"Alice," I assure her.

"Alice. I was just giving Alice some toggery for the Salvation Army."

"The Salvation Army?" Roger looks confused; his grooves sink deeper into his face.

"My job," I say rather convincingly.

"A do-gooder." Roger squeezes me toward him. "I knew that about you."

I look up at the TV. There is footage of the entrance of the fifth precinct.

"Once again we bring you live coverage of the escape of the very dangerous murder suspect Alice Teakle."

There's Mother in front of the precinct: "This has all been a terrible mistake. Alice would never harm anyone."

Barnes is standing behind her, saying, "Alice led us to believe that she and Polly were working on a project together."

The crawl at the bottom indicates that it is two degrees Fahrenheit in New York City.

The next shot is of Jean. "I'm not going to comment, but you guys are barking up the wrong tree."

They show Seminara, the officer who initially interviewed me. "Many sociopaths come off as harmless, and just because someone looks like a nice young lady doesn't mean she can't have the heart of a killer."

And then he adds, "The murder suspect is not charged with anything, so we need for the people not to panic."

The reporter says that Humphrey Dawson has placed a fifty-thousand-dollar reward for my capture. The story concludes with a pretty good drawing of me; the police were unable to take my picture before I escaped and I guess Mother didn't turn anything over.

"My oh my. The girl in that picture looks like you, except you are prettier."

"I've been hearing that all day," I say as calmly as I can.

"Hey, guys," Roger screams to the room, "doesn't that look like Alice?"

No one looks at the TV. Roger doesn't have much authority. I panic.

I appeal to Roger's ego.

"So, Roger. Tell me what happened between you and—" I nod in the general direction of the three girls who got me in here and who have not separated since we got to the party.

"It's a long, long, long story," Roger says, poised to start it from the very beginning.

I glance around the room. I've been unobserved for quite a while, but now I distinctly feel the stares of some of my fellow revelers. Moreover, Roger's proximity is making me ill.

"I think I need some air," I tell him.

"Do you want me to go with you?" His reluctance to release me results in a revolting caress of my forearm.

"No."

I gather my horse gear and head to the door. Top Hat is available, so I ask him for Diane Paynter's coat, while I slip on my sneakers. He gives me the coat. I open the door and barrel down the stairs.

"Alice, wait," Roger hollers.

"What?" I freeze up. Did I leave something behind?

"I wanted to get your number," he screams.

"My phone is broken," I yell.

"Here's my card." Roger folds his card into an airplane and

throws it down to me. "I still have to tell you that story," he says hopefully.

"Yeah."

I'm on the street. I have no money. And now I can't use my MetroCard.

I walk up Broadway. There are many pedestrians hunting for the hot party or the swinging bar. There's a lot of pressure to ring in the New Year in a fabulous way—unless you're on the run. I have other priorities. I just want to stay warm. It's cold. Two degrees, according to CNN. My face is under a wind attack. As people exit their cars and step out of buildings, they gasp. I fight back and walk at a good clip. I create makeshift gloves by pulling the sleeves from my large dress down over my hands. I wear the helmet on my head. The bags of horse gear, though cumbersome, force me to expend more energy and keep up my body temperature.

When I hit Union Square, I veer right to Park Avenue South. I know to stay away from the West Side. Too many cops trickling down from Times Square. I'm on Twenty-ninth and Park when the New Year begins. I can tell because I hear horns and screaming coming from the windows above me. I think about the Siskins, and wonder if their party will receive better reviews this year. It wasn't awful. I liked Jill, and if I weren't a murderess at large I would have liked to have joined her book club. I think of Roger and the path of pockmarks that dominate his face, and I wonder if he is clinking glasses with a woman, an interested one. I wonder if he'll achieve his New Year's resolution.

I wonder if I'll achieve mine.

I reach the Grand Hyatt on Forty-second Street. It has an unsystematic, sprawling lobby. I land on a soft, cushy chair, unnoticed.

It's six A.M. when a member of the Grand Hyatt's crack security team wakes me up.

"Party's over, miss, you'd better get home."

Home.

Then the party would really be over. I trudge on up to Sixty-fifth Street and park myself outside of Charlie's house. I wrap myself up in Felisha's horse blanket; it doesn't smell of horse. Phew. I leave my helmet on—good protection.

Somewhere around three, Charlie emerges. I was certain he would. He's my only hope. Even though he doesn't know it, Charlie and I are connected. We have Harvard. We have Pennington & Litt. We have Kovitz.

And Charlie's a lawyer.

A lawyer with nothing to do.

I still get heart palpitations when I see him, even though I know he's probably not looking his best. He's wearing blue sweats and a blue down jacket. His jacket is open, and he looks as if he's wearing a flannel pajama top underneath. It could be an old shirt; I'm too far away to distinguish. He heads east. I stuff my horse blanket into the bag, and follow him. He goes into a Food Emporium on Third Avenue. It's so cold that even though I'm wearing my helmet, I go inside after him. Whenever I go to the grocery store with Jean it's an event—like she has never been in a grocery store before. She examines each item—except for anything relating to cleaning—and discusses whether it's delicious or has the potential to be so when mixed in with the right food. Figs, for example, don't do much for her as a snack food, but earn all sorts of culinary honors starring in a Moroccan stew. Charlie is more like me. He's at the cashier in less than three minutes with a half gallon of skim milk, Life cereal, and Pringles. I wait at the cashier reading my horoscope.

Apparently, I have a lot of "energy to apply to my work," but I "have a more complex agenda than others realize."

We go back to Charlie's house. Well, he does. I just wait outside.

It's January 2 and the streets have come to life. There are more pedestrians trolling the streets today, and, well, more cops, too. I'm fine for now. I changed out of the dress and into Felisha's riding britches. If you look at me, it's unclear whether I'm homeless or I fell off of my horse.

But no one does look at me. I'm ensconced in the sparse shrubbery. To take my mind off the increasingly cool wind, I think about the position I've put myself in. I have to come up with the most propitious time to approach Charlie, but I cannot imagine what time that will be. I am on the street, without shelter, without money, without the freedom to roam around. Meanwhile, I have to figure out how to deal with a day consisting of all these "withouts."

I have to find some way to move around without getting picked up by one of Kovitz's minions. And I really must develop a method for cleaning myself up.

Where on earth do the homeless relieve themselves?

The plethora of large department stores in Manhattan comes to mind, and I feel absurdly relieved to have had one productive thought. Because the streets contain so many souls who have no way to live, I feel increasingly sure that I can remain here safely for as long as I need to.

Then I feel guilty. After all, here I am benefiting not only from Felisha's ordinarily objectionable noblesse oblige, but from the rampant state of homelessness that has suddenly become my greatest ally.

Charlie emerges in the early afternoon. Unlike me, he's wearing the same outfit he was wearing yesterday. He walks east again, but makes a right on Lexington Avenue and heads into a little coffee shop called Eat Here Now. I have long digested the food from Felisha and Justin's and would give my britches for a plate of eggs. Charlie peers into the window. I do the same. We look at a woman sitting in the back corner. She has dirty-blond hair. I mean blond hair that is dirty. She wears a tight orange sweater that doesn't quite cover her belly. It's unclear whether it was designed that way or whether her belly is simply too large.

If I sound jealous or mean, maybe it's because this is Charlie and, despite my drastic circumstances, I see him in a romantic haze.

This couldn't be a date. The two certainly do not look their best, and when Charlie takes a seat, he doesn't kiss her or touch her. Within minutes, however, he seems to be interrogating her. I can't see her face. From my angle, all I get is the back of his head.

He moves away and for a second, I see her; she's crying. Has he broken up with her? Is she pregnant? Is he the father? This has to be personal, doesn't it? This can't be related to his job. From what Jean tells me, he's still unemployed. They talk for thirty minutes or so. Charlie doesn't eat anything. The blond girl eats a cheeseburger deluxe and a slice of lemon meringue pie. Charlie summons the waiter, gets the check, leaves a twenty on the table, and the two get up. The two leave the restaurant. The blond woman looks apologetic. She's crying. Charlie looks angry.

I'm so confused that I'm no longer cold. Charlie returns to his quarters and I to mine.

I think about Charlie and the handful of times when our paths have crossed.

In the winter of my sophomore year, when I was dating Mark the diagnostician, I was up late studying for my Japanese history exam in Hilles Library in the old Radcliffe Quad. I was getting ready to leave and I donned my grungy blue down parka with an enormous round hood when I spotted Charlie in the carrel across the aisle. His legs were up on the desk and his head was tilted back on the chair. I felt nervous just looking at him. Mark never made me feel nervous. Mark just made me feel alone. I tried to avoid looking in Charlie's direction, but as I was heading past him, I heard him snoring very loudly in his carrel. I paused for a second to glance at him, hoping that his sleep would shield him from learning of my intrusion. I got a pretty good look at him, though I admit he looked a little less dashing with a trickle of drool streaming down his cheek, and that the accompanying sound effects were similarly unenchanting.

Before I could step away, Charlie woke up. It was so abrupt. I didn't have the wherewithal to smile at him. I just stood there mortified in my jacket, looking like Violet Beauregarde from *Willy Wonka & the Chocolate Factory.*

Charlie smiled, though. He looked around his pockets. When he realized he didn't have a Kleenex, he wiped his face with his sleeve.

"My mother would die," he chuckled.

I couldn't laugh or smile. I simply admired his handling of the entire situation. Realizing my speechlessness would continue, I turned around and left the library.

Later, when I told Jean, she was unimpressed. "What do you care about him?" she admonished me. "He went out with Polly Linley and you have Mark."

I hang outside Charlie's house for several days, but the climate has taken a turn for the worse. My hands have transformed from severely chapped to raw and bloody. My fingernails, which for the past thirty-two years have shown remarkable resilience, are now brittle and jagged. I've managed a couple of sink baths in the ladies' room of Grand Central Station; walking to and from provided some much-needed exercise. To relieve the boredom of sitting in the cold twenty-three hours out of each twenty-four, I've taken some cards and a pen from the lobby of the Roosevelt Hotel, and have compiled lists of my favorite restaurants, the smartest people I've ever met, and dogs and cats I have loved. I am planning to pick up some more tomorrow, and to start in on the meals I most wish I were eating.

It's snowing pretty steadily, but even in the inclement weather, Charlie leaves his apartment at dawn to go for his fifty-minute run. It would be futile to attempt to keep up. My sneakers, which were in pretty poor condition when I was taken to the precinct, have disintegrated. Although Felisha's riding boots are a full size too small for me and make long walks an unattainable dream, they are perfectly suited for keeping me warm. I have also wrapped Felisha's red silk pajama top around my frozen legs.

As usual, Charlie has gotten up at six-thirty for his run. I take this time to sift through the garbage in an attempt to see if I'm still a front-page story. Luckily for me, a fraudulent financier who cheated Wall Street investors of millions has fled the country and a famous Swedish athlete has claimed to have seen a UFO. I appear on page eight for several days in a row.

I wait until Charlie returns from his run and is comfortably upstairs before I head out on my own constitutional. By ten-thirty my blood is back in full circulation and I make my pilgrimage to Bloomingdale's, where I scrub myself in their rarely trafficked seventh-floor restroom. It's a mile closer than Grand Central and just as anonymous. Once I feel clean and warm, I go back to my Sixty-fifth Street residence, where I keep an eye on Charlie and imagine that he might come to help me.

I shrug off several attempts to enlist me in a homeless facility by saying that I've been beaten and robbed in the shelters. A homeless man overhears me and gives me the schedule of a kindly driver on the Lexington Avenue bus.

"He don't ask for no bus fare," he whispers, "and if you smile pretty, he'll give you some bread." At this point, my informant reveals to me his huge black-gummed toothless grin. "With those"—he points to my intact teeth—"he may even give you a loaf."

His information is correct. The bus driver takes me around for a couple of hours. When the bus is empty he gives me a couple of hot dog buns.

"My wife gets it for the birds." He doesn't speak directly to me. "But I have better uses for it."

He's a very nice man, and I think when I get out of my situation that I will thank him and his wife.

I was at Pennington & Litt before Charlie even got there. I went right to that firm just after graduating from college. In fact, they recruited at Harvard, hoping to get a bunch of bright, energetic twenty-one-year-olds, and work them to death for a year before they quit and sought some other career.

Jean had gone right to Harvard Law School and she liked the idea of my becoming a paralegal.

"You'll totally want to go to law school," Jean assured me, hoping that I'd follow her.

The one thing I learned at Pennington & Litt was that I would never go to law school. I can't confront anybody and the work seems boring.

After I'd been at the firm for two years, I was in the office library fetching a book for an attorney when I heard a somewhat familiar voice.

"Is this a good place for a nap?"

It was Charlie, and for a moment, I thought he was remembering our little encounter in Hilles Library four years before. But no, he was talking to Lydia Stone, a stiff beauty from Human Resources. She didn't respond to the nap comment but instead told him about the state-of-the-art library at Pennington & Litt. Charlie chatted with her amiably.

When the snow clears, and there are dry patches on Charlie's block, I return to my surveillance. It's not long before I follow him back to Eat Here Now. He's there with another woman. Again, he doesn't eat anything and she eats a huge plate of food. This one has short dark hair and her face is covered in makeup. At first, she's very flirtatious with Charlie, putting her hand on his, touching his face. I'm not jealous this time because it is clear that Charlie is uncomfortable, like he wishes he had some bacterial soap or at least a moist towelette. As they interact, he gets increasingly angry with her.

I had another interaction with Charlie about eight years ago. I know this appears to be pathetic and desperate, but I'm aiming for honesty here. I was still a paralegal at Pennington & Litt. I was terribly bored. I even confided to Mother that the most exciting part about the job was leaving. Mother, who has been busy every minute of every day since her depression ended, convinced me that my life would improve if I were to enhance myself creatively. At that time, she was taking a jewelry-design course at the New School. She was "working in metals" and presented Barnes and me with weekly gifts of cuff links, earrings, and other items. Jean was always happy to get what I didn't want. Mother suggested that I take a bead-stringing class to help me open myself creatively. She said that bead stringing was a form of artistic meditation and that my questions about my future would be answered.

Over a choker?

Mother signed me up for the class and presented me with a list of tools I would need to get started: a crimper, some pliers, an awl, and, of course, beads. She instructed me to go to the bead district. (The bead district, if you're not familiar with it, is really a couple of stores in the West Thirties, but Mother calls it the bead district to make her projects seem more compelling.)

I didn't tell Mother but I had all but taken the nonpaying job with K.I.N.D. the week that the jewelry class was to begin. The only problem was that I had avoided quitting my paralegal job, fearing it would lead to an unpleasant confrontation with paralegal management at Pennington & Litt. I had never had a real office job before working at the law firm, and so I had never left one before. I was hoping that my job performance would be so disgraceful that I would get fired: It would be their decision. I started coming to work especially late, leaving especially early, and forgetting to complete many of the tasks the lawyers had assigned me. Of course, you can get lost in the big law firm shuffle. Especially if you are me. So, unfortunately, no one seemed likely to fire me any time soon.

My class was to start at ten after five in the afternoon, and I still hadn't gone to the bead district to purchase the supplies. My job was in Midtown, the class was downtown, and the supplies were somewhere in between, so I left work at three-thirty. And it was clear I was leaving. I was wearing a raincoat, carrying an umbrella and my briefcase. Mother had gotten it for me when I started working as a paralegal so that I would take my work more seriously. I had all but sent a mass e-mail announcing my departure.

To alleviate my self-consciousness, I pulled out my supply list in the elevator and studied all of Mother's required and recommended items. I hadn't known that beading was so complicated.

"Where are you going?"

It was Charlie.

"Huh?"

"I'm sorry to distract you. But I figured with that level of concentration you must be going somewhere interesting."

Charlie looks really good in a suit.

"I am going to the bead district," I told him.

He thought I was kidding.

"Oh, while you're there, pick me up some beads."

So I did.

Buying beads for Walter Redwin, a.k.a. Charlie, was probably the craziest thing I had ever done. In fact, it almost seems more plausible to me that I killed Polly Dawson than that I would buy Charlie a gift.

But be clear: I didn't do the former.

And I did do the latter.

I went to the bead store, I purchased all of the items on Mother's list, and then as I was checking out I saw a little jar marked SELECT GLASS BEADS $7.95. I thought it would be sort of cute to present them to Charlie. So I bought them.

I was so freaked out after my purchase that I never went to the bead class. I went home and stared at Charlie's present for a couple of hours and failed to return Mother's call about my review of the class. I went in to work at six-thirty the following morning, placed the jar on Charlie's desk, and ran home.

In retrospect and after the benefits of several months of therapy, I may have committed the act to expedite my job transition. You see, I never again went back to Pennington & Litt. I didn't call in sick. I didn't leave a note. I suppose I would have sent an e-mail if that option had been available to me. But it wasn't.

I'm sure nobody noticed anyway.

So I will never know what Charlie's response to the beads was. I wonder if he remembered the conversation in the elevator. Don't get me wrong. I was incredibly curious, but not curious enough to face him or to confide to someone else at the firm what I had done. I didn't even tell Jean. She was at Harvard Law School, and I was cutting bead class.

I'm still outside. I've been hanging outside Charlie's house for a week now, keeping warm with Felisha's horse gear, riding the bus with an occasional trip to Bloomingdale's.

Charlie has met with eight different women now. I can't figure him out. Is this a fetish? They don't look alike—they're all different colors and sizes—but they have a similar quality. And they all play out a similar scene with him. They eat a big meal; he has a cup of coffee. They cry at some point, and he gets angry at them. And then he leaves a twenty-dollar bill on the table. I feel like I am back at Mona Hawkins, watching a series of types all read for the same part in a movie.

But what is the movie about?

I know I can't do this for much longer. I was never much of a camper, and this is so unpleasant. The warmer weather is about to change. Snow is starting to fall and flurries cover the street. They could be the start of a blizzard. I don't know; I haven't watched TV in over a week. I cross the street to a row of garbage cans, which abut Charlie's front door. Maybe there will be a newspaper in one of them with a weather report. I lift the lid and carefully dip my hand inside. Sometimes, as Freud might say, a newspaper is just a newspaper, but sometimes it's a receptacle for dog shit. And while my hygiene is below acceptable, I don't wish to add more gross things to my personal odor. I imagine what it's like to be a surgeon. One false move and—

"Who the fuck are you? And why are you following me?"

Charlie is yelling at me.

THREE

• •

CHARLIE

I'm sitting in Charlie's living room. He's not saying anything, and I'm not saying anything. I see a phone, but he doesn't use it. He's not staring at me, but he has his eye on me, just in case I may want to escape. He doesn't realize this is exactly where I want to be.

He finally speaks.

"Who do you work for?" His voice is deeper and gruffer than I remembered.

I don't think he wants me to tell him that until recently I worked for Mona Hawkins Casting.

"I don't work for anybody," I tell him.

"Are you with the FBI?"

I don't answer.

"Are you?"

"No. I'm not with the FBI. May I use your restroom?"

"No."

We sit in silence. I stare at my surroundings. Charlie's living room is really dark, which I find cozy. And it has a fireplace, which for now is posing as an obsolete-computer receptacle. There is one big empty brick wall, and the other three, which may have been painted white at one time, have evolved into aged bone. His only wall hangings are maps of famous World War I battles: Marne, Ypres, Verdun, and Lutsk. There are books everywhere: On the shelves, they are neatly categorized. I take a moment to notice that Charlie's interest in history didn't stop in college. He has a whole wall devoted to Europe 1700–1945. Another to law books and journals. I notice only a small section of fiction.

Charlie's clearly not a fan. There are weathered copies of paper-back Shakespeare plays and random copies of American classics, college souvenirs more than anything else. The floor is littered with more history books: memoirs and biographies. Some are dog-eared, others are stuffed with old bills and credit-card receipts.

At least Charlie's not a neat freak.

I'm wobbling in Charlie's not-so-state-of-the-art desk chair as I manage to check out a pile of photographs. Some of the faces look familiar; they're the women that he met at Eat Here Now.

"What's your name?"

I look up at him, careful to maintain my balance.

"Alice," I say softly.

"Alice what?"

"Teakle," I tell him. I can tell by his response that he doesn't recall my name at all.

"Well, Alice Teakle, could you please tell me why you have been stalking me?"

I really wouldn't characterize my behavior as stalking, but I don't want to argue with Charlie.

"I need your help."

Charlie laughs at me.

"You need my help?"

"Yes," I tell him.

It's clear that Charlie doesn't believe me, but he's willing to hear me out.

"The police are after me. They think I killed someone, and I didn't."

"The police think you killed someone?"

Pause.

"Yes."

Pause.

"So why didn't you call a lawyer? Why did you come to me?"

I answer him very clearly.

"You're a lawyer and you know Kovitz."

"Phil Kovitz? How do *you* know Phil Kovitz?"

Charlie raises his voice.

"He may be in charge of my case. He thinks I'm a killer."

Charlie leans into me and puts both of his hands on the arms of the desk chair. It stops wobbling.

"Don't lie. How do you know Kovitz?"

"I don't know him. He came to my house; he took me to the station."

Charlie's hands are a hair's breadth away from my neck.

"You're lying to me. You aren't wanted by the cops. How stupid do you think I am? Who are you really? Don't lie to me. I will kill you."

I believe him.

"My name is Alice Teakle. I gave you beads."

Recognition.

"What?"

"My name's Alice Teakle." I'm saying the words faster than I can think them. "I gave you beads at Pennington and Litt. They think I killed Polly Dawson."

"Polly Dawson? Why would you kill Polly Dawson."

His opening statement.

"They think I did it. Kovitz is already ironing my prison wear." I'm not fully ready to disclose their flimsy evidence. "But I didn't do it. There's no changing his mind. I saw you and Kovitz having lunch at Mee-Hop a few weeks ago, and now I'm hoping you'll believe me and get Kovitz off my back. I thought you could convince him. I don't know him. You know him."

Charlie doesn't say anything. He steps back. I hope that our Mamet-like exchange has ended.

"Is it okay if I use your bathroom?"

"Sure. It's over there." A weary Charlie points to a closed door.

————————

I've scrubbed myself to the best of my abilities in Charlie's guest bathroom sink. There doesn't appear to be a lot of visitor traffic here. I take a deep breath and explore my surroundings. There are no towels unless you count two disposable and dusty American flag hand towels on the sink. Either Charlie's a major patriot or the last time he visited his second bathroom was on July Fourth, the year to be determined. The only thing in the medicine cabinet is a three-inch Ace comb. I run it under hot water and attack the knots in my hair, one by one.

I'm tempted to use an unopened toothbrush, which is sitting on a little shelf next to the mirror. But that would be stealing, and I want to come off as someone with integrity so that I can offset the fact that Charlie found me going through his garbage less than an hour ago.

I return to the room, my face raw from scrubbing and my hair wet, unsnarled, and unclean.

It turns out that Charlie remembers that I left the beads.

"It was so odd," he calmly explains to me. "I came to work, and there was a jar of beads sitting on my desk. I had no idea how they got there."

"You didn't remember our conversation about the bead district?" Indignant, I forget for a moment that I'm defending my life.

"Only vaguely. Months later I was heading to a meeting in the West Thirties and I saw bead stores with little jars in the windows just like the one on my desk, and I had a flash in my head—a woman telling me about the bead district. But I couldn't recall who I was talking to."

I know this is ridiculous given my situation, but my feelings are hurt.

Charlie gets up from the couch, and leans toward me at the desk.

"If this makes you feel better . . ."

He leans lower into me and puts his hand by my leg.

I'm really uncomfortable. I've gotten used to my smell by now, but I know it must be awful. Is Charlie giving me a belated thank-you kiss for the beads?

No. He opens the drawer by my leg and pulls out the jar of beads I had purchased for him eight years before.

I'm moved. I'm trying to figure out how to tell him that without sounding utterly ridiculous when Charlie interrupts me—

"Now tell me why you're living on the street."

I try to tell him everything from the beginning. My first account is spotty. I omit the following Polly part. I tell him how someone has framed me for Polly Dawson's murder. I tell him about the planted museum pin and the matchbooks from the Four Seasons and Lever House. But when I get to the story about Otto & LuLu's I can't seem to do it without explaining that I had followed Polly to that store. So I tell him the truth.

"Well, I had this little habit."

"What kind of habit?"

"Oh, not drugs or anything if that's what you are thinking." I can tell it is, because Charlie suddenly looks relieved. "I had taken to"—I gulp —"following Polly."

"What do you mean?"

"I'd been following Polly around for a few weeks."

"Why?"

How do I tell him the answer to this when I myself am not sure? Because I'm curious. Because I'm nosy. Because I wanted to see if I could.

"For sport, I guess." I then tell Charlie that I'd decided I no longer wanted to follow Polly on the day she was killed.

"You want me to believe that you followed Polly Dawson around because it was fun and that she happened to get killed the day you thought it was no longer fun, but that you happened to find the body?"

He cross-examines well.

"Yes."

"How did you know about me and Kovitz?" Charlie is once again suspicious. "Were you following me?"

"No. Believe it or not, Polly was having lunch in Mee-Hop when you were having lunch there. Do you remember? It was about two and a half weeks ago. It was a deceptively beautiful day. Everyone was underdressed because the sun was so strong but the temperature could not have been higher than thirty degrees. You were wearing only a light Windbreaker. It was royal blue." I come close to telling him that that particular blue suits him. "I recognized you and was hoping you wouldn't recognize me because I didn't want to draw attention to myself. I was also hoping you wouldn't recognize Polly, but she was pretty well disguised."

"How did you know that I was eating with Kovitz?" At least he's not alluding to my accurate recollection of his attire.

"I saw his badge, and it said Kovitz. I remember little details like that."

"Did you happen to hear our conversation?"

"No way. I was too focused on Polly."

"I see. So you weren't following *me* at all?"

He's actually getting it.

"Yes. It was just Polly, and then I ended up on the unfortunate end of a really bad coincidence."

"Is this something you do all the time?"

"Oh, God no."

"You mean you've never done it before?"

"Well . . ." I'm about to deny it, but I decide to go for broke. After all, I'm in his apartment, sitting on his couch, and I've already gone through his garbage. "I went through a phase in my adolescence."

"What was in it for you?"

This question is a little much for a relationship that started five minutes ago.

"I don't know. I wish I could tell you." I look at him, asking for understanding. "It turned out to be really interesting. One afternoon, I was walking home and I saw the Clover School mafia. They were the girls who always beat us in field hockey. I guess I must have been bored because I just started following them."

"Because you were bored?"

"I'm not defending it. You asked me and I want to be truthful. Should I go on?"

Charlie hesitates but I can see that he's curious.

"They kept darting in and out of stores, laughing, cracking each other up. They'd be in a store for two minutes and they'd come running out. I finally followed them into this boutique called Divertissement. They were stealing. Each one took a container of chocolate-chip-flavored lip gloss from the counter."

"Chocolate chip lip gloss?"

"You've never been a twelve-year-old girl."

"And was that the only time?"

I'd been so lonely that I actually followed happy families on occasion. But I am not about to be quite that honest.

"No."

He pauses for a second.

"Then why have you been following me around for the last week?"

I pause.

"That was stalking." I'm a tad more impudent than I want to be. "Not in the bad way. I was waiting for the perfect moment to ask your advice about Kovitz."

"What advice is that?"

"How can we convince him that I didn't kill Polly Dawson?"

"We?"

"Well, I couldn't do it myself, but maybe we could team up like *Remington Steele* or something. He would think *you* were solving a crime but in reality *I* would be. Do you have a snack?"

"What is *Remington Steele*?"

"What is *Remington Steele*? Where were you from 1982 to 1987? The TV program about the brainy PI who, for some reason, was not taken seriously by potential clients and the authorities. So she made up a fictitious boss, Remington Steele. And then a charming, handsome thief assumes the name Remington Steele for himself, and pretends he's her boss and she ends up doing most of the actual detective work."

"I never watched that. And I'm not sure I see the comparison."

Only that I loved Pierce Brosnan, the star of *Remington Steele,* and I love *you.* But I can't tell him that.

"Well, I would do all the work to clear my name, and you could be my ambassador to the authorities, like Kovitz. And you'd get all the recognition. You could be famous."

I realize from Charlie's sunken expression that he has no desire to be famous.

"Or you could get me a snack." I say it as a joke, but I'm actually famished.

"What makes you think that I can convince Kovitz?" Charlie heads back toward the kitchen.

"First, you know him."

I'm shouting to compensate for the volume produced by what sounds like a flurry of opening and closing cabinets in what I think has got to be his kitchen. "Second, he doesn't think you're a criminal. Third, you're a lawyer, and have at least some experience in the convincing department. I'm not so good."

Charlie comes back in the room. In one hand he has a canister of Pringles and in the other, a warped wooden bowl. He plops them on the table. "You want me to be your lawyer?"

I can't tell if he is asking me or accusing me.

"Well, I—"

"Do you want me to be your lawyer?"

He says it more softly this time.

"I don't know if I want that exactly. I was thinking of you as a conduit to Kovitz. I can't afford a lawyer. I can't afford a MetroCard."

Charlie glances at the mound of papers on his desk. "How about we trade services?"

I don't get it. Does he need a casting assistant? I empty the chips into the misshapen bowl.

"I'm not sure I follow you. Pringle?" I reach out to him with the bowl in my hand.

"You don't need to follow *me*." He ignores the chips completely. "I want you to follow other people."

Is this the point where I remind Charlie that following was what got me into trouble in the first place? And that despite my decline in well-being, my mental health may be taking an enormous leap forward. Do I go that far?

"What kind of people?" I query as I try to elegantly place some Pringles in my mouth.

"Streetwalkers."

I think I know where this is going and I nod, my mouth full, so that Charlie can continue with his request.

"I need you to check out some prostitutes for me." His face reddens. "Not in the way you might think. You see, I think they've been paid off in a conspiracy against my father."

"Your father?" I ask as if this is the first I've heard about the scandal.

"Yes. My father has been the COO of Kelt Pharmaceuticals for twenty-three years. And he's good at it. When he started, the company was worth just under a billion dollars, and now it's worth forty-seven billion. Now everybody wants his job. The younger people in the company are greedy, and they're trying to pass their greed off as concern for the company. Because the finances are what they are, and because my father likes his job, they have to attack my father personally. What they're doing is sick." Charlie's anger peaks, and then he stops speaking.

"What are they doing?" I ask as gently as I can.

"They fabricated a story to embarrass him." Charlie lowers his voice.

"What kind of story?" I take another handful of chips.

"They say my father frequently visited prostitutes."

He pauses. This must be so difficult for him. Of course Charlie doesn't want to be famous. His family is already infamous.

"They said he violated some sort of morals clause in his contract. They used a whole team of so-called investigators to manufacture a case against him. They presented him with the package of evidence and he refused to leave. More recently, they have called in law enforcement so they could make all of this stuff public and humiliate him. He was told that all sorts of charges were pending against him. He left the office in disgrace."

"Is he going to go to prison or anything?"

"No. Surprise, surprise. The second he quit his job, the charges were dropped. Apparently there was not enough in the company's paperwork to go forward with any of it."

"But if he didn't do anything criminal—"

"The trumped-up solicitation is a crime. And the mere suggestion that he has been with hookers demonstrates that his judgment is impaired and he's unable to lead the company. It's completely ridiculous. My father's totally depressed—even worse than when my mother died. And I want to help him."

"Can't you get your law firm to hel—" I want to tell Charlie how sorry I am that his mother died, that I lost my father at eight. That I know his pain.

"I have no more law firm. My biggest client was Kelt Pharmaceuticals. I brought them in—not my father's idea, but I had gotten to know their general counsel through him. And when Kelt got rid of my father, they hired a new law firm. So Pennington and Litt had no use for me. The managing partner told me I should 'keep a low profile for a few months—maybe take a vacation until this whole thing blows over.' My name would be bad for business."

"Unbelievable," I say, although I've known all this for weeks.

"All because of the greed of these guys."

"So what are you doing?" I ask.

"Well, I want to nail these guys."

I'm almost finished with the chips and am still hungry.

"Does this have anything to do with your meeting with Kovitz?"

"Yes. I knew him way back. We worked together when I was an assistant in the United States Attorney's Office before I started at Pennington and Litt. We were buddies. And when my father got railroaded, I asked him to look into it."

"And did he?"

"The problem is that Kovitz is a New York City cop. Somehow the guys at Kelt handed this over to the FBI because there was some interstate activity, and Kovitz is having a really hard time getting the feds to talk to him. Those guys are arrogant."

"So is Kovitz helping you at all?"

"In a limited way. He did a few background checks on all the women they say my dad hired. Stuff I couldn't get."

I look at the heap of papers on Charlie's desk. It's topped with the poor copies of the photographs.

"Are those the women you took out to lunch?"

Charlie shoots me a look. He suddenly remembers that less than two hours ago, he was ready to kill me.

"Yeah." He pauses and decides whether I am worthy of this next level of information. He decides that I am. "I'm trying to figure out why they're lying. Why they told the investigators that my father did this."

"Are you sure that he didn't?"

Charlie looks at me as if, well, as if I accused his father of maintaining a whore habit.

"I'm sorry," I tell him. "What have the hook— I mean the women said?"

"They told me that they were professional escorts and that they were paid by my father to have sex with him."

I don't say anything.

"I asked each of these women if they had any agreement with the government or the scumbags at Kelt in terms of testifying against my father if this were to move forward in any way. And what a coincidence. They all do. It seems that prison isn't in their cards if they pin the blame on my dad."

Here I can sympathize. It sounds like Charlie's dad has no way out. I suddenly realize that if Charlie's dad, who has the lawyers and the connections, can't get out of some sex scandal, how is a nobody like me going to escape a murder charge?

After Charlie and I have exchanged our tales of woe, he sets me up in his apartment. He points to a big fluffy navy couch in his living room.

"You'll sleep there."

He clears a bookshelf and tells me I can put the extra stuff that Felisha gave me there. He refers to it as "luggage."

I give the living room another look. I look outside the arched windows onto Sixty-fifth Street. I am looking at the very spot I was inhabiting for the last five days. Of course Charlie had seen me there. I was impossible to miss. No wonder he's so mistrustful of me. When I was staring up at the building from the street,

I had envisioned him as being much farther away. I couldn't even imagine what was behind the window. I pictured only Charlie and not his warm bookish environment. His living room, lit only by his halogen desk lamp and the natural light of the day's conclusion, is a symphony in brick and books. The room is brightened to a small extent by a red Azerbaijani dragon rug. His old wooden coffee table, covered in books, looks like something his parents must have given him when he set out on his own. In the corner of the room is Charlie's desk, covered in papers. The man was clearly not expecting company.

"I really like your place."

"I like the neighborhood," Charlie tells me, as he hands me a clean bisque-colored towel and matching washcloth, "but I guess you know it better than I do."

I laugh a little. "It is really safe."

"If you don't count the wanted murderer taking residence in your apartment."

"Or living on the street."

"What was that like?" Charlie asks me. "Living on the street."

"I wouldn't recommend it, especially if you have an alternative that includes heat and a shower, but after I inured myself to the cold and dirt, I was okay with it."

"Really?"

"Under normal circumstances, I probably wouldn't have made it through a night, but because I have been so focused on fleeing the police, I didn't focus on the cold, the dirt, or the hunger." I don't tell Charlie that the highlight of my day was using the public restroom on the theory that he might find me gross.

"I'll say." Charlie is staring at me.

Of course he's staring at me. I'm still filthy.

"Would you like a shower?" he asks.

"I thought you'd never ask."

Charlie informs me that I can use the guest bathroom as if it is my very own, adding that he never uses it. I have to ask for soap, shampoo, toothbrush, and toothpaste.

Boy, am I dying to brush my teeth. The Pringles were not a good idea.

I am still wearing Felisha's riding pants. They could use a wash, too.

"You don't by any chance have any clothes that I could wear?" I ask Charlie shyly.

"Sure, I have some white capri pants and a pink eyelet top."

Wow. Charlie's funny.

"Do you have sandals that match?"

"Nah, I think those riding boots finish the outfit."

"True, and they are more weather appropriate," I add.

Charlie heads into a closet and produces a pair of jeans and a black cotton turtleneck. He throws them to me.

"I left this stuff in the dryer too long. They're a little small on me. It's the best I can do."

Just hearing the word "dryer" is exciting to me. I can't wait to wash.

"How was the shower?" Charlie asks me as I emerge in his still-too-big jeans and roomy turtleneck.

"It was the best thing that ever happened to me," I say. "I'm ready to get to work." I'm referring to Charlie's father's dilemma.

"How about we get a little food?" Charlie says. "You're obviously famished. Those Pringles were twelve years old."

"Really?"

"I have no idea. They were here when I moved in, and that was about eight years ago."

"You're kidding me," I say, starting to feel a little less good.

"Of course I'm kidding you. You wolfed them down." He's smiling.

I like the sight of him up close. His hair, in need of a good combing, is thick and full. His fair skin has been temporarily dimmed by what looks to be a day or two of dark brown stubble. His clear light brown eyes, slightly creased on top, maintain an air of sadness despite his genuine but possibly fleeting grin. It's his first smile since I got here, but I guess having a stranger stalking you after months of family turmoil wouldn't exactly be mirth-producing.

"All that running from the law can really build up a girl's appetite."

Wow. Charlie and I are chatting as if we are friends. This is so weird. I want to call Jean and tell her all this.

Charlie grabs his phone. He calls Eat Here Now. It's on his speed dial. He orders two cheeseburgers deluxe, a chocolate milkshake for me, and four cups of coffee.

"I don't have a coffeemaker," he explains. "This way we don't have to go out later to get the coffee."

The cheeseburger is heaven. How could I never have eaten at this restaurant? The fries are perfect. Even the coffee, cold as it is, is rich, and heartwarming. I concentrate on Charlie as he tells me everything he can about his father's case. Charlie thinks he's being framed by Kelt's new CEO, Remy Spencer. Of all of Kelt's executives, Remy seemed most anxious to get William Redwin out of the company and he immediately took his job. Charlie has a file on Remy, which he hands over to me. As I scrutinize, I see that there is nothing incriminating about the guy. To be sure, there are many articles that profile him. They say little about his personality.

"I want you to comb this for clues," Charlie says. "I have found nothing." I'm sliding my last french fry through the little mound of ketchup on my plate.

This could be fun. I'm still hungry, though. Charlie stopped eating ten minutes ago. It would be a shame to let those fantastic fries go to waste.

"Do you mind if I have some of your fries?" I ask Charlie. I don't even wait for his response as I dig in.

I've been staying in Charlie's house for more than a week, and we are making small strides. I've tailed Remy, and I see nothing that could link him to a prostitution ring or to anything else incriminating. Frankly, the man is boring. He lives on Sutton Place, not too far from here. He has the same schedule every day. He leaves his house for work at eight-fifteen every morning. He's easy to spot. He's on a bicycle. Although I know his choice of transportation is both healthy and environmentally laudable, I still think he looks silly in a charcoal gray cashmere coat and men's leather dress shoes for a third-of-a-mile ride on a pricey hybrid bike. I'm able to keep up with him if I walk quickly because the traffic is so terrible. If I ever meet Remy and strike up a close friendship with him, I will point out that he should consider walking. Kelt's offices are located at Fifty-ninth and Park, just about six blocks from Charlie's apartment.

It was hard for me to leave Charlie's house the morning after my first night with him. I had passed out on my couch bed right after dinner. I slept twelve hours. When I woke up, I knew I had work to do, but I was scared that once I set foot out the door, the entire New York City Police Department would be standing outside Charlie's door, ready to fire.

"For some reason, you're off their radar," Charlie assured me.

"I know, but I want to stay off." I wanted to luxuriate in the proximity to Charlie as well. I wasn't able to fully internalize my recent rooming situation last night before I fell into a deep slumber.

"Just don't go killing anyone and you'll be fine," said Charlie, as he handed me a huge scarf to put over my face and a knapsack with a lot of Swedish writing on it, which a foreign-exchange law student had left in his home five years ago. I was wearing Charlie's weathered orange jacket, the baggy pants, and my now-dry sneakers. I looked like a student.

Remy Spencer hasn't noticed me. Frankly, I've hardly seen him. He hasn't left his office, even for lunch, in the past three days. He goes home at seven-thirty, and, from what I can see, he stays there. I pulled an all-nighter on his street two nights ago to make sure he didn't leave at an odd hour.

"If Remy has done anything wrong," I tell Charlie, "it's in the past. He hasn't had any outside human contact all week."

"I figured he would be a long shot. Now that he's paid off the hookers, he probably wants to keep his distance so no one suspects."

I agree with Charlie, but I'm also determined to make sure Remy doesn't slip up. From everything I've read, he's a meticulous fellow. If he did frame William Redwin, he's probably covered his tracks beautifully.

As far as my own situation goes, my story's not getting the coverage you might think. Charlie says that this is because the police are probably embarrassed. He has warned me, though, that this could turn. An ambitious reporter could do a huge story about me to highlight the inadequacies of New York's finest.

Don't get me wrong. The story has been on the news every day, but it's usually about eleven or twelve minutes into the program when the viewers are poised to hear the new guidelines for the food pyramid. It's presented as a nonstory. A reporter announces that it has been this many days since Polly Dawson was murdered, and Alice Teakle is nowhere to be found. There are no quotes or video footage. Not even a picture of me! Just a wedding picture of Polly and Humphrey.

———

We've given up on Remy for the time being, and Charlie is now handing over folders on each of the women who have given a statement to the police. There are Rosalie, LaDonna, Charisse, Doreen, Carly, Oxanna, Trini, and Justine. They have all told the police the same thing: that they had met with William Redwin, on a regular basis, in exchange for cash. In addition, William Redwin furnished lavish gifts upon them. Not of a romantic nature but rather items like high-end televisions and home appliances. Carly received a Sub-Zero refrigerator. The women all worked for an agency run by an older woman named Henrietta Murch. Charlie also keeps a file on Murch. She too has talked to the police and has admitted to taking twenty percent of the cash paid by Redwin to each of the girls, which she insisted was quite generous of her.

Further, Murch told the police that she didn't exact any payment from her girls with respect to gifts that Redwin had given them. "I don't touch their tips."

I ask Charlie if he has spoken with Murch, and he says that she refuses to speak with him. She has threatened him with an order of protection if he goes near her. He wants me to see what I can do.

"Work your magic," he tells me.

He's referring to my following. I don't remind him that following Remy Spencer produced nothing.

Charlie and I have established a routine. He gets up every morning at six-fifteen and goes for a six-mile run. Then, he returns home and works at the computer. To relax, he reads World War I history. He's currently obsessed with the Battle of Verdun and plans to visit there when this whole thing with his father is behind him. Like me, he's not a big phone talker. He occasionally takes a call from his friend Mark, a professor of medieval studies at Haverford College. Their conversations usually involve a "What's up" and a "Not much."

Flattering.

I am typically gone all day. I have abandoned Remy, for the most part, and am now staking out Henrietta Murch's Williamsburg apartment. She lives above a bar right next to the bridge. She doesn't exactly fit my stereotype of a madam. She's about four foot eight, eighty pounds, with a Dorothy Hamill haircut. She wears no makeup, and when she leaves her house, she wears a navy peacoat and mom jeans. From far away, she looks like she could be a twelve-year-old girl. She doesn't look like a fifty-three-year-old curator of prostitutes.

Murch stays close to home. We've never gotten on the subway together and she leaves her house only for light household errands. During the day, she spends about three hours cleaning a sparse no-nonsense bar called Basura on the bottom floor of her apartment building. Maybe that's where she conducts her business.

I wait for the bar to open. Murch doesn't come down. The bar patrons are Williamsburg hipsters, men and women, clothed in expensive yet unpleasant attire. Even though it's freezing, most of the clientele stays outside the bar, opting to smoke on the street.

The bar is packed by midnight. Murch stays in her apartment. I can see her through her small, well-placed dormer window. She has been watching the Food Network all night.

I stay until three A.M., when the bar finally closes.

"Maybe she's not even a pimp," Charlie says the next morning. "She's being paid to play one to frame my father."

And while it certainly looks that way, I can't imagine anybody pretending to be a criminal even for money. But Charlie is the one with experience in law enforcement.

"Did you see anything like that when you were a prosecutor? People saying they committed crimes even though they didn't?"

"Nothing like that. But I did see a lot of fraud."

I spend very little time in Charlie's apartment. Once I am confident that I won't be recognized, I alternate my time between Murch's place and Remy's, hoping for contact between the two. There is none.

I report my findings, or lack thereof, to Charlie.

"I was hoping that since they are confident that no one is suspicious of them, they would continue to stay in contact," he says, thinking aloud. "But then again, they were successful in their mission. My father is out. They have no need to talk to each other."

"True. But if I've learned one thing from *Law and Order,* it's that criminals slip up even after they have completed their crime."

Charlie and I are not up late nights gabbing incessantly about philosophy and our childhoods. When I'm here, we spend most of the time talking about his father and, to some extent, my fugitive status. Sometimes we hang out together in the living room: He scours the Internet and I watch television. Charlie's one of those people who owns a television set but doesn't use it. When I got here, the television was in a corner behind a bookshelf. There was no place to sit comfortably and watch. I asked him if I could move it from the corner to a more suitable spot. There's no seat in the living room that has been appointed for good viewing. The couch was certainly in the wrong place. Although he wasn't too taken with the intrusion, he acceded.

I still have a crush on Charlie. I'm less speechless around him these days but remain disquieted by his presence. I wish I could talk to Jean about it. For that matter, I wish I could talk to Jean about anything. It has been weeks since I have spoken to my best friend. I'd like to call Mother as well, but then she would tell Barnes, and Barnes, without a doubt, would call Kovitz.

It's not that Barnes would want me to go to jail. He just wouldn't want his relationship to be inconvenienced by my disappearance. It would be better for him for me to be in Kovitz's

custody than to have to deal with Mother, who I can quite se-
curely say is distracted by my circumstances. And Mother is
much more likely to put him first if I'm locked up somewhere. I
do without a call to Mother.

For now, Charlie and his television will do.

The most important thing is that Charlie believes me. I'm not
sure why he does. I think it's somehow tangled up with his belief
in his father's innocence. He's channeling his ire with his father's
accusers into helping me with my case. He refers to the cops as
"bastards." Except Kovitz. He likes Kovitz even though I know
he's useless.

"He's a victim like we are," Charlie reminds me.

I can't see how Kovitz could possibly be a victim, but I keep
quiet on this. I need Charlie's full support and if he wants me to
sympathize with Kovitz, I will.

I've been here for ten days and Charlie finally asks me why Mona
Hawkins fired me.

So I tell him my story.

"Mona fired me because I told an actress who had auditioned
for a role in the film that even though she had done a great job in
her audition, the director had selected another woman for the
role."

"Isn't that what casting directors tell people?"

"Yes, of course," I tell him, "but I told Lissa—this actress—
that the audition itself was a sham."

"Why'd you do that?"

"Because it was true. Because I felt for her. Because I didn't
want her to think that she was untalented."

"Wait." Charlie starts pacing his living room. "Why would a
production company waste time and money on auditions if they
already had an actress lined up for the part?"

"It's a publicity thing," I tell him. "Jenna McNair is the actress who ultimately got the part. She had been demanding more than the producers would pay. So they did this whole public stunt with 'auditions' just to get her all fired up so she would agree to their offer."

"And you told this to Lissa?" Charlie asks me.

"Yes."

Charlie starts pacing again. I don't know if Charlie thinks I am a decent person or not, but I know that he is thinking less of me now.

"Did you know Lissa?" He's cross-examining me.

"I got to know her because she came in so many times to audition and Mona always made her wait so long."

"Why would you risk your job for someone you didn't know?"

"I felt sorry for her. She needed to know she did a good job. I saw it all the time. These actresses, coming in day after day. So hopeful and so prepared. And Mona would tear them down. Actors too, but Mona is a misogynist. So she was generally harder on the women."

I recall the countless times Mona reprimanded these earnest young things in her office. She began every casting session with a negative assessment of their appearance. When I came in to interview with her, she thought I was coming in to audition for a sitcom she was casting.

"You've got to be kidding me," she said when I walked into her office.

"I'm not quite sure I understand," I told her.

"You're all wrong. I'm casting a waitress. In television talk, that means good legs. Dancer legs. When was the last time you went to the gym?"

"Umm . . ."

"If you have to think about it, you're wrong for the part.

You're thin enough, but you carry yourself like a big fatty and the hair needs work. Uncombed is never in. The clothes don't work, either—you look like an office assistant, not a waitress."

"That's why I'm here," I managed to say while Mona paused.

"We're not casting an office assistant. Jed! Jed!" she bellowed. "We have a situation."

An earnest twenty-something-year-old appeared out of nowhere.

"Oh, Mona. This is Alice. She's here to interview for Katie's job."

"Oh." Mona looked at me as if in a whole new light. "Hire her," she said to Jed.

I wasn't sure whether to take Jed's offer. The interview was so unpleasant.

"Life is unpleasant," Barnes had said to me when I asked Mother her opinion later that day.

"Just go until you find an alternative, Alice. It will give you the structure you need until you have a vision for yourself."

I explain all this to Charlie. Then I describe my first days at Mona Hawkins. My role was ordering lunch. Every morning, I was required to review the three-ring binder filled with laminated menus from restaurants that delivered to our office. I was required to call each of these restaurants—there were more than twenty—and ask about the daily specials. I then had to type an unabridged account of the specials and place an asterisk next to any dish that included goat cheese or fennel, as Mona was partial to those ingredients. Mona would spend a good part of the morning considering the menu, both to herself and out loud. At 11:45 or so, Mona would call me into her office, command me to shut the door, and announce her order, which routinely consisted of two appetizers and two entrees.

I can tell that Charlie is poised to ask me if Mona is fat. I tell him that she looks like a cadaver.

Again, I intercept his predictable question about an eating disorder.

"Not really." I explain how lore at the office had it that until five years ago Mona had maintained a weight of 298 pounds.

Mona's most trusted assistant, Jed Rausch, used to imitate Mona's proclamation:

"I find eating very sensual." Then Rausch would dribble some bread product out of his mouth and say, "Delicious, delicious, delicious."

Five years ago, Mona announced to the office that she was taking a little leave to have some gallbladder surgery and would be out of the office for five weeks. She was back at work in a month: fifty pounds thinner.

"I had a big gallbladder," she told suspicious employees.

Energized by her weight loss and restricted by her egg-sized stomach, Mona limited her meals to small series of bites of food. It was more pleasurable for her to have one bite of eight foods, she would lecture to no one in particular, than eight bites of one.

"I still love food," she proclaimed. She had come clean about the nature of her operation after losing one hundred pounds.

"I just want to taste it all."

Mona has maintained her current weight of 119 pounds through this tasting method.

On my first day of work Mona had given me a lecture about the lunch order and her philosophy behind it:

"I rather enjoy looking at all of the food I don't eat. Instead of food controlling Mona, Mona controls— No ... no ... Mona *conquers* food."

"I hope that woman has an account with some local food shelter or Meals on Wheels," Charlie says after I have told him all this.

I think of my recent days on the street and how much I would have appreciated just a few of Mona's leftovers.

"No. Part of Mona's regime was that she didn't want *anyone* to have the food."

"You're kidding."

"No. One time I tried to take some of the food to a soup kitchen on my way home and Mona caught me and threatened me."

"I can't believe directors and producers hired her." Charlie's incredulous.

"Me neither. There was this rumor that she was involved in the gay porn industry for years and years. And then suddenly, one day she set up shop in legit film, made some lucky choices, and became a premier casting director."

"Why would anyone work for this monster?" Charlie asks me.

"It's a pretty good starter job for people who want to go into casting or get into other parts of show business. One of Mona's assistants was a script supervisor in Hollywood. Another went off to cast some stuff of her own. Some leave show business altogether because they realize it's not for them."

"That's you, right."

"I guess."

"When this all blows over are you going to go back to show business?"

I don't tell Charlie that I never thought of myself as in show business. I worked for Mona, hoping what Mother had hoped: that it would lead me to realize my true calling.

"Let me take this one step at a time," I tell Charlie, and he senses that I don't want to talk about Mona anymore.

Charlie's busy at the computer writing notes on his father's situation. He looks particularly defeated this evening.

"It makes no sense," he confides to me. I resist reaching out to him and instead let him continue speaking. "It's impossible to picture my father doing any of that stuff. He's still mourning my mother. I can't even picture the man on a date with another woman. They were married for thirty-seven years."

I have so many things I want to tell Charlie. Not just about his father but about mourning a spouse—what it can do.

"It sounds like your parents had a great marriage," I say, thinking of my parents. "My mother and father had one, too. Whenever I tell people this, they tell me that I'm romanticizing their relationship because I lost my father at such a young age. But I look at our old photo albums and family movies and I know they were meant to be."

"I didn't realize that. I'm sorry. Was he sick?"

"No, he and my older brother were killed in a plane crash when I was eight."

Charlie doesn't speak right away.

"That must have been a very lonely time," he says finally.

I nod.

"It was. Sometimes it's still that way."

"A pain you never get over." His voice is flat.

"But you do learn to live with it," I reassure him.

"So how come you seem so normal?" he asks sincerely. "I mean except for the obsessive following."

I tell Charlie about my childhood friends.

"I kind of went from one house to another. My friends liked it because it was a prolonged slumber party and the parents didn't mind because I tried to be a perfect guest."

"And what does being the perfect guest entail?" Charlie is smirking.

"I stayed out of everyone's way and when appropriate I would tell a funny story."

"I can believe that," Charlie says. "You are, in fact, hilarious."

"Oh, you should have met me in high school. I was in my humor prime. I wrote parodies for our school literary magazine. In fact, that's how I ended up at Harvard."

"You attached a parody to your application?"

"Oh, no. I hadn't even considered going to Harvard. I had always thought that I needed a smaller, more nurturing school. But one night, I wrote a parody of my friend Daphne Feller's personal essay, entitled 'Semper Amabo Harvard.' I wrote it in Latin and it had fourteen footnotes. Daphne dared me to send it in. She even did all the typing."

"You actually wrote something in Latin?" Charlie is clearly impressed.

"Well, once I had the idea, I had to execute it."

"What happened to Daphne?"

"She went to Stanford. She's a doctor. Her parents just celebrated their fortieth wedding anniversary."

"Did your mother ever remarry?"

Speaking of pains I can live with.

"Yes." I tell Charlie about Barnes, the god of all things foolish. He is somewhat cheered.

I like this moment we're sharing. Charlie puts his arm out as if to give me a comforting hug, but catches himself.

"I'm going to do some work on the Internet."

That's my cue to watch television.

"It has got to be someone from the film," Charlie tells me this morning.

"What?"

I'm not awake yet, and Charlie's lack of coffeemaker is not acceptable. He's fresh faced from his post-run shower, wearing what I call his uniform: jeans and a blue rugby shirt. The neatness of the navy is nicely contrasted by his intense expression and his floppy hair. He's eager to tell me his theory and drags me to Eat Here Now. I'm wearing one of his thick flannel shirts and Felisha's riding pants and boots.

"The killer has got to be somebody from the movie you were working on."

I have known this to be a possibility, but how could Charlie be so certain?

"Too much of a coincidence," he tells me. "The person has been staking you out and has been staking Polly out. The killer has to have wanted you persecuted or Polly dead. It seems unlikely that someone would want to hurt you."

A compliment!

Charlie is still talking. "But the killer may have had a beef with Polly, or likelier yet, her husband. What better way to torture a person than to kill the person he loves?"

I knew Charlie was a romantic.

"And the killer must have seen you hanging around Polly. You could've been anybody. Just a nice easy fall guy for this killer."

I don't know whether I should delight in Charlie's assertion that I'm not hateable or bemoan the fact that he thinks I'm a bit of a milquetoast.

Charlie continues to ponder this.

"What about Lissa, the scorned actress?" Charlie asks, excited.

"You clearly have no experience in showbiz," I tell him. "Actresses are routinely fired for no reason, not hired for no reason, and treated like garbage for no reason."

"Yeah. But what if this one was a nut?"

"They're all nuts. And her beef would probably be more with Mona than with Humphrey. After all, Mona was the mastermind who decided to use Lissa as a pawn in the negotiations. If Lissa wanted to kill, her target would be Mona."

"Maybe she hates you. Maybe she's *framing* you," Charlie tells me.

"No. Actors know that the casting assistant is a nobody. It would be a waste to frame me."

"Don't sell yourself short. You are not a nobody."

"I will take that as praise."

"You should," he says seriously.

I don't know why, but I blush.

Charlie has clearly not thought this through. The killer could have been stalking Polly for days and noticed that Polly had another "fan." This opens up the list of possibilities as to Polly's murderer. But I don't want to overwhelm the guy. He has his own mystery to solve.

"I've made up a list in my head," I tell him, "of all the people who might want to kill Polly. Only one is from the film."

"I'm all ears," Charlie tells me.

Maybe I'm wrong, but I think he may be enjoying this just a little bit.

"Well. I'll admit that I have never liked Polly Dawson. She's led a charmed life, but has left a wake of disgruntled friends, colleagues, and maybe lovers. In the last couple of weeks alone, I saw Polly's actions inspire extreme reactions in people." I'm tempted to ask Charlie about his college romance with her, but I refrain. "I know of two men who may have been in love with her and two women who hated her."

"Okay. Ladies first," Charlie says.

"The first one is D.M." I point out that that is my name for her. "I think she may be one of Polly's business partners," I tell him. "She's older than Polly, fatter than Polly, and far less refined."

"You have just described ninety-nine point nine nine percent of the female population. That's hardly a reason to kill her."

I tell him about Polly's flaunting her trim little figure in front of her friend, who, by all appearances, has to struggle with her weight. I also tell him about our museum trips. Polly always ignored the line to pay for their admission, leaving D.M. to take care of it.

"I wouldn't think that poverty was one of Polly's problems," Charlie says.

"Oh, Polly was much meaner than that."

I tell him about one interaction I'd witnessed. They were standing in front of *Le Déjeuner sur l'Herbe*. D.M. said she wasn't sure that the general public would be familiar with Monet. Polly almost spat at her.

"No problem there, because this is *Manet*. You should educate yourself."

"You couldn't miss the festering animosity," I tell him.

"Polly was horrible," I continue. "She said something to D.M. like 'It's one thing that you've never been exposed to any sort of culture, but you've known for weeks about the importance of these trips to the museum. The least you could do is a little reading.' "

"Whew," Charlie says.

"She told D.M. that she embarrassed her."

Charlie looks totally fascinated, so I go on.

"Polly always ordered a huge meal when they were out together. She would order the Lever House hamburger and french fries. When we went to the Four Seasons, she would get the whole pheasant and whipped potatoes. As they sat there, Polly would play with the food rather than eating it. When the busboy would come to collect her plate, she would clutch her stomach a little too dramatically and say something like, 'I'm so so so full; I couldn't eat another thing.' " I shake my head disgustedly. "I swear, she put on this performance to torture D.M.

"She would sit over her steamed greens looking longingly at Polly's uneaten burger. Polly would pretend to be oblivious to all of this, but she had a habit of stabbing a forkful of the most presentable portion of food and then waving it in her friend's face and then placing it back on her plate."

Charlie looks doubtful. "That's no reason to kill someone," he says.

"You didn't see it," I tell him. "They had this kind of emotionally abusive thing. Polly put down everything that this woman did. Polly was nasty and this woman just took it. Maybe she snapped."

Charlie may not be sold on this theory, but he types into his computer: *Suspect Number One. Name: D.M. Blondish female. Motive: Weird woman friendship or business relationship.*

"Next?" Charlie says.

We're still on the female suspects. I think for a moment.

"Jenna McNair," I say.

"Who's that?"

"You'll like her for the murder," I say in detective show lingo. "She's from the movie. She's going to be a very big star."

"Go on."

"Jenna McNair. She's the one who got the part that Lissa tried out for."

"Why would she kill Polly?"

"I got the vibe that the two hated each other." I start to tell Charlie about how I went to the mayor's mansion for a cocktail party and about the icy connection between the two of them. "When Polly left, I saw Jenna mouth the words 'What a bitch.'"

Charlie seems less interested in Jenna McNair than in my crashing a private party at Gracie Mansion.

"No one arrested you for trespassing?"

"Ummmm. No."

"You were at a city party with city officials and security and guest lists and cameras, and you didn't get caught?"

"They had guns, too," I say enthusiastically, "and bats and walkie-talkies and bomb-sniffing dogs."

Charlie looks at me and takes a deep breath. "You *are* good," he says in awe.

I feel tingly. But we have to get back to Jenna.

"I don't know why, but those two women didn't like each other."

Charlie, still awestruck by my mayoral coup, continues typing into his computer. *Suspect Number Two. Jenna McNair. Motive: The two don't like each other.*

"Is this really a strong motive?" he asks. "You said yourself that Polly Dawson must have a long list of women who don't like her."

Charlie's right. I think of Jean and me, for example. I have despised Polly for years and Jean's hatred of her is almost pathological.

"I know," I tell him, "but the timing with Jenna would be right. For example, my best friend, Jean, and I have always hated Polly. It's been a constant. It would seem weird that out of the blue, for no reason, either of us would kill her. Polly wasn't a new character in my life."

Charlie interrupts me. "Yes, but the theory is that you always hated her and then your getting fired triggered a murderous event. That makes your motive stronger than Jenna McNair's."

"So I got fired," I say matter-of-factly, "from a position I didn't even enjoy. And why would I kill Polly? She's not in casting. Under your theory, if I were to kill anybody, it would be Mona Hawkins. Jenna just met Polly. Who knows? Polly may have realized that her husband was working with a woman who was more beautiful than she was and made her life miserable."

"This one seems thin to me, but we'll keep it." Charlie is poised for Suspect Number Three.

"We're on to the gentlemen," I say. "I guess the number-one suspect has to be Polly's cute young lover."

"I like it," Charlie says. "More."

"Polly was sleeping with a guy. He must have been twenty-three, twenty-four years old. She used to go to his apartment almost every day and the two would spend hours up there."

"How did you know about him?"

"I was lucky. I was vigilant about following her to this one building over and over again. Most would have given up." I say this as if my behavior were normal. "One day, they must have discovered they were hungry because they actually left the premises and ventured into Chinatown for a meal. In fact, that was the day I saw you having lunch with Kovitz."

Charlie seems a little flustered. "So, she was having an affair. That's it?"

"It was very intense. All that time in his apartment—only one meal?"

"I need more."

"My gut told me that the affair was not going to last. She was a hot businesswoman. He had that young-nothing quality to him," I say. I realize I sound kind of snobbish, so I decide to leave out the part about his ghastly soul patch. What if Charlie went through a soul patch phase himself?

"So you think she may have broken things off, and then he killed her?" he asks.

"Sure. It happens all the time on *Law and Order*."

"But it doesn't happen all the time in real life. Alice, if every spurned lover committed homicide, there would be ten times as many prisons and graveyards, and New York City would be empty."

"This guy was young. He was impressionable, and Polly was probably the most fascinating person he would ever meet. And she was probably two-timing even him."

"What makes you say that?" Charlie asks me.

"Well, there was this guy in the public library," I say.

"A librarian?" Charlie asks me.

"No—a guy. Suspect Number Four, in fact. Someone at the library. But he looked out of place there. He was wearing a very expensive suit. He didn't look like the kind of guy who ever goes to the library except to attend five-thousand-dollar-a-plate library benefits. He wasn't there to read. He wasn't there to research. He just seemed to be doing some weird library mating dance with Polly."

"Did they interact?"

I pause. I reach into my pocket. I graze my hands over the crumpled piece of paper, and in my head I see her message: *12/20 Tender Dutch.* She had left it for him in the card catalog. I decide in a split second that I can't tell Charlie about the note. I'd have to tell him that in addition to following Polly I was reading her private written exchanges. This definitely falls outside the category of trying to learn about my life through learning about hers. I will have to keep this a secret for now.

"They didn't interact. But they were together."

Luckily, Charlie believes me. He types into his computer: *Suspect Number Four: Library guy. Motive: Alice will make one up.*

"Any others?" Charlie asks.

"Nothing comes to mind. I mean, she was incredibly flirtatious with every male cast member from her husband's film. Did one of the stars kill her out of passion? It just seems unlikely. They all worshiped her husband, and while her behavior was highly annoying and even reprehensible, I didn't see her spend days on end with any of them the way she did with the young lover," I tell him. "Then again, my reconnaissance lasted only a few weeks. It's likely that Polly made a trillion enemies before I entered the picture."

"Well. This is a good start," Charlie says.

"It is," I agree. "But we better take a page from von Schlieffen."

"Schlieffen, as in the Plan?" Charlie asks, energized.

"Yes," I say, "we have to fight this war on every front."

"I thought I was the only World War One buff in this house."

"Oh, you are. I have limited enthusiasm for World War One." I pause. "No offense or anything."

"How do you know about the Schlieffen Plan?"

"Once I hear it or see it, it stays there," I say, pointing to my head. "We have to plan our strategy. This is where you come in."

"Look, I was the one typing the suspects in the computer and asking the probing questions about their motives."

"And you did that well." I note that I have never until this moment been condescending. "But now you have to take it up a notch."

I tell him he has to call Kovitz and see what he can get from him. Any clue would be helpful.

"Do you suggest I just call Kovitz and say 'Hey—so interesting about that Polly Dawson murder. Could you hand me your files?'"

"You could do something a little more subtle."

"Subtle?"

"Yes. How about something like, 'Hey, I saw you on the news. You're very telegenic. I dated that murder victim Polly Dawson when we were in college, and I think I may also know your suspect. She and I worked in the same office for a while. I could ask around for you.'"

If Charlie were drinking right now, he'd be doing a spit take.

"How do you know that Polly and I *dated*?"

"I remember Polly crowing that she dumped you."

"I remember that, too," Charlie laughs.

"Well?"

"Well what?"

"You dated Polly. Did you have a relationship with her? Are you sad that she's dead?" I sound a little more fishwife than houseguest.

"As long as you're asking, I went on exactly two dates with her. I had no relationship with her, or interest in her, for that matter. And I'm not sad that she's dead, but I feel for people who might be."

"You had no interest in her? You must have at one point."

"Sure. When I first met her, I thought she was pretty, smart, and ballsy. Then about five minutes into our first date, I realized she was not for me."

"How so?" I can't help myself.

"She was entitled and agenda-laden."

Ooh, agenda-laden. I like that. I can't wait to tell Jean.

"Not my type," he continues.

Is this the part where I tell him that I have a negative sense of entitlement and had to go to therapy to develop an agenda?

"But you went on a second date with her?"

"We made two dates when I asked her out initially. It would have been ungentlemanly of me to back out of the second date, which by the way, involved prepurchased tickets to something."

An a cappella concert offered by the Krokodiloes at Memorial Hall, I'm on the brink of saying. I keep my mouth shut, however. Sometimes it's better not to advertise the Olympian memory.

"Did you ever see her here in New York?"

"On the side of a bus from time to time. But that was it. No. Frankly, I never even thought about her."

I wish I could say the same.

"So will you talk to Kovitz?"

"I will. Do you really think I have to tell him that he looks telegenic?"

"Flattery will get you everywhere," I say, quoting Mother.

"And . . . ?"

"And then you ask him for the file."

"How do I do that?"

"You're the lawyer. I can tell you that on *NYPD Blue* they say things like 'Whaddya got?' "

" 'Whaddya got' is good."

"Thank you."

We return home—Charlie's home. He puts on his headphones and resumes his work. He spends at least five hours a day listening to recordings he made of the conversations with his father's escorts. I'm not sure what he thinks he'll hear today that he didn't hear yesterday, but I don't ask him. It's his way. I do, however, need him to make a move on my situation. Don't get me wrong. I'm grateful for the shelter, and I'd be happy to live forever on the couch that belongs to the man I love. But at some point, he's going to resolve his situation and ask me, as he did once before, "Who the fuck are you? And why are you following me?"

Once I'm certain that Charlie will not be disturbed, I turn on his television. I'm gauging the progress on the Polly Dawson murder investigation. I'm still the number-one suspect according to the press and law enforcement, but the story and my sketch don't seem to fascinate journalists. CNN keeps showing the same shot of Humphrey Dawson thanking the public for its support during this trying time. The story then glides into a still photo of the fifth precinct station house accompanied by a reporter's remarks that the police "failed to maintain the suspect."

"Failed to maintain the suspect." I escaped. And they don't even name me or show my sketch. I'd be insulted if I weren't so grateful. Last week, they aired a quick interview with Mother. Only Mother didn't get a word in. Barnes did all the talking.

"I can assure you, *we* have done nothing illegal."

"Wow. He doesn't exactly have your back," Charlie noted.

"That should be our family slogan," I said.

"I'm sorry about that, Alice." A short phrase, but with his intense delivery, I believed him.

As for my coverage today, the local news is only slightly more detailed.

"We are pursuing all of our leads," Kovitz tells the camera.

The newspapers have dropped the story. *The New York Times* carried the item on the front page of the Metro section the day after this occurred; the *New York Post* and the *Daily News* had a sketch of my face on New Year's Day, and for the next week focused more on Humphrey. Six days after his wife's murder, the *Post* had a picture of Humphrey with the headline SINGLE AGAIN.

I am exhausted. I am currently knee-deep in Charlie's case. Oxanna, Trini, and Justine seem to have fled New York City—or at least their official residences. Last week, I waited in a cramped stairwell across the street from Oxanna's apartment for twenty-seven hours with no results. It was brutal. I was also tired and would have fallen asleep except for two things that kept me conscious. First, it was freezing and I had to keep my body parts moving. And second, I didn't want to let Charlie down.

I waited so patiently, but no one went into or came out of her small Inwood tenement. I didn't see lights of any kind turn on or off. I gave up when it was clear that a pub owner down the street had spotted me and begun making inquiries among the locals.

I went back to Charlie's to warm up a little before I went to Gravesend, Brooklyn, where Trini supposedly lived. That was a short visit, as I saw a pile of mail addressed to her on the steps of her deserted building. Once assured she was nowhere to be found, I went back uptown again, to East Harlem. Justine lives there. Or should I say lived there. Someone else was looking for her, too. A nondescript man seemed miffed that he couldn't find her.

"She'll be outta town for a few weeks," a clerk from the bodega next door told him. "I look after her bird."

"How convenient that all of these girls skip town within three weeks of a tenuous accusation," Charlie says. "This is very suspicious."

I agree. It is suspicious.

Remy is still in town, though. He faithfully rides his bike to work every morning. And Charlie has been combing industry periodicals and blogs to see if he has made any changes at Kelt.

"So far the only change he's made is to ruin my father," Charlie says.

I have taken a few trips to see Henrietta Murch, and she is still staying close to home. I haven't seen her make contact with anyone other than clerks in her local Duane Reade and Shop Best, and an attendant in a Laundromat.

"Maybe they are speaking in code."

If Charlie knew a thing about TV, I would swear that he has watched too many episodes of *Alias*. I can pretty much bet my freedom on the fact that they aren't speaking in code, but I know how badly Charlie needs answers so I promise him that I'll keep following.

Today, Charlie brings home a copy of a tabloid that describes Polly as a sex addict. It goes on to say that friends of hers who refuse to be identified have detailed a series of Polly's extramarital relations.

"What do you make of that?" he asks me. He's drinking his third cup of coffee from Eat Here Now.

"As someone who's not above gossip, I make nothing of it," I tell him. "Have you ever thought of investing in a coffeemaker? It could save you a lot of money."

"Nothing?" He's ignoring my appliance input.

"Nothing. All famous married people cheat on each other according to those rags. The people who write that junk know that readers will believe anything as long as it is typed. I know for a fact they make stuff up."

"How do you know that?" Charlie asks me in that cross-examination tone.

"I read it somewhere," I tell him.

"How do you know that the somewhere that you read it didn't make it up?" Charlie asks, half lawyer, half kidding.

I crumple the tabloid and throw it at him.

Our first fight.

"Oh, and by the way," he says seriously.

"Yes?"

"I'll get a coffeemaker, but you have to make the coffee."

I turn on the city's twenty-four-hour news channel, New York 1. I learn that there will be a memorial service for Polly Dawson next Thursday.

I call Charlie's name: "Walter?"

Nothing.

"Walter."

Nothing.

I go up to him. He's wearing his headphones and writing furiously in a notebook. I know the only way to get his attention is to make physical contact. And even though I'm sleeping in his living room, wearing his clothes, and trusting him with my life, I'm nervous about touching him. First, it seems like an intrusion, and second, I fear that in touching him, I'll give myself away. Charlie can't know that I love him. He might question my motives for staying here, which I promise are genuinely separate from any romantic feeling. This is information I don't wish to share with him.

I tap him awkwardly on the top of his shoulder. He gasps slightly and looks at me in horror. Not quite the reaction I wanted. I was looking for something a little more neutral.

"Sorry, I didn't mean to scare you."

"No—it's just that I was deep in thought. I had missed something Doreen said, and I was able to catch it this time."

Doreen was the first woman I saw Charlie with at Eat Here Now. We had no address for her.

"Anything good?"

"I'm not sure. When I questioned her about my father, I asked her what she knew about him, and she kept referring to my mother as if she were still alive."

"Oh," I say, knowing this is a sensitive subject for him.

"It lowers her credibility," he says to me. "If she was connected with my father at all, she would know within minutes that he is a widower. She obviously has the wrong guy."

"Maybe your father wouldn't tell her about your mom." I know this is a mistake once the words escape my lips.

"You don't know my father. And you didn't know my mother"—Charlie raises his voice with me—"and you didn't see how they were together. My father wouldn't disrespect her by paying for sex and pretending that she was alive."

I've let Charlie down somehow, implying that Doreen is more credible than his father.

"I'm sorry," I tell him, "but it sounds like she will ultimately be helpful."

"She'll be helpful. After I ruin her. They're all lying, I assure you."

I believe Charlie. I believe him because he believes me, and this agreement we have is what keeps us committed to seeing this thing through. Besides, it's Charlie.

I change the subject.

"Guess what I saw on New York One?"

"They caught the killer and you're exonerated."

"No, close. But there will be a memorial service for Polly next Thursday."

"Where?"

"Undisclosed location."

"That's helpful." Charlie puts his headphones back on and starts taking notes. I tap him again without any hesitation.

"What?" he asks as he takes one speaker off his ear.

"We're going." I'm surprised by my command.

"What?" He takes the headset off. He looks cute when he's scruffy.

"We're going to go to the memorial service. It will be a way to get information."

"We don't know where it is, and you're running from the law. The place is going to be packed with police."

Charlie does have a point.

"You're right. You should go."

"I should go?"

"Yes, go. It couldn't be more perfect. Talk to Kovitz. Get a sense of the crowd. Look for suspicious people."

It sounds dumb as it comes out of my mouth. The only person who successfully assesses suspicious people is Lieutenant Columbo. The runner-up is a tie between Adrian Monk, the hero of the USA Network, and Robert Goren, Vincent D'Onofrio's character on *Law & Order: Criminal Intent*. Charlie, for the record, is nothing like either of these characters. But it's a start.

"How am I going to figure out where they are holding the service?"

"Easy."

Charlie looks unhappy. I can't have an uncommitted player on the team.

"Look," I continue. "Trust me, please. I've gotten this far. This apartment is one block from a police station. And yet, undisguised, I remain undiscovered. With an extra brain—yours—we can not only run away from the law, but we can make them scratch their heads as to why they ever considered me a suspect in the first place."

"Huh?"

"Just follow my lead," I tell him.

"Okay," Charlie says. I think he might be smiling. He puts his headphones back on and returns to his notes.

I'm getting a little bored. We are in the midst of an ice storm. No one is going anywhere today. There will be no following. Charlie takes a break from his "research" and is reading *The Complete History of World War I*. He says it relaxes him. I look in the kitchen to see if there is anything to eat. The refrigerator is empty except for a small square of cheddar cheese. I look in the freezer, hoping there might be an entire Carvel cake. There's nothing but frozen peas and spinach, both of which are severe victims of freezer burn. The cabinets have to have something. Oh, good, *Rice-A-Roni* . . . "the San Francisco treat." I'm now humming the old ad. Jean used to live on that stuff in law school. I grab the box. Damn. It expired last April. There's a can of chicken broth in the back of the cabinet. It still has two more good months. And that's it. I can't believe this guy has no food in his house.

I notice there is another cabinet on top of the cabinet. I climb onto the counter to open it. And voilà: salt, pepper, and nutmeg. Nutmeg? There has got to be a story behind that one. I take them down, along with the can of soup. And I realize that after more than a week of burgers and omelets from Eat Here Now, I've probably had no vegetables in close to a month. I'm not a health nut or anything, but that can't be good for you. I grab the peas, the spinach, and the cheese.

"Everything okay?" Charlie asks me from his desk.

"Yes. I just thought I would make myself a snack."

"We could order from Eat Here Now."

"No thanks," I tell him as I boil some of the chicken broth.

"Don't you need ingredients for a snack?" Charlie screams.

"All taken care of." I put the spinach in the broth.

"Good luck."

"Thanks." I chop the cheddar into small pieces and I put the peas in the spinach broth mixture. I have no idea if this will be tasty, but I need the vitamins. I take a chance by adding the cheese and the nutmeg. I pour half of the mixture into a bowl.

Charlie walks into the kitchen.

"Smells good in here."

He comes over to my shoulder.

"Whaddya got?"

"I thought I could use a vegetable."

"Is there enough for me?"

I want to lie and tell him no. But the man has been letting me stay in his house.

"Eat at your own risk. I'm not a chef." I hand him a bowl. I'm mortified. I don't even know what nutmeg is for.

Charlie eats a few bites but doesn't say anything.

"This could use one more ingredient." Charlie leaves the kitchen.

I'm a little offended. After all, I used every ingredient in his house.

"If you are thinking of adding the Rice-A-Roni, it expired nine months ago."

Charlie can't hear me. He's left the kitchen. My friend Cecily told me that when she was growing up, her mother used to take all of the most delicious food items and lock them in her room so the "help" wouldn't steal them. Meanwhile she left expensive jewelry and other stuff lying around the house. Maybe Charlie will come in with some veal shanks or a wild boar.

But no. Charlie is more normal, thank God. He returns with a wine bottle. And for a second I don't know the appropriate reaction. My friend Jean always cooks with alcohol. Even if she is making a can of soup, she always tosses in some wine. Last year she made oatmeal raisin cookies and soaked the raisins in rum for twelve hours beforehand. "It gives them a bite," she tells everybody.

"Maybe we could use a little," Charlie tells me as he leans toward me and reaches over my head for a second. Suddenly he steps away with two glasses in his hand.

I nod to let Charlie know that I'll have some wine.

We sit in his living room for a few minutes without saying much. I feel uncomfortable discussing anything other than our respective police investigations.

"You're pretty resourceful," Charlie says out of nowhere.

"Huh?"

"This food. Who would have known there could be a meal waiting for me in my kitchen?"

"I take it you're not a cook."

"A fine observation."

"Don't you snack? I understand the no cooking thing, but there's not a pretzel to be found."

"Yeah. My ex-girlfriend lived here with me for a while and she was terrified of bugs and mice. So we weren't allowed to keep anything in the cabinets."

Ex-girlfriend? Of course Charlie has an ex-girlfriend. He probably has several ex-girlfriends. Even though I've admired him from afar for all of these years, I never pictured him with anybody specific. Now I have this image in my head of Charlie dating this freaky vermin-phobe.

"I guess it's a waste of valuable real estate."

"Huh?" I'm not really listening to Charlie as I try to picture him and this girl in the living room: *my* living room.

"You know, having a kitchen with nothing in it. Some people live in apartments the size of this kitchen, and I've abandoned this promising space."

"Oh," I say. I'm still thinking of Charlie's ex-girlfriend and am therefore incapable of discussing his insufficient use of his kitchen.

"I'm going to cook more from now on."

"I'm glad I could help."

"Good," Charlie says.

"Good," I say.

We experience a pause that lasts as long as Handel's *Messiah*, the extended version, before I gather the courage to reintroduce conversation to the table.

"So, here's how we are going to get to that memorial service . . ."

Charlie and I are standing over his desk staring at his state-of-the-art phone. I press the speaker phone button and dial Jean's office phone number. It's a number I have been dialing for years.

It's likely that the police are monitoring Jean's phone calls. I can tell Charlie is nervous.

The phone rings once before she picks it up.

"Jean Middleton."

I'm comforted by Jean's voice.

"Hi, Jean. I don't know if you remember me. My name is Walter Redwin. We went to Harvard Law School together."

Jean pauses for a second. I know that she's dying to get in touch with me to tell me that my Charlie called her.

This is where Charlie's part gets tricky.

"You may know me as Charlie."

Now, I know you may be wondering how I managed to get Charlie to identify himself by his crush-name.

"Just introduce yourself to her on the phone," I instructed him casually just minutes ago. "And then tell her that she may know you as Charlie."

"Why Charlie?"

"Oh, it's this thing with me and Jean."

"What kind of thing?"

A thing where I made up a name for you when I decided to become obsessed with you.

"I promise I will tell you the second I get out of trouble." Curiosity is a great motivator.

So here we are standing over Charlie's desk as he identifies himself as Charlie to Jean.

Jean pauses even longer this time.

"Oh," and I can tell by the tone of her "Oh" that she knows. She knows. She knows. Jean knows I'm with Charlie.

"What can I do for you?" I can hear the excitement in her voice.

"I was working until very recently at Pennington and Litt and am currently on a leave of absence, and I was hoping to change jobs. I was looking at the Harvard Law alumni bulletin and I saw . . ."

"Yes!" Jean just wants him to cut to the chase.

"I was wondering if I could take you out for coffee and pick your brain."

"Sure. I'll be there," Jean says.

"Can we set up a time?" Charlie asks.

"How about tomorrow?"

"Thursday's better," Charlie tells her.

"Thursday it is. Ummmm." Jean pauses. "Walter?"

"Yes?"

"Is everything okay?" Jean's asking about me, of course. She shouldn't have done that. If her phone is bugged, they could realize she is asking about me.

"Yes." Charlie saves it. "I just need a job change. That's it."

"I'm sure I can help you," she says very professionally.

Charlie turns the speaker off and hangs up the phone.

My plan is working.

Jean is waiting for Charlie at the café at Barnes & Noble in Union Square. I know that she'll drink an enormous espresso and she'll study the entire pastry selection before telling the cashier, "No thank you; it's not like I need one." Charlie got there ahead of time to make sure the place wasn't being monitored by the police, although I think they would change out of their uniforms for something like this. In fact, I haven't seen a cop make an arrest in uniform since *NYPD Blue*. The ladies of the *Law & Order* franchise dress better than any of my friends. But the place looks clear. Charlie has reported that there are three women with strollers arguing about who has the least baby-friendly husband. There's also a student-looking guy slumped over a chair in the back. The cashier is a twenty-something African-American woman, eager to serve her customers so that she can get back to her stack of bridal magazines.

I wait on the first floor next to the stairs in the self-help section, pretending to read books about getting the love I want, and Pilates. I notice the top two sellers: The First is *The Way: Part Two* by Dr. Michael Ledyard. He's The freak I keep seeing on the talk shows promising to cure gay people of their homosexuality. A few days ago, he was on television hawking the book while Charlie was reviewing his files at his desk. He told me that if I didn't change the channel he would have to turn me over to the cops.

And then there is this woman's book. I keep seeing it on *Oprah* and *The View*. It's called *Men Fight, Women Bite*. Clarissa Winnick. That's her name. Her premise is that fighting like a girl is actually extremely effective if women just own it. She says that women have to develop their Trifecta Defensive: the shrill piercing scream, the shocking bite, and the annoying kick. She claims that women have evolved over the millennia with increased Trifecta Defensive potential.

"The female shriek has grown in decibel level over the years, and though we do not have the benefit of early female *Homo sapiens* recordings, anecdotal information suggests that the woman's shriek has become a huge advantage in physical combat."

Too bad they have no female recordings—or as I call it, evidence—to support her theory.

Winnick has no support for the evolution of the female bite and kick, which she claims can disable the most evil attacker. As examples, she has warded off rehearsed attacks by news and talk personalities with her Trifecta Defensive. Matt Lauer and Diane Sawyer both fell to the ground last week: Matt on Tuesday and Diane on Wednesday. Needless to say, neither of them had a gun.

If everything is going as Charlie and I planned, he and Jean are making small talk. Jean is chattering about the merger market and Charlie's speaking in the abstract about his need for a career move. Charlie asks Jean to write him a list of contacts and presents her with a note from me, of course.

Downstairs in self-help; need it as I am being framed.

Jean can't wait to see me. I can feel it, and Charlie must do his best to contain her. He asks her if she knows of any literature that could be helpful in his career change. She tells him that first he has to figure out what he wants.

"I suggest you look in the self-help section; I can help if you want," Jean is probably telling him at this moment.

I see the two of them coming down the stairs as I peruse *Who Moved My Cheese?*

"I think it's over here," Jean says as she comes toward me. I lift my eyes for a second, and then go back to the book.

He hands her the book; she opens it, and reads my note.

J.

I'm alive. Charlie's helping. In 10 mins, leave Barnes & Noble and go to Mona's office. Wait outside the building in a taxi. You'll see Mona. She's skinny, skinny with an enormous head (think Nancy Reagan, the First Lady years) and will be wearing all black w/ an enormous purple tote. She'll get into a car service car—it might have a little lobster on the windshield. Your taxi must follow her car. Charlie'll be in a taxi following you. You'll hopefully be heading to the memorial service—Never thought that would happen, huh? Try to get info on the deceased. Say that you're a lawyer who worked for the company. Talk to the most attractive people there; they're actors and will spill their guts.

Don't drink any alcohol!!!!

Can you believe this?

A.

P.S. Remember, don't drink any alcohol!

The "this" in "Can you believe this?" refers to my dire situation and my proximity to Charlie, but of course I had to review the note with Charlie before he passed it along to Jean. What if she needs him to help her with my instructions?

There she is. There she is. It's Jean. "Hey, Jean," I mouth to myself. I feel better just seeing her. She looks great, by the way, wearing a sleek black leather coat offset by the beautiful aquamarine cashmere scarf that I got her for Christmas last year. It looks great with her superdark curly hair and her blue-green eyes. They look great together. Charlie, for the first time since I've been staying with him, is wearing a suit. It's charcoal gray.

"Is the color too boring?" he asked me this morning.

"No—you are going to a memorial service. The idea is not to look fashionable. You are supposed to be sad."

"Gray is sad," he noted.

"You can jazz it up with a red, happy tie," I told him. "But not too red—maybe a little crimsonish."

Boy, does he look good. Tall and lanky, with not such good posture. I like that. It could be because I am no Jack LaLanne myself. Also it makes him look like a man with a purpose.

My best friend and my lifelong crush. Together. How weird is this? I'm a little envious of Charlie and Jean. Not because I think they could fall in love or anything. I kind of want to follow Mona Hawkins, too.

So, I do.

I'm confident that Mona will be at the memorial service; she doesn't miss any public event that relates to showbiz. She assumes that every function is planned for her benefit. And I'm sure this one is no exception. When I worked for her, she always spoke about "Humpy" as if he were new to show business, when in fact he had won two Oscars for Best Director.

I hop in a cab behind Charlie. Our caravan heads up Park Avenue and we make a left onto Twenty-third Street. Then we head west.

How can I pay for the taxi when I don't even have the money for a MetroCard? I know this is embarrassing, but two nights ago, Charlie announced that he would give me an allowance.

"Let's just call it a stipend," he assured me as he gave me twenty-five ten-dollar bills. "You may need it for the work you're doing for me."

So here I am in the taxi, heading up Madison Avenue, hoping to learn a little about my case so that I can in turn help Charlie with his. I assume we're heading to Frank E. Campbell, funeral home to the rich and famous. Obviously, I can't go in. P.S. 6 is just across the street. Maybe I can lurk there and pretend I'm a parent, like Meryl Streep did in *Kramer vs. Kramer*.

But the caravan stops a mile sooner—at Sixtieth Street and Madison. I can't see Mona, but I do see Jean, and then Charlie disembark from their respective vehicles. Why did we stop at Barneys? Maybe Mona needs to buy a lipstick for the occasion, but as I study my surroundings, I see a deluge of limousines.

Of course, the memorial service is at Barneys.

Barneys, as I recall, was the first major retailer to carry Polly Dawson's lingerie line before she started her own chain. Polly was obsessed with the place. I know that because I followed her here at least a dozen times. I see police barricades surrounding the entire block. There are hordes of cops as well, although I don't see my team: Kovitz, Seminara, and Bristol. They must be inside.

I worry a little about Charlie and Jean. Charlie isn't much of an actor, and Jean gets nervous quite easily. A few years ago, Jean decided to throw a surprise birthday party for her then-boyfriend, Lee. She had invited about twenty-five of Lee's friends, and me of course, to wait at her apartment while she and Lee were supposed to go on a date. They were to meet at Lee's office in the West Fifties and then go out for a drink at a bar near Jean's house. Jean was supposed to pretend that she forgot her purse at her apartment and then bring Lee up for a big *surprise*.

Unfortunately, when she told Lee that she forgot her wallet, he offered to pay for the drink. She immediately blurted out that they had to go to her house because twenty-five people were waiting to surprise him.

Charlie and Jean. The Dynamic Duo.

They're all I have.

I stand across the street, with my scarf over my neck, pretending to wait for a bus in front of the Cole Haan store. I know that watching them puts me in no better position than they are. But, alas, I'm compelled.

People continue to stream into Barneys for forty-five minutes. I knew Mona would get there early; she always gets to these things early. Ironic, considering that she would let her actors and actresses wait at least an hour before she waltzed into a casting session.

There's a little slice of glass that isn't covered by the Barneys window display, and I see the crowd thinning from the first floor. They must be heading up to the lingerie department on six.

I wait two hours exactly. I have memorized every shoe and bag at Cole Haan. I must leave. Soon, I'll be a suspected shoplifter and the nervous salesgirl will call the police.

I go to get a pretzel from the vendor across the street, and I notice more movement through my little slice of glass. The cops seem to have gone in the store, so I can peer in for at least a while. The entire first floor of Barneys has been transformed into a huge party space. I feel as if I'm spying on a wedding—not a funeral. Hunky men in white ties and tails are handing out what appears to be a stunning array of hors d'oeuvres, as well as champagne cocktails. People are in deep conversation, laughing or networking. There's a huge spread of food set up where all the jewelry is supposed to be. There, I see Mona, with that skinny little body and colossal head, helping herself to a teeny taste of everything.

Mona loves buffets.

I see Jean. She must have checked her coat. She's wearing her superexpensive Yves Saint Laurent graphite-hued wide-legged trousers with her signature silk brocade jacket. Oh, I see she bought the ridiculously expensive Wilmer Heiker mary jane pumps, which I know for a fact set her back $640. That's Jean. Offsetting her haute ensemble is the can of Diet Coke in her hand. Phew. Jean is not so good with alcohol. She gets a little chatty. After two glasses, I'm afraid that she'll spill my secret. Oh, good. I see Charlie in charcoal. I can't figure out whom he is talking to, but I think it's Jenna McNair, the lead actress in *Only at Sunrise,* beautiful nemesis of Polly, and Suspect Number Two. If you're wondering whether I'm jealous of Jenna, I think the answer is no. I'm so focused on getting myself out of this that I'm immune.

And then I see *him.* I wasn't sure if he'd be here. In any event, I was not one hundred percent confident that I would recognize him. Here he is. Polly's little boyfriend. He's a little more dressed up than he was the day I saw him with Polly Linley—now Dawson—now dead. Suspect Number Three is pretty handsome from afar. He smiles and waves at a couple of the other mourners. He looks serious, but he doesn't look morose.

He does look young, though.

Polly Dawson's secret young lover sure had a lot more reason to kill her than I did.

Jean walks by. She looks at the young guy for a second. It seems at first that she might know him. It's hard for me to read because I'm standing outside the window. But she stares at him for a second longer than you might look at a stranger. But this is my boy-crazy best friend, and the guy is pretty good-looking.

To Jean's credit, Polly's lover gives her the once-over. Go Jean!! You just got checked out by Suspect Number Three.

He disappears pretty quickly after that.

I try to train my eye on Jean but she's disappeared from my

little window. I see Humphrey; he looks genuinely sad. He's flanked by several gorgeous women I don't recognize. They must be models for Polly's lingerie catalog. Movie star after movie star appears in my line of vision. There's Kelly LeRoue. She seems more interested in the Barneys accessories than in being at Polly's service.

Finally, I see Jean again. She's no longer drinking Diet Coke. She has a glass of champagne in each hand. Why is she doing this? Jean, I try to telepathically convey, you know you can't be trusted to drink. But I realize I'm too late. Jean is already tipsy. Five minutes out of my sight, and she has morphed into the Drunk Lady at the Memorial Service. And then I see why. She's in deep conversation with Preston Hayes. Preston was one of the four male costars in the film. And the hottest. He enjoys the reputation of being the biggest womanizer in show business. And he just happens to be talking to my friend Jean. She's laughing with him; his hand is grazing her arm. Well, this ought to help her get over her twenty-three-year-old paralegal. Hayes gives her a business card and then moves on. Phew. I don't want her wasting time with him when she could be doing some real sleuthing.

Okay, now Jean is talking to Humphrey. They speak for about a minute or so, and then she gives him a sloppy long hug. He has no idea who she is. He moves on.

Charlie's a little less outgoing. He's talking with a woman I don't recognize. They have been immersed in conversation for about ten minutes now. He lets her eat off his plate. It seems a little intimate for me, but I can't concern myself with that now. If I'm not jealous of Jenna, I'm not going to be jealous of this woman.

I see Preston Hayes again. The man is positively gorgeous. Thick, wavy black hair, tanned skin, a half smile, and bedroom eyes. He has one arm around each of the models. So much for his moment with Jean. I look around for the other stars and I can't see them. Maybe they're still upstairs.

Charlie's back in my line of sight. He is talking to, of all people, an un-uniformed Kovitz. I knew Kovitz would attend. He's at the service for the same reason we—I mean Charlie and Jean—are. I wonder if Charlie is doing a decent job of justifying his presence at Polly Dawson's memorial service. I can't tell from the expression on either of their faces whether this encounter is a potential problem for me.

I see D.M., Suspect Number One, entering Barneys. She moves very slowly. I'm trying to get a look at her face to see if I can make out any expression, but she's too far away.

Taupe is not her color. I can say that. At least she's not wearing beige, but a simple black might have been an improvement. All in all, she looks terrible. Her eyes are swollen and she looks dumpier than she did when I was trailing her. She heads straight to Humphrey. The two embrace for at least a minute. They break apart only because Jenna McNair, Suspect Number Two, mourning stylishly in a low-necked black sheath dress with short capped sleeves, cuts in. I have a perfect view of them. She's telling Humphrey something. Jenna and Humphrey then embrace. Their contact seems more furtive. She even strokes his face. But she darts off and suddenly ends up on the street. We're right next to each other. Jenna does not recognize me. Not from Silvercup, not from the mayor's party, not from the newscasts. Now that Polly is dead, Jenna is the principessa of self-absorption.

I peer inside. Suspect Number One is at the buffet table loading her plate with all of the food Polly would never eat. Her eyes are filled with tears.

Suspect Number Four, the library man, is nowhere to be found. Perhaps he's keeping his distance. I reach into my pocket and find the crumpled note she has left him: *12/20 Tender Dutch*.

Oh, no. I see a cavalcade of news trucks heading up Madison Avenue. All I need is some earnest young reporter recognizing me from my minimal coverage. This is my cue to leave. I have to get back to Charlie's house.

I'm lounging on Charlie's couch watching coverage of the memorial service when Charlie and Jean walk in the door. Jean rushes to me; she's screaming.

"Oh my God. Oh my God. Oh my God."

I try to calm her down, but she continues:

"Oh my God. I can't believe it. Oh my God."

"I know," I tell her. "Weird, huh?"

"Tell me everything," Jean urges me as she kicks off her Heiker pumps. Charlie, who has until this point been standing quietly in the doorway, goes into the kitchen to see if I've made him some lunch.

I have.

As Charlie is digging into his farfalle with butternut squash sage sauce, I tell Jean everything. I tell her about the following, and finding Polly dead in Otto & LuLu's. I tell her about my near arrest and my escape. And then I tell her about my week of homelessness and subsequent rescue by Charlie.

"I can't believe you're staying here," was all that Jean could whisper.

"The funny thing is," I tell her, "after all I've been through in the last months, nothing seems weird."

"That, my friend, is because you're in shock. If weird were a play, this would be it."

"So?" she asks as Charlie heads back into the kitchen.

"So?"

"Anything?"

"Yes, Jean, we're making passionate love every night right after we strategize how to keep me from going to prison for the rest of my life," I say.

"Nothing?"

"I don't even think about that right now."

"You liar."

She's right. I'm fibbing a little, but we could spend the whole afternoon examining and analyzing Charlie when we should be figuring out how to clear me.

"What did you learn?"

"Well, we were only there for a few hours, but I think Humphrey's genuinely distraught over his wife's death."

"I agree," Charlie says as he walks in the room eating from a batch of chocolate chip cookies I baked last night. I've silently been appointed cook-in-residence. Amazingly, I find myself loving it.

"But I don't know if Polly would be so sad if this tragedy befell her husband."

"Oh?" I ask, knowing that Jean was cheating on Humphrey with her young Chambers Street boyfriend.

"I don't know," Jean tells me. "I got a lover whiff from a lot of the guys there. For example, every star of the movie except for Preston Hayes stayed away from Humphrey. I didn't see one of them express their condolences to him."

"And he's their director. I agree it's a little strange." I go into the kitchen to fetch us all coffee from Charlie's trusty new coffeemaker.

"Yeah, I heard the same thing," Charlie breaks in. "I was talking to Merilee, Polly's former personal assistant, and she said that a lot of people were 'close' to Polly." Charlie puts quotation mark fingers around the word "close."

So that was the woman who had monopolized Charlie.

"That could mean friendship," I tell him.

"It could, but in this case it doesn't. I asked Merilee if Polly had a lot of friends, and she said, 'I wouldn't call them that.'"

"Sounds like Polly hasn't changed," Jean quips. "Did you get any names?"

"Nothing. I'm surprised she told me as much as she did. I think she was, too. I told her that I was at the memorial service with my sister, who had been chummy with Polly as a teenager."

"She must've loved that." I didn't realize Charlie was such a good liar.

"I think she was surprised. She said that she didn't think Polly remained in touch with anyone from before she made it big."

"Sounds like she didn't like Polly."

"I don't think she liked her, but she wasn't broadcasting that at the woman's memorial service. She kept telling me that Polly was a great boss."

"Oh good, I told everybody I was in the counsel's office at Polly's lingerie company and what a great boss she was," Jean chimes in. I picture Jean, the bad drunk, talking on and on about Polly, making a misstep with every word.

"That was risky." I try not to berate Jean. She's taking these risks for me.

"I know, but I thought if I said I did legal work, I wouldn't get all muddled up in a lie. I was able to talk about myself pretty openly without having to worry about contradicting myself." She's still slurring her words.

"What about that cute guy from the beginning of the party. I saw you making eyes at him."

"What are you talking about?" Jean asks rather defensively. She even appears to have suddenly sobered up.

"The really cute guy. I couldn't see what he was wearing, but he was the only person at the entire service who had a soul patch. Also, his hair definitely needs a trim. I thought I saw him kind of looking at you. I think he was . . ." I'm trying to find the words here. "I think he was admiring you."

Jean is about to say something, and then I interrupt her.

"He was Polly's lover."

"I have no idea who you are talking about."

I can't read Jean here. Does she not believe me? Is she thinking that I killed Polly and am fabricating a lover? My warm and fuzzy drunk friend has been replaced by a slightly clipped shrew.

We're silent for a moment. Jean takes in a deep breath.

"If it makes you feel any better," she changes the subject, "I just got this general sense that nobody except maybe her husband was that bummed out about her death. So in that way, my friend, you don't have to feel guilty about murdering her."

Charlie looks alarmed, but I start to laugh. I think it's my first big belly laugh since Polly's death. I go over to Jean and give her a great big hug.

"I talked to Kovitz," Charlie breaks in.

I pull away from Jean.

"And?" I feel my heart pounding in my throat. Kovitz could be my key into or out of prison.

"And, you're still their Suspect Number One, but they're trying to play down anything having to do with you because your escape looks bad for the precinct."

"When you say Suspect Number One, does this mean that there's a Suspect Number Two?"

"No one specific that he mentioned, but Kovitz said that the department had reason to believe that Polly Dawson had a lot of enemies."

"Well, at least I'm not the only one who thinks that." I'm excited for a moment. "Do they know about any of the stuff I told you about D.M., Jenna, the young lover, and the library guy?" I realize that I only know about these people because I was tailing Polly *before* her death. They all managed to keep a pretty low posthumous profile. "How about her husband? Don't they always look at home?" I ask.

"I asked him that, but Humphrey was on location in Maine the day Polly was killed."

"He could have hired someone," Jean offers. Jean does not yet know about our other list of suspects.

"No. The way she was stabbed it was personal." I clearly remember Polly's mutilated body.

"I told you," Jean says, "I'm really good at this. My guess is that our murderer is one of Polly's lovers; a spurned lover, a lover's lover, something like that."

I agree with Jean. I saw the stab wounds. This is personal.

"Maybe it's a lingerie competitor," Charlie offers.

"That doesn't sound right," Jean says dismissively.

Again, I agree with Jean. No wonder we are friends.

"I don't think we should rule it out," Charlie counters. He sounds wounded. We've ganged up on him. And I realize that Charlie believes his father was framed by a competitor, and that he may take our dismissal of his theory as a vote of nonconfidence in his father.

Charlie, I've learned, is extremely sensitive.

"Maybe Jean could look into this stuff."

I give Jean a look that says she has to go along with me.

"Absolutely."

Charlie looks relieved. So I fill Jean in on my theories. I tell her that Jenna McNair may have killed Polly over some beautiful successful woman turf war, that D.M. could have murdered Polly because she couldn't take her anymore, that Polly had a young lover who could have killed her for a million reasons: She loved him too much, he loved her too much.

Jean is quiet during this part of the discussion. I think she's still recovering from being dumped by the paralegal.

I tell her that Polly may have had another lover. I describe the man at the library, but I withhold from Jean, as I had withheld from Charlie, the critical information about the "Tender" note.

"Doesn't sound like anything," Jean tells me.

"No—if you had seen them . . ." I try to convince her.

"No. There is no *them*. A man was in the library while she was in the library. What about all of the other reading enthusiasts?"

"That's just it, Jean. They weren't reading. Everyone else was. They were both just there at roughly the same time and left at roughly the same time."

"But they didn't come in together?" Jean asks.

"No."

"And they didn't leave together?"

"No."

"So, in conclusion, you have nothing."

I give up. I will tell Jean about the note when I get more information.

I glance at the clock. It's three-thirty in the afternoon.

"Jean, shouldn't you go to work?"

"Are you out of your mind? I took a personal day. For weeks I was thinking that I would never see my closest friend again or, at best, I would be talking to you through one of those Plexiglas windows with a hole. But here you are. And I get to schmooze with celebrities, no less."

"I'm still a murder suspect," I remind her.

"I know, but we both know it's ridiculous. So let me enjoy the moment."

Jean has a point. This should be the worst time in my life: I have no home and am instead completely dependent on a man

with whom I've been secretly in love for years and years, who is
being kind to me because he is kind. And because he thinks that
I have some special power that can save his father. I may be days
away from a humiliating investigation and trial, and weeks away
from life in prison. And yet, I'm actually enjoying myself. I'm
living in the moment. Funny how Mother and her acting squad
were always talking about living in the moment, and I dismissed
it as actorspeak, and yet I take delight from one instant to the
next.

"Let's go out and celebrate," Charlie says.

"Eat Here Now?" I ask.

"Of course." Charlie smiles at me.

This is one of those moments.

I resume working on Charlie's case the day after my reunion with
Jean. The weather is clear and I'm energized. Kovitz has admitted
that there is a possibility that I am not a murderer, I have made
contact with my dearest friend, and Charlie and I seem more comfortable around each other. And, not that I'm bragging, but I notice that more and more of Charlie's clothes are making their way
onto my little shelf.

Charlie also seems to respect my investigative skills.

"Follow the whores," Charlie cheers me on. Charlie, by the
way, is wearing a towel around his waist. Okay. I admit he's wearing a T-shirt, too. But the towel around the waist could mean one
of two things: On the one hand, it could indicate some level of
intimacy; on the other, it could be that he doesn't even regard me
as a woman.

"Follow 'em until you find something," Charlie says. He's
brushing his teeth.

He definitely doesn't regard me as a woman.

———

I leave Charlie's apartment. I'm lucky it's winter because I can hide myself in my hat and scarf. Actually, it's Charlie's hat. It's blue with a white snowflake pattern and a pom-pom.

"Very pretty," I told him when he pulled it off the top shelf in his closet.

"Very funny. It's a ski hat," he told me.

"Are you a skier?"

"No," he told me.

"Then it's not a ski hat; it's just a pretty hat."

"You win, Alice. You can have the hat."

I'm also wearing my newest pair of Charlie's old jeans.

"From when I was skinny," he told me.

I wanted to tell him that he was still skinny, but men don't appreciate that. They like words like "lean" and "fit."

"You seem lean and fit to me."

Charlie smiles at me. "You're just sucking up because you want my sweater."

"You read me well," I told him. "And I am partial to the pumpkin-colored merino V-neck."

So here I am outfitted in complete Charlie-wear trying to find today's hooker. Charlie has finally gotten Rosalie's address. She lives in my neighborhood. Or should I say my former neighborhood. I take a cab to Fifty-second and Eleventh. I get out and I wait. Or should I say I lurk. Because that's what it feels like in this part of town. Charlie thinks that Rosalie is the hooker who's most likely to break.

"She seems to feel for my father," he told me.

I'm not sure if my tailing her will produce any signs of her empathy. But Charlie's hoping that I catch her conspiring with executives of Kelt Pharmaceuticals. And if I don't see Rosalie engaged in any conspiratorial acts, then I will simply move to the next one on the list.

Wow, this is my first time back in the neighborhood, and I kind of miss it. Don't misunderstand. I love staying with Charlie, but it probably would have been better if our cohabitation was born out of our desire to move from being boyfriend and girl-friend to the next step rather than my desperate attempts to avoid jail. I guess I miss my stuff. I miss my little apartment. Jean used to call it my cave because the windows face a brick wall. Never a fan of natural light, I was fairly comfortable in my studio. I had my trusty TV, my only slightly splintering hardwood floors, and an ample supply of books.

Mother was not a big fan when I first moved there. Although a lot of her actor friends lived in Hell's Kitchen, she thought it wasn't necessarily the place for her daughter. The neighborhood, which at one time was inhabited only by prostitutes and drug dealers, has recently become trendy. It still retains much of its seediness, as Mother was well aware. It was Barnes who con-vinced her that the apartment was perfect for me.

"Angela, this is a very busy street. It is also quite elegant," Barnes told her. "The building across the street is an exquisite and rare example of urban Gothic architecture."

Despite his pedantry, I appreciated Barnes's enthusiasm. When I signed my lease, he offered to buy me drapes to lend a little drama to my room. I think Barnes really liked the apart-ment, but he also liked the fact that it wasn't right next door to Mother's. Getting from Hell's Kitchen to the Upper East Side is time consuming. Barnes knew that if I moved into their neigh-borhood, I would probably be around a lot more. Barnes and I got along better when geography was on his side.

Whether it is a passing feeling of fondness for Barnes or vague sentiment, I have a hankering to check out my street, my building. But I am certain that I'll be spotted by McGruff the Crime Dog or the neighborhood watch. I just have to remember that I was lonely there. And now, lonely I'm not.

So here I am in the no-man's-land of Eleventh Avenue. I'd fear for my safety if not for the dog park across the street. I see two boxers pummeling a German shepherd mix. I think this is supposed to be fun for the dogs, but it makes me uncomfortable.

It's been two hours and Rosalie hasn't emerged. I hope to have more luck with her than I did with Oxanna, Trini, and Justine. I could be here for days, but it's the least I owe Charlie. The man has given me his clothes, for crying out loud.

I'm lucky. Rosalie finally exits the building. She walks east up Fifty-second Street, trying to negotiate her way through broken bottles and used condoms. She makes a right and goes into the ninety-nine-cents store. I follow her in. She buys some junky-looking floor cleaner; I get a soda. We both leave. She heads back to Fifty-second Street, but keeps going east all the way to Eighth Avenue. She heads uptown. We're dangerously close to my apartment. She stops at the Duane Reade on Fifty-third Street. Again, I follow her in. This would probably be a good time for me to buy some hygiene products for myself, but I don't want to get distracted from Rosalie. Also, this was *my* Duane Reade. I don't know if the cops have come by and told the cashiers to keep an eye out for me. I guess it depends. She goes to the baby section and pulls a jumbo-size package of Huggies diapers. She pays for them and heads back to her apartment.

I wait outside for several more hours. I see that the boxers have returned. They are a little less vicious this time. Or maybe I have become hardened to it over the course of the day.

It's eight P.M. now. Maybe there'll be more action now that it is nighttime, but I wonder what Rosalie does with the baby.

Maybe I'm wrong to assume she has a baby. Maybe the diapers are a gift or something.

It's midnight, and there has been no movement. I head back to Charlie's house.

He seems disappointed.

"Walter," I'm starting to get used to his name, "this is going to take a while."

"It has been a while," Charlie tells me. "I've been patient. I've tried to put faith in the system. That failed me. I've tried to appeal to these girls on a personal level. That has failed me. I don't think I can move on with my life until I get to the next level."

"Not to be insensitive, but you're not accused of anything here."

"True. But I did lose my job over it. And it's bigger than that. I'm a lawyer. That's all I've done. I've always wanted to be a lawyer. I'm one of the few that considered it a noble profession. Not anymore. I've invested my trust and time into the system and it has failed me. Whether or not they take me back at Pennington and Litt, or I find a new job at some other place, is irrelevant. I can't continue to practice law if I think it produces this kind of injustice."

Charlie, motivated by his own speech, starts reviewing his notebooks.

"Maybe if we go through the police reports to see the supposed times these woman were 'dating' my father, you can narrow your tracking to that certain time."

"Sounds good to me," I tell him.

But it doesn't.

My brain has finally started to function again. I realize I have a resource that is better than Charlie, better than Jean, better than

Kovitz even. Charlie's computer. I convinced him to let me use the Internet for one hour a day. Let me digress for a moment to say that Charlie's only flaw is his possessiveness over the computer.

"It's the only thing I have left," he said with despair. "Now that I have no job, no business at all, it's the one thing that is mine."

"On the one hand, I understand you," I finally told him. "On the other hand, you are telling this to a fugitive from justice." I then gave him a pretty good sob story about how I too have nothing, except for confidence in my own innocence, and that is all I need to feel whole. Clearly moved, Charlie caved.

"One hour a day. The Internet. You start your own account. I don't want you going through my stuff."

"But going through your stuff is what I do," I joke with him. He doesn't laugh.

"One hour, and if you abuse it, no more."

So here I am, attempting to do investigative work without moving my feet. This is not my forte. Where to begin?

First I have to create my own e-mail account. I could use my old account, but it's more than likely that the cops are tracking it to see if I have accessed any of my e-mail. I'm certain that it's what led them to Dr. Moses. They're probably reading all of my messages to see if they can provide any clue as to my whereabouts or any evidence against me in Polly's murder. Too bad for them, I'm not a big Internet user. As I said, I like to do my research on foot, and when I'm trying to relax in front of a screen, I will undoubtedly choose to watch TV.

If only I had mentioned following Polly to Dr. Moses I might not be in this boat. She could be my alibi witness. But if I had told her she would have directed me to stop, or at the very least made me feel guilty about following. Of course, then I wouldn't have been in Otto & LuLu's when Polly was killed, Kovitz would never have investigated me, and I would be back in my own apartment.

And Charlie wouldn't even know I'm alive.

I can't worry about this stuff. I set up the account. It's easy. My user name is TheFollower. How could it not be? My password is Charlie. (My password has always been Charlie—at Mona's, at K.I.N.D., even at Pennington & Litt.) All set. Then, I do a Google search. I type in Polly Dawson's name. The number of results is practically infinite. I decide to go to the Principessa Web site. Who knows where that might take me?

The Web site hasn't been updated since Polly's death. This is kind of eerie given Polly's narcissism. There are three photographs of her on the home page alone: Polly as a sexy Santa, Polly as a sexy reindeer, and Polly as a gift—sexy, of course—because she is wearing nothing but a huge red bow. I go to the Principessa collection. Polly models most of her own lingerie. I read about Principessa. This is supposed to be about the lingerie collection but it's really all about Polly. There's a whole biography of Polly and the site gives you the option of playing a musical accompaniment while reading. I choose not to, in fear that it will be Polly herself singing and that she'll have a perfect voice.

So far, nothing.

Finally, the site does have a little contact option. It says that I can e-mail polly@principessa.com.

At least we have an e-mail address.

The site does little to assist me in my investigation, but it does remind me of why I disliked her so much.

"Time is up." Charlie is standing behind me.

"But I was just getting started."

"Tomorrow." Charlie comes over to me and pulls my arm a little.

"Okay." I give in. And in truth, I was a little stuck as to what to do next.

I go to my spot on the couch and pull the blankets over my chin. I turn the television on with the volume muted so that I don't disturb Charlie while he researches on the computer. I love hearing him type. Maybe because I am the worst typist in the world. That's one of the reasons a casting job seemed so appealing to me. Of course, I didn't foresee the amount of correspondence and notes involved in my job. And then there were the menus. Mona told me she was helping me by forcing me to practice.

"Your fingers lack grace, Alice. It is very unbecoming."

I usually dismissed these types of comments as sheer Mona-isms. But as I hear Charlie, I know exactly what she was talking about. I listen to the little ballet his hands do as they partner with the keyboard. I don't need the TV volume. This is my lullaby.

I'm asleep when I hear the doorbell ringing. And I just start to wake up when I hear Jean's voice coming from the kitchen.

"I've completed my first assignment," she says proudly. She starts handing out coffee and bagels as I walk into the kitchen dressed in Charlie's pajamas. Charlie's with her.

"I hope you didn't think your first assignment was catering," I tell her.

"Well, don't you two make a perfect pair?" Jean says to us, referring to the fact that Charlie and I are wearing the exact same pajamas.

Charlie laughs, but I just feel embarrassed.

Jean senses my discomfort and starts our meeting.

"I conducted my own investigation, and I found out that Polly was about to sell her company."

"Any reasons?" I ask.

"I fished around a little. This lawyer from another firm is working on a deal with me, and, coincidentally, he represents a potential buyer for Polly's company. He wasn't really close with her, but he has been friends with her lawyer for years. And she was definitely on the verge of unloading the entire thing."

"Any reason?" Charlie asks my question.

"My source says that Polly was fickle." Jean has relaxed again. "I think the term he used was 'a fucking yo-yo.' One moment she'd become obsessed with something and then after a while she'd get bored. I asked how she could've achieved so much. He told me that she was one lucky bitch. He liked to swear. She was thinking of moving into interior design."

"As opposed to posterior design." Charlie seems so proud of his joke that it makes me laugh. The aroma of French Roast fills the room.

"Did your source say that her volatility extended to her personal relationships?"

"Do you mean was she sleeping around? He didn't say."

"I guess you guys are focusing on the love kill theory," Charlie concedes. I feel bad for him. He was counting on his theory about the business competitor. "So where should we start?"

"She could have been sleeping with anybody." Jean takes a huge bite of bagel. "Should we just go through the phone book?"

"No, let's start with what we know. I feel as if her extracurricular romantic life was related to *Only at Sunrise*. We know that Polly was spending an inordinate amount of time on the movie set. Let's start there. We still don't know the identity of the Chambers Street fellow. Do you want to look into that?" I ask Jean.

"I would rather look into Preston Hayes," Jean says a little too quickly. "I mean, we had that connection at the party."

I give her a slightly condescending look.

"I would hardly call Preston Hayes a contender." I may sound a bit too dismissive. "I don't even think he slept with her. Even if he did, from what I read in the paper, he has these meaningless flings on a weekly basis. He probably doesn't have the passion for Polly that would inspire him to kill her. Or he never had anything to do with her."

"So you think these other male stars didn't talk to Humphrey at the service because they killed his wife?" Charlie asks me, incredulous. "Maybe they just hated Humphrey after working for him."

"You put that aside when there is a death," I say. Although I know I would shed no tears if Mona Hawkins were to die.

I'm just theorizing, but as the words trip off my tongue, they make so much sense to me.

"What if Humphrey was having the affair, and it was a woman who killed Polly?"

"I didn't get that vibe at the service," Charlie says.

"It would have to be a strong woman. That body was attacked pretty hard." I think aloud as I hand him his extra-sweet, extra-light cup of coffee and start to prepare my own.

"But the police think *you* were strong enough to do it?' Charlie looks at me.

"The police are fools," I say. "I saw the body. If the killer was a woman, she did not have this body."

I acknowledge my wimpy physique to my best friend, who by the way is still in perfect shape, and to the man I secretly love.

"That," I continue, "was somebody strong and somebody who was filled with rage. They think I was that distraught over being fired from a job as a casting assistant."

"Look at the people who are fired from assembly lines and then they go and kill all their coworkers," Jean says.

"Maybe you can say that when you are called as a witness for the prosecution," I tell her, "but remember those people are *always* men. I don't recall a woman ever going on a killing spree after being terminated."

"What about Mona?" Jean asks. "You say she is mean and has a temper, and that she's always in love with all of these guys.

Maybe it finally got to her. She may have thought that the only thing that stood in the way of a delicious future with Humphrey was his wife."

As much as I long for Mona to go through the public humiliation of a murder trial, I know she didn't kill Polly.

"She doesn't have that stabbing personality. She's without passion. She's more likely to watch you get run over by a car and laugh. But let's check out some of these other leads, too. That D.M. woman seemed to really detest Polly. Maybe I could find something out about her. At least preliminarily it looks like an Internet job, and since I'm sort of housebound, I can do that one. As for you guys, Polly seemed to be spending a lot of time over at Silvercup Studios, hanging around the movie set even when Humphrey wasn't there. Maybe she was cheating on her downtown boyfriend with one of the movie stars. You guys can get close to them and do some poking around."

"That sounds easy, because movie stars typically befriend just anybody who wants to get near them," Charlie says.

"Oh, I forgot. It's National Sarcasm Week," I say. "Please do what you can. You guys were so amazing at the service. I have utter faith in you."

"Why don't we focus more on these men who are involved with the movie?" Charlie says. "I'll see if Kovitz has anything. He told me I could call him."

"I know you guys don't believe he's a suspect, but I was wondering if it was a conflict of interest for me to see Preston Hayes?" Jean says. "He asked if he could see me again."

I look at Charlie.

"Please," Jean says. "You'll like this, Alice. He lives in your neighborhood, just two blocks away from you. That way, when everything is normal again, and Preston and I are an item, I can see you all the time!"

"Sure, use my plight as an opportunity for romance."

"I'm not the only one," Jean says, and she looks from me to Charlie.

Charlie doesn't notice.

Jean's back at work today. I miss her.

And I miss Mother. I wish I could include her in our little sleuthing party, but I'm not sure she would keep her eye on the prize. And, there is a 97 percent likelihood that Barnes would turn me in.

Am I sure that Mother will tell Barnes my whereabouts? I am. When I was eighteen years old and a senior in high school, all my friends had "boyfriends." These were boys that they met on vacation or at school dances or in after-school programs. My then–best friend, Daphne, was totally in love with Stan Markham, the man she would marry five years later. My other close friends were involved in much less serious, albeit time-consuming romances. I felt left out. Mother, who by this time had been dating Barnes for three years and was fairly happy, noticed that I wasn't myself. I confided to her that I was the only one without a boyfriend.

"Don't worry, you're a fantastic girl, Alice, you'll meet someone," she said. I wanted to tell her that it wasn't so much that I didn't have a boyfriend myself but that I felt abandoned.

Before I had a chance to respond to her, Barnes showed up.

"What are you two young ladies talking about?"

"Nothing," I said quickly, and gave Mother a look to indicate that I didn't want Barnes in on this conversation.

Six hours later, Barnes came into my room. He told me that I shouldn't feel weird about not having a boyfriend. He said it in a way that made me feel like a loser.

He chuckled a little and said in a casual tone, "Your mother doesn't keep secrets from me, *capiche?*"

So now I keep secrets from Mother.

I've given up on Rosalie. If she was ever a prostitute, she's taking a sabbatical, and I don't see her talking to anyone who might be in on the Kelt conspiracy. Today, it's LaDonna's turn.

I have a bit of a spring in my step as I head over to the subway. Charlie has given me a present. Gloves. Two nights ago, when I got home from my freezing night outside Rosalie's apartment, Charlie was staring at my hands.

"Are you okay?" He immediately grabbed my hands and buried them in his.

"Oh, it's fine. They'll thaw in a few minutes."

But Charlie wouldn't let go. He held on to my hands until they no longer felt like icicles—about twenty minutes. Actually, it was about seventeen minutes, but I let my hands linger a little, just to see what it felt like.

It felt pretty good. In fact, I found myself flustered when Charlie asked about my progress. I gave him one-word answers and refused to look into his eyes. I was too close to giving myself away.

So, this morning, Charlie let me sleep in a bit and when I woke up, he was at my feet.

"I got you something," he said.

Was I dreaming?

"Here." And he threw the gloves at me.

"What if I hadn't been here to defrost you? That could have been a disaster," he said.

I'm trying not to analyze this statement. Was Charlie trying to tell me that our little hand snuggle was unpleasant? Was he trying to be romantic?

"He's a nice guy," a voice in my head tells me. "You were cold. He bought you gloves."

I listen to that voice as I head down to Bloomingdale's. It's a beautiful day, unseasonably warm for the last week in January. I'm not even sure I need to wear Charlie's gloves, but I have no idea how late this'll go, and this unexpected warm front may disappear. I head down into the subway station and take the N train to Astoria. LaDonna is the only hooker from Charlie's list who lives in Queens, which is fine by me. I always get lost there. Even after weeks of going to Silvercup, I still try to avoid that borough.

LaDonna has given the strongest and most detailed evidence against Charlie's father. I'm reading the file right now. It looks as if LaDonna and Charlie's father met once a week. She'd go to the bottom of the Clark Street subway station in Brooklyn and wait for Charlie's father's train, which usually arrived at five minutes after seven even though their appointment was seven o'clock. She'd wait for him to get out of the train. The two would linger separately by the train tracks until all of the other passengers went up in the station elevator, and then they would wait to go into an elevator together. When the elevator reached the station lobby, the two would go to a livery cab station one block away. They'd go into the back of the cab and he'd ask the cab driver to drive around. At the end of the "ride," he would furnish her with cash. After it was over the two would get out of the livery cab. LaDonna would get on the train back to Astoria, and he'd hail a yellow taxi and take it, presumably, back to his apartment in Manhattan.

I get out of the train at Thirty-first Street. I have to follow the little map I drew from the Internet to get to LaDonna's apartment. It's easy to find because she lives above Classy Girl Tanning Salon. I can see the bright orange sign from a block away. I wait outside the apartment, pretending to review LaDonna's file, which I've memorized at this point. I'm lucky. She comes down within twenty minutes, and even on this winter day, she looks ready for work. She wears a very short down coat and something shorter (at least I hope there's something) underneath.

I follow her back to the N train. I'm lucky once again; a train comes just as we get there. LaDonna sits down and starts to read *People* magazine. It's the plastic surgery issue. I wish I could get a little closer and check it out; there are some stars I have questions about.

We get off at Fifty-ninth Street, where I started. LaDonna goes to the uptown express platform. I notice that she helps herself to a pack of wild cherry Life Savers from a newsstand just before gliding onto the Number 5 train.

Our first stop is Eighty-sixth Street.

Please get off here. I'm not in the mood to be so far from headquarters. We head toward the next stop. It's almost two miles to the 125th Street station, and the ride seems long.

Please get off. Please get off. Please get off.

LaDonna doesn't move. In fact, her eyes are closed. I hear the conductor's voice over the speaker. It's inaudible except for the words "125th Street." A group of passengers gets up and forms a line to exit the train.

LaDonna's still there.

The doors open. All of a sudden, LaDonna is on her feet, rushing to exit. I just make it.

We head west on 125th Street. First we go to a donut store. LaDonna gets a cherry-filled donut. For the record, she pays for it. I get a cup of coffee, which is so clear, it looks like tea. But I'm afraid it's going to be a long night.

LaDonna heads to the stairs to the Metro North platform. I follow her. I wonder where we are going. Westchester? Connecticut?

And I'm really hoping that this does not involve some sort of overnight stay. I don't feel like sleeping in someone's backyard. That part of my life is behind me.

It crosses my mind to wonder why LaDonna chose to pick up Metro North here in Harlem. Grand Central Station is one station stop on the downtown express from where we got off the N train. Also, when you go to Grand Central, you don't have to go outside in this cold February air to get on the train. And you can get a better seat on the train if you get on at its point of origin. But then again, maybe LaDonna is running late and felt that going to 125th Street by subway is faster than getting there by train and going downtown.

Sure enough, as we reach the top of the stairs, a train is pulling into the station. I look at LaDonna's face to see if there are any signs at all of urgency that she needs to catch this train right away. I hear the conductor announce that the train is going express to White Plains. LaDonna doesn't budge from the platform. The doors close.

Good. I'm not in the mood for White Plains anyway.

Another train pulls into the station. Destination: New Haven.

LaDonna doesn't budge.

Where are we going, LaDonna?

A bunch of passengers get on the train. One gets off.

LaDonna remains behind. In fact, LaDonna heads down the stairs of the train station. She is following the one man who has gotten off. They don't say a word to each other. LaDonna moves toward a cluster of livery cabs parked under the train station. The cars are all dark, beat-up Ford Crown Victorias. While they don't share the medallions that identify all of the city's yellow cabs, they all seem to purchase the same car deodorizer that hangs from the front mirror.

LaDonna opens the door to the first livery cab in the line, and the man follows her inside.

I don't know what to do. I can't get into another livery cab and ask the guy to follow this one. This isn't the right neighbor-hood for that. The driver may be up to no good.

Worse yet, the driver may think I am up to no good and call the cops.

So I stand in the spot where LaDonna has picked up the car. I'm frozen.

"Hey, pretty girl, you want a ride?" I hear a West Indian ac-cent coming from behind me.

I turn around, and am relieved to see that it is coming from this cluster of livery cabs. The driver is boldly smoking a joint, and I notice that his car is missing the deodorizer.

"No, thank you," I tell him.

"What, you scared?"

Yes, of course I am scared. "I'm waiting for someone."

"Who?"

"Immigration."

"Bitch," he says.

Oh well, at least he thinks I am pretty.

I've been here close to an hour. I don't want to give up. But it may be fruitless for me to stay here. For all I know, LaDonna and the man have taken a taxi to his house, and I'll never see her again. But I'm compelled to stay.

A car pulls into the livery area. LaDonna gets out. She heads over to the 125th Street station steps and I follow her. I guess we're going home. I turn around for a second, and I see the man get out of the car and pay the driver from the outside window. The man turns around and hails a yellow taxi cab. I see his face.

I recognize it.

William Redwin.

Charlie's father.

———

LaDonna and I take the same express train down, but we don't share a car. It's not necessary. Besides, I need to be alone to reflect on my circumstances. I'm at a loss. Could Charlie be wrong? He was so sure of his father's innocence.

How will I tell him?

Or do I tell him? Charlie is, after all, my link to freedom.

Maybe that guy wasn't his father. I didn't even get a good look at him.

But in my heart I know it's Charlie's father. I have a good memory.

Why do I know what William Redwin looks like? Last summer before Polly was murdered, before I started following Polly, before I was fired even, Jean tried to fix me up with one of her boyfriend's friends. Her boyfriend at the time was the oh-so-rich and powerful Hugh Price. Jean wanted me to date someone in Hugh's circle. That way we could spend more time together, as Hugh had pretty much monopolized all of her free time since he had first taken a shine to her.

"He's going to bring a friend to dinner," Jean told me. "No pressure. I don't even know him. But Hugh is always talking about him as if he were some kind of folk hero. His name is William. He's rich. I think he's a little older than we are."

A little older. William was old enough to be my father.

That said, I wish he were my father. My stepfather, I mean.

I saw his allure immediately. William was the gentlest person I had ever met. And like me, he noticed things. Things men don't typically notice. Jean and Hugh were so involved in each other that William and I were forced to spend the entire evening together.

"Maybe we should get them their own table," he joked.

"Or a room."

William laughed. "It must be hard to lose your closest friend to Hugh Price."

"Oh, it's not like that with me and Jean."

"Forgive me. I didn't think so. But Hugh's a very charming guy and he likes to have a monopoly in all arenas of his life. You probably don't get to see your friend much."

William was right. I was happy for Jean. The whole thing was exciting, but I couldn't help thinking our friendship had become a casualty of their relationship.

"All things considered, I'm happy for her."

"That's magnanimous of you."

William was a charming companion. He asked me about my job. I ended up telling him all about Mona: her bizarre eating habits, her power trips, and her fascination with "yummy actors."

"I take it she's not a role model."

"Not at all." I said it in an uncharacteristically wistful way.

"It will happen for you," William said, as if he knew me.

And I felt as if I knew him. I didn't know what it was, but I had an affinity for him. Nothing romantic, but he made me feel at ease.

And he seemed so familiar.

The next day, I received a handwritten note at my office.

Dear Alice:

It was lovely to meet you last night. You are a delightful and beautiful young woman. I haven't laughed like that in months. Hugh was right when he said that I would find you very appealing.

Having said that, I must be honest with you. When Hugh told me that he wanted me to meet someone, I thought he was referring to your friend Jean. I was unaware of his matchmaking ambitions. And while I'm flattered that Hugh thought we would make a fine pair, it is impossible for me to think of that sort of relationship right now. I recently lost my wife and a romance with another woman is unimaginable.

I did not mean to meet you under false pretenses. Please excuse me.

Maybe we'll meet again under other circumstances.

William.

William Redwin! It had to be Charlie's father. Of course he looked familiar. He was a grown-up version of his son. Not exactly. William and Charlie both had a full, floppy head of hair, a lean physique, and a slouch. Jean hadn't told me his last name; Hugh probably hadn't told her.

Charlie's dad. I went on a blind date with the father of the man I have loved quietly for over ten years. I'm not one of those "this is a sign" people. But this had to be a sign.

We're back in Charlie's living room. Jean is presenting a very detailed account of her date with Preston Hayes.

"Normally, I would blow off a guy in a vest. But he looked really sexy in it."

I look at Charlie. He's tuning Jean out.

"Earth to Walter," I say to him gently.

"Oh, huh," Charlie says. He's especially quiet. I wonder if he knows I'm lying to him about his father.

"Everything okay?" I ask him.

Charlie takes another bite of lasagna. I made it yesterday after I found a bag of dried porcini mushrooms in his overstuffed desk drawer. I almost missed them as they were housed in an old empty wallet, with long-expired credit cards and a $2.60 taxi receipt. I may as well admit to snooping. I've never been the jealous type, but I keep replaying that conversation we had in his kitchen over a week ago when he told me about the vermin-phobic girlfriend.

So I checked out Charlie's desk drawer to see if I could find a picture of the mysterious ex. I'm not sure what I hoped to find.

I couldn't find any pictures of her, but I did spot some porcini mushrooms. How bizarre to find porcini mushrooms in a desk drawer.

"What are you doing in my desk?" Charlie asked me.

"I was looking for these." I held up the porcini mushrooms.

"You knew I had porcini mushrooms in my desk?"

"I smelled them."

"You smelled porcini mushrooms from my desk?"

"Yes. I cook with them a lot, so I'm very in tune with their aroma." I felt so guilty lying to this man who has opened his home to me. But I couldn't very well ask him about the ex.

"Well, make something with them. You're the cook."

Wow. He believed me. He didn't even question me any further about the mushrooms. I made up this thoroughly preposterous story, and he trusts that I'm telling the truth.

So here he is eating my porcini lasagna. I've never cooked a porcini mushroom in my life, but I do have a safe meat lasagna recipe. I replaced the meat with the porcini mushrooms after I soaked them in one of Charlie's fine cabernets.

"Everything okay?" I repeat to Charlie.

"Oh, yeah. I'm just waiting for her to get to the good part." Charlie points at Jean.

"The good part is," Jean says, "he is *H-O-T*."

"Jean, I didn't risk my freedom, your freedom, and his freedom"—I point at Charlie—"just so you could improve your social life. The big question is whether Preston gave you any scoop."

"That's the best part. He did. He took me for drinks at the Campbell Apartment in Grand Central Station, which as you know

I may normally think is a little *turista*. But let's face it, Preston Hayes could make a Bennigan's seem romantic."

"Yes." I gently guide her back to the point. "What happened at the Campbell Apartment?"

"Well, in the one-jillionth of a second that we stood in line before they recognized him and whisked us to a table, he had his hand on the small of my back."

"I think she wants to know about the murder," Charlie suggests, picking up on my impatience.

Don't get me wrong. In other circumstances, I would pay money to hear about the minutiae of Jean's date with Preston Hayes. It's only because I'm a wanted killer that I've lost interest in Jean's colorful romantic life.

"Yes, please," I say. "Did he give you anything?"

"Oh, that." Jean takes a huge bite of lasagna. "Total scoop." I love when Jean talks like a valley girl.

"And?" Charlie's paying attention now.

"According to Mr. Hayes, Humphrey Dawson's not the weepy widower everyone claims."

"What do you mean?" Charlie and I ask in unison.

Jean makes a face to me indicating that she thinks Charlie's and my synchronicity is meaningful.

"Humphrey Dawson was having an affair."

"Did Hayes say with whom?" Charlie asks before I do.

"No. He just said it was common knowledge. Humphrey would disappear for hours at a time, he had lipstick on his shirt, and he always acted strange around his wife."

"How?" I need more information than the word "strange." I'm strange.

"Whenever she'd come to the set, he would avoid her. She was clearly checking up on him, and when she started showing up more and more, he'd become irritated. He'd complain about it to all the guys. The guys were pissed off about this, and that is why they did not approach him at the Barneys thing."

I love Jean. This explains so much.

"Did he tell the police?"

"Of course he told the police," Jean says. She hugs me. "I think this nightmare is going to end soon. Even if Humphrey's girlfriend has nothing to do with this, the cops have got to think there are other people who had a bigger motive than you."

Charlie ignores our glee. He too is digging into the lasagna.

"Did you ask Hayes whether she was sleeping around?"

"Yes, and he said that Polly would flirt shamelessly with all of the guys on the set just to get a little attention from her husband. He said that he felt for her, that some might think she was pathetic, but that she was a woman in love who had put all of her trust in this man."

I don't say anything. I'm still elated, but I try to think of all the ways this information can play out. Jean's still talking.

"He so gets it," Jean says. "Here he is, a heartthrob, but he gets it. I can't believe I go out with these schlumpy lawyers. No offense, Walter," she says when she realizes that Charlie is a schlumpy lawyer. "And they don't understand a thing about feelings. He could have anyone he wants, and yet he gets it."

"He's an actor," Charlie says, "and he wants to get into your pants."

"No, he was the perfect gentleman. That's the thing."

"What about his hand on your lower back?"

"The small of my back," Jean corrects him.

"Okay, the small of your back." Charlie titters. His leg touches mine for a second.

"That," Jean pronounces, "was a gesture."

"Let's get back to my plight," I say, annoyed. "Did Hayes give you any idea who Humphrey was sleeping with?"

"No. But I sensed that he knew."

"Did Hayes say that he thought that Humphrey killed her?"

"No. I couldn't bring it up. I don't want to seem obvious. This lasagna is so good. You should be a chef."

"You mean instead of a murderer."

"That is what I love about you, Alice Teakle, your perspective."

"That is what you love about her?" Charlie asks, annoyed.

"Yeah," Jean is equally annoyed, "is that okay?"

"Sure," Charlie says.

And he's quiet.

I want to have a little conversation with Jean to see if she caught Charlie's mood change. If I had more self-esteem I'd think that maybe he conjured up a million other things about me to love more than my perspective. And I want to know if Jean caught this as well.

I break the silence. I report my discovery of the day.

"I've figured out Polly's computer password."

"How'd you figure it out?" Charlie asks.

"You're in the presence of greatness, don't you know?" Jean tells him. And then she looks at me to make sure I understand that she's just done me a favor.

"Of course I do," says Charlie.

I try to make eye contact with him to see if there is any more to this than empty conversation. "But I like to know some of the secrets." He continues to direct these conversations to Jean.

"Well, as you know, she has—or I should say had—an e-mail address at Principessa, where people could contact her. So she may have a mailbox full of evidence in some other section of cyberspace, but—"

I pause. I'm really enjoying the attention.

"But . . . ?" Charlie seems impatient.

"Yes," says Jean. I think she's surprised to see me revel in the spotlight.

"After several tries I got her password."

"Let me guess," Jean says, "'Jack Birnbaum'?" Jean's never gotten over Polly "stealing" Professor Jack Birnbaum from her.

"No."

"Let me try," Charlie says. "'Humphrey.'"

"No."

"Okay. This game has gotten boring," Jean says. "Spill it."

"You guys have to think like Polly. Polly's password wouldn't be other people's names—she's far too narcissistic. Her password is simple—her birthday."

"How do you know her birthday?"

"Easy," I say, "it's my birthday. April second."

"Her password is zero-four-zero-two-one-nine-seven—?"

"No, silly. Polly would never remind herself of the year she was born. She wants to have the option of lying to herself about her age. Her password is just April second."

"Score one for Nancy Drew," Jean says. "Now tell us what was in the e-mail?"

"Lots of fan letters. I'd probably be vain too if I had that many people writing to tell me how much they loved me."

"Are you sure they were fans and not love interests?" Jean sounds nervous. I wonder if she's concerned that Preston had a thing for Polly.

"No, there was nothing from Preston Hayes, if that's what you're thinking."

Jean doesn't say anything.

"There was one from a Yahoo! account that said 'I am way ahead of you, princess, we're off.'"

"'We're off'?" Charlie says. "What does that mean?"

"I don't know—it sounds too curt to be a break-up note," I say.

"I agree. Why not say 'we're *over*'?" Jean offers. "Unless he's foreign."

"Whatever it is, it does sound suspicious," Charlie says. "We may have a Suspect Number Five here."

"This could've been written by one of the existing suspects. It could be from D.M. She was tired of being pushed around," I say.

"No," Jean says. "From what you have told me, I don't think D.M. would ever confront Polly verbally."

"But she would stab her?" Charlie says.

"Yes. I think she's been too weak to ever say anything to Polly, but maybe she had this rage that took her over physically."

"Now who watches too much TV?" I joke with her.

Although, the scenario is remarkably similar to last year's sensational news item about the murder of the rich and glamorous hotel tycoon Sherry Butters. Apparently, Sherry's personal assistant had tired of her boss's contemptuousness and killed her with a free weight after being scolded.

"This just doesn't seem like a D.M.-ish note," Jean insists.

"But you've never even seen her."

"I know," Jean tells me. "But I know her type. The jealous underdog friend who does everything while the vapid beauty takes all the credit."

"Kind of like you and me," I joke.

"I don't think Jean's jealous of you," Charlie says seriously.

Jean and I were thinking that I was the jealous underdog. I don't know if I should be flattered that Charlie thinks of me as a beauty or disappointed that he thinks of me as vapid.

"In any event," I say, putting aside that thread completely, "this note could've been written by anyone."

"Do you remember the exact address?" Charlie asks me.

"I do," I say, "it's four dollar signs, then 'at yahoo dot com.' And no, I can't think of anybody that would tie this in with the suspects we have or anything else about Polly that I previously noticed."

"Well, one thing's for sure," Jean says, "that message seems to indicate much more of a motive than your being fired."

"The only thing now," I say, "is to figure out how to get the cops to read this message. Hint, hint, hint: Talk to Kovitz," I say directly to Charlie.

"So, are you seeing Hayes again?" Charlie changes the subject.

"He said he would call me," Jean says. "And as a certified interpreter of manspeak, I can tell you that could mean one of two things. Either he will call me or he will not call me."

"I hope he calls you," I tell her.

"Me too. It would be a nice pick-me-up after being dumped by a twenty-three-year-old who staples for a living."

Jean looks at me and remembers that I was once a twenty-three-year-old who stapled for a living.

"And does it badly," she adds.

I don't say anything.

"Speaking of calling, your shrink has been calling me."

"Dr. Moses?" I panic, wondering if Charlie will judge me for going to a shrink. But then again, he seems relatively okay with my lurking outside his apartment just days after my Polly gig ended.

"She's worried, and she wants to know if I know anything."

"How did she get your number?"

"She said you talked about me in therapy and she looked me up in *Martindale Hubbell*. Frankly, I was flattered she remembered me. Do I have a big part?"

"Of course, Jean, you are the lead. I am the supporting player. We talked about your problems for forty-eight minutes and sprinkled in stories about me, the wacky friend."

"Very funny. She just sounded kind of great on the phone. As if she was genuinely distraught over your disappearance and well-being. I don't know if my shrink would do that, and we've been together for years. It made me a little jealous."

"Maybe when we figure all of this out, you guys can go to Moses for couples' therapy?" Charlie suggests.

Charlie and I have been making some progress on our list of suspects. I think we've almost ruled out Jenna McNair. I've been doing some simple research about her on the Internet and she's been popping up on all sorts of plastic-surgery-gone-awry Web sites. According to plasticdisasters.com and leave.my.face.alone .org Jenna was in Zihuatenejo, Mexico, enjoying a teeny bit of liposuction and a faulty nose job at the time of Polly's death. Leave.my.face.alone.org actually videotapes movie stars as they exit and enter plastic surgery vacations and then posts the video on the Internet. According to the date that was flashing on the tape, Jenna checked herself into Dr. Pedro Trujillo's office on December 24. She's seen leaving his office with a small Band-Aid on her nose on December 30. She's limping.

"Is it possible that she came back to New York during that time, killed Polly, and then hopped on the plane?" Charlie asks me, hopefully.

Normally I'd say yes. But her nose does look different. It would mean her coming back to New York very soon after surgery.

"Let's assume she had the surgery. Let's assume that she left the office a little earlier than scheduled to come back and kill Polly. I don't know that she'd have been able to muster the force necessary after having surgery done on her head and midsection."

"People can muster a lot of strength when they're angry."

Charlie and I continue to do our research on the Internet. I'm pretty certain we have identified D.M. She is Doris Meisel. According to a couple of articles in obscure business magazines, Doris has been Polly's business partner for more than ten years.

And wouldn't you know it, but the Principessa stores were her brainchild. This information, however, isn't repeated often. I can only guess that Polly silenced Doris in the presence of reporters. There are few pictures of Doris in Principessa articles. After all, who would photograph an average-looking middle-aged woman when a hot charismatic number was available? This piece of research has only confirmed for me what I had previously interpreted as Doris's resentment of Polly.

"Enough to kill her?" Charlie asks as he pushes me off his computer chair so that he can take his proper place.

"We'll only know that when I can continue with my research," I say, lobbying for more than an hour a day.

It's been a week since I saw LaDonna and what looked to be Charlie's father at the 125th Street Metro North stop. I haven't gone back there. I've parked myself outside Rosalie's house, in large part because I think it will provide me with no more damaging information about Charlie's father.

"I thought you said you were through with Rosalie?" Charlie asks.

"I was, but I reviewed her files and I get a lying vibe," I say, even though I'm the one who is lying.

"I trust you," Charlie tells me.

Doris has agreed to meet me at a diner for lunch. I knew from her eating habits with Polly that she wasn't happy going to fancy power spots for her midday meal. I also figured that she would be relieved to avoid sucking on a lettuce leaf, surrounded by skinny women.

So we're at the Delish (by the way, they have the greatest chicken wings), sitting across from each other. I can tell she doesn't recognize me in the slightest. I'm not Alice Teakle of murdering fame, but rather Theresa Olson of Rockport, Illinois. I'm blond today. Thanks to Charlie. He bought me a wig as a gift. I was concerned about my outfit, but he surprised me with a wrap dress.

"I thought this would look good," he said. But I couldn't tell if he meant good as a disguise or good good.

"Men really do prefer blondes?" I said.

Charlie doesn't say anything.

"Thank you," I told him, deciding not to pursue it.

"What exactly do you need to know?" Doris asks me. She looks more relaxed than I've ever seen her. She's let her straight orange bob grow into a multihued, scattered head of hair. And she's wearing colors: mostly navy, a little white, and a spot of yellow. No beige in sight. She's two inches shorter. Gone are the pumps. Doris is wearing clogs. The twenty-five pounds she had to lose before is easily up to thirty-five, and she's sans makeup.

In spite of this, she's glowing.

"I don't know if I told you in our previous phone conversation, but I'm new to this city. I just started at Columbia Business School. We're doing a project for one of our classes where we set up a model business." I'm able to fudge my way through this conversation because this was exactly the course my father taught at Northwestern before he left. "I've been researching successful and powerful women in New York City, and your name keeps popping up."

"It does?" Doris is clearly used to being the unknown talent at Principessa.

"Well, yes. In business school we look at all sorts of business models and you seem to be the brains behind the Principessa success story."

"That's arguable," Doris says candidly. She's not used to a flood of compliments.

"I picked you and your company because I'm thinking of going into business with my closest friend. Her name is Jean." I use Jean's real name to give a feeling of authenticity. "But I wanted to know if that was a mistake. I mean, is it better to go into business with someone I only know professionally— Is it even a mistake to go into business with a woman?"

Doris thinks about what I'm saying.

"You should be more concerned with the kind of personality you do business with rather than the manner in which you know each other."

At this point I take a huge bite of my chicken pot pie. "Mmm," I say. "Nothing better than comfort food."

"You really want to avoid a difficult personality," she adds.

"Now, have you worked with another woman?" I say as naively as I can.

Doris looks shocked and doesn't say anything.

"Oh. I'm sorry," I say. "Did I have my information wrong? The files at Columbia are so untrustworthy." I fuss with my purse.

Doris gives me a well-deserved look of disbelief.

"You mean you didn't know?"

"Know?"

"Oh—I worked with *Polly Dawson*." Doris underscores Polly's name with her tone. "Principessa was her company."

"Oh." I try to drum up only a flicker of recognition in my eyes.

"You don't know who that is, do you?" she says.

"No. I'm so embarrassed. I guess I spend too much time studying and not enough time living in the world," I say. "That's why I want to go into business with Jean. She's all 'world.'" I mime quotation marks. "And I'm all 'books.'" I giggle self-deprecatingly.

"I don't know how to say this," Doris says gently. "Polly Dawson died a couple of months ago."

"Died? Oh my. That's horrible." I gulp. "Was she ill?"

Doris thinks about this for a moment, and then says, "No, she wasn't ill. She was killed."

"Oh my. I'm so sorry. Are you okay? Was it business related? Are you scared?"

Here, I sound inauthentic.

"No. As a matter of fact I'm not scared at all. It was some deranged classmate of hers from college."

"Wow," I say, doing my best not to seem deranged.

Doris interprets my silence to mean that I'm suddenly awkward over the unexpected news of her friend's death.

"We've all been coping with the loss." She says this with an air of someone who has gotten over it.

"I do hope you're okay," I say sympathetically.

"I am okay. Between you and me, Polly Dawson was one of the most fascinating people with whom I have ever worked, but she was also one of the most difficult."

"That can be complicated," I agree.

"Yes. Very." Doris is licking her hand after downing a particularly sauce-laden chicken wing.

"If it's not inappropriate, I'd still like to get some advice."

"No. It's not inappropriate at all." Doris is now grabbing my french fries as if they were hers from the start.

We're friends.

"Thank you. You're saying it's okay to work with my friend as long as she's not difficult?"

"I guess that's what I'm saying. And you should make clear to each other what your roles are. Sometimes if there is an imbalance of power, one of the partners ends up treating the other one like a doormat."

"I hear you. Between you and me, Jean is the charismatic one. I have a feeling I will be up late crunching numbers while she's at cocktail parties." I'm only slightly misrepresenting our relationship here.

"If I were you, I would have a talk with her now. Otherwise you may want to end up wringing her neck."

"That's really good advice. Thanks." Can Doris see me shudder?

"You are very welcome. I don't know. Something about you. You have a very promising future."

The something about me is that I'm wanted for killing her business partner.

One thing is for sure, Doris Meisel isn't remotely distressed by Polly's death. Does that make her a killer?

It doesn't rule her out.

Today is Charlie's meeting with Kovitz. I can't focus on anything else. I brief him on all of the key questions he must ask:

Am I still the number-one suspect?

Are they still looking for me? And to what extent?

Who else do they suspect?

What do they have on anyone else?

Have they followed up on the tip that Preston gave about Humphrey's gal pal?

"I'll do what I can," Charlie tells me. "I also want to talk to him about my father."

"How did you and Kovitz get so tight, anyway?" I ask him.

"When I was in law school, I worked in a legal clinic that represented a bunch of cops who were accused of stealing drugs from suspects and then selling them on the black market. Kovitz was lumped in with those guys, but insisted that he knew nothing. But he was with them all the time. He had complete faith in all police officers and was blind to their wrongdoing. All of the accused were being investigated and tried at the same time. Some flipped early and everyone was implicated except Kovitz. The DA, for whatever reason—I think economy—refused to believe in Kovitz's innocence and pushed for trying him along with all of the others. Sometimes the jury has a hard time parsing one defendant from another. It was my first real legal work. I got the judge to grant a motion severing his trial from the other guys. It eventually came out that Kovitz really was innocent. He says it may never have come out if not for me. I don't know."

"That must have been a good feeling."

"It was. In fact, since that time, I did three busy years in the DA's Office and even made it to partner in one of the best firms in the country, and it still tops my list of my most satisfying career moments. Too bad it happened before I even passed the bar."

"Some people never have those moments," I say, thinking of myself.

"Some people don't look for them," Charlie tells me.

"Do you look for them or do they just come to you?"

"I think I keep myself open."

"Yeah, I remember in college when they wrote that article that profiled you in *The Crimson* as the man who saved Francisco Pena."

"You remember that?" Charlie asks me.

I could practically recite the article word for word. When Charlie was a senior, he exposed the mistreatment of a freshman named Francisco Pena by the university police. Pena was among the many undergrads who rode his bicycle on university paths that were, according to the school, exclusively set aside for pedestrian traffic. Although hundreds of students violated this rule, Pena was repeatedly singled out. The police never stopped any other students. One day they had enough of his insubordination. They asked Pena to step off his bicycle. They impounded the bicycle and detained Pena for two hours. It turns out that Pena had his organic chemistry final that day. He was over an hour late. He received a failing grade.

Charlie filed a complaint with the university, exposing the

differential treatment Pena received. Pena was targeted, according to Charlie, because he was Hispanic. The school made sure that Pena was permitted to retake his exam. And more significantly, he received a public apology from the university police and Harvard's president.

"I can't believe you remember that," Charlie says.

I have a fantastic memory. Besides, it is a pretty incredible story.

I keep having the same dream. I'm walking in the dark with my father. I think we're in a church. Mother and Paul are half a block ahead of me. Paul looks as he did at his tenth birthday party, wearing perfectly pressed khaki pants, a light blue button-down shirt, and shiny new brown loafers. Mother is in an airy gown. I look over at my father; he is wearing a new tuxedo, and smiling his big smile. I look down. I'm in a bridal gown. It is big and princessy, but I *love* it. I look up and I see Charlie, standing next to my brother. He's wearing the same tux as my father. It is my wedding day.

Suddenly, my father's hand lets go of mine and my brother disappears from the scene altogether. Mother is still ahead of me, and, as I walk toward her, Barnes appears, wearing a velvet dinner jacket and an ascot. We are still walking forward, but there is no altar. In the middle of the church are two caskets. I don't look inside, but I recognize the mahogany from the funeral twenty-four years ago. Barnes is tending to Mother as she cries violently. I look around for Charlie and he has disappeared. I am alone.

I've had this exact dream four times.

I am trying not to be too hopeful about Charlie's meeting with Kovitz today. First, I may still be their only viable suspect. My excitement is also tempered by what I'm pretty certain is going on between William Redwin and LaDonna. But I can't go to Charlie with this information until I'm absolutely sure.

The only way to be sure is to follow William.

It's funny. Charlie hasn't given me a folder on his dad: where his dad lives, his phone number, his car make and license plate. He wants me to clear his dad without even looking at him.

Does this mean that on some level Charlie thinks he's guilty?

Then again, Charlie isn't investigating me, either.

But Charlie didn't see what I saw. He didn't see his father driving around Harlem with a prostitute.

I don't even know where Charlie's father lives. He didn't tell me. I look him up in the phone book, and I realize that he's on Eighty-ninth and Park, not much more than a mile from here. I just have to see if he's home. I call his number. Realizing I am probably the only person on the planet that doesn't have caller ID, I press *87 to privatize Charlie's number. (It's a trick Jean showed me when she was obsessively calling an aloof boyfriend three years ago.)

It's ringing.

Ringing.

Ringing.

"Hello."

"Oh, ummm, hi." I don't really have a game plan. "May I speak with Nicole?" I disguise my voice just in case he recognizes it.

"I'm sorry. What number are you calling?"

I tell him a number. Unfortunately, I panic and I give him his number.

"You've got the right number but there's no Nicole here."

I want to die, I'm so embarrassed. Charlie would kill me.

"I'm so sorry. I thought this was the number the phone company gave me, but sometimes I transpose the numbers wrong."

I hang up the phone and grab my coat.

I get on the express train to Eighty-sixth Street. When I get out, I walk one block over to Park Avenue and then just a few blocks to Eighty-ninth Street. Charlie's father lives four blocks from Mother. I suddenly long to take a detour and knock on her door, but Barnes will most certainly turn me in.

It's hard knowing that Mother and I are so close—geographically.

I wait outside his building for a while. It's difficult to be on Park Avenue because there are no stores or restaurants to provide a legitimate justification for loitering. I didn't bring anything to read, either. I hope I don't look too creepy. I'm wearing oversized corduroys and a ski jacket. I run down to Lexington Avenue. I go into an old drugstore and search for a prop. I find it: a crappy sketch pad and a box of pencils. The sketch pad has been sitting on the shelf so long that even though it advertises white paper, the sheets are a pale yellow. But the price is right: $1.19 for the pad, and the guy tells me I can have the box of pencils if I throw in eighty-one cents. I give him two dollars in change, and then run back, crossing my fingers in hopes that William Redwin hasn't left his house in the last thirteen minutes.

I glance at the front door of William Redwin's building. The doormen are changing shifts. The stout older guy is replaced by another stout older guy and the young buck is also replaced by a nearly identical colleague. I think of the doormen at Mother's. It has been the same group now for as long as I remember. They always give me that look that says, How come you keep coming back here by yourself? All of this building's other graduates have families or, at the very least, a life. I always feel as if I should offer to take the service elevator.

I'm sitting on the edge of the sometimes-grassy area on the island that divides Park Avenue from itself. I'm drawing with one hand and covering the page with the other. I hope this will be interpreted by all who see me as modesty.

I'm a terrible draftsman.

I draw for just over three hours before William Redwin exits the building. He's wearing a long dark overcoat and a cap. He makes a left and walks downtown on Park. I'm relieved. I thought for sure that we'd be taking a cab up to the Metro North station in Harlem.

Redwin walks.

And walks.

And walks.

He turns left on Seventieth Street and walks east. He must have a destination; we've been going for almost half an hour now. Maybe he sees me tailing him. No. He would recognize me. And then, even if it would draw attention to himself—negative attention—he would turn me in. Despite my being "delightful" and "beautiful."

Okay. We're on York Avenue now. We must be near our destination. We can't go any farther east because we will end up in the river. We make a right. We are on Sixty-eighth Street now— just a few blocks from Charlie's house. William abruptly goes into a building. I know this building. It is Sloan-Kettering Cancer Center.

Does William Redwin have cancer?

I can't follow him any farther. I've already invaded his privacy enough.

I hear the security guard talking to him.

"Nice to see you, Mr. Redwin. You're a little late today."

It seems odd that the security guard is so involved in Redwin's cancer treatment.

"I know, but I'm here."

"Oh, sir. It is very nice, sir. I can take you there now, sir. Let me just get someone to watch the desk for a sec." The security guard picks up the phone. "Karl. It's Zona. Mr. Redwin is here. I'm going to take him to the Falls. Can you come over here?"

I wait on the other side of the desk, careful not to catch anyone's eye. They always ask for identification in places like this, and I'm not going to risk producing a document with a picture of me on it.

Karl shows up within two minutes.

"Hello, sir."

He extends his hand to Charlie's dad, who grasps it warmly.

"Let me show you up," Zona says as she leads Redwin up the escalator into the front lobby. I scurry in after them as Karl gets himself settled.

We walk into the upstairs lobby and there is a beautiful waterfall in the middle of the floor. Bright purple orchids punctuate the streams of water that continually pour down the huge rock formation. Next to the waterfall is a plaque:

IN MEMORY OF EMILY REDWIN

Redwin stares at the plaque for some time. After a few minutes, he turns to Zona.

"Thank you."

"You're welcome, Mr. Redwin. Do you need me for anything else?"

"No, Zona. Thank you."

"My pleasure, Mr. Redwin. We'll see you tomorrow?"

"Yes."

"Okay then."

Okay then. And off we go. Mr. Redwin and I. He hurries out of the hospital and waves his hand anxiously for a taxi. He gets in. For a moment, I forget my discretion and I stand too close to the door.

I could swear William Redwin is staring right into my eyes.

I'm lucky to get another taxi right away.

204 • KAREN BERGREEN

"Follow them," I say to the cab driver, hoping that he's not an undercover cop.

We make a right on Sixty-eighth Street and sit in traffic for about ten minutes. I think about William Redwin and how much pain he's in.

"My father hasn't been this way since my mother died," Charlie had said. And William told me himself in his note that finding romance was "unimaginable."

William, it appears, makes daily trips to the hospital where his wife died.

As the taxi heads up First Avenue, I'm hit with the rage that's been fueling Charlie. These people are pushing him out of the company, *his* company, months after losing his wife. This is outrageous. Of course I'll help Charlie. I'll follow all of those girls on that list to see what kind of payoffs they are getting. That man I saw the other day with LaDonna could not have been William Redwin. It was some other WASPy white guy getting his rocks off under the 125th Street station.

It was probably some jerk from Kelt Pharmaceuticals doing just what Charlie has been thinking all along: paying the hooker off in some sort of conspiracy.

We're making our way slowly up First Avenue. I guess I'm going to have to walk from Park and Eighty-ninth back to Charlie's house. I don't want to spend all of his money on cabs. We head up First Avenue past Eighty-ninth Street.

"I think he missed the turn," I tell my driver.

The driver doesn't say anything, but he does something with his shoulder that appears to be a shrug.

We go by Ninety-first Street. Nothing.

We keep going. The traffic has thinned out some.

We keep going.

I know when we'll turn. But I don't tell the driver because I don't want it to be true.

It is true.

We turn at 125th Street and head west.

To the Metro North station.

William Redwin gets out of his taxi.

"Sixty-fifth between Park and Lexington," I tell the driver.

I'm no longer worried about how much this will cost me. I have other problems now.

It's just after six when I return to Charlie's house. I have no idea what to tell him about his father. You were wrong about him, but please don't give up on me. And that's just the selfish part. I don't want to hurt Charlie. I love him. Not just in the crushy way. I love him in a way that I know it will hurt me to hurt him.

I decide to be angry with William. He has put me in this position. If he had just been honest with Charlie from the get-go, I wouldn't be dealing with this unpleasantness. What was he thinking? Going to prostitutes. I look at Charlie's files. Descriptions of back alleys and underpasses. William Redwin doesn't need to go to prostitutes. He certainly doesn't need to go to cheap ones. He's an attractive, rich, successful man in a city filled with women looking for attractive, rich, single men. And it didn't need to be sordid. The man wasn't cheating on anybody. According to the files, William went to these women only after Emily's death.

He chooses prostitutes when he can have anybody.

I think of Mother. She chose Barnes when she could have had anybody. He wasn't such a plum choice, either.

But their liaisons were legal.

When I get home, Charlie isn't here. Good on two fronts. First, I don't really feel like telling him about his father right now. And second, I can use the computer without his timing me.

I've made significant headway with respect to Doris, and I've all but ruled her out as a suspect. On the one hand this does not bode well for me. If I could just find the real killer, I could give all of the information to Kovitz, turn myself in, and then join Charlie in holy matrimony.

I figure if I'm going to dream, I'm going to dream big.

I don't really want the killer to be Doris. I like her. I am Doris—without the extra weight and the success. But the way Polly treated her reminds me of the way Mona Hawkins treated me. And now Polly is dead, and Doris is free. I want her to get her life back as I'm trying to with mine. I log on to Charlie's computer to step up my research.

Oh my. Doris and I are nothing alike.

Doris is a chess freak.

I have happened upon an obscure dating Web site, Chessmates: *If the only King in your life is two inches tall, or if your romance is in a stalemate, don't despair. Come to Chessmates: For chess enthusiasts who are looking for real-life Kings and Queens.*

There she is, sitting at a table with a chessboard, looking up at the camera. She is listed as *Doris Meisel, 47, businesswoman (lingerie).*

From what I can tell, Chessmates is a dating service for chess enthusiasts. I click on Events. There's a chess retreat scheduled for next weekend. There are chess cocktail parties every week. I click on Event Archives. Oh my. There was a Chess Christmas Cruise. I click it. There is a gallery. And there she is: Doris. Still middle-aged, still overweight, but there's something different about her.

She's happy.

There's no Polly harping at her side. She looks interesting and interested. She's in almost every photograph. The Chess-mate photographer obviously loved her. And the cruise looked beautiful. Where was it? I look at the dates.

It looks as if Doris is innocent after all. She was sailing through the Panama Canal on the day Polly Dawson was murdered. I'm happy for her. Elated even. Now that Polly's dead, she can enjoy the rest of her life. And she has an alibi.

But where does that leave me?

Charlie walks into the room beaming. He has just returned from his meeting with Kovitz.

"What?" I tuck the William Redwin files under my bottom so he doesn't ask me about them.

"Polly Dawson was pregnant when she was murdered."

So now I'm looking at one of those double homicide charges.

"That's not the great part," Charlie says.

"I figured."

"Humphrey Dawson's infertile."

"So he is . . . was . . . not the father?"

"Very good, Dr. Ruth."

"So the cops know Polly Dawson wasn't faithful to him."

"Better. Humphrey knows Polly wasn't faithful to him. He has taken his reward for your head off the market."

"That's great news."

"I guess Preston Hayes isn't such a reliable source after all."

"I guess not."

"I have more." More. Charlie has more. I take a moment to praise myself for loving him all of these years.

"According to Kovitz, something didn't seem right at the memorial service."

"That's crack detective work." I can't help myself. "Why don't we start with the fact that it was at Barneys?"

Charlie ignores me.

"It seems that they have added to their list of suspects."

"Added? As in I'm not the only one?"

"Yes, Alice. You're still holding first place. Your position is strong due to the fact that you haven't turned yourself in."

"I might have been more cooperative if they hadn't been so eager to convict me within thirty seconds of questioning."

Charlie ignores me again. I become concerned.

"Are you trying to get rid of me, Walter?" I say, trying to be coy to cover my desperation.

"Kovitz has some others in mind." Charlie doesn't address my question. "Now that it's clear that Polly wasn't a faithful wife, the list of suspects and motives is growing. According to witnesses, Polly was continually cheating on Humphrey. It was as if she wanted him to find out."

"Maybe he was withholding, and she just wanted to make him think she was sleeping around so that he could be more attentive," I offer. My friend Debbie Gold had done this exact thing with a boyfriend so that she could get him to propose to her. And it worked.

"Well then, how would that explain her pregnancy?" Charlie says in a Miss Marple moment.

"I'm just covering all the bases," I say, but Charlie's detective skills are improving.

"Kovitz had a huge emergency and had to cut our meeting short, but he assured me that we could meet tomorrow and he would have some really good information for me."

"Did he give you a hint?"

"No. He was in a hurry."

"Of course he was." Kovitz never ceases to let me down.

"But," Charlie repeats, "he's going to tell me more tomorrow."

"Let's just hope that he doesn't change his mind," I say.

"Don't worry. I know how to get anything out of Phil Kovitz," Charlie assures me.

"How are you getting this stuff out of him?"

"Kovitz is partial to Jack and soda, and he thinks he can hold his alcohol better than he can. And so, after three of them I told him that I was a big fan of Humphrey Dawson movies and that I had always had a little thing for Polly."

Oh, that's a point of vulnerability for me, but I must press forward.

"And then what did he say?"

"He said that I wasn't the only one and then suddenly he started opening up to me, telling me that Polly slept around quite a bit and that she did it right on the movie set."

I think back to when I followed Polly at Silvercup Studios. I saw the hair flipping, the lip biting, and the flirting, but really nothing else. I guess I'm not the detective I thought I was.

"Apparently she was caught the day before her murder with one of the stars, Ian Leighton, in the hull of the boat used for the film."

My first thought: That sounds so unappetizing. The movie is about a lobster-fishing family.

So she did have a thing with Ian Leighton. And I missed it. But Ian does work fast. Everybody at Mona Hawkins Casting knew it. First, there was a story floating around that Ian had actually slept with Mona. I couldn't believe it until I had a conversation with Julia Wechsler, one of Mona's nineteen-year-old interns, who had slept with Ian a few times. He dumped her without warning; she couldn't understand his behavior.

"The man is a sex addict," she told me after she'd been in therapy for three months and was completely over him. "Attractiveness doesn't make a difference. Mona was there and she was probably touching him. It was inappropriate for Ian to sleep with the casting director, which fueled his need to have sex with her."

"Gross," the Janus-faced Jed Rausch had said.

I had met several girls who had been Ian's victims. He made them feel incredibly special for short periods of time and then moved on. I always wondered why Ian never made a move on me. He hit on practically everyone else in our office. I secretly wondered if I was so undesirable that a sex addict wouldn't hit on me.

"You have nothing to do with it." Julia, who had become something of an expert on the topic, had read my mind. "It's about him. It's about the danger and the inappropriateness of it. You and Ian are roughly the same age. That makes it less exciting for him." Julia explained that the fact that Ian was in a "committed" relationship with someone else increased his need for sex.

Now that Ian is single, he's probably more drawn to married women. And with Polly, married—to his director no less—and flirting, one thing led to another.

But on a movie set?

"I wonder what kind of perversity leads someone to be so cruel as to flaunt their infidelity."

"Maybe she wanted attention," Charlie says.

"Or maybe she was just really selfish," I say, speaking ill of the dead. I realize that I still dislike Polly. She's the one who got me into trouble in the first place.

I get back to Kovitz.

"Did he tell you if he knows when Polly last saw Ian Leighton?" I ask.

"According to Leighton, the night before she was murdered."

"So, Polly was cheating on her lover."

"The guy from the Chinese restaurant?" Charlie asks.

"The very one. And I know Ian Leighton. He is nothing like the young buck from downtown."

"But maybe Mr. Leighton could have angered your young buck," Charlie says.

"He is so not my young buck. And Ian would not have been looking to steal Polly for any extended period of time. That's not his MO," I tell him. "But the young buck would not know that. Ian, if you don't know his backstory, is hot and successful. The young guy could have felt threatened. Very threatened. Suspect Number Three is looking good."

I remember to follow up on Jean's lead.

"Did you ask him if Humphrey was faithful?"

"I did, and he told me that to the best of his knowledge, Humphrey was. He hadn't heard anything to the contrary."

Anything to the contrary? Helllllooo? "What about the tip from Preston Hayes that Humphrey had a girlfriend?" I knew I was a better investigator than Phil Kovitz.

"I couldn't tell him that I knew about the tip because he'd get suspicious, but he said that he definitely heard nothing about Humphrey being unfaithful. In fact, he heard quite the opposite. Humphrey was very devoted."

I've got to press Jean on this. She seemed fairly certain that Preston said that he had given the cops a tip. Maybe he said that he was going to give them a tip some time in the future. But I don't want to dwell on this.

"So?" I change the subject. "When are you meeting?"

"Tomorrow."

"Around what time?" I ask, trying to sound as nonchalant as possible.

"Why are you so curious?" I think he is a little suspicious.

"Why am I so curious?" I buy a little time so I can figure out why I'm so curious. "Because my future is at stake."

"Noon."

"Noon it is," I say under my breath.

Charlie and I are getting dressed. Not together, unfortunately. But we could be twins. I'm wearing his jeans, his down jacket, his flannel shirt, his hat, his gloves, and even his sneakers. Charlie gave me a pair of his old blue Nikes, and I stuffed the tips with toilet paper. I'm sure I'm doing permanent orthopedic damage.

"What are your plans, exactly?" Charlie asks.

We head out his front door. It's snowing and his tree-lined street is blanketed in white. In other circumstances, we could be a Christmas card, Charlie and I. But Christmas is over, and I'm on the run.

To stay with you until I'm exonerated, and then get married.

I explain to Charlie, as we muddle through the flakes, that I'm off to follow a new lead. And although my outfit provides some camouflage, I'm worried that she's going to think she's being stalked by a boy.

"I don't know, Alice. If you look really hard you can see the contours of a woman's body."

Is Charlie suggesting that he is looking hard at my contours? I blush.

"Stop making me so self-conscious. My lack of self-consciousness is why no one has ever caught me."

"I caught you," Charlie says quickly.

"Maybe I'm too self-conscious in your presence." I decide to withhold any explanation of this comment and instead enjoy the awkwardness of the moment.

We walk our separate ways. At least for a moment we do. I've convinced Charlie that I'm walking across Central Park. Charlie's heading down to meet Kovitz in Chinatown. They've agreed to meet at Mee-Hop at noon.

Charlie heads into the restaurant. I follow him. This is a particularly difficult task, given that Charlie knows my hobby and I am wearing his clothes. But I'm here, and I'm rather enjoying this challenge.

Kovitz is there. From what I can see, he and Charlie have a

warm relationship. That doesn't surprise me. Charlie's a very nice person. If anyone can get to Kovitz, it's Charlie.

The two eat their lunch: vegetarian chow mei fun and vegetable hot and sour soup. Charlie told me last night that Kovitz was a vegetarian.

"I would never have guessed that," I told him.

"People are full of surprises," he said. "Who would have known you were a murderer?"

What can I say? I love this man.

I don't even know why I'm here. Mee-Hop is extraordinarily loud and I dare not remove my hat. Plus, Kovitz and Charlie are speaking in soft voices. At times like this, Jaime Sommers and her bionic ear could come in handy.

Kovitz is obviously risking his career to confide in Charlie. This makes me love Charlie even more. I wonder what it would be like to wake up with him in the morning. I mean in his bed. Looking at him.

"Alice."

He will say my name.

"Alice."

He will say it again.

"Alice. Why are you dressed like that?"

Okay. This isn't my fantasy. That voice is real and it isn't Charlie's.

"Roger." He says it. Not me.

Oh, no. I try to look down.

"Alice. It's Roger. From Justin and Felisha's New Year's party. If I recall, you are my New Year's resolution."

If I recall, *my* resolution was to get myself out of my mess. Roger's doing nothing to help matters. He's blocking my view of Charlie and Kovitz. More significantly, he has a booming voice. And he just blasted my name in front of the cop who has it out for me.

"Alice, don't you think it's kismet that we reconnected?"

"Huh?" If I go to jail, it's going to be this loser's fault.

"Alice, can you hear me?"

And if I go to jail, this guy's going to be my only visitor.

"I thought we connected on New Year's Eve. And wow. You look great. The boy outfit on you is kinda sexy. I always knew you were a woman of mystery."

He always knew? The man met me for six minutes.

He is still talking.

"If I didn't know any better, I would say you are working undercover."

I laugh uncertainly.

"There you go. I just got you to smile. That's because we have something, you and me. And that something is called chemistry."

I am for a second tempted to scream Kovitz's name and throw myself upon the mercy of the court. The room is spinning and my heart is beating in my ear.

"We had this moment."

Roger's voice is booming now.

"But then, Alice, you were out of there so fast."

"Like this," I say.

I put a ten-dollar bill on the table and run out onto the street as fast as I can.

Roger doesn't follow me. But from the street I hear him shouting my name over and over again.

I'm in a lot of trouble.

I'm in Charlie's living room when he returns. Dr. Michael Led-yard, the man who claims to cure gay people, is on *Oprah* promoting his book *The Way: Part Two*. I have never seen Oprah so angry. She uses the word "inauthentic" a lot and she directs it toward the "doctor." His theory is that if you live as if you are straight, you are straight. And if living this way is hard, life is hard. He has brought several guests to the show. There they are all lined up, claiming to be cured of their sexual "oddities." They all look as if they could be in the chorus of *La Cage aux Folles,* but there they are, each limply holding the hand of a female companion.

Charlie bursts in. "Alice," he says, half Ricky Ricardo, half Jackie Gleason.

"Yes," I say innocently.

"What was the point of that?" He's referring to my presence at Mee-Hop.

"I don't know," I say truthfully. "I guess that I wanted to be in on it?"

"How much more in on it could you be? You are the number-one suspect in a murder case."

"I'm sorry," I say. I'm quite somber.

Silence.

"Really sorry." More somber still.

More silence. I change my approach.

"I'm the level of sorry that I have to be to find out what you learned from Kovitz."

"Alice. This isn't funny," Charlie says. "I'm going out on enough of a limb by harboring a fugitive. And now I don't know if you have some sort of death wish for us. You're lucky Kovitz had a couple of drinks in him."

"You're right," I say.

Silence. This time I know not to say anything. Charlie's face softens before he speaks. Phew. I knew we'd be fine.

"I forgive you. I have to, because this is really good."

I can taste my freedom. "Do tell."

"Remember when Jean told us that she knew a lawyer who said Polly was looking to sell her company?"

"Yes," I say, almost breathless.

"Before she was ready to sell, she was engaging in some illegal activity. I'm not really sure what she was doing, but she ended up as an informant for the government."

An informant.

"Like a spy?" I ask.

"Sort of. It seems that Polly was doing business with a big Wall Street muckety-muck who was getting greedy. She was about to sell her company to a big retail organization. She was knee-deep in an insider-trading scam when the FBI and the U.S. Attorney's Office nailed her. To avoid prosecution, she agreed to cooperate. She was going to rat on this big white-collar criminal. The government wanted him way more than her.

"A first tender offer was scheduled for days after her death. She had told this guy about the offer, and he was going to invest at twelve dollars a share when the market share was twenty dollars. She'd gotten him to agree to split the difference."

I don't say anything. Why is all of this sounding so familiar to me? I can't quite place it.

"Who's the muckety-muck?" I say, borrowing Charlie's quaint verbiage.

Charlie sits at his computer and starts typing. "His name is Ralston Brown. He's pretty famous."

Charlie types in the letters *R-A-L-S-T-O-N*. A picture pops up. "There he is."

My heart stops. "It's him. It's him. That's the library guy."

"What are you talking about?" Charlie asks me.

"That's the guy from the library. Suspect Number Four. The one I said had a relationship with Polly. Now it makes sense."

"To you," Charlie says. "I have no idea what you are talking about."

I reach into my pocket and I show Charlie. *12/20 Tender Dutch.*

"You see, I pulled this out of the card-catalog drawer. Polly had written it for the guy, but for some reason he left it there. I thought it was a love note. I thought they were going to make tender love on December 20 and either they each pay for the date or they would fly to Amsterdam. But it is clear: The tender offer was for twenty-dollar shares and an inside price of twelve dollars. And Dutch means—"

"Dutch means that she offered to split the profit with him," Charlie says.

"Huh?" Reason Number 235 that I should have taken Economics in college.

"If Ralston Brown hadn't been on the inside of the deal, he would have had to pay twenty dollars per share of Principessa. As an insider, she was offering him a huge discount, a huge illegal discount of twelve dollars. He saves eight dollars per share. But not really, because he has to split the eight dollars—"

"Oh. So she gets four dollars of every eight that he saves?"

"Precisely, my dear Watson," he says warmly.

"Hey. How come I'm Watson?"

"Because Sherlock is the one who knows the basic principles of insider trading."

Fair enough.

"So this wasn't an affair at all?"

"Doesn't look like it."

"But I was right that there was something between the two of them. I just thought it was something romantic, when it was really something criminal."

"So the thought is that Ralston may have been so angry with Polly that he killed her?"

If there were a big cartoon lightbulb over my head right now, I wouldn't be surprised. I'm picturing the e-mail to Polly at $$$$@yahoo.com, the one that says "I am way ahead of you, princess, we're off."

Way ahead of her. As in he knew she was going to send him up the river for the rest of his life. That's a motive to kill.

I tell Charlie that Suspect Number Four, Ralston Brown, may have implicated himself on the World Wide Web.

"Looks that way," Charlie says unenthusiastically.

He's not looking in my direction.

"Walter," I say. When he's wearing his stern face, I use only his real name.

He doesn't respond.

"You're angry with me, aren't you?"

"I am," he says without emotion.

"I'm really sorry that I waited so long to tell you about the note."

"Alice, you make it sound as if you volunteered the information out of the blue. If I hadn't told you about this information from Kovitz, you would never have told me about the note."

He's right.

"Sorry," I say pathetically.

"I don't want sorry. I want to rethink this partnership. I'm not sure I trust you."

I want to tell Charlie that he's mistaken, that I'd take a bullet for him. Instead, I don't say anything.

"I don't trust you, Alice, because you don't trust me. I went to lunch with Kovitz this afternoon, and you followed me. Even though I gave you all the information that he gave me. But you weren't equally forthcoming. You kept this note from me for some reason. It makes me wonder what other information you're withholding."

"I kept the note from you because I was embarrassed."

"You were embarrassed about the note?"

"I didn't want you to think I was that nosy."

"You've got to be kidding. You stalk a woman for weeks and

weeks, following her every move, and you don't want me to think you're nosy?"

"N-not just nosy. I used the term '*that* nosy.' Somehow, I drew the distinction between following Polly and reading her mail. Reading the note seemed more intrusive. I didn't want you to think I had boundary issues."

Charlie starts laughing. I want to defend my statement, but I realize I'm ridiculous. Of course I'm intrusive. Of course I have boundary issues. I start laughing, too. My laughter makes Charlie laugh more. I realize I've never seen him in this state. At best, generally, he looks amused. I feel very close to him right now.

"I'm sorry," I tell him. "I do trust you. It wasn't about trust."

"I think I understand," he says, "but why don't we agree that we'll tell each other everything, good and bad?"

"It's a deal," I say.

Charlie grabs my hand. I'm certain he's going to pull me into him and kiss me. But no. He just shakes it.

It is, however, the longest handshake in history.

I'm at Charlie's computer again. I wasn't as thorough as I could have been when I was reading Polly's e-mail. I was dismissive of correspondence that bore any resemblance to fan mail. Even though Polly is dead and I'm alive, I find the public adoration annoying. If, however, reading a few fan letters could ultimately exonerate me, I'm willing to be annoyed. I can tell the fan mail because it comes mostly from personal e-mail accounts. The subject lines usually say: "We ♥ Polly Dawson," or "We ♥ Principessa." I read all of them. Most of them praise Polly for being so beautiful, and more than a few of her fans were surprised that someone with her looks was Harvard educated. They all praise her for the social good that she did. What social good? This is why I get annoyed.

There are several e-mails from happycamper@yahoo.com. They date as far back as October, and it looks as if Polly opened the letters and saved them along with her unread mail. I look at the first one. "That was great, baby. Anytime." I open a second. "You're more beautiful today than you were yesterday." Not exactly a poet, but he doesn't sound like a psychotic fan, either. I see more: at least ten. All of them are short and complimentary. Several just say "great." Happy Camper addresses her as Baby. Here's a longer one. "Tomorrow, Baby, I'm taking you out. Not a hot spot—unless you're describing the sauce. So don't worry about being noticed."

"I'm taking you out." Does he mean he is going to kill her? No. Happy Camper seems like a straight shooter. Not a hot spot except the sauce. He must be talking about a spicy restaurant. And one that isn't glamorous. Mee-Hop.

Happy Camper is Polly's young lover. The one from the Chambers Street apartment.

I go through every e-mail carefully. They all have that slightly enthusiastic albeit blasé tone. And they stop somewhat abruptly. The last one reads. "Hey Baby; cool to slow things down right now. But I was serious about what I wanted to do with us and this girl from my office."

As if Polly would ever have shared that spotlight.

The e-mails from Happy Camper stop, and I don't see any others that look remotely suspicious.

Conclusion: Happy Camper, a.k.a. Polly's young lover, didn't kill Polly. Even if he were the father of the baby, he had no idea. No, I suspect Happy Camper is keeping company with another beauty. Who knows, maybe he found two.

"If we can identify the father, we might be able to identify the murderer," I tell Charlie as he walks in.

Charlie sighs.

"You disapprove of this, don't you?" I say.

"It makes me uncomfortable. It's so sneaky. I've had bad luck with sneaky."

"Let me guess," I say. "Your housemate? The one who hated to have food around." I can't bring myself to say "ex-girlfriend."

"The very one," Charlie says.

"Not all sneakiness leads to broken hearts," I reassure him.

"That's what I keep telling myself," Charlie says.

Charlie's in the shower. He's singing. I can't tell if he is off-key or if I don't know the song. I don't want to ask him though because he may stop. And I like it.

He seems happy.

He thinks we're making progress on my case, and he wants to celebrate.

"You know what tomorrow is?" he asked me just before he went into the shower.

I had no idea.

"Tomorrow is Valentine's Day. You're so good with food and all. Maybe you could make us some yummy treats."

Valentine's Day. I've always hated Valentine's Day. It's God's way of punishing people for being alone. But now Charlie wants me to make treats for us. Does this mean we are Valentines?

Now I'm confused, a whole new reason to hate the holiday.

I want to call Jean to ask for her advice, but Charlie could come out of the shower anytime. She thinks Charlie is fixated on me. That he thinks I'm some kind of Superwoman.

"Superwoman?" I asked her.

"Yes," she told me, "he thinks you have magical abilities because you can follow people without being seen."

I blushed when Jean told me this, and then I changed the subject.

The truth is that even though I love Charlie, I can't even try to be his Valentine until everything is resolved. And I don't just mean my precarious legal situation. At the moment, I'm more concerned about what I know about his father. I can't tell him. I can't hurt him.

Now we have a whole new lead on our case. Polly Dawson was pregnant. And the father of her baby was not her husband. Wow. And Polly knew her husband was infertile. Her husband knew he was infertile. Frankly, the whole world knew he was infertile.

What if the father of Polly's baby *was* her young lover? What if Polly had told him that she was going to tell her husband, leave him, and have their baby? What if the actor didn't want a powerful director like Humphrey to be his enemy? What if that actor was Ian Leighton?

That's a pretty good motive for murder. Better than being a fired, disgruntled casting assistant.

And there's Humphrey himself. While it appears he didn't kill Polly, he may have been someone else's motive for murder. That's not so far-fetched. Kovitz thinks I killed Polly because I was fired from Humphrey's movie (and because I hated her).

Was he cheating on Polly?

According to Jean, Preston said he was cheating and Preston had given the police that tip. But Charlie said that Kovitz didn't mention anything about Humphrey's infidelity. So that means:

A. Kovitz is lying.

B. Charlie is lying.

C. Jean is lying.

D. Preston Hayes is lying.

E. This is all a big misunderstanding.

I'm not inclined to think that Charlie or Jean is lying to me. Kovitz could be withholding that particular piece of information from Charlie for some reason. But what reason? He was so detailed about everything else. And then there's the possibility that Preston Hayes was lying. But why would Preston lie to Jean? Maybe he had a fling with Polly, and he's trying to justify it by saying that Humphrey is a philanderer. They were together about as often as she and Ian Leighton were, and somewhere along the line those two ended up doing it in a lobster boat. But Preston Hayes doesn't have the reputation of being a sex addict.

Just a womanizer.

Maybe he's a gossip.

I call Jean on the phone and tell her that I think Preston Hayes is a bad lead. He told us that Polly was faithful when she wasn't.

"But I kinda like him," Jean tells me. Jean "kinda likes" a lot of people. She has a very welcoming heart.

"I know, but I don't think his information is good," I tell her. "Maybe you can date him after this whole thing is over."

The truth is, I learn, nothing has even happened between Jean and Preston. He's rubbed her lower back three times and run his fingers along her forearms twice. He's sent her a dozen roses, but he hasn't said anything to her about Valentine's Day.

"I've Googled him every day, and it doesn't look as if he has a girlfriend or anything. He's always linked with models, but they usually show up with him to fundraisers and charity events. He never seems to go to a private dinner or on a vacation." Thus spake Jean.

Preston Hayes may link himself with models to garner press attention because he's two starring roles away from being an object of the paparazzi. *Only at Sunrise* is his second major feature film. He was something of a hit in last summer's blockbuster, *Frolic and Detour,* where he played a hot young cable man who slept with all of his female customers. Critics unanimously agreed that the script was awful but that Hayes's charm kept them in their seats.

Mona was quite taken with him as soon as she met him. "Delicious," she said. "Where has this man been all my life?"

I picture Mona on a date with Preston, ordering eight meals for herself and asking for a shopping bag for all of the leftovers.

I can't tell Jean to terminate her budding romance because it's not helping me, but I do tell her that he may not be as astute as he comes off.

"He is an actor, you know," I tell her.

"I know."

I also tell Jean that it's likely that Preston had a fling with Polly Dawson.

"I don't want to judge him for that," she says in a way that indicates to me that I have to keep my mouth shut. She knows I will. You can't fault a man for loving Polly Dawson. I don't fault Charlie for loving an untrustworthy woman who refuses to have food in her home.

I whisper to Jean that Charlie wants me to bake him something for Valentine's Day.

"Make him cupcakes with sexy messages," she tells me.

I want to ask what sort of sexy messages, but Charlie's suddenly standing next to me.

"Sounds great," I say to her in a loud voice. "Bye, then."

I turn to Charlie.

"Jean wants to continue to see Preston Hayes even though I told her he may be useless to us. She says she 'kinda likes him.'"

"Who are we to interfere with affairs of the heart?" Charlie says soberly.

"We're the number-one suspect and her accomplice in a murder of a celebrity," I tell him.

———

I'm mixing the ingredients for the cupcakes. This could be a good distraction for me from Ralston Brown, whom I now consider our number-one murder suspect. Especially now that we are pretty sure that Jenna McNair was redesigning her body, D.M. was playing chess, and Happy Camper had moved on. Although, now that he's looking good for the murder, there are some other people that we should also consider, like Ian Leighton, potential father of Polly's baby. There also may be people from Polly's life to whom I was not privy: any of the other male cast members, another old boyfriend, or business partner, or some crazy fan. Just thinking about all the work ahead of us makes me nervous. I need the baking diversion. It'll be fun. I like Jean's idea. Write sexy messages on a cupcake. Sounds good, but it's hard to fit a sexy thought onto that small surface. What'll I write? "Bra"?

I could always go for the more traditional "Be Mine" and "Love."

But that's so impersonal. I need something that has to do with *our* special circumstances. Like "Innocent!" Or "Unfair!" I'm hoping it'll come to me as I am cooking.

I have a bottle of Grand Marnier in front of me. Maybe if I take a shot or two, I'll be inspired. Wasn't Hemingway an alcoholic?

I've found this recipe on the Internet: chocolate Grand Marnier cupcakes. I'll serve them on a platter surrounded by clementines. I haven't baked anything in so long. This recipe's easy enough. Right now I am sifting the flour, the baking soda, and the salt. Easy. Now I get to melt the chocolate with the Grand Marnier. I dip my finger in. Mmm. Now all I have to do is to mix the sugar, the egg, and the sour cream.

Wait. Sour cream?

226 • KAREN BERGREEN

I could have sworn it said heavy cream. I only bought heavy cream. I look in Charlie's refrigerator to see if there's any sour cream inside. Nothing. Of course not. The man is not exactly a collector of ingredients. I know I should go back to the Food Emporium. But it's so cold outside and I can't deal with the long line there. I know it's just a couple of blocks away, but it'll add a lot of unexpected time to the cooking project. And, I'm starting to feel the Grand Marnier. My little buzz will be ruined by a trip to the store. I could just use the heavy cream. Cream is, after all, cream. The cupcakes will just be a little less sour.

I pour the mixture into pretty orange cupcake wrappers and put them in the oven.

Life is getting better.

Maybe tonight will be "the Night" for me and Charlie, after all. I'll tell him that I've always loved him, and he'll tell me that he knew there was someone right under his nose, and that it wasn't until he found me going through his garbage that he knew that I was that someone. Then we'll kiss, but I'll have to tell him that we need to be strong until our lives are straightened out. He'll agree, but he'll also confide in me that this is the hardest test of them all.

The buzzer sounds. The cupcakes are done.

I go into the kitchen. All I have to do is ice these things and then write the romantic messages.

I open the oven.

Oh no. They don't look like cupcakes at all. They're just flat stumps.

The cream! It was the cream. I should have bought the sour cream. I look at the clock. Charlie will be here in forty-five minutes. I need at least two more hours if I'm going to start all over again.

Maybe I can save them. I'll just create little domes out of the chocolate orange buttercream icing.

The icing isn't thick enough to give the cupcakes their necessary heft. So, I have to present Charlie with the stumps.

And now, it's going to be that much harder to include a romantic message in the icing. I was counting on a fairly ample diameter on which to fit the appropriate tidings. Without that, I don't know what to write.

I hear the door open.

"That smells amazing."

It's Charlie. I don't have much time to come up with something pithy for the stumps.

"Alice, I'm starving, and my mouth is watering."

I write the only words on the cupcakes that I can think of as I place them on the platter with the clementines.

Charlie walks into the kitchen. And he's staring at them. Twelve mutant cupcakes filled with self-revelation.

Charlie starts reading the cupcake messages aloud:

"'Oops.' 'Uh-oh.' 'Yike.'" He looks at me. "I think it's 'yikes.'"

"I know, but I couldn't fit the S there, and that made it even more descriptive."

Charlie starts laughing.

He keeps laughing.

"The recipe calls for sour cream, and I used heavy cream." I confess all.

Charlie keeps laughing.

He takes a bite of an OOPS.

"They taste delicious."

"You must like icing," I tell him.

"I love icing," Charlie says, "and I love these cupcakes. The little messages are perfect."

Perfect. Charlie thinks they're perfect. I'm so excited, I almost miss his next comment.

"I wanted to do something nice for you on Valentine's Day," he says.

I get nervous. I wish Jean were here to help me script an appropriate reply.

I say nothing.

"I thought about it," he continues, "and I think I thought of a really good gift."

I'm going to faint. Is it the Grand Marnier going to my head?

"I'd like to watch television with you."

I'm stunned.

"Is that your gift?" I ask him. I sound a spot ungracious.

"Yes. I see you parked here in front of the tube, dying to talk to someone about all of these programs you watch. You can't call anyone because you're a fugitive from justice. So, I thought I'd donate my eyes and ears for an evening."

I don't remind him that if I'm desperate I can always call Jean. "Sounds like a gift more for yourself than for me."

But it isn't. I know. Charlie has no interest in television. He's trying to do something nice for me. He has shared his apartment with me; now I can share my hobby.

"Who knows? Maybe I'll get hooked."

"Don't get too invested in the guilt of anybody the police peg early on."

I'm explaining to Charlie how *Law & Order* works. "If you know who does it in the first ten minutes, then NBC thinks you'll switch to another show for the remainder of the hour."

We're sitting on his couch, my bed. I'm wearing one of Charlie's pajama tops and a pair of his jeans. He looks as if he might have dressed and shaved for the occasion: a black cashmere turtleneck and a new pair of thick winter khakis. We're sitting as close as two people can without any physical contact.

"But they have pretty good evidence here," he tries to persuade me. "This killer has a motive: It's his wife's lover, he has no alibi for the time of death; and he works in a lab that has the capability of producing the poison that killed him."

"No, the detectives have missed something. They always miss an important piece of evidence. This guy isn't guilty, I will bet you. And don't think the next guy will be guilty, either. They always have to go through a few of them before they land on the real killer with the obscure but much more sinister motive."

"When you say bet, I was wondering what you could offer. You've already moved in here, I've given you half my wardrobe, and I've put you on allowance."

"Do you want me to move out?" I panic.

"No, Alice. I like having you around." And after he says it, he smiles a little. Our legs touch.

My stomach does about six somersaults.

I wonder if I should tell him that I've loved him from afar since college. And I realize he's still talking.

"Who knows? Maybe we could sell your story to *Law and Order* and you could pay me rent."

Maybe I should wait before professing my love.

Law & Order goes into a commercial break when suddenly the local anchorwoman bellows: "Another murder in Manhattan: Could this be another bizarre plot of Polly Dawson's twisted killer?"

Another murder? The news break ends and a car commercial comes on.

"Change the channel," I tell Charlie. He starts pressing buttons on the remote. Obviously the wrong ones, because the car commercial is only getting louder. I grab the remote from him. I turn to New York 1; they call themselves New York's only twenty-four-hour news station. It's got to be there. No, it's a one-hour sports special. Since when is sports news? I turn to CNN; Michael Ledyard is on again. I turn to MSNBC. I know it is hopeless. That channel never has any news. Clarissa Winnick, author of *Men Fight, Women Bite* is on explaining her Trifecta Defensive. She's sitting on top of the current darling of World Wrestling Entertainment, Doctor Power, discussing the importance of the shriek, the kick, and the bite.

I turn to Charlie to share my frustration. He's not on the couch. Is he irritated that I grabbed the remote control from him? I am desp— Oh, there he is at his desk sitting in front of the computer.

"I just logged on to the Internet." He turns around. "Mona Hawkins is dead."

Mona Hawkins is dead.

Dead.

The story is now on TV: Mona Hawkins was found dead in her office. Stab wounds. The killer left no clues this time. The newscaster is reporting that according to preliminary forensic reports, the knife wounds were consistent with those inflicted on Polly Dawson. But the murder weapon was different.

Of course the murder weapon was different. The Polly Dawson murder weapon is at the fifth precinct station house. I should know: It was found in my living room.

The newscaster is talking.

"An NYPD insider reports that Mona Hawkins was stabbed at approximately six this evening. So far there have been no clues as to the killer's identity or motive in the killing. Police are not saying whether they believe at-large suspect Alice Teakle is responsible for this killing. Teakle was brought in for questioning on December 31 of last year, but she escaped police custody. Until now police have been silent as to whether Teakle was considered a danger, but after tonight's events, they will broaden their search. It turns out, police tell us, Alice Teakle was formerly employed by the murder victim and was fired only several months before she allegedly killed Polly Dawson, who was married to the director of the film she was casting. It is believed that Ms. Teakle may blame Humphrey Dawson and Mona Hawkins and others associated with the film for her unemployment."

Six P.M.! I was frosting the mutant cupcakes at six P.M., just moments before Charlie got home. Our cupcakes. Charlie knows that I was here. He now knows for sure that I'm innocent. Of course, he can't go to the cops with this information. It'll ruin everything. They'll arrest him for being an accomplice for obstruction of justice or something like that.

"This may put a wrench in suspects one through four," Charlie says as if I hadn't thought of it, "but we have a new angle. All we have to do now is find out who killed Mona," Charlie tells me. "Whoever did this, he or she is really lucky to have you. You are the perfect scapegoat."

"Maybe I'm being framed by Suspect One, Two, Three, or Four," I tell him. "Look, the killer left all those clues the last time. And the clues pointed only to me or to somebody who'd been tracking my whereabouts. And now Mona's dead. She's the one who fired me, which is apparently the reason for my killing spree."

"Let's put our suspects aside for a second. Does anybody have a beef with you? An old work rival? A former boyfriend."

I don't know how to tell Charlie that I don't think I made that kind of imprint on anybody. My old boyfriends seemed to have gotten over me before the relationships ended. A work rival seems drastic.

"I don't think so," I answer.

"Could there have been something going on with the movie? Something we didn't think of. Something illegal. And the killer thinks that you know about it, and he's trying to send you some kind of message."

"That one *Law and Order* episode must have had an impact

on you," I tell him. "It's just so far-fetched. The director wasn't killed. None of the producers were killed. It was the director's wife and a casting director."

"How about the spurned lover angle? Suspect Three, the young lover. And then Ian Leighton, and any other man she may have seduced?"

"I buy that for Polly. But Mona Hawkins's closest thing to a lover was a profiterole."

"Maybe it's just a coincidence," Charlie offers.

"Not if the report was correct that that knife went in the same way." The truth is I know nothing about knives and how they're supposed to enter a victim. Maybe there are only a couple of knife entry routes, but the reporter made the match here seem significant.

Too bad I am such a *Law & Order* fan. I wish I watched *CSI*. I need a show with some forensic assistance. Even *Quincy M.E.* would be more helpful to me at this point.

I want to call Jean, but she's on a date with Preston Hayes. He came through, finally, and invited her to a star-studded Valentine's Day party. She took a day off from her job to primp.

"I need to buy new underwear," she told me this afternoon. "Just in case Preston makes his move."

It's really weird. Preston Hayes, the new Mr. Hot Hot Hot, is romancing my friend. He has been on five outings with her. He has taken her to big fancy parties, and last week the two spent an evening with another couple, Preston's best friend Ted Swinton, the new It novelist, and his wife in Park Slope. Jean has an annoying habit of talking about Ted Swinton as if they are best friends. She casually throws his name in every sentence. Two days ago she was referring to a cabernet he recommended.

"My impending murder conviction is doing wonders for your social life," I told her as she was deciding between two teddies.

"I'm sorry, is it insensitive of me to be asking you for lingerie tips?"

"Go ahead. This whole thing is surreal."

And I wasn't lying. I may be jobless, homeless, on the run, facing a life in jail, but I'm enjoying myself. Something I don't recall ever doing before. Maybe it's because I have a sense of purpose now. I'm still fascinated with Jean's romantic life, and not because Preston Hayes may be my ticket out of a guilty verdict. No. I think I am no longer living vicariously through her. Instead, I'm relating to her. I've become acutely aware of every interaction I have with Charlie. I notice, for example, that his leg was touching mine just minutes ago on the couch. I notice that he has started talking to me about topics other than his father or my plight. I notice that he now stands a little closer to me when we speak than he did when I first moved in. Then again, when Charlie found me I hadn't bathed in over a week and I was wearing a riding helmet.

I told Jean to wear something comfortable. She's going to be at a party all night and she doesn't want Preston to see her fiddling with her underthings.

"But what if we go back to his apartment?" Jean asks.

"He's not going to be examining your underwear. You can worry about that when you get engaged."

"You don't think we are going back to his apartment, do you?"

The truth is I don't. Preston has gone on five dates with Jean and hasn't made a move. Jean notes that he has touched her suggestively on her forearm, her back, her face, and her hair.

"We held hands in front of his best friend," she reminded me.

True, but my gut is telling me that Preston will not make any move tonight.

"You think he's encumbered?" Jean asked me.

"I do," I told her. "Maybe an on-the-way-out girlfriend or a secret wife." Or he's pining over the death of Polly Dawson.

"Or a secret life?"

"Maybe you are transmitting 'don't touch me' signals," I told her. A lot of men have told me that I frequently send off this signal.

"Could be. I mean, I really like him, and maybe I'm just getting smarter about jumping into bed so quickly."

I wonder if Preston is making a move right now. Someone should be having a successful love match. Whoever killed Mona also killed my hopes for romance tonight.

Charlie has gone to sleep early. There was no point in prolonging this ultimately unpleasant evening. I sit by his phone and his computer waiting for Jean to call or e-mail. If things with Preston have moved on to the next step, then she might not have turned on a TV or logged on to a computer in the last few hours. But most certainly Preston would find out. The casting director for his movie was murdered less than two months after its director's wife was killed. Surely, someone contacted him.

I keep checking the Internet for updates on Mona's death. "We are all very shocked and saddened," Jed Rausch, one of her former assistants, has told the press. Jed Rausch was the guy who gleefully told me about Mona's stomach surgery and her ties to the gay porn industry.

"She was a brilliant casting director," Farron Moore, a casting rival, said.

I wish people could be honest in these interviews. She was a despicable freak and at least two hundred people will be dancing on her grave. As for motive, we all had it, but only one person was brave enough or grandiose enough to kill her.

There's little information about the killing. The most recent report says that Mona was killed inside her office at six P.M. None of her employees were there.

"She told us to go home; it was Valentine's Day," Jane Somers told a reporter. I had never met Jane. I assume she was hired to replace me.

Valentine's Day? Did Mona Hawkins have a Valentine? Stranger things have happened, i.e., my life. But Mona. Mona's romantic dinner date would be the dinner itself. I have seen the woman undress a guinea hen with her eyes. True, she lusted after some men, but they were only a fantasy. I think she may have actually gotten off on food.

But even a nine-course tasting menu at Jean Georges could not have inspired her to let her minions leave early for the day. She was never generous. She never even wanted to *appear* generous. No, Mona wanted the office empty for some reason. But what reason?

She must have been meeting someone there.

But who? Surely not a lover. If there were such a tasteless individual, he would have met her in her home. Maybe he was an actor trying to seduce her for a job. Better to send her a tin of assorted mini muffins than to arrange a rendezvous. No, there was some kind of meeting. And the police, who didn't know Mona, don't find it odd that she had emptied out her office. Of course it makes sense to let everyone out early on Valentine's Day—if you have a heart.

Mona was meeting someone and she didn't want anybody to know.

We have to go to Mona's office.

I tiptoe into Charlie's room, immediately feeling bad about waking him.

Charlie's bedroom is huge. I've been inside it a handful of times, mindful that we don't share the same property rights here. His room is bigger than my room—his living room, I mean. It could use a little work, though. And though the living room may not be featured in *Architectural Digest,* its homey combination of academic and personal clutter is endearing. His bedroom, however, is positively austere. The bed is right next to the door, and across the room are two enormous windows, which lack any treatment whatsoever. The rest of the room is filled with dead air.

"Did your ex-girlfriend take the window dressing with her?" I will ask him after we get engaged.

On the wall adjacent to the bed is a huge fireplace. Charlie uses it for storing clothing; my guess is that it is laundry because Charlie has not done any since I moved in. I grab a shirt from the pile. Without thinking, I bring it to my face. It smells like Charlie.

I hear a little mumble from the bed. Charlie is turning over in his sleep. I smell his shirt again, and I'm tempted to crawl into the bed with him. There are sounds coming from across the alley. They're loud enough for me to detect music of a sort, but too soft to determine any specific tune. I take in a deep breath, accidentally inhaling Charlie's scent from his shirt.

I love this moment.

How crazy am I?

"Walter?" I whisper.

Nothing.

"Walter?" A little louder.

"Hmmmm?"

"Walter. It's me, Alice."

"Alice." Charlie is whispering my name.

"Can you help me?"

"Come to bed, Alice."

Come to bed?

Charlie's eyes are closed. Is he asleep? I lean into the bed to see if he's awake, and Charlie grabs my waist and pulls me on top of him, our legs entwined.

We are kissing.

I can't believe this. My lifelong dream is happening as I am on the precipice of prison.

"God, I've been wanting this," he whispers in my ear.

I know I should stop. Time is running out. Boy, can he kiss.

"I . . ." I start to say, but Charlie is kissing my earlobe.

"We have to . . ."

What is it we have to do again?

He pulls me in closer.

"Walter. I am sorry to do this, but I need you to help me."

He's still kissing me. I have been waiting my entire adult life for this moment, and it's happening. I guess I could have this one night with him before I get carted off to prison. At least I'll have memories. My arms go around him as he holds me closer still. His mouth is doing something magical to my neck as his knee comes between my legs.

Then, the thought of eternal confinement endows me with a large dose of reality.

I get up abruptly.

"We don't have to do this," Charlie says. His chest is bare and he is gently holding my leg. I must have pulled his shirt off.

"Oh, no," I tell him. I'm staring at his shoulders. They're lean and muscled, like a swimmer's. "I want to do this." More than you possibly know. "But we need to go to Mona's office."

"Mona's office." Charlie repeats this robotically.

"Yes." I touch his leg. "I'm really sorry. But we have to go check out Mona's office to see if the killer left any sorts of clues."

"Alice," Charlie is fully awake now, "we both saw the same news report. They said the killer left no clues."

"Let me explain something to you." I'm sitting up but taking care not to move my leg, lest Charlie remove his hand. "A. The news gets everything wrong. B. The police think I'm the killer and they might not be looking for the right stuff. And C, I know the Mona Hawkins Casting office better than any cop."

Charlie gets up. He grabs a pair of corduroys from the clothing tower and pulls them over his pajamas. He sees me looking at him.

"It's cold out. Okay?"

I don't say anything.

"Well?" he asks.

"Well what?"

"Is that what you're going to wear to the crime scene?"

I take a look at myself. I'm still wearing Charlie's pajama top. It is fully unbuttoned, and I am suddenly self-conscious. I run out of the room speaking loudly about the importance of hurrying.

We're two blocks away from Mona's office. Nineteenth and Sixth. There's going to be a security detail there but Charlie tells me that he doesn't think there will be more than one or two officers.

"Are you sure?" I whispered to him in the cab downtown. I know there is evidence in Mona's office, and I have to get it before the police mess up the investigation. Or the killer plants more incriminating evidence against me.

"I'm not sure, but it seems they have an idea that this is about revenge and not about robbery. So, the police may not stay on location for too long."

Add that to the fact that it is 3:15 in the morning and their resources may be thin.

Charlie and I discuss our plan. He'll distract the cops and I'll get into Mona's office.

"I feel like we're in an episode of *I Love Lucy*," Charlie tells me. It's probably his only TV reference point—especially since we didn't even get through an entire installment of *Law & Order*.

"Did they ever have an episode where Lucy gets the chair?" I ask.

"No. And lucky for you, the death penalty was imposed a lot more in New York during that time than it is now."

"That's cheery," I tell him.

Charlie grabs my upper arm and looks me in the eye. He holds my gaze for an extra second.

He pities me. He loves me. He pities me. He loves me. He pities me. He pities me.

I gently pull his hand off my arm. "We should get moving."

"So, it's as we discussed?"

"As we discussed," I say.

Charlie hands me his keys and his wallet, and turns to leave.

"Wait," I tell him.

"What?"

"This." I run my hands through his hair for a second before I move it around a bit.

"I wanna rough you up a little."

"You're right," Charlie says, his voice coarser than usual. "Maybe we should make it look more authentic."

And I can't figure out quite how he does it, but Charlie falls to the ground.

What I hear next is a cross between a groan and a cry.

"What happened? Are you okay?"

I can't see anything because it's so dark. Charlie moves into the light of a streetlamp and I can see that his forehead is bleeding. He shows me the heel of his hand and there is a pretty substantial gash and three small scratches. I'm about to tell him that we should call the whole thing off, when I see that he's smiling.

"There," he tells me.

"What have I done? I've turned this sweet straitlaced lawyer into a con artist."

"No, the folks at Kelt Pharmaceuticals did that."

I'm brought back to reality. Charlie isn't flagellating himself for me; we made a deal. He gets the cops off my back and I help his father. His father who drowns his pain from his wife's death by frequenting hookers.

"Go to it," I tell him.

And Charlie runs off. I hear him from afar seconds later.

"Help! Help! Help! Please! Is there a police officer around here? Somebody, help!"

I can hear voices but I can't make out the words. It's most likely the cops that are guarding Mona's town house. They've rushed to help Charlie. Charlie's telling them that he was mugged. They took his wallet and his keys. He describes the mugger. A Russian guy, he thinks. Some sort of Eastern European accent. Charlie tells the police that he's okay. That not much money was involved, but that he's spooked. The guy has his keys. The cops take his statement and are kind to him. Charlie told me that they'll discourage him from pressing charges.

"It keeps the crime rates low. The police try to convince you not to report anything. They especially discourage it if they think they're not going to solve the crime," Charlie told me in the cab just minutes ago.

"Are you sure? That seems so wrong."

"Only to the extent that Kovitz was telling me the truth."

Kovitz. Mr. Reliable. The one who suspected me, and the one who couldn't effectively keep me off the streets. Let's hope he has gotten this one right, otherwise poor Charlie is going to have to go to the precinct.

As Charlie leads the officers away from the town house, I creep up slowly. They've left their post completely, and there's a field of supposedly vacant space surrounding the entrance. I rush to the door. I don't have the key anymore; Mona made me hand it to her the day she fired me. As if I'd come back to the place.

As if.

Mona was short-sighted, though. She forgot that intimate knowledge of her nighttime alarm system trumped the key. Basically, she just didn't want me to come in while she was there. I know that she would never have changed the security code. I press it: 276119. That is, 276 standing for her former weight and 119 standing for her current one. Or should I say, current as of about nine and a half hours ago? The alarm is now off, and the door is unlocked. I go in. There's police tape all over the place. The reception area is filled with it. Is this where Mona was killed? I walk by the reception area—my old desk. I look at it. There is a note in Mona's awful handwriting.

> *Jane,*
>
>   *Make sure you remove the menus off the ring binders that are closed.*

Did I mention that Mona has—had—the worst grammar on the planet? The note is written on a pad of paper that says A DOG'S LOVE IS PAWSOME.

Obviously Jane's.

I snoop around Jane's desk. There's a picture of her—I recognize her from the news—with her boyfriend, I presume. He has his arm around her. They look as if they are attending a theme banquet at a beach resort: many tan people in hats, and Jane and the boyfriend are holding up drinks with umbrellas in them.

Mona's office door is closed and there is police tape tied in a bow around the doorknob. But the door's not locked. I open it. I'm wearing Charlie's gloves. The office looks as it always does. There are pictures of Mona covering the walls. Mona with Tom Cruise. Mona with Michael Douglas. Mona with a variety of soap opera stars. I see that Mona has added a picture of Preston Hayes to her wall. Too bad she didn't live long enough to know that he's hot and heavy with my best friend. That's not bad revenge.

Although killing her makes more of a statement.

But I didn't kill her. And I don't even know if her killer wanted revenge. A restaurant strike would be more effective.

The ring binder with the menus sits on her desk. There is an e-mail from Will Smith. It looks as if he was checking out her availability to cast his next movie. "I'll make the availability," I can hear Mona saying. "For Will-icious Smith, I'm always available."

From the looks of things, it seems that she was stabbed in the hallway. But why the tape on the door? I check it a little more carefully. Maybe she and the killer spent some time in there before they went into the reception area. Maybe she was stabbed here and dragged there. Maybe the killer wanted something from the office. I give it another look just to make sure. Everything seems normal to me.

Mona's file cabinet is opened slightly. This raises a red flag for me because Mona wasn't one to use the file cabinet with any regularity. Everything is on the desk; the file cabinet is more of an archive. I doubt that Mona herself was dealing with any of her stuff. She considered that to be a summer project. She'd get an intern from NYU film school to file all of her papers for free. The intern's job was pretty easy. The films were alphabetically filed and all Mona kept were copies of pictures of attractive male actors who had auditioned and any clippings praising the casting of a given film.

The interns were instructed to stay away from a large accordion file tucked away behind the *XYZ* files. This instruction was easy to follow, as the file was overstuffed and messy. I was always tempted to check out the file. We all used to speculate on what was in it. Jed Rausch, mourner extraordinaire, swore that it was related to Mona's work in gay porn. But he never had any substantial evidence. It's more likely filled with old restaurant menus. The whole gay porn rumor seemed a little far-fetched to me. Why would a gay porn producer go into legit films and why would she go into casting? Why not production or direction? Something with more power. On the other hand, Mona does enjoy looking at men. And she really preferred looking at the straight ones. Maybe she actually thought she had a chance with them. I recall her looking at Thom Reuter when he came into our office.

"Delicious," she whispered to herself, and licked her lips. Did Mona think that Thom could possibly have been interested in her?

I look across the room at Mona's couch. A casting couch? No way. I don't see it. These guys flirted. They all did. I remember Preston, for example, bringing Mona roses right before his screen test. They all did things like that. Roses and teddy bears. The really smart ones brought food. But the women did it, too. No, Mona did not sleep with these guys.

And I refuse to believe Ian-sex-addict-Leighton was any different.

I go through the files to see if anything is out of order. The most recent intern did a great job. Liam was his name. He was incredibly organized. I think he ironed the wrinkled papers. Everything from *A* to *E* looks good. I keep going. It's taking me longer because I'm wearing gloves. The last thing I need is a paper cut with my DNA-filled blood seeping onto the dead woman's files. *F–L* looks good. I wonder what'll be done with these files now that Mona is gone. What will be done with her office? She had no family. No loved ones. No friends even. She just had these people whom she simultaneously air kissed and back stabbed. *M–R* looks untouched. Just the way it was last summer before I was dismissed. Will there even be a funeral for Mona?

I think of Polly's funeral. All the people who went, even

though she was so flawed. But Polly had a husband. She had lovers. I think of Charlie's dad and his dead wife. She has a waterfall. There's definitely not going to be a waterfall for Mona. Everything looks good until Z. I stick my arm in behind the Z file.

The accordion file is missing.

I'm back at Charlie's house. He hasn't returned yet. I cross my fingers, hoping that our little plan hasn't backfired. I need to talk to him about the accordion file. It's missing. Or at least I think it is. I mean, I have not been back at that office for four months now. Mona may've taken it home with her or she may have thrown it away. But it's suspicious. I pause to think about our assessment of Polly's murderer. Charlie, Jean, and I have been assuming that it was one of Polly's lovers. But why would one of Polly's lovers kill Mona Hawkins? Could the answer lie in the missing accordion file? Could Mona and Polly have known a sinister secret about one of the actors—either in *Only at Sunrise* or some other Humphrey Dawson movie?

Even though it's after four in the morning, I'm hungry. I go into the kitchen to prepare myself a little snack, and I see the mostly uneaten cupcakes on the counter. I think I had eaten just one bite when I learned that Mona was dead.

She would've been proud. I only had a taste.

I clean up the mess in the kitchen. Maybe I should make Charlie some scrambled eggs when he gets home. If he gets home. What if Kovitz was staking out Mona's office and then he sees Charlie? Suddenly, the casual inquiries about Polly's death might not look so casual when he shows up right next to a related murder scene.

Charlie is risking a lot for this. Not for me, I have to keep reminding myself. But for his father. We made a deal. Charlie's the guy who lives up to his end of the bargain.

Not me.

I wish there was some other explanation for William riding in a livery cab with a hooker. But I know there isn't.

I have to tell Charlie.

Charlie is home. I can hear the door downstairs. I'm afraid for a second that it's the cops, that Charlie is locked up downtown and he told them that they could find their fugitive here. But no. I can tell by the footsteps on the stairs. Charlie walks up four steps really fast and then pauses before getting to the fifth stair. Then he goes four steps fast again. He opens the door.

"Mission accomplished?" he asks.

"Mission accomplished."

I look at Charlie. The left side of his face is covered in blood and dirt. His shirt is ripped. He smells like smoke and BO. Someone else's. The pockets of his pants are inside out and hanging. Despite this, I want to hug him, to thank him for doing this and to protect him from the news I'm about to tell him about his father.

"Sorry I took so long," he says.

Sorry he took so long. The guy just risked his life. Okay, maybe not his life, but his freedom, his dignity, and comfort for me.

"But . . ."

I realize he is still talking.

"I realize that I wasn't able to come through on the Valentine's Day gift: watching TV with you. So I got you these."

Charlie steps inside his front door and hands me five roses.

"The cop couldn't leave his detail, and I didn't want to file an official report. So he loaned me ten dollars for a cab home. I walked. And then I was able to buy you these. Not exactly a dozen, but I figure you've been here five weeks and there's one rose for each week."

He walked home. He walked from Nineteenth and Sixth to

Sixty-fifth and Lexington. That's almost three miles in the middle of the night.

"Wow." I'm not much for extemporaneous speaking.

"Maybe I'll take a shower," he tells me. Then he kisses me. It lasts about a minute and a half. Then he walks toward his room.

"Okay." I'm still stunned. I think my eyes are tearing, but I don't want to check.

"Is it all right with you if I go straight to bed?" he asks. "I mean, sleep. I'm dead on my feet." He sounds sincerely sorry about this. "Tomorrow," he adds.

I nod. I've been waiting for this for years. I can go a few more hours.

Charlie goes into his bedroom. I take a glass out of the kitchen to put the flowers in, as there is no vase in sight. When do I tell him about his father? If I do it now, it'll kill him. Not right now. Tomorrow.

For tonight—despite the murder, the break-in, and Charlie's injuries—has been perfect.

I can hear Charlie in the bathroom. He's singing something. From the living room, I whisper, "I love you and I'm sorry."

Jean calls first thing in the morning. Charlie is still asleep.

"He told me he loves me," she screams after I answer the phone.

"Isn't it a little soon?" I ask, trying not to sound judgmental.

"He said that, too," she tells me. "I was where you are, Alice. I was thinking that there's no way that this guy loves me. I told him that. He said he was dealing with a lot of loss. That all he used to think about was being famous and being a star. That he didn't have time for love and all of that. But now that he has a taste of his dream, he realizes that it's empty. That you 'don't die with your Oscar.' He loves that I'm not in show business and that I'm a boring corporate lawyer . . ."

I want to ask Jean if she slept with him, but I can't because Charlie might have woken up. For that matter I want to tell her about the flowers.

"You'll never guess what happened last night." It's my turn to give her some news.

She beats me to it.

"Mona Hawkins was murdered."

"How—?"

"Preston told me. I think that was why he told me he loved me. He was so overcome with emotion. I mean, it's just so creepy. The casting person for his movie and the wife of the director of his movie are murdered. No wonder he wants to be with an outsider."

"I know how he feels." I sense that Jean is so caught up with Preston that she has lost sight of my perilous position.

"Yeah," she sighs.

"They think I did it."

"They do? How do you know?"

"The TV, the Internet, I imagine the newspaper."

"Oh. Alice, I'm so sorry. We were at this party all night. No TVs or anything. It was like we were cut off from reality. Preston didn't even have his cell phone. And I just got into work, I haven't even logged on to my computer. Tell me everything."

So I tell Jean about the break-in.

"And how was Valentine's Day?" Jean asks.

Of course I want to report to Jean my developments of last night: the fallen cupcakes, the *Law & Order*, and the kiss. But Charlie could hear us.

"Uh-huh," I say.

"Oh, is Charlie there?" she asks me.

"Uh-huh," I repeat. "Wait, how did Preston know that Mona was killed when you guys were so cut off from reality?"

"That's the difference between people like us and people like Preston. They always have ways of finding this stuff out. Is the Charlie thing good?" she asks me.

"Yes. Except for the fact that they now think I've committed two murders instead of one."

"I know, honey, but as Preston says, the truth will come out."

Preston said what?

"In what context?" I ask Jean.

"I'm hoping you don't mind, but I kind of told him about your situation. I didn't go into detail. I just said that I had a friend that the police were talking to."

Mind? Of course I mind.

"Jean? Are you insane?"

"Alice, we can trust Preston. Remember, he's been giving us information about Polly. And now he can give us information about Mona. He's so on our side. He told me she was dead, basically, before he said hello."

I don't trust anybody.

"Jean. The information he gave us about Polly was wrong."

"It was a little wrong, but then when I told him about you and how it was important to *me* that we set the record straight he told me that his number-one priority was helping *me,* that means *you, Alice,* out."

"Jean. I can't believe you didn't consult with me on this."

"And I can't believe you're angry with me. I am trying to help you. Charlie's about one hooker allegation away from landing in a mental institution, and you're just sitting there wide-eyed, watching him, while I'm out investigating. You should thank me for gaining Preston's respect. He's our ticket out of this thing."

"It doesn't matter if Preston is helping us. I pulled you into this under strict confidence, and now you're confiding in some actor you don't even know."

"What? You've confided way more in Charlie. And you told me yourself he's best friends with that Kovitz. He may be setting you up."

Best friends with Kovitz. Jean is prone to exaggeration. Not to mention I can't believe she betrayed me.

"No wonder you don't practice criminal law," I tell my best friend, "you don't know how to keep your trap shut."

"At least I don't sit and judge anyone who tries to help me without moving forward with my life. Maybe you can sit and play house with Charlie instead of having a real relationship with him."

"Oh, and you have a real relationship with Preston? Why, because he takes you to a glamorous party at the last minute? Oh, and that part about how he loves you. He's an actor, Jean. Actors tell everyone they love them—read Lee Strasberg."

"You asked for my help, Alice, and now you don't want it. Why? For the same reason you can't stick with anything: therapy, jobs. Limbo is your heaven, Alice."

Jean hangs up the phone. I can't tell if she has slammed it or not. I want to call her back and slam the phone. How dare she? She violates my confidence and then basically condemns me for a situation in which I'm the complete victim. She knows she was wrong to have told Preston. Instead of admitting her error, she took the immature path of attacking me. She wants to protect this new "relationship." A relationship that is three weeks and six dates old, with an "I love you" and maybe some fooling around. She's willing to trade in her best friend for that.

Well, she's either really lonely or she really doesn't care about me.

"Everything okay?" Charlie is indeed awake.

I don't tell him that Jean has told Preston. I'm afraid that he's going to ask if he can confide in someone, too.

"Yeah. It's just a little tense."

"You're telling me," Charlie says, and he heads back into his bedroom. I think about what Jean has said, that Charlie was a foolish choice for a confidant. She thinks I picked Charlie because of an old crush. She's got to be kidding. Charlie was the only person I knew who had any connection to Kovitz, the man who arrested me. And, even though I didn't really know Charlie, I've overseen the general trajectory of his character for years. Jean has known Preston Hayes for a minute.

And now she has blabbed to him. Who knows what Preston Hayes will do with this information? He may dump Jean and fall in love with a lady cop and tell her. Or he may spill to a reporter or a friend. The point is, my secret is out. Jean has put me in jeopardy. And now Charlie is potentially in trouble, too. After all, he has been harboring me. Jean should be looking after herself, too. She has withheld vital information from the cops. Even I know that, and I didn't go to law school.

Charlie comes back into the living room. He's showered and looks more relaxed than he has since I moved in, despite the bruises and scrapes on his head. He's wearing a bathrobe. I look at my own outfit: It's an old Charlie shirt. I've been sleeping in it since I got here.

"What's our plan?" Charlie asks me, pulling me into a hug.

I don't know. I don't tell him about Jean. Even though I'm angry with her, I feel the need to protect her.

"Well?" he says.

"I'm thinking," I tell him.

And I am. About what Jean said. That my trust in Charlie is based on an unrequited, immature, and stale crush.

I back out of the hug and head toward the bathroom.

"I'm going to do some stuff," I tell Charlie. "You can call Kovitz or something."

I don't look back at him, but I sense that he's hurt and maybe a bit confused.

"You're the boss," he tells me.

I'm outside.

Charlie thinks I am on a mission either to help his father or to do some work on my own situation. I just needed to leave his house and clear my head. To mull over my friend's stinging comments without trying to be a polite houseguest. And whatever romantic thoughts I may have been entertaining about Charlie must be quashed. Charlie is a means to an end for now, the end being my freedom. The day I am exonerated and Jean apologizes to me is the day I renew my crush.

I'm outside to think. How dare she? How dare she take away that fun little fantasy I've been having while my life is a mess.

Now I have to deal with reality.

I don't want to.

Urgh.

It's time to tell Charlie about his father.

I run back to the apartment.

I turn the key in his lock and push the door open with intensity.

"I need to tell you somethi—" I start to say, but I realize that Charlie's not alone. Standing in his living room holding a cup of coffee in one hand and a half-eaten cupcake in the other is William Redwin.

"Hi," I say.

"Hello?" William stops there.

I don't say anything. Charlie rescues me.

"Dad, this is my friend Alice from college. We're working on a project together."

I take off my coat. I'm wearing Charlie's shirt.

"What kind of project?" he asks, slightly amused. He's not going to mention our "date."

"A legal thing," I say, trying to sound professional.

"Are you a lawyer?" William asks me.

"No, I am a—" Charlie cuts me off.

"She's my research assistant."

"I didn't know lawyers had research assistants." William winks at me. This is too uncomfortable.

"We're working on a special project."

"Oh," William says, as he looks at his OOPS cupcake.

I smile awkwardly.

"You look familiar," William says. Is he enjoying himself?

"A lot of people say that," I say.

Nobody says it. I wonder if he knows that his "delightful" blind date is a potential murderess, or at the very least, has witnessed his secret life.

"I have one of those faces," I add.

Charlie cuts in. "Dad, what are you doing with your time? I worry about you when there's no structure."

"This and that," William says. I guess he doesn't even tell his son about the visits to Sloan-Kettering.

"Maybe you should take a trip or something. Then when you get your job back, you'll be relaxed from a nice vacation."

"I may not get my job back," William says.

"Dad. This thing will blow over."

"It may not blow over," William says.

"Dad. I don't want you to give up. I haven't," Charlie tells him.

"You need to be realistic, Walter."

"I'm being realistic. These women are going to start feeling guilty about lying, and then they'll recant and you can sue Kelt Pharmaceuticals to get your job back."

"They may not recant," William says.

"They will," Charlie says. He is determined.

William doesn't say anything. Instead, he turns to me.

"Tell me about yourself, Alice. It is Alice, isn't it?"

"Alice is a great cook," Charlie says.

"Oh. That's always a plus," William says.

"Shall I go into the kitchen and whip something up?" I need to escape.

"No thanks. I just had something."

"How about a drink, Dad?" Charlie says.

"No thanks."

"Water?"

"No thanks." William is not listening. He's staring into space.

"So what kind of research are you guys doing?" William asks Charlie. He thinks we're a couple. He thinks Charlie isn't telling him for some reason.

Charlie doesn't answer right away, so I interrupt.

"New York," I tell him. "We're researching New York."

"What for?" William asks.

I'm stumped. Charlie looks at me, though, giving me permission to say whatever I please.

"We're preparing a pamphlet about New York neighborhoods for new businesses," I say, thinking I can probably remember a few things I wrote at K.I.N.D.

"I didn't know you knew anything about that, Walter."

"He didn't at first," I said, "but I've been helping him learn."

"I thought you said she was your research assistant," William says to Charlie. Why doesn't he just say he knows we're lying?

"She is. She knows more about these kinds of books, but I have the legal expertise for start-up companies." Charlie's body language is way too uncomfortable for the casual conversation we need to present.

"You're a litigator," William says.

"For companies, Dad."

William seems to drop it. But I notice he's looking at me. I know he's trying to communicate something, but either he can't or I'm illiterate.

"Dad?" Charlie says.

William's not listening. He is looking at me.

"Dad?"

Nothing.

"Dad, are you okay?"

"Of course I'm okay." William gives me a little smile—I think.

"Maybe I should leave you guys alone for a bit," I say. "I'm going to go do some research."

"What'll you do?" William asks me. He knows I'm in trouble. He must've seen it on the news.

"It's a book about New York. We're in New York. I'll walk around."

Charlie doesn't stop me.

I want to go home. And I don't mean Fifty-fifth Street. I mean to Mother's house. I don't care if Barnes lives there. Seeing Charlie with William reminds me how I miss my own flawed parent.

And, for the first time, I feel bad about following Polly. I still don't like her—didn't like her. But who am I—who was I to invade her privacy? She didn't invite me to watch her every move, listen to her conversations, and monitor her purchases. Yet I derived parasitic pleasure from gluing myself to every detail of her life. It would make me sick to receive that kind of attention.

Maybe I deserve to be punished. Polly wasn't a good person, but my actions were inexcusable.

However, I didn't kill her.

I'm ten blocks away from Mother's house. It's Wednesday, and Barnes will most likely be at Chelsea Piers playing golf. He never misses a golf appointment. His wife's kid is a fugitive from justice and I can guarantee you his score has not changed. Mother will probably be at her ballet class. She's religious about her ballet.

"It's gotten me through a lot of painful times," she has told Barnes and me. Even he can't coax her into missing a class.

Sophie is probably upstairs; that is, if Barnes hasn't driven her out with his bigotry. I smile as I think back on the first day I met Sophie. I had come by Mother's to pick up a check from her. This was when I was working at K.I.N.D. for free. Barnes was angry with Sophie because she had put his dress shirts in the wrong closet.

"I have made it clear to you, have I not, that my dress shirts go in my dress closet. They do not go in the closet with my casual clothes."

"I am sorry, Mr. Newlan." Sophie was genuinely apologetic, as this was her first transgression.

"Need I draw you a map, Sophie, of the proper dwelling for each article of clothing?"

"Dwelling, sir?" Sophie couldn't understand Barnes's singular style of speech.

Barnes looked at Sophie, trying to assess her question.

"Are you mocking me, Sophie? Please don't mock me."

Sophie didn't say anything. I think, like me, she was trying to stifle a laugh. Barnes sensed this.

"Sophie." Barnes is at his most condescending when he overuses a person's name. "I am really trying to help you, to teach you. Isn't that why you left Puerto Rico in the first place, so that you could have a better life here in our country?"

"Yes, sir," Sophie said.

"I guess your 'teacher' needs to be taught that Puerto Rico is part of the United States," I whispered to Sophie.

"He needs to feel like he's king of the castle," Sophie said.

"I think you mean king of the dwelling," I corrected her.

The problem is that I have to get past two doormen and anyone else who might be lingering in the lobby. What do I say to them? Hey guys. I bet the cops have told you that if I come around here, you're supposed to call them, but I've always been amiable—sort of—and I didn't murder Polly or Mona. I was framed. So if you could just let me go upstairs and see Mother and refrain from calling the cops, I'd be ever so grateful.

I don't think so.

I have an idea. I am at the corner of Eighty-third and Madison. And I've finally found a working pay phone. I dial Mother's house.

It's ringing.

"Hello, Newlan residence." It's Sophie.

I hold my nose. "May I speak with Sophia Marino, please?"

"This is Sophia Marino."

"This is Edna Applebaum from the INS, that is, the Immigration and Naturalization Services."

Sophie pauses for a moment. "Yes."

"We're calling to inform you that one of your people is down here. Could you come get her? She says it's a little cold. Could you bring a shawl?"

"I'll come right away, Ms. A-Applebaum."

"Good. We are on the eighty-third floor."

Now I know there is no eighty-third floor in the Jacob Javits building. And I'm hoping that Sophie knows that, too. She's no dummy. I'm sure she picked up my hint, as we have been joking about her immigration status ever since Barnes lectured her. Unfazed by trash, I pick up a *New York Post* from the street and hold it up to my face as I wait for Sophie and her shawl.

I stay on Eighty-third and Madison. And I wait.

There she is trotting toward me with a shawl and a little bag. We greet each other enthusiastically but quietly.

"Thank you for coming. I was hoping you wouldn't tell the police."

"Why would I tell the police, Ms. Alice? I might get deported." We both burst into laughter.

"Here. I brought you something from your mother's closet." Sophie reaches into the bag and pulls out one of Mother's old wigs. Good thinking, Sophie, I left my blond wig at Charlie's house. I put the wig on. I put the shawl over my coat and make it look like a really big scarf. I walk back to the house with Sophie.

I'm in Mother's kitchen drinking hot chocolate and reading an old issue of *Vanity Fair* when I hear the door open.

"Anyone home?"

It's Barnes.

"Just me, Mr. Newlan."

I hide in Mother's laundry room. Barnes never goes in there.

"Is my wife back yet?"

Obviously he wasn't listening.

"No, Mr. Newlan. Just me."

"Any calls?"

"No, Mr. Newlan. No calls."

"I see on the caller ID that someone called about twenty

minutes ago. I thought you said there were no calls, Sophie."
Barnes's tone is professorial.

"That was a wrong number, Mr. Newlan."

"Sophie. When I ask you if someone called, you have to tell
me, 'Yes, Mr. Barnes, someone did call, but it was the wrong
number.' When you say that no one called and someone clearly
did call, that is not an answer that is completely forthcoming."

No response.

"Well?"

"Yes, Mr. Newlan. There was a call, but it was the wrong
number."

Just so you know, Barnes is not interrogating Sophie like this
because he thinks *I* might have called. The man is a control
freak.

"Sophie, when you are ready, I will have my lunch."

"Yes, Mr. Newlan." I listen as Sophie prepares Barnes's standard lunch. It's tuna with low-fat mayonnaise on whole wheat
bread with a small bag of baked potato chips and a Red Delicious
apple.

I try to think of a game plan. How will I speak to Mother if
Barnes is at home? He's sure to call the cops right away.

"Sophie."

"Yes, Mr. Newlan."

"This apple isn't as shiny as usual."

"Yes, Mr. Newlan." I imagine that Sophie is heading over to
his lunch table and shining the apple for him. I'm hoping that
she uses her spit to give it that extra shine.

"Sophie, do you know when my wife will return?"

"She should return very soon."

"Sophie, I don't want you to think I was simply scolding you
before. I was trying to impart to you the importance of being
precise. I'm sure that your intentions were honest when you told
me that there were no calls, but you were incorrect and impre-

cise. If you ever want to advance yourself in our country, you have to be more precise."

Barnes often gives Sophie advice on how she can "advance" in this country. Usually it relates to completing a menial task for him.

"Yes, Mr. Newlan."

Mother will be coming home shortly. The question to ask is, when will Barnes leave again? Sophie comes into the laundry room. I make an obscene gesture in Barnes's general direction, and Sophie chuckles.

"Sophie."

"Yes, Mr. Newlan," she calls from the laundry room.

"Were you speaking to me?"

"No, Mr. Newlan. I was not."

"Oh. I thought I heard something."

"You did, Mr. Newlan."

To be precise, you heard a chuckle, I want to add.

"Everything all right in there?"

"Yes, Mr. Newlan." I mouth it as Sophie says it.

"You know I don't like to be disturbed during my lunch."

Funny, I think, because you are inviting disturbance.

"I understand, Mr. Newlan."

The front door opens. "Hello, hello, hello!"

It's Mother.

"I'm back, my darling."

Mother seems distraught.

"Anything?"

"Yes. Angel. Sophie took one call. She failed to mention it to me at first, but after I taught her the importance of precision, she was able to inform me that it was a wrong number."

"Barnes. It could have been Alice." Mother starts shuffling about.

"Sophie would recognize Alice's voice. Would you not, Sophie?"

Would you not?

Before Sophie has a chance to answer, Mother interrupts.

"It must have been Alice. She may be trying to convey a message to us. She may be in trouble."

"Angel, Alice will contact us when she is ready to face the consequences of her actions. She's probably doing some long and hard soul searching."

Little does he know, I'm doing it in his laundry room.

"I just hope she's all right," Mother says.

"Of course she's all right. We would get a call if there were something wrong. Maybe we should try to take your mind off of all of this. Maybe we could go on a vacation. I've been dying to try that new place on St. Kitts."

"I'm not going on a vacation while my daughter is missing."

Thank you, Mother!

"Angela. Try not to be so dramatic."

It was a mistake to come here.

I'm on my way back to Charlie's house. This is the second time I have run back to him today. I imagine his visit with his father will have ended. I can't wait to tell him about Barnes's most recent lecture to Sophie. Charlie calls him Lord Ridiculous.

I walk in the door. I was right. William isn't here. But Charlie is. He's sitting on the couch. I like to think of him as sitting on my bed. It seems more intimate. I realize that except for our *Law & Order* date last night, Charlie hasn't sat here since I've been staying in the apartment. Maybe his visit with his father has pushed him to confront his feelings for me. Maybe his father has seen that we should be a couple together and told him that we should move this relationship forward.

I'm not sure I want this. I mean, maybe I've loved Charlie all of those years because he was unavailable and maybe my feelings for him have intensified these last few weeks because he's the only person who knows the truth. Well, Jean knows, but she betrayed me. But Charlie has been helpful and warm, and re-spectful and lovi—

"Alice, we need to talk."

Here it is. He's about to confront me. There's going to be a long declaration on his part. Then I will have to say a few words. Like I have always loved you, too; I have never before felt this way. Or something more mysterious like I know. I know. I know. Then we'll kiss.

"Alice, I have to have a frank conversation with you."

Here goes.

"I need you to answer me honestly."

Oh, no. He is putting it on me. I have to declare my love for him before he does. Maybe it's all for the best. Maybe I've finally learned that it's good to take risks.

"Are you asking me to say what I think you are asking me to say?" My voice almost doesn't sound familiar. It's all husky.

"I'm asking you to be honest with me, Alice." Charlie's voice sounds the same as it always does.

Here I go, I love you I love you I love you. I've always loved you. Loved you loved you.

But it doesn't come out. Charlie is speaking.

"Alice. My father told me that what they say is true."

What who says? That I'm a killer?

"That he's been paying these girls."

I'm not sure how to react. Do I console him?

"At least you know," I say to him meekly.

"I wish I had known sooner," he says.

I don't say anything.

"If I had known sooner, I could have helped him. Really helped him. Saved his job, and saved my job. And his reputa-tion."

And your reputation, I think to myself.

"Maybe he wanted to protect you."

"From what?"

"From knowing that he's flawed. He doesn't want to admit that he has some kind of problem. He was probably really lonely after your mother died and he couldn't have a real relationship with a wom—"

"No, Alice, that's not it."

It is it, Charlie. This is why your father kept it from you.

I don't say anything.

"Alice, you followed my father. You knew he was seeing these girls. I asked you to follow *them,* only them, to get dirt on them, but you didn't trust me and you went after him. My father told me. He recognized you. And you know how he recognized you? Not just because of your recent notoriety but also because you and my father know each other. Apparently, you went out on a date. You went out with my father and didn't tell me."

"I wouldn't call it a date . . ."

Since when does a meeting with a mutual lack of interest become dating? Under that definition, Charlie and I have been involved in an intense affair.

Charlie ignores me.

"We were mutually uninterested. He was obviously mourning your moth—"

"Don't say anything about how he mourned my mother. I will tell you how he mourned my mother."

Charlie has tears in his eyes.

"Emily, my mother, was a social worker. She worked right up until she was so sick she couldn't move. For the last eight years of her life, she had been helping girls in trouble. For the most part, they were prostitutes. Most of them had been abused or were drug addicts, and my mom helped them to transition out of their careers. For many, the change was easy. For others, it didn't

work. My mother had been working with Rosalie, Doreen, La-
Donna, Trini, Carly, Justine, and Charisse and Oxanna right until
the very end. And, for various reasons, they couldn't make the
transition. She couldn't get them to quit. When she knew she
was dying, she told my father that her greatest regret was that
she had failed these women. My father promised her that he
would do it for her. He would do whatever it took.

"Then my mother died, and my father was devastated, but he
kept going. And he decided he was going to carry out my mother's
last wish. He collected her files and sought out these women. He
obviously couldn't communicate with them the way my mother
had, but he went out with them. He paid them. He paid them to
talk to him. There was no sex.

"He paid them a lot. And, as the police reports said, he got
them appliances. The police reports failed to mention that he
also got them books and job applications. He even helped
Trini, Justine, and Oxanna to get their GEDs. He ultimately told
each of the women who he really was and why he was doing
all this.

"This was all happening while he was being investigated, but
he didn't care. He had made the promise to my mother, and he
was going to see it through even if he went to jail. He was afraid
that if he told the police what he was doing, they would throw
the girls in jail."

"But why did the girls rat on him? He was helping them."

"They were scared. They were accepting his money, and they
thought that if Murch found out they were taking the money
without providing any services, she'd have her thugs take it all.
Murch was tough on them."

So Henrietta Murch *was* dirty!

"Why did he tell you this now?"

"He wanted to wait until everyone had quit the business and
they were safe. LaDonna was the holdout, but she has finally

quit. She's moving to Washington to be with her aunt. Now that they're all safe from Murch, he's told the police the entire story. He would have kept silent forever, but he realized what this was doing to me."

"Wow," I say, "your father is a hero."

"You say that now," Charlie accuses.

"I'm not sure what you—"

"What? You're not sure what I mean? You saw my father with these women. He saw you outside his apartment. He saw you when he was on one of his 'excursions.' He didn't know why you were stalking him. He thought maybe you were in love with him and couldn't take rejection. He saw you, Alice, at the hospital where my mother died. I can't believe you fucking followed him to the hospital where my mother died."

William noticed me.

"When he was convinced that you weren't a stalker, he thought you were coming to him for help. He knew you were in trouble."

"Walt—I'm sorry. I was going to tell you, but—"

"But what, Alice? What? You thought my father went to prostitutes—that he had sex with them. Even after I told you that it was impossible. You didn't take me at my word, Alice. I have believed you from moment one.

"And then I think to myself, Okay, so she thinks my father is some kind of Eliot Spitzer, why wouldn't she tell me the truth? I'll tell you why. You thought I'd be so depressed that I wouldn't help you, or worse, that I would kick you out. Or that I would think that everybody around me is a liar and then I would most certainly kick you out. I don't know, Alice, if I would have done that stuff. But now I do know. You're a liar. You lack moral courage. You can't be truthful with anybody because then you won't be able to get what you want from them."

"I wanted to tell you, but you were so certain—"

"Certain? Certain of what?" Charlie is yelling now. "Certain that my father was a law-abiding citizen. Certain that my father, who I believed was a faithful and loving husband for thirty-seven years, wouldn't date a girl young enough to be his daughter, or worse, step near a hooker. Wow. I must have been living in a bubble, Alice, to be so naive about my father."

"That's not what I'm saying." I'm trying to calm Charlie down. His face is purple.

"Alice, I don't fucking care what you're saying. Because it's all a lie. A lie to get me to house you and help you. How do I know you didn't fucking kill Polly Dawson? I wasn't there. How do I know you didn't kill Mona Hawkins? Because you were supposedly baking flirtatious cupcakes for me? How do I know you actually baked them? You could have bought those cupcakes. The fact is, Alice, I know nothing about you. I thought I did. I thought you were this delightful flower that had been waiting to bloom. As you stayed in my house, I added water and sunlight, and started to feel close to you."

A blooming flower? He does love me. No man uses floral terms to describe a friendship.

"But no, Alice. You're a weed."

A weed! I can't believe that Charlie just called me a weed.

"I want you to leave."

"Where will I go?"

He'd better not say, "Frankly my dear, I don't give a damn." The flower analogy was cliché enough.

"I don't give a shit. Why don't you turn yourself in? Maybe you should make today a lesson in honesty. If you're innocent, the truth will come out."

"The truth?"

"The truth," he says. "Why don't you try it?"

"Okay, Mr. Honesty. Here's the truth. I went out with your father on a 'date.' I did it as a favor to Jean—while she was dating Hugh Price. He was wonderful. He seemed like a really nice man, a really nice father, in fact. He reminded me of my father. And that was it. He had no interest. I had no interest. And I didn't tell you because it wasn't worth mentioning, and all of us would have been embarrassed."

And now for the hard part.

"I did follow your father. I followed him a lot. I saw him with one of those women on your list. I knew he was grieving. I know what grief can do. It turned my mother, my fantastic, loving, devoted, and responsible mother, into a zombie who ultimately remarried the first person she saw—despite his ambivalence about her kid. So, meaningless sex with anonymous people didn't seem so bad to me. I admired your father no less. I am sorry about my intrusion at Sloan-Kettering, but I wanted to clear him for you. I wanted so much for him to be innocent. Not for me. But because I didn't want to hurt you. Because, and here it is, Walter . . ."

I can't believe what I'm about to say to him.

"Because I love you. I loved you when I first saw you in Professor Flatineau's class at Harvard and then when I was a paralegal at Pennington and Litt. That's why I gave you beads. And I quit after I gave you beads because I was mortified. And then, when you took me in, the shallow love I had for you filled out and became a real thing."

Charlie's stunned. I haven't spoken this many words in my entire stay.

"And another thing," I tell him.

"What?"

"The name Walter doesn't suit you. You should consider changing it." I slam the door behind me.

I'm outside Charlie's house now. I feel the way I did on New Year's Eve. I have nowhere to go. Maybe Charlie's right. Maybe I should turn myself in. Then the police would have the truth.

The problem is that the police are never going to believe my story. I don't believe it and I lived it. They're never going to understand why I followed Polly. I was in therapy the whole time and I didn't even mention it to Dr. Moses. And as much as I'm disappointed in Charlie right now, I would never divulge to the cops that he's my alibi for the Mona Hawkins murder. Despite his having thrown me out, I don't want to get him in trouble. He let me stay with him for six weeks, and I can't put his future in jeopardy simply because I don't like the way he reacted to my withholding the information about his father.

Was I right about keeping the stuff to myself? In hindsight, no. Charlie says I lack moral courage.

Maybe he's right.

I'm going back. Back to Mother's house.

I still have the wig that Sophie gave me. The doorman accepted that I was an extra cleaning person when Sophie took me into the building with her. Most of the residents in that building have a staff. I put the wig on right outside Charlie's house. It's actually keeping my head warm.

I'm outside Mother's apartment. I walk right in and nod, with my head already down, to the doorman. He remembers me from this morning and tells me to go on up. I get in the elevator and press the six. We live on six. Or I should say "they" live on six? I haven't lived here for fourteen years.

I ring the doorbell. Sophie answers in less than a second. When she sees me, she tries to stop me from coming in.

"It's not a good time," she whispers.

I know why she's saying this. Barnes is standing right behind her.

"Hello, Barnes," I say.

"Alice, we've been worried sick," Barnes tells me.

I skip the niceties.

"I'm here to see Mother." I look right at him. "Don't call the police."

Mother comes running in. She's crying.

"Alice. Is that you, sweetheart?"

"Hi, Mother," I say. We hug. Mother continues to sob.

"I thought you were dead," she says.

"We were worried sick." Barnes actually looks relieved.

"Sorry," I say.

"Sorry?" Barnes says. I can tell that he's about to embark on a self-righteous monologue.

"Sorry? You disappear for months after police question you for your involvement in that poor woman's death. You don't contact us. We haven't been able to function."

"Why can't you just say, 'Alice, we're so glad you're okay?'" I say to Barnes.

"Naturally we're glad you're okay." Barnes surprises me. "I'm elated, but I'm also angry. You could have called."

I'm touched by Barnes's concern. It seems legitimate.

"Barnes, I'm terribly sorry." I turn to Mother. "Mother, I am really sorry for what I have put both of you through. I know that you've been crazed. But I thought it would be too dangerous to contact you over the past few weeks."

Mother keeps crying.

"I know that you're wondering what my involvement is in these two murders, and all I can say is that I was at the wrong place at the wrong time. I've been hiding out for a while, hoping that the police would find the real killer in the meantime."

"The real killer?" Barnes says. He can't possibly think I did this. I ignore Barnes.

"And Mother. I'll answer anything you need to know, but I'm asking you not to call the police. I just need to sort out a little information. Once I have it, I will go to them."

Although Mother's sobs continue, I can see that she is nodding in agreement.

"We most certainly will not agree to that," Barnes exclaims.

"I wasn't asking you," I tell Barnes, dismissively.

"Well, what is to stop me from calling the cops?" he asks.

"Mother will stop you," I say.

"What?" Mother stops crying rather abruptly.

"Mother will stop you from calling the cops," I say to Mother. "She will because she owes me."

I keep talking. I haven't prepared this speech so it comes out a little weird.

"When Mother married you, I didn't say anything. Because I knew that you had rescued her from terrible grief. I was aware, Barnes, that you didn't like me. I don't just mean that you didn't want to take responsibility for me. You didn't like me personally, which is weird because I had never had that effect on anyone in my entire life. But you loved Mother, and more important, she loved you, so I made a promise to my dead father that I would keep my mouth shut. I kept it shut through elementary school when you undermined me, I kept it shut in high school, I kept it shut in college when you kept Mother from visiting me. And I've kept it shut for the last ten years or so even when I see your eyes roll in my presence. But . . ."

I look at Mother.

"I'm not keeping it shut now. I figure my father will forgive me for breaking my promise under the circumstances."

I continue.

"What I'm trying to say, Barnes, is that you can be a jerk. Despite this, I get why Mother loves you. You're supportive of her career and you make her feel pretty, and necessary. I wish you would do the same for me."

I turn to my mother.

"Mother. You've always told me that I'm too passive and that I need to learn passion. You paid for all of that therapy, and now, I think I know what you were hoping I would find. And I found it."

"Oh, Jesus." Barnes rolls his eyes. He was never a fan of therapy.

"No, not Jesus." I am irritated. "Me. And Mother, when this is all over, I would love to tell you every delicious minute of the past weeks. But I ask you now if it would be okay to hold off on contacting the authorities. You say I never finish anything. Let me finish something. Let me clear my name. Let me do it. Give me two days. If I'm still number one on the most-wanted list, call away."

"You're not going to let her do this," Barnes says.

"Yes, Barnes, I am."

"Two days. She could be on another continent in two days."

"Barnes. It has been seven weeks, and here she is in our living room. And she's not here for money or help. She's just here to check in."

Barnes leaves the room.

By instinct, I am tempted to apologize to Mother. I really didn't want to hurt her feelings.

"Alice, sweetheart."

"Yes, Mother?" It comes out like a question. Am I in trouble?

"You look wonderful. Don't tell my husband, but I'm very proud of you."

I look at my reflection in the mirror above the fireplace. My wig is on crooked, and my face is a little dirty.

"Mother?"

"Yes?"

"Can I have twenty dollars?"

I'm out on the street again. I actually managed to get Barnes to leave the room. Mother is proud of me. Yay!

Reality check: I'm still on the run, and I have no place to live and only twenty dollars to my name. More important, my best friend hates me and Charlie hates me.

It starts to snow, and my wig is providing me with less warmth than Charlie's hat. I need to be indoors. I run into the Barnes & Noble on Eighty-sixth between Lexington and Third. I realize I haven't read a book in months. A distraction. I look at their new fiction. The store is doing a big-time promotion of *The Golden Pillow*. That was the book Polly was reading. The cover gives little away. The author is Ted Swinton. Ted Swinton? Where have I heard that name before? Ted Swinton. I turn the book over. "Advance Praise for *The Golden Pillow*." Hmm. *The New York Times* says that it is "haunting." The *Detroit Free Press* calls it "astounding . . . a colossal effort." The *San Francisco Chronicle* says, "Swinton may be the best novelist America doesn't know about." I scan down the back cover. I can't afford to buy the book; I might as well see what it is about.

For years, Theo Barlow basks in the naïveté of youth. He is the star of his high school football team, the highest-ranking student in his class, and possibly the most charming teenager in the quaint little village of Melting, Connecticut. And then the morning he is to graduate from high school, he makes a gruesome discovery: On the night before he was born, his parents suffocated his brother.

Not a promising premise.

I look inside the book jacket. And I see a picture of the author. My first thought is that he's cute. My second thought is that he's gay.

I know him. That's my third thought. I mean, I don't really know him. I've just heard about him from Jean. Ted Swinton is Preston Hayes's best friend. I look underneath the photo. It says Ted Swinton lives with his wife, Carolyn, in New York City. They have two bulldogs.

I'm dying to call Jean. I feel connected to her somehow through this picture of Ted Swinton. I open up the book and read the acknowledgments page. It looks as if Ted Swinton has thanked everyone he has ever met for helping to make his book possible. He thanks all of the publishing people, his agent, his parents, his wife, Hank and Frank (the dogs?), a bunch of other people, and finally a big thank-you to Dr. Michael Ledyard for "showing me the way."

Dr. Michael Ledyard?

He's the one I keep seeing on TV, saying he cures homosexuals. Ted Swinton is gay. I knew it.

Why else would he be thanking him in the book? Thanking him for showing him "the way."

I scan the acknowledgments again for Preston Hayes's name. According to Jean, the two have been best friends for years. I think she said they were roommates at one time. I check the list several times, but Preston's name is not on it. Maybe Preston isn't really his name. I mean, who comes out of the birth canal with a name like Preston Hayes? He was probably born Egbert Jones or something. But, even if Preston were an Egbert, he would've told Jean. It sounds like they're at the confiding stage. She certainly had no trouble telling him my little secret. He should tell her this one. I mean, if he's so taken with her.

Is he?

FOLLOWING POLLY · 273 ·

I walk around the store a little longer. I go to the self-help section looking for a book on how to be your best fugitive. Instead I see Dr. Ledyard's latest book, *The Way: Part Two*. Catchy title.

I don't even want to pick the thing up, but I'm curious. I had heard that this guy wasn't really a doctor. He got some sort of advanced degree from the University of Phoenix, a.k.a. the Internet. I look at his picture to make sure that he's the same guy I saw on TV. He is. He's incredibly unattractive, which may explain why he was able to cure his own homosexuality. Everyone knows that women are more forgiving in the looks department than men. If Ledyard had been a hot, popular gay man, he might not have wanted to cure himself.

I look at the book. There are no chapters. Just a quick author's note and pages of "reader" questions. The author notes that "We don't intend for *The Way: Part Two* to be a sequel to *The Way*, but rather we intend for it to be an appendix."

Wow. A $33.95 appendix. And who is "we"?

I open the book to the first "reader" question.

Dear Dr. Ledyard:

I engaged in a homosexual lifestyle, but then I read your book and I changed my ways. I am now happily married to a very nice woman. But sometimes I see my old boyfriends out and about. Do I say hello to them? It is very awkward.

Bruce C.
Dayton, Ohio

Dear Bruce:

Congratulations on your incredibly successful marriage. And I thank you for your letter. I have received many letters asking the very same question. I see no problem saying hello to or even socializing with a person from your past as long as that person is married or is in a serious relationship leading to marriage. Social interaction with a pre-Way single of your gender may be dangerous and tempting. But not if that person is with someone else. Then, he is cured.

Good luck, Bruce.

Dr. Michael Ledyard

I guess his advice isn't unreasonable. If I ever got married, I'd probably feel more comfortable with my husband's ex-girlfriends if they were already married. But that doesn't really cure a gay person. It's more of a way to repress them. And frankly, Dr. Ledyard isn't the first in the field of gay repression. But I do admire his marketing technique.

I'm surprised that someone who seems as hip as Ted Swinton would have fallen for Dr. Ledyard. But we all have our secrets.

I suddenly have a new thought. Maybe Ted has a bigger secret. Like Preston Hayes. He didn't thank Preston in the book because he didn't want the world to make a connection between the two of them. Then again, he did thank Dr. Ledyard. It's only logical to believe that he's a "recovering" homosexual.

But what if the absence of Preston's name from that list was not Swinton's idea at all, but instead it was Preston's? He's an author, after all, not an actor. It is not career suicide to be a gay writer, but it can be catastrophic for an actor, especially a male romantic, straight lead. The actor will have to go to lengths to maintain his heterosexual image. So he finds a girlfriend. She's pretty, nice, and completely outside the showbiz machine. And best of all, she has the worst judgment in men. This, I begin to think, is the situation between Preston Hayes and my ex–best friend Jean.

Okay. I'm getting way ahead of myself. Just because the author looks a little effeminate and he thanks a gay healer in a book acknowledgment doesn't mean he's gay. Just because his best friend is instantly involved with my best friend, but they have no physical relationship, does not mean that *he's* gay. Maybe he just wants to take things slowly.

But it does seem really suspicious, doesn't it? I'm not surprised Jean hasn't had this thought. She's so bad at this stuff. I think of Bram. Not that I'm an expert. I've been, I know, pining for someone for fourteen years. At least Jean actually gets involved with these guys. At least she accrues some experience. All I have is a nervous feeling in my stomach from time to time. And anyway, this isn't really about me. It's about Jean, and I guess my question is, do I tell Jean? She may think I'm making this all up because I'm angry with her about telling Preston.

And worse, she could decide she doesn't believe me and then tell Preston my whereabouts. He may rat me out. It would certainly help his image. I can see the headlines.

STRAIGHT HEARTTHROB NABS MOVIE KILLER.

What do I do?

I believe that Mother will not call the cops. And I also believe that she will force Barnes to hold off, as I had asked, for forty-eight hours.

I have forty-seven hours to find Mona's and Polly's killer.

But I don't know who it is.

Ralston Brown, the vindictive insider trader, is looking good to me. He had a very strong reason to kill Polly. Moreover, as far as I know from Kovitz's conversation with Charlie, he has no alibi. But why would he kill Mona? Did he realize that the police were onto him, and so he just picked someone involved with Polly's husband's movie so that he could appear less guilty?

It doesn't sound right.

Besides, how would he know about me?

So what about the Polly lover angle? I've eliminated Suspect Number Three, her young lover, the soul patch. He just didn't seem passionate enough about her. He looked enamored, but not obsessed. And the fact that he wanted to do a threesome with her and some girl from his office—it just doesn't seem as if he has the requisite passion in his blood.

But would he become murderous if he learned that she was pregnant?

I don't know.

Of course, it's likely that there are other candidates for the baby's daddy. Ian Leighton, for one, and any of the other hunks that she may have taken in, so to speak.

I'm baffled. I feel powerless.

I decide that the best thing for me to do is to tell Jean. Even if I end up behind bars, she will be spared a portion of the devastation of an inevitable breakup. I won't tell her that Preston Hayes is gay, because that is not an actual fact. It's merely a conclusion that I have come to based upon the facts Jean has given me, and my discovery of Ted Swinton's book.

But maybe I'll just ask Jean if she has considered the possibility that Preston Hayes is a homosexual who's using her to appear straight as his breakthrough movie is wrapping. She told me that I should tell her when I think she's involved with an inappropriate partner, didn't she? Even though she hates me now and she may not want to hear what I have to say, I have to do what I have to do. After all, I may be going to jail in forty-seven hours and then I will have to stop thinking about my friends and focus instead on who can help me out of this disaster.

But it's still too dangerous to go to her house. I head to an

Internet café on Second Avenue and Eighty-third Street. I can send her an e-mail. So far, I think my handle is still secret. Maybe instead of telling her that I think Preston is gay, I'll simply give her the information and let her reach that conclusion herself. I know what you're thinking: Jean already has most of this information and it still hasn't occurred to her that Preston is gay. True, but she doesn't have this information served to her cold. She only has it in the context of the fun time she has been having.

I go into the café. I'm afraid that they'll ask me for a credit card or something so that I don't walk out with the computer, but a girl in a floppy hat with a lip ring merely points me to the back wall. I ask her the cost of getting online. She opens her mouth to tell me that I pay at the end. I see her tongue is pierced, too.

I head to the back corner. I log on to CNN.com's news headlines to make sure that there have been no new developments in my case. There's always the chance that Barnes will take offense at Mother's newly discovered defiance and call the cops on me anyway.

I'm clinging to my freedom for at least a few hours. But for the first time since New Year's Eve when I ran from the fifth precinct, I don't feel particularly attached to the notion of freedom. I had my time with Charlie, and I blew it. My best friend hates me. And, even though I feel a certain weightlessness from having confronted Mother and Barnes, I don't long to spend any time with them.

I want to help Jean. Even though she may hate me, she's still my best and dearest friend.

I log on to the computer. The computer asks for my username. I type in *T-H-E-F-O-L-L-O-W-E-R*. It asks me for my password. Easy. *C-H-A-R-L-I-E*. The computer indicates that I have mail. I click Read Mail hopefully, only slightly expecting a come-back-to-me note from either Charlie or Jean. But no—it is just some unpronounceable series of letters and punctuation marks offering me discount vicoden, which they should have at least spelled properly. I click on Write Mail.

To: JeanMiddleton@lwm.com

I'm not sure if Jean went into the office today, but I choose to send this sort of personal note to the office because I know she gets office mail at home, whereas I don't know if she gets personal mail at the office. I try to make the mail sound as impersonal as possible.

Jean:

I'm not trying to retaliate with this note. I'm worried. I need you to consider these factors about the new b-f.

1. *Has not mauled you—and you (as we both know) are maulable.*
2. *He's in Hollywood and needs a certain image.*
3. *Best friend is Ted Swinton.*
4. *Ted Swinton thanks Dr. Michael Ledyard in book.*
5. *Dr. Ledyard claims to cure gays by encouraging them to lead straight lives.*
6. *And why didn't he sleep with Polly Dawson?*
7. *Just a feeling . . .*

Please, oh please, be careful. Me

I click Send, and I wait a minute or so. I'm hopeful that I will receive the following message.

My Dearest Friend:

Thank you. Although I'm somewhat disappointed, I appreciate your saving me from a greater sadness down the line. And

how thoughtful to think of me when times are so tough for you.
You really are the best.

Me

The screen, though, remains blank. Do I send an e-mail to
Charlie? I could write "I'm sorry" nine thousand times, but I
know my betrayal has been too recent for him.

My work here is done.

I leave the Internet café. It's starting to rain.

I have this fear. What if Preston's at Jean's house? What if she
has left her e-mail visible? What if he's nosy? After all, I'm nosy.

I'm not far away. It's cold, but it's bearable. I'll just let myself
into Jean's apartment, turn off her computer, and hope that she
sees the e-mail while Preston is not around.

It's less tricky getting into Jean's apartment than you might
think. Jean lives in a swanky, overpriced Upper West Side edifice
along with dozens of other well-paid cool urban types who need
a roomy granite kitchen to store their myriad takeout contain-
ers and that one box of baking soda. The security in the building
appears tight: There is a doorman and a concierge, but they are
more interested in their epaulets than in keeping out the wanted
murderess lurking at Eighty-third Street and Columbus. Jean's
neighbor runs a nanny employment agency out of her apartment,
so there are always a slew of women showing up in the building
lobby asking to be allowed to go to the eighth floor. The elevator
requires the doorman to unlock each floor.

I go in and announce myself. "Hi," I say with a little youth in
my voice, "I'm looking to go to eight B. My name is Celia."

I thought Celia sounded child friendly.

The doorman isn't even looking at me.

"Go on up," he says. "She's expecting you."

Remind me to put him on my security team.

I take the elevator to the eighth floor. I get out, wave to 8B's front door, and head over to 8A.

I turn the knob. Jean always leaves the door open. She, for some reason, is under the false impression that her building is secure. Jean's computer is in her bedroom. I have to walk through her hallway and past her kitchen to get into the bedroom. I peer into each of these rooms as well as the living room to make sure that I'm alone. I hear a rustling in the kitchen. I tiptoe in. It's empty. There are, however, two coffee cups in the sink, in addition to a couple of empty wineglasses. There are three bottles on the counter.

Jean loves to drink.

Once I'm confident that nobody is there, I head over to Jean's bedroom. The computer is shutting down as I enter. I would normally find this very odd, but I'm momentarily distracted by a pile of photographs casually lying on Jean's shelf. I pick them up. The first one is of Jean standing in front of her Wall Street offices wearing a sexy but conservative Tahari suit. She really is beautiful. She has that 1940s starlet look in photographs; pale, thin, and sharp.

Oh my God. Why does Jean have a picture of Polly's young lover, a.k.a. Happy Camper? Not just one picture, but two. I know Jean's standards run the gamut, but I would have thought she would be repelled by the ambivalent chin hair. I would recognize that soul patch anywhere. His rubber-band body is another giveaway. Yes, it's definitely Soul Patch. And she's in the pictures with him. They were taken months ago. I can tell. Jean was still wearing her fall clothes. Happy Camper isn't even wearing a jacket, but he is wearing his cargo pants and hiking boots. The ones he was wearing when I saw them in Mee-Hop the same day I saw Charlie eating with Kovitz. Ooh, here he is in

Jean's office. Happy Camper is going through Jean's filing cabinet?

Polly was sleeping with Jean's paralegal. I start to remember everything. Jean telling me that her paralegal was an aspiring moviemaker. He was working as an intern on a movie.

He must have been working on *Only at Sunrise*. And that's where he met Polly.

Things were good with him and Jean, but then he started to pull back. That usually happens with Jean. Just as she starts to really fall for someone who should be a fling, the guy pulls back. Or cheats. Happy Camper went for the latter with Polly. I know because I saw them together only days before Jean told me their relationship was souring.

But he did want to do a threesome with Polly with *some girl from his office.*

Jean?

Too much information.

I wonder if Jean knew about this. The only thing worse than getting dumped by a little boy is getting dumped by a little boy who prefers to be with Polly Dawson. That would have killed Jean. Did she have any idea? She must have. She saw him at the Barneys grieving bash. They looked at each other. I thought he was checking her out, but he wasn't checking her out at all, he was acknowledging her—the way you do an old lover. So why didn't she tell me? She knew I would be sympathetic to her. Polly had swiped her boyfriend. Maybe she was embarrassed. Maybe she didn't want me to know that Polly beat her.

"She'll get hers." That's what Jean always said to me. "Polly Dawson will get hers."

And what a coincidence! She did get hers.

Maybe not such a coincidence after all. I don't like what I'm thinking. Jean has always hated Polly. She hated her more than I

282 • KAREN BERGREEN

ever did. Polly seemed to have everything Jean wanted, even Professor Jack Birnbaum. After college, Jean kept waiting for Polly to fail. But it never happened. She led a fairy-tale life. Then, when Jean met the guy she wanted to take home for Christmas, it was Polly who took him away from her. And Polly didn't even need him. She was married to the perfect man. And she had another lover. The timing was perfect. When Jean learned that Soul Patch dumped her for Polly, she was ready to get even. This was exactly when Polly ended up dead.

Jean, a murderess?

I look at the picture of the two of them together. Jean is wearing a tank top. Her arms are in perfect shape. She's very strong. She could probably carry out serious stabbing. I might not have the physical abilities to murder Polly, but Jean does.

Okay, so let's say Jean killed Polly in a psychotic rage. What I can't understand is how she is letting me take the fall. How she is letting me face a lifetime in prison for a crime she committed. I can't reconcile that with the Jean who's been my closest friend for almost fifteen years. Did she actually kill Mona to resurrect law enforcement interest in me? Charlie had told us that Kovitz admitted I was looking less obvious as the killer, and then, what a coincidence, Mona ends up dead. Jean knew I hated Mona. Jean knew where Mona's office was. And Jean knew that Mona Hawkins was murdered last night. "Preston told me." She said it casually. But that was only minutes before she told me she couldn't get in touch with me because Preston had taken her to a party where there was no access to televisions or newspapers. And when I pressed her on that information, she threw a bogus that's-showbiz type of answer at me.

Jean was the one who said that Preston had given the police a tip that Humphrey was sleeping around. I had always assumed that Preston was lying. Maybe it was Jean. Maybe she made it up to make it look as if she were actually helping me.

I rush out of her apartment. I hop in a cab and spend my last seven dollars going to the only place I call home.

I go to the place where I feel best: my little campsite across from Charlie's house. It must be after five now. It's dark, and the rain is starting to thicken. If I can just make it to my spot without getting too wet, I can rely on the canopy for some shelter.

I'm here finally, and I'm pretty dry if you don't count my feet. Felisha's riding boots are just yards away from me, inside Charlie's front hall closet. But they might as well be in Yangon. The shoes Charlie gave me are soaking wet, as are my feet. I remove the shoes and the socks, and am able to dry my feet with my wig. I stick both of my feet inside the little hat of hair. Hey. I'm not going anywhere.

I think I've been asleep for several hours. The rain, now that it isn't coming down on me, is serving as a sleep aid. I've been dreaming of Charlie.

It's still dark, and there's someone next to me. A male someone.

"Walter," I whisper, hoping that Charlie will whisk me upstairs and pull me into his bed. Of course we'll have to share a hot bath first.

"Shhh," he says. And it's very sexual. With a little more edge than our brief moment last night.

"I'm sorry," I say.

"Shhh," he says, even more forcefully this time. He puts his hand over my mouth. Maybe he's afraid that if I speak, we'll only start fighting.

I push his hand away. Or try to anyway, but he exerts more force.

"We both know I'm stronger than you, Alice Teakle." A shiver goes up my spine. This is not Charlie. This is not a make-up call. I look over at his face.

Oh my God. It's Preston Hayes.

I try to think quickly.

"My friend is meeting me here," I say, knowing that the rain will drown out my voice.

"And which friend would that be?" Preston laughs. "Robbie the Rat? He doesn't wake up for at least another hour."

Boy, is he not funny.

"Clever," I say. "Why are you here?"

"I'm here about a nasty little e-mail you wrote to a certain friend of yours."

I decide to play dumb. After all, my name isn't on the e-mail.

"I don't know what you're talking about," I tell him.

Preston squeezes my arm even more tightly.

"Would you like me to read it?" he says. "Actually, I'm an actor and a quick study. I have it memorized."

"I still don't know what you're talking about."

As Preston recites the e-mail I wrote to Jean, I realize he's not at all in love with Jean. He and Ted Swinton were or are lovers. He was using my friend to cover up his sexuality because he didn't want to jeopardize his burgeoning career as the next "It boy." I had written the e-mail to Jean merely to inform her that Preston would probably not be the One, as she had hoped. Preston's interpretation made my e-mail sound more sinister. Or more to the point, it made him seem sinister. I mean really sinister.

It dawns on me as Preston is finishing up: I'm being hushed up by a man who will do just about anything to keep his secret.

"You killed Polly," I whisper to him.

Preston doesn't say anything.

"You killed Mona," I whisper even more softly.

"You know what they say about trouble?" Preston pauses. "Trouble comes in threes."

Trouble comes in threes. It sounds like an Agatha Christie novel. And I smile for a second, forgetting that my life is on the line. Preston Hayes could be an Agatha Christie killer—except for the gay part. You didn't get to be gay back then.

"I understand," I tell him. "I understand why you did this."

And part of me does understand.

"Polly Dawson came on to you, didn't she?"

Preston is silently concurring, I can tell.

"You must have turned her down. She was able to flirt shame-lessly with you at Silvercup. But it didn't amount to anything. She was relentless, and when you wouldn't budge, she figured it out. She probably taunted you. She was probably taunting you for weeks. When I saw you two exchange glances at Silvercup, you looked worried. But you weren't concerned that she was go-ing to dump you or that her husband would find out. You were worried that she would expose you."

"She was mean enough to do it," Preston says as if in a dream.

"It pissed you off. And you were worried."

"I was this close to being an A-list star, and this slut was going to ruin it."

"So you started following Polly. Not like me. You weren't trying to find purpose; you had purpose! You needed to make sure she stayed quiet."

"I even asked her nicely," Preston whines.

"You looked for secret information on Polly to keep her

quiet. You tracked her every move. And then you noticed me. There was someone else following Polly. Someone who was leaving her footprints all over the place. I was blithely swiping my credit card at all of Polly's favorite haunts."

"You have to admit, you made it very easy. In your next life, you should pay cash."

"And then she went to see you. Not at the movie set but at your home. Jean had told me that you lived two blocks from me. Polly had been carrying *The Golden Pillow,* Ted Swinton's book. She must have figured out that you and Swinton were lovers, or former lovers. And you didn't have to blackmail her. There was an easier way out. You could kill her. No one would believe that you would do it. Especially when there was a far more attractive suspect in the neighborhood."

And when I say "attractive," I mean "likely to kill." For, even as he is trying to kill me, I make note that Preston Hayes is a very handsome guy.

"So you gathered little souvenirs when you could from places where you'd followed me and Polly. You picked up matchbooks from Lever House and the Four Seasons. You even made sure to pick up a museum pin from the Metropolitan Museum of Art. You knew that it wouldn't matter to law enforcement that *I* hadn't picked them up. You planted them at the crime scene, and my credit-card receipts corroborated my presence at these places."

"And as luck would have it, you put your fingerprints all over the murder weapon," Preston whispers.

I start to shiver, and I can feel myself crying.

"You must have been sure that you'd gotten away with murder. You were a shoulder to cry on for Humphrey."

"And you brought me Jean, a delightful yet gullible patsy."

"But you were still obsessed with keeping your secret. Who else knew? Mona Hawkins for sure. With her ties to the gay porn industry, she would figure out the truth about you. Mona had a big mouth, plus an even bigger accordion file. You had to stuff the former and steal the latter.

"You'd already killed once.

"So on Valentine's Day, you made an 'appointment' with her. You probably flirted and brought her snacks. Then you killed her. And you took the file! You hurried out to be with your beard, Jean. But you made a mistake. You told her about Mona's death in the early evening before it was made public—a breaking-news halftime story during a ten o'clock episode of *Law and Order*. And now Jean's friend is on to you. You'll kill me."

"And I think I might have to then kill Jean," he says without affect.

Jean.

Jean. How could I have considered even for a second that she was a killer?

In a sick way, I admire him. I've never been ambitious enough that I would kill for something. This guy is willing to do it four times.

"Your secret's safe with me," I plead. "I won't tell anyone."

"No, you will, Alice. You already told Jean."

I panic. I told Jean right away. In fact, the second I thought of it.

"That was before I realized how important your secret was." I pause. "It's just Jean. It's not like Jean can do anything for you. She's not a mover and a shaker like Polly Dawson or Mona Hawkins." I can see Mona smiling as I refer to her as a mover and a shaker.

I hope Preston will consider this for a moment. But he starts pressing on my neck.

"That's not a risk I am willing to take," he says. "You're simply not worth it."

Is he right? Am I not worth it? Certainly the lives of Polly and Mona were more valuable than my own. Polly was a major breadwinner and the subject of much public discussion. And Mona, while despicable, did certainly have her place in the biz. I'm unemployed, and frankly, my only claim to fame is as a murderer.

So he does have a point.

But what about Jean? She needs me now. Not only to warn her about Preston, but also to help pick up the pieces when she realizes that she has been dumped by another guy. There's no reason to tell her that I considered for a moment that she could be the killer.

What about Charlie? He hates me now. But I feel as if it's not over with him. We haven't seen this entire thing through. And here is Preston trying to cut things short.

I guess what I'm saying is that I'm not ready to die. I doubt that Mona and Polly were ready when Preston Hayes slaughtered them, but this is my story.

Preston has experience with this. He has killed two people already. I have only gotten credit for it. How do I fight him?

And then it flashes in my mind. Clarissa Winnick. The overly pale self-defense guru and author of *Men Fight, Women Bite*. I picture her pinning Rosie O'Donnell, a woman twice her size, to the ground.

I hear her whiny voice. "Fight like a girl. Fight like a girl." And so I do. First, I scream. The most unattractive shrill voice to hit the Upper East Side. Preston starts to grab my neck even more tightly, but I take my free hand and pull his hair. Really hard. Because it's so thick and full, it's easy to pull. He clamps harder on my neck, but the force on his scalp distracts him a little and I bite his hand hard. I even draw blood.

"You bitch! You bitch! You bitch!"

Sticks and stones . . .

I kick him in the shins. I'm able to disable him for just a little bit. So then I knee him in the balls. He lets go of me, desperate for even a few seconds to tend his fresh wounds. That's when I start to go for his eyes.

Wow, this Clarissa method really works. Maybe I'll go on *The View.*

And then everything goes black.

FOUR

· ·

MY LIFELONG DREAM

open my eyes. The first thing I notice is that everything around me is white. Am I dead? Is this heaven? No, I can't be. I'm realizing this as I process my second sensation: discomfort. I turn my head. Ooh, a TV. Maybe it *is* heaven. But there's no program on the screen. Instead, the screen displays only three different-colored lines and some numbers. I'm not looking at a television; I'm looking at a monitor.

I'm in the hospital.

The fact that this has taken seconds to digest means one of two things. One: I'm drugged. Two: I'm badly brain-damaged.

"Help!" I try to scream but my voice sounds small and farther away from my ears than it's supposed to be.

The door opens. Oh my God. Blue hats. Blue attire. It's the cops. I can't get away physically, but I can mentally. I'll do my best amnesiac.

"Hello, Officers," I say, half polite, half lady in distress.

The officers—there are two of them—pull out their walkies and speak softly and in code.

"Where am I?"

"New York Presbyterian Hospital."

"Oh," I say. And then I give them an exaggerated confused look.

"Do you know your name?"

"No," I lie.

The door opens.

"Alice Teakle." It's Jean. Did she call the cops?

"Huh?" I continue my charade.

"Alice. It's me, Jean. Jean Middleton. Your best friend."

Some friend. She might as well be working for the cops.

"Jean?" I try to revive my childhood acting skills to present myself as a woman searching her memory.

"Alice, I'm so happy you're alive. We were so worried."

"Worried?" I'm really good at this.

"You are a very lucky lady." I know that voice; it doesn't belong to Jean. It belongs to Kovitz.

Jean is working with Kovitz. She turned me in because I didn't approve of her boyfriend. And then it comes back to me. I was right not to approve of that boyfriend. He was a two-time killer and he almost murdered me as well. Boy, is Jean going to feel like a jerk when she finds out that my instincts were correct. And she is going to be feeling pretty terrible about betraying me to Kovitz.

"You're a very lucky lady. You came this"—and then he makes a pinching motion with his hands—"close to being rubbed out by Preston Hayes."

"So you figured out that he killed Polly Dawson and Mona Hawkins?" I say, shedding my amnesiac persona.

"So you know?" Jean trills. "You know me. You know us." She does a little dance. Okay, maybe I was wrong. Maybe she didn't turn me in.

"Of course I know you," I say dismissively. But then I rethink it. I look at Kovitz and try to widen my eyes. "The name Preston Hayes made it all come back to me."

Jean comes over to my bed and hugs me. "Will you ever forgive me, Alice?"

"Yes." I turn my head in Kovitz's general direction, hoping that he will ask me the very same question. "Don't you have something to ask me?" I say to him with a newfound snottiness.

"Oh. Yes, Ms. Teakle," Kovitz says earnestly.

This is what I've been waiting for. I'm going to get the apology that will have made all of the nights on the street and the running from the law worthwhile.

"How do you suggest we dispose of these running-from-the-law charges?" he adds.

"Detective Kovitz, I've watched enough legal shows on television to know that there are no 'running-from-the-law' charges in New York State. I wasn't under arrest when I slipped out of your grasp." I'm fully alert now. "I admit that what I did was slightly cheesy, but you're not a member of the Etiquette Enforcement Agency."

"And if you were," Jean puts on her lawyer voice, "you would issue Ms. Teakle an apology right away. By intimidating and harassing her, you put her in harm's way. You're lucky we don't sue you."

"Yeah, that," I say.

Kovitz holds up his arms in the universal "halt" position. "Look, nobody is suing anybody here." I admit Kovitz's take-charge manner is preferable to what was becoming a high school feud. "Ms. Teakle." Kovitz looks at me. "What you did was very brave. True, it was incredibly stupid, but you got guts. The city owes you a great deal of thanks for assisting in the capture of a very dangerous man."

So there it is. My apology. My cheeks flush. Kovitz is human. Suddenly, I realize I don't know what happened.

How did I end up in the hospital, and where is Preston Hayes?

"Hayes is in custody," Kovitz says. He can read my mind now that we're best friends.

"Last I recall, Preston Hayes and I were wrestling, he was winning, and he won—or so I thought."

"Hayes knocked you out. Lucky for you, a Good Samaritan happened to be passing by. He slugged Hayes, just hard enough to knock him out, and then he called us. Another five minutes out there, young lady, and you would have been having cocktails in heaven with Polly Dawson and Mona Hawkins."

I doubt very much that Mona Hawkins is anywhere near heaven right now. The food is probably better in hell. I'm not so sure that Polly Dawson made it up there, either. Also, cocktails?

"Wow, I still can't believe it was Preston Hayes."

"Alice, I'm so sorry that I doubted you. I guess I got carried away because he seemed so great. I really believed that I liked us together. If only he had been straight and had lacked homicidal tendencies . . ."

"I know what you mean."

I'm not lying to her. I took all these risks these last few weeks because I was so focused on Charlie. It never occurred to me that someone would try to murder me. I was too busy planning our meals and our children.

Speaking of which, I wonder if Charlie knows that I'm in the hospital. I can't call him and tell him the latest development. He thinks I'm a weed.

"He can't possibly be angry still," Jean says.

She's brought a huge box of newspaper and magazine clippings with her. It seems that William has become quite the hero. A few days after I landed in the hospital, Kovitz, despite Charlie's instructions to the contrary, leaked the truth about William Redwin to the press. He became an overnight phenomenon. Readers, exhausted from a consistent barrage of human weakness, were drawn universally to this story about a man's quiet goodness. Women saw his actions as romantic and wrote him love letters and delivered casseroles; men saw him as rehabilitating the tarnished image that their gender had suffered over the last few decades. One of Tuesday's *New York Times* op-ed columnists said he brought honor back to the name Bill. *People* magazine did a photo retrospective of William and Emily's marriage.

"I don't understand the fuss," William told *The National*

Observer. "My wife worked with these women for years. Where are her front-page stories?" And of course that comment spurred on a whole new heap of praise, calling William the new face of feminism.

I wonder how Charlie is taking his father's celebrity. Most of the articles make a passing reference to Charlie and his non-wavering faith in his father's innocence. Others simply mention a son. I wonder if Charlie still has all of his files on the girls. Has he cleaned his apartment yet?

I wonder if Felisha's riding boots are there. I picture him throwing all of my stuff, including the wig, the dress, and the gloves, into a plastic bag and giving it to the real Salvation Army. The TV is most likely back in its former, useless location.

I'm certain he'll keep the coffeemaker.

Jean's telling me that Mother has come by several times.

Sans Barnes. Hard to believe that Barnes would allow Mother to enter my little drama without him. Maybe he's making her wear a wire.

"I'll call her later," I tell Jean.

"I wouldn't do that if I were you." Spoken in a distinctly unfamiliar Jamaican accent. I look behind me. It's a nurse. She's holding a clipboard and taking notes on all of the information on the computer monitor.

"Huh?" Is she about to tell me that I'm going to die after all and that I should make peace with Mother?

"I don't mean to be enterin' your business, you know, but your mother—she's very worked up 'bout all of this." The nurse has come over to the side of the bed. She's beautiful; a little older perhaps. But she has beautiful skin and perfectly molded features. Come to think of it, she looks like a black version of Mother. "She wants to know you're all right."

"Why don't you tell her then?"

"I think she means all right in the head." The nurse taps her own head on the off chance that I didn't understand the meaning of the word "head."

"I'm all right," I tell her. "She just has an albatross of a husband. He puts me in a bad mood."

"You tell her that," the nurse says in a very kind tone. "Your mother. She love you very much. She want you to get better and be happy."

"Thank you."

I'm suddenly very tired. I'm really cold. "Jean. Can I go to sleep?"

"Of course, honey. But I'm going to stay right here with you."

And as I'm falling asleep, I want to ask my best friend for the name of the Good Samaritan: the man who saved my life. I should send him a gift basket or something. But I'm way too sleepy to form any sentences. At least any spoken ones. I drift off.

"Alice, honey, are you awake? Alice, dear. Are you waking up?" The proximity of the voice is startling and comforting. It moves away a bit. "I think she's awake."

And I wake up. I know something huge has happened.

Mother is standing over my bed. She's weeping. And she looks weird to me.

She looks kind of ugly. I don't mean like a monster or anything. It's just that Mother is possibly the comeliest woman in the tristate area, and the way I see her now, no one should see her like this.

"Are you okay?" I ask her.

"Oh, Alice dear, I should be asking you that question. We thought we lost you."

We! I wish our conversations didn't always involve Barnes.

"Didn't we, Jean?"

"Where's Barnes?" I say flatly.

"He's at home," Mother says.

"Is he sick?" I can't imagine that Barnes would be mentally healthy enough to allow a mother-daughter visit without his officious presence.

"No. I instructed him not to come."

"Really?" Jean perks up. I must admit, this is getting juicy.

"Are you two not getting along?" I ask.

"Nothing like that. You were right, Alice. Barnes and I have been doing a lot of soul searching. He agrees that it's time you and I have some time without him, while he's at a backgammon tournament or reading the newspaper."

"Wow." This is bigger than the whole Preston Hayes being a gay murderer revelation. Barnes is letting me have some Mother back.

"Now, Alice." She interrupts my thoughts. "I love Barnes. I guess all these years I wanted him to love you and you to love him as—" Mother starts crying again. "—you and your father felt about each other. I kept thinking that if the two of you just gave each other a chance it would happen."

While I can't for the life of me see what any human being would find positive to say about Barnes Newlan, I know that Mother is being honest.

"I'm so sorry, sweetheart." Here comes the monologue. "For all of the junk I have put you through." That doesn't sound like a Mother monologue to me. "From now on, Alice, Barnes will have no say in decisions regarding you. He's not allowed to give you advice, unless you ask him for it. And he's been in therapy for two weeks now."

Ahh, therapy. I need a seventeen-hour session with my shrink.

"I keep telling him about your fantastic results with Dr. Moses."

"Fantastic results? I was framed for murder and nearly died!"

"From what I've seen, it was after you started therapy that you started to deal with your problems. We call it acting out."

We, meaning those who aren't licensed in mental health.

But she is right in a way. Maybe the visits with the therapist made me feel safe enough to engage in the psychotic following episodes. Maybe the visits with the therapist made me feel confident enough to stalk Charlie.

I smile at Mother. "Maybe you're right."

I look over at Jean. She's bawling. And suddenly I realize I'm crying, too.

I've lost all track of time, but I know that I stay in the hospital for almost a month. I was out of it for the first two and a half weeks. No one is using the word "coma" because they think that will scare me. Funny, though, they have no problem throwing around terms like "hemorrhage" and "bleeding of the brain." My head seems to be under control now, thanks to my neurosurgeon, Dr. Manuel Reiter. I've met him exactly once, but, according to Mother, Jean, and Nurse Jennifer, he was here all the time when I was "out of it." I stay in the hospital an extra two weeks or so because I have a phantom infection. Or at least I did. And no one could find its source. They've finally figured out that it was in my spleen, but the doctor told me yesterday that they were able to save it. I know this is probably not a good time to ask the doctor what the spleen does. He may think I am ungrateful.

Mother comes to visit me every day. Our conversation is stilted at first. I have forgotten how to talk to her. All those years of adjusting my conversation to accommodate the fact that Barnes was in the room. So I start at the beginning.

I tell her that for years I missed being with her, just her. I tell her that I sensed that Barnes hoped I would go to prison so that he could have her all to himself.

"What you understood to be control, Alice, I recognized as protection. Barnes knows that my biggest enemy is free time. He's afraid that if I'm not working or being attended to constantly, I'll go back into my depression. To some degree, he feels the same about you. When you got fired, he was terrified that you would go into a very dark place. I admit he's not so good with the mother-daughter thing. He doesn't have his own kids and doesn't understand the complexities of those relationships. What you might see as privacy, he sees as secrecy. And he's not comfortable with that."

To some degree, Barnes was right. I was keeping secrets. Suddenly, I long to tell Mother everything. I start with my following Polly. I tell her how it began. How I detested Polly in college and how easy life seemed for her. I wanted to figure out how she "did her life." So I could do mine the same way. And then I got caught up in her double, make that her triple life.

"I love it," is all Mother can say. "I hope you kept a journal."

"It's all in here," I say as I point to my head, "or at least what's left of it." I suspect my memory is intact, since I'd spent at least an hour the night before remembering almost every word of Daphne Feller's little sister's graduation speech.

And then I tell Mother about Charlie. I begin with Professor Flatineau's History of Paris class. I tell her about how I loved Charlie from the moment I met him.

"Like your father and me." I notice that Mother is crying. I try to cheer her up.

"I gave him beads," I say.

"That's big," she replies somberly.

I tell her how I dreamed of Charlie during my involvement with other men. I tell her that I dreamed of him when I was running from the police, and that when I finally found him, I was truly happy, despite my impending prison time or death.

"You must really love him," she says.

"I do, but I did a terrible thing." I recount how I was afraid to tell Charlie what I thought to be the truth about his father because I thought he would hate me or lose faith in me or both. "It was weak and selfish," I say.

"Alice, you were in love."

"I hope he'll forgive me."

"He will if he's the man you say he is." Mother is more serious now than I have ever seen her.

Mother thinks I should be a private investigator. She thinks that following people is my calling. I'm just happy she hasn't asked me to create a watercolor of all of the scenes I had witnessed these last months.

"I can help you," she says. "I know people."

I'm going to look into this.

Mother has a good idea. I could continue to intrude, but with a purpose. I wouldn't feel as morally bankrupt if my spying could help someone and was income producing.

The phone rings.

"Why don't you answer that?" Mother says.

I pick it up. "Hello."

"Hello, Alice." It's Barnes.

"Hi, Barnes."

"I trust you're feeling better," he says.

"Yes."

"Good. Well then. I have a question for you. I will be attending a French decorative arts auction this evening, and I was wondering if you could remind me of Napoleon the Third's chief architect."

"Baron Haussmann," I say suspiciously. The man has Internet access.

"Thank you, Alice. I really appreciate that," he says. "Well, good-bye, then."

"Good-bye." I turn to Mother. "He really appreciates me."

"He's trying," she says.

Dr. Moses has stopped by a couple of times. She was there when things were really bad, according to Jean. I am a little embarrassed to see her.

"Are you mad at me?" I ask her.

"No, I'm relieved. We have a lot to talk about when you start back in therapy."

"Just so you know, I really did think we were making progress. I have my lifelong dream." I'm still not ready to say Charlie's name yet. "Or at least I had a lifelong dream, but maybe we can come up with another one."

"Let's work on this one first," Dr. Moses says, smiling.

I could swear she's wearing hemp.

I think I have everything. At least I hope I do. I'm in the lobby of the hospital. I've said good-bye to the doctors. We never developed much of a relationship. Apparently my case was fairly unremarkable from a medical standpoint. But I have a hard time leaving Jennifer. I wish I could take her home with me, so she could take care of me until I figure out what I'm going to do with my life.

"Oh. You all say that. Then a week goes by, and you say, 'Jennifer who?' " Jennifer has wheeled me down to the lobby exit of the hospital and is now hugging me. "You be good to your mother, now. She needs you. And you need her."

———

And so I leave the hospital. Just like that. Jean took my stuff back to my apartment last night. She and Mother both wanted to take me home, but I told them I would rather take them up on their kindness later in the day. I haven't been in my apartment for almost three months. Mother paid all my back rent and helped convince the landlord to let me stay in the building. She told him that he'd be helping a New York hero, and then she slipped him five grand. "It costs more to move," she assured me.

Jennifer had instructed me to get into a taxi the minute I leave the building, but the March weather is so enticing, I decide to take my chances and walk a bit. The sky seems especially low today. The clouds move quickly and change their formation every minute or so. It's like watching a movie in the sky. It's cold, but a lot warmer than I remember. Spring is imminent.

Spring: my new start.

I shiver.

Someone is following me.

Who?

Preston Hayes is in custody. I must be imagining it. I must have a little post-traumatic stress disorder coming to me.

I cross the street to Sixty-fifth and York. If I keep walking west, I'll walk into Charlie's house—my former, albeit temporary, residence. And the home of the only man I've ever loved.

Charlie may never speak to me again, even if he no longer resents me for withholding the information about his father. After all, our quandaries have come to their respective resolutions. Now we have nothing that binds us.

I don't know if I'll recover from this loss. I don't recover from relationships as quickly as Jean. In case you were wondering, she has been seeing my neurosurgeon, although she is reluctant to use words like "love" and "obsess" and has taken a shine to the phrase "we'll see."

I'm on First Avenue now, and I am certain I'm being followed. Despite my discomfort, I take pride in the knowledge that whoever is following me lacks my stealth. This one is too close to me—too desperate.

I have no choice. We are on a very busy, very public street. No one can kill me here.

I whip around. "Stop it."

"I didn't mean to scare you."

I'm looking at Charlie.

"Hi," I say shyly. "Sorry, I thought you were someone else."

"Just how many people make pursuit a hobby?"

"You'd be surprised."

"You look good," Charlie says.

"So do you." Of course he does; he looks like Charlie. He's wearing his blue down jacket and jeans and hasn't combed his hair since yesterday.

"You feeling okay?" he asks.

"I just got out. I thought I'd walk a bit."

"Be careful. There are a lot of nutcases around."

"Yeah," I say.

"You want an escort? After all, you've been in the hospital for a month."

He knows.

"You know," I say.

"I do."

"So you know everything?"

"I do."

"I'm sorry the way things turned out," I tell him.

"Not everything, I hope."

"No—I'm okay with the fact that I'm not dead."

"Yeah. It was touch-and-go there for a while."

How does Charlie know that? He probably called Kovitz for an update.

"I guess I was out of it for that part," I say, referring to my coma.

We stop at the red light.

"We were all pretty worried. I can tell you now because you're walking around, but I was sure that you were dead."

When exactly was that?

"What do you mean?"

"You know, when I disconnected you from Preston. I couldn't tell if you were breathing or not. There was a lot of blood."

I'm obviously way less interested in the volume of blood in this memory than I am in Charlie's presence there.

"You were the Good Samaritan."

"I was the person who, from his window, saw his houseguest getting clobbered."

The light turns green again, but we're just standing there.

"But Kovitz didn't identify you. He just said that a Good Samaritan found me."

"Oh. That's because I didn't want my identity to become public—you know, with the reporters. I could see them pursuing a human interest story. Frankly, there have been enough Redwins in the public eye."

"How's your dad?"

"He's doing great. He's relieved the whole thing is over, though he wishes that the celebrity treatment will end. I assure him that it will. A big movie star will have triplets or a cabdriver will return someone's wallet. Kelt offered him his job back."

"Did he take it?"

"No, he says he's done with that chapter. He's at a smaller company that is working on anti-cancer drugs."

"He's a really wonderful man. I'm glad for him."

"Me too."

"Walter, I'm really sorry I didn't tell you."

"I think I know that. If I didn't know my father so damn well, I would have jumped to the same conclusion."

"He is kind of a perfect person."

"No, if he were truly perfect, he would have convinced La-Donna to clear him before he lost his job," Charlie says, chuckling. "But in my own hiatus from work, I've had a lot of time to think. More than enough. In fact, I realized that I acted very badly toward you. You did nothing wrong. I was just really angry. Angry that my mother died and that my father couldn't have handled it more nobly. You happened to be there during the worst of my rage storm."

"This is not nec—" I interject.

"Let me finish. While I was thinking about how I was going to apologize to you, I saw you there with Preston. There you were in mid-pummel, covered in blood. It was too much. The anger about what had been done to my father, to me, and to you. I don't know where I got the energy; I ran downstairs, out the door, and I punched him in the neck and knocked him out."

"And you called Kovitz."

"Yup. And Kovitz called his buddies from the nineteenth precinct. As soon as they grabbed Hayes, one of the guys took me in his squad car to New York Hospital. We didn't even wait for an ambulance."

"So you came with me to the hospital?"

"I did. My father had some connections over there and we got you the best neurosurgeon."

"Dr. Reiter. Not much of a bedside manner."

"No, but that's not his job. Besides, you got all the bedside manner you needed from Jennifer."

Jennifer? How did he know Jennifer?

"You knew my nurse?"

"Yeah. She was pretty strict, though. She had all sorts of

rules. Stay two feet from the bed except for your mother. She was allowed to touch you. Jean and I had to stay back."

Wait, he was there with Mother and Jean?

"Yeah, and we couldn't say anything that was not positive. 'I don't want no gloom and doom.'"

"So you met Mother?"

"I did."

"Why didn't she tell me?"

"I asked her not to. And Jean as well."

The two largest mouths in New York failed to utter any of this to me.

"I can't believe this."

"I wanted to talk to you."

"Why weren't you in the hospital when I woke up?"

"I was on the way, and then I heard you had an infection. I was afraid my presence would compromise your immune system."

"Why?"

"I thought you would never forgive me."

"Forgive you? You saved my life."

"For kicking you out in the first place. For putting you at risk. I should have predicted that someone might go after you. After all, you were framed. I wanted to be able to ask for your forgiveness when you were strong enough to grant it. And if you aren't strong enough today, then I don't want you to have to make a decision."

As Charlie is saying this, I realize that I'm exhausted.

"I'm a little tired." I say to him. We're on Sixty-fifth and Lexington, just yards from his house.

"Well, don't say anything."

"Oh. I'm not too tired to forgive you. I love you. I just happen to be tired."

There it is. It just slipped out. For the second time. The first time I told him, I was angry. Today it just came out so matter-of-factly. Naturally. As if Charlie and I had been saying "I love you" to each other for years, and we just completed a squabble over dry cleaning. I can't un-say it.

Charlie doesn't say anything.

Well, I'm thinking, spit it out. Just say that you can't see a future or you don't like me or I'm ugly or something.

"Do you want to rest at my house?" he asks softly.

Now it's my turn not to say anything.

"I moved all of your things into my room."

I'm shocked.

"But I don't have any things in your house."

"While you were in the hospital, Jean let me into your apart-ment and helped me get some of your stuff. Actually, she selected it. I just packed and carried it."

"My stuff is in your apartment." I don't even consider asking him what he would have done if this conversation had gone differently. It never would have.

And he knows it.

"I got you something else," Charlie tells me.

"What is it?"

"A DVR. And I've been watching all your programs for the past month. I've seen sixty-eight episodes of *Law and Order*. You're right. It *is* a good show."

My stuff is at Charlie's house and he has become a TV watcher. Maybe Kovitz was right and I'm in heaven.

"I can't believe this."

"I can't either. But as you said, I love you."

Without thinking, I turn to Charlie, and I kiss him. And he kisses me back.

For five minutes.

"Let's get you to bed, Alice Teakle."

"Okay, Walter Redwin."

"Call me Charlie."